THE
GIRLS HE
ADORED

THE
GIRLS HE
ADORED

A NOVEL

JONATHAN NASAW

POCKET BOOKS

New York   London   Toronto   Sydney   Singapore

POCKET BOOKS, a division of Simon & Schuster, Inc.
1230 Avenue of the Americas, New York, NY 10020

ISBN: 0-671-78726-8

POCKET BOOKS and colophon are registered trademarks of
Simon & Schuster, Inc.

Printed in the U.S.A.

For Susan

THE
GIRLS HE
ADORED

1

"I'LL SAVE YOU SOME TIME," said the prisoner, shuffling into the interview room in his orange jumpsuit, fettered and manacled, wrists cuffed to a padlocked belt around his waist, and a scowling sheriff's deputy at his elbow. "I'm oriented times three, my thought processes are clear, and my mood and affect are appropriate to my circumstances."

"I see you're familiar with the drill." The psychiatrist, a slender blond woman in her early forties, looked up from behind a metal desk bare except for a Dictaphone, a notepad, and a manila folder. "Have a seat."

"Any chance of getting these things off?" The prisoner rattled his fetters dramatically. Slight, an inch or so below medium height, he appeared to be in his late twenties.

The psychiatrist glanced up at the deputy, who shook his head. "Not if you want me to leave you alone with him."

"I do, for now," said the psychiatrist. "He may need a hand free later for some of the standardized tests."

"I'll have to be here for that. Just pick up the phone when you're ready." A black telephone was mounted on the wall behind the psychiatrist. Beside it was an inconspicuous alarm button; an identical button was concealed on the psychiatrist's side of the desk. "And you, siddown."

The prisoner shrugged and lowered himself into the unpadded wooden chair, tugging with manacled hands at the crotch of his jumpsuit, as if it had ridden up on him. His heart-shaped face was just this side of pretty, with long-lashed eyes and lips like a Botticelli angel. He seemed to be bothered by a lock of nut brown hair that had fallen boyishly across his forehead and over one eye, so as the guard left the room, the psychiatrist reached across the desk and brushed it back for him with her fingers.

"Thank you," said the prisoner, looking up at her through low-ered eyelids. The glitter of mischievous, self-satisfied amusement had faded from his gold-flecked brown eyes—but only for a moment. "I appreciate the gesture. Are you a defense whore or a prosecution whore?"

"Neither." The psychiatrist ignored the insult. Testing behavior, she told herself. He was trying to control their interaction by pro-voking an aggressive response.

"Come on, which is it? Either my lawyer hired you to say I'm insane, or the DA hired you to say I'm not. Or were you appointed by the court to see if I'm fit to stand trial? If so, let me assure you that I am perfectly capable of understanding the charges against me and assisting in my own defense. Those are the criteria, are they not?"

"More or less."

"You still haven't answered my question. I'll rephrase it if you'd like. Have you been hired by the defense, the prosecution, or the court?"

"Would it make a difference in how you respond to my ques-tions?"

The prisoner's demeanor changed dramatically. He lowered his shoulders, arched his neck, cocked his head to the side, and formed his next words carefully, almost primly, at the front of his mouth, speaking with just a trace of a lisp. *"Would it make a dif-fer-ence in how you respond to my questy-ons?"*

It was a remarkably effective imitation of her own bearing and manner of speaking, the psychiatrist realized. He had her nailed, right down to the hint of sibilence that was, after years of speech therapy, all that remained of a once ferocious, sputtering, Daffy Duck of a speech impediment. But the parody was more affection-ate than cruel, as if he'd known and liked her for years.

"Of course it would," he went on in his own voice. "Don't be disingenuous."

"I suppose you're right." The psychiatrist sat back in her chair, trying to maintain a professional demeanor despite the hot blush blooming in her cheeks. "That was an excellent imitation, by the way."

"Thank you!" Jail garb, fetters, and circumstances notwithstanding, the prisoner's grin lit up the bare room. "Want to see my Jack Nicholson?"

"Perhaps some other time," she replied, sounding to her annoyance every bit as prim as his imitation of her. She caught herself touching the top few buttons of her beige blouse with fluttering fingertips, like a schoolgirl who'd noticed her date glancing surreptitiously at her chest. "We have quite a bit of work ahead of us today."

"Oh! Well then, by all means, let's get on with it." The prisoner flapped his manacled wrists, as if he were shooing pigeons away; his chains rattled musically.

"Thank *you*." She leaned forward and pressed the power button on the voice-activated Dictaphone. "I'm Dr. Cogan, by the way."

The psychiatrist had been hoping he would respond in kind—thus far the prisoner had refused to give his name to the authorities. But all she got from him was a cheerful "Pleased to meetcha," and a cavalier, if truncated, wave of his cuffed right hand.

She tried again, more directly. "And your name is . . . ?"

"Call me Max."

"I notice you haven't quite answered my question."

"I notice you haven't *quite* answered mine. Who hired you?"

She'd been hoping he'd let it drop; now she had to answer, or risk losing his cooperation. "The court, indirectly: I was hired by a firm that contracts its services to the county."

He nodded, as if she'd confirmed something he already knew. She waited a moment, then prompted him. "And your name?"

"Like I said, call me Max." He looked up. Really, that's the best I can do, said his embarrassed grin; I win, said his eyes.

The psychiatrist moved on. "Nice to meet you, Max. As you're probably aware, we have some standard tests we need to get through—"

"MMPI, Rorschach, thematic apperception, maybe a sentence completion if you're really trying to pad your hours—"

"—but first let's just chat for a few minutes."

"By chat, if you mean conduct a clinical interview, beginning with a question to be asked in an open-ended manner and designed to elicit the patient's own perception of the problem"—he had to stop for a breath—"or difficulty that has led him or her to seek treatment, let me save you some time: My diagnosis is dissociative amnesia, possibly a dissociative fugue state."

Then you're not really oriented times three, are you? thought

Dr. Cogan, breaking off eye contact to look through the manila folder. "I'm curious, Max. You seem to be quite familiar with psychiatric terms and procedures. Might you have worked in the mental health field?"

"Might have." Then, thoughtfully: "Of course, I also might have been a patient in a locked facility. I mean, considering the circumstances under which I was found."

"That sounds like a good place to start. Tell me about the circumstances under which you were found."

"Well, Dr. Cogan, it's like this." The prisoner leaned forward in his chair. His breathing had grown shallower, and the glitter in his eyes was darker and more pronounced. The psychiatrist had the impression that for the first time since he'd entered the room, his interest was fully engaged. "The first thing I remember is finding myself sitting in a car next to the body of a young woman who had recently been disemboweled."

Disemboweled. It struck Irene Cogan as odd how one simple word could be so much more evocative than a three-page coroner's report describing in clinical detail "a semicircular ventral incision beginning one and a half centimeters above the right iliac crest, extending downward to three centimeters above the pubic symphysis, then describing an upward arc to the top of the left iliac crest, with resulting extrusion of both large and small bowel. . . ."

She looked up from the manila folder. The prisoner was waiting for her next question with an eager grin, his gold-flecked eyes shining, looking for all the world like a man enjoying a terrific first date. Momentarily jarred out of her professional detachment, Dr. Cogan switched onto automatic pilot, lobbing one of the interviewee's last words back at him in lieu of a real question. "Recently? How recently?"

The prisoner shrugged easily—or as easily as the fetters would allow. "I dunno, thirty, forty seconds. She was still sitting up."

2

THE BUREAU LIKED ITS AGENTS to be young and fit, to wear conservative suits, and to carry regulation weapons in over-the-kidney holsters. At fifty-five, Special Agent E. L. Pender was two years from mandatory retirement, overweight and out of shape, and beneath a plaid sport coat his boss had once described as being loud enough to spook a blind horse, he carried a SIG Sauer P226 9mm semiautomatic in a soft calfskin shoulder holster.

"Enjoy your stay in San Jose, Agent Pender," said the young flight attendant, giving him the obligatory doorway send-off. What with all the forms that had to be filled out in order to carry a weapon on a commercial flight, it was impossible for an armed FBI agent to travel incognito these days. "Thank you for flying United."

"Thank *you*, dear." Pender tipped his trademark hat, a narrow-brimmed green-and-black houndstooth check with a tiny feather stuck into the band. Beneath it, he was bald as a melon. "You know, the time was when I'd have asked a pretty gal such as yourself for her phone number."

"I'll bet." The stewardess smiled politely.

"Would I have gotten it?"

The smile never wavered. "My parents didn't let me date much when I was seven, Agent Pender."

Pender's luck wasn't much better at the rent-a-car counter. The clerk knew nothing about the midsize sedan that was to have been reserved for him, so he was forced to squeeze his six-four, two-hundred-and-fifty-pound frame behind the wheel of a Toyota Corolla.

At least the car had AC and a respectable sound system. Pender set the temperature control to blue and the volume control to high, found an oldies station on the FM band, and sang along in a sweet, surprisingly soulful tenor as he drove. A full hour passed before they played a song to which he didn't know all the words.

Strictly speaking, from the standpoint of professional courtesy, Pender should have notified the local FBI resident agency before showing up in Salinas to interview a murder suspect currently being held in the county jail. But according to the grapevine, the RA's collective nose was still out of joint from the previous summer, when the bureau had brought down agents from the San Francisco field office to take over a high-profile kidnapping investigation—they wouldn't be likely to welcome an interloper like Pender with open arms.

Also strictly speaking, Pender should have checked in immediately with the Monterey County Sheriff's Department. But before he requested an interview with the prisoner, he first wanted to speak to the arresting officer, and local cops tended to be overly protective of their own.

According to Pender's information, obtained for him by one of Liaison Support's overworked clerks, Deputy Terry Jervis lived in a town called Prunedale. They'd had a few chuckles over that back in Washington. "Prunedale, home of regular folks," and so on.

He found the place without any difficulty—one thing about working for the government, you could always get hold of a decent map. The house was a small, well-tended ranch with sprayed-stucco walls and a few rounded arches thrown in so they could call it mission style, perched on a hillside in the sort of semirural neighborhood where half the houses were trailers, and half the trailers were probably meth labs. A spindly lemon tree was tied to a stake in the middle of a rocky but carefully trimmed front lawn; tidy flower beds lined the short walk from the driveway to the front door.

Pender rang the bell, then backed down from the low doorstep so his height wouldn't be intimidating. The woman who opened the door as far as the chain permitted was black, solid, broad in the beam, and low to the ground. It occurred to Pender that this might be Jervis—she had a cop's wide ass, and the arrest report hadn't been gender-specific.

"Yes?"

"Special Agent Pender, FBI. I'm here to see Deputy Jervis."

"Terry's resting. Could I see your shield, please?"

If not the cop, then the cop's wife—only a cop's wife would say "shield" instead of "badge." Pender tinned her, flipping his wallet open to show her his old Department of Justice badge with the eagle on the top and the blindfolded figure in the pageboy haircut holding the scales of justice in one hand and a sword in the other.

"You have a photo ID?"

"Here you go."

She glanced from the picture on the laminated card to his face and back again, then closed the door. The chain rattled; the door opened wider. "Come on in."

Pender took off his hat as he stepped through the doorway. "Thank you, Mrs. Jervis."

The woman frowned. "I'm Aletha Winkle."

Pender winced exaggeratedly. "Sorry. That's my job—stumbling to conclusions."

She ignored the apology. "Hey, Terry," she called over her shoulder. "There's an FBI man here to see you."

The response was a muffled "Okay." Pender followed Winkle down a short hallway, past a small living room furnished largely in wicker, and into a white-and-pink bedroom—everything from the bedclothes to the bureau, the rug to the ceiling fixture, was either white or pink.

Pender froze in the doorway—the pale woman sitting up in bed was pointing a semiautomatic pistol at his midsection. He threw up his hands. "FBI—take it easy there, Deputy."

"Sorry," Terry Jervis hissed through clenched teeth, lowering the gun. "They tell me the guy was making threats—we were worried he might send somebody to carry them out."

Deputy Jervis had spiked blond hair and washed-out blue eyes. The lower half of her face was heavily bandaged, and her jaw was wired shut. Her pajamas were pin-striped, black on pink.

"I understand." Pender lowered his hands. "Does it hurt to talk?"

"Some."

"I apologize in advance—I wouldn't be here if it weren't important. I'd be grateful for anything you can tell me."

"This is where I get off," said Aletha Winkle. "Call me if you need me, honey." She stooped, plumped the smaller woman's pillows, kissed her high on the forehead. On her way out of the room she waggled her forefinger in Pender's direction. "Don't you tire her out, now!"

"Scout's honor," replied Pender.

Jervis smiled weakly. "Aletha's a little overprotective."

"I noticed—and God bless her for it." In Pender's experience, some lesbians, like most minorities, tended to regard even a pleasantly neutral tone as barely disguised disapproval. But Pender was a proponent of what was known as the affective interview, so he made sure to add an extra dollop of warmth to his voice as he returned the grin.

"Take a load off." Deputy Jervis pointed to the small, pink-cushioned chair in front of the pink-and-white mirrored vanity, then set the pistol down carefully on the bedside table, next to a framed photo of herself and Winkle, posed in front of the house with their arms around each other's waists. It had probably been taken on the day they moved in—a yellow Drive-Yr-Self moving van was parked next to a green Volvo station wagon in the driveway.

"You really need that?" asked Pender, nodding toward the gun. He knew the model well—Glock .40s were now standard issue for recruits at the FBI Academy.

Jervis nodded sheepishly. "I know it's dumb, I know he's behind bars, but he's still got me spooked. If you never saw the fucker, then you can't imagine how fast the fucker can move."

"Probably not." Pender picked up the delicate-looking chair, positioned it a few feet from the side of the bed at a forty-five-degree angle—the recommended interviewing position—and sat down carefully with his hat in his lap.

"Have your people found out anything more about the son of a bitch?"

Pender shook his head. "Dead end. He wasn't carrying any ID—no wallet, just a roll of cash—and it was the victim's car. His prints are a mess, old grafts on the interior surfaces of both hands. No matches so far—the lab's working on a reconstruction." Pender scraped his chair a little closer to the bed—a signal to the interviewee that it was time to get down to business. "Tell me about the bust—how'd you take him down?"

"Routine traffic stop. Eastbound maroon Chevy Celebrity with California plates rolls through a red on Highway Sixty-eight, near Laguna Seca. Male driver, female passenger. I hit the lights, he hits the gas. I call in the pursuit; he pulls over a few seconds later. As I'm approaching the vehicle, I see the driver leaning over toward the female passenger—I figure he's fastening her seat belt for her.

Then he turns toward me, big smile, what's the problem officer? At this point I haven't even unsnapped my holster. Routine traffic violation, maybe a warning on the seat belt.

"But when I look in, I see this blond girl, couldn't have been more than eighteen, she's sitting straight up holding her stomach with both hands. She's wearing a white sweater that looks like it's dyed in overlapping bands of red at the bottom, and she has the strangest expression on her face. Just, you know, *puzzled*—I'll never forget that expression. I ask her if she's okay, she lifts up her sweater with both hands, and her guts spill out onto her lap."

Jervis closed her eyes, as if to shut out the memory. Pender wouldn't let her. "What happened next?"

"He has the knife in his left hand—before I can react he brings it up so fast and hits me so hard I thought he shot me at first. It was like my mouth exploded—I'm falling backward, spitting out blood and teeth, trying to draw my weapon. He's on top of me before I hit the ground. I can't get my weapon out, but I'm hanging onto the holster for dear life."

Jervis winced again; her hand went to her jaw. "That's all I remember—they tell me he was trying to yank my belt off when the backup unit pulled up, and I was holding onto the holster so hard they had to pry my hands away."

"But you're down as the arresting officer."

A rueful chuckle. "Charity collar. It was a twelve-inch bowie knife—a souvenir from the Alamo, I heard. Busted out all the lower molars on the right side, all the uppers on the left. He just barely missed my tongue or I wouldn't be talking to you now."

Her pale complexion was turning chalky; her glance strayed toward the bottle of Vicodin on the white wicker bedside table.

"And here I promised Miss Winkle I wouldn't wear you out," said Pender. He knew he didn't have much longer; he cut to the question he most needed to ask the only person who'd seen the victim alive. "One more thing, then I'll leave you in peace. It's about the girl. You say she was blond?"

"Yes, sir."

"Could you be a little more specific—was it platinum blond, ash blond, something like that?" Careful not to lead her where he hoped she'd take him.

And she did: "No, sir, it was more of a reddish blond."

"Would that be the color people sometimes refer to as strawberry blond?"

"Yes, sir, that's it exactly." It was obvious that every word was causing her pain.

Pender patted her pale freckled hand as it lay on the pink comforter. "That's okay. That's okay, dear. You've been a great help—you don't have to say another word."

Aletha Winkle gave Pender a dark look as she bustled into the room.

"I'll let myself out," Pender said.

"And next time call first."

"Yes, ma'am, I'll be sure to do that," replied Pender meekly.

Pender's chagrin didn't last long. In fact, as he strode down the flower-lined front walk, he was tum-te-tumming "And the Band Played On," a tune written by Charles B. Ward and John F. Palmer in 1899, but still familiar enough nearly a century later that at the 1997 inaugural meeting of the team charged with investigating the disappearances of nine females from nine widely separated locales over the past nine years, Steven P. McDougal, chief of the FBI's Liaison Support Unit, was able to recite the first few lines of the chorus by heart, confident that it would be recognized by every agent in the room:

Casey would waltz with a strawberry blond
And the band played on.
He'd glide 'cross the floor with the girl he adored
And the band played on.

Thus McDougal dubbed the phantom kidnapper Casey, after the only characteristic the missing females had in common: the color of their hair. But it was Ed Pender who sang the next two lines of the song in his sweet tenor:

His brain was so loaded it nearly exploded
The poor girl would shake with alarm.

The room went dead quiet; McDougal broke the silence.

"Ed has a bad feeling about this one, boys and girls," he announced, leaning back in the leather chair at the head of the conference table, peering professorially over his half glasses. "Let's help him make it go away."

Since that initial meeting, two more strawberry blonds had been reported missing under suspicious circumstances, but the FBI still hadn't gone public with the investigation, largely because not a single body had come to light. Then in June 1999, Monterey County sheriff's deputy Terry Jervis made what she thought would be a routine traffic stop, and everything changed.

Casey, you son of a bitch, thought Pender as he squeezed himself back into the blue Corolla. You son of a bitch, we've got you now.

3

ON A RIDGETOP HIGH IN the Cascade Mountains of southern Oregon, a strawberry blond in her early fifties, wearing a high-necked green silk gown and matching surgical mask, stands in the middle of a chicken yard, scattering feed to a flock of golden-plumed Buff Orpingtons.

Her movements are awkward—she bends and turns stiffly from the waist—and the hands emerging from the long sleeves of the gown are freakishly skeletal, smooth shiny skin stretched tightly over fleshless bone. She spills nearly as much feed as she sows. As the birds crowd around her ankles and dart under her gown to peck at the fallen seed, she scolds them mildly.

"Now, children, there's plenty for everyone." Her voice is muffled behind the green silk mask and has a peculiar timbre, thin and unresonant—the converse of nasal. "Vivian, mind your manners—no shoving. And you, Freddie—try to show a little self-control. Remember your position."

Freddie Mercury is the lone rooster in the hen yard, a strutting dandy with flowing plumage of antique gold and a proudly erect crimson comb. When the woman ducks into the dark coop, he follows her, clucking soothingly to the brooding hen inside to reassure her that her egg will be safe.

And indeed, the woman's bony fingers pluck only the unattended eggs, all brown, some still warm, from the dirty straw of the roosts, and deposit them gently, carefully, into the shallow basket hanging from her forearm. When she has finished, the rooster accompanies her to the gate and stands guard, facing his flock, to prevent any of his plump golden wives or buff chicks from escaping with her.

From the hen yard it is a hike of a few hundred yards through a shady wood of old-growth Douglas fir to the kennels next to the embowered, double-gated sally port, where half a dozen amber-eyed, black-and-brindle Rottweilers with barrel-like bodies, powerful, wide-skulled, flattened heads, and massive jaws capable of crushing a sheep's skull or a bicycle with equal ease greet her noiselessly, wagging their stubby tails and wiggling their broad behinds.

Eerily silent, eerily patient, the dogs stand at quivering attention while the woman opens a wooden bin containing a fifty-pound bag of dog chow, scoops the dry kibble into six individual bowls, each labeled with its owner's name—Jack, Lizzie, Bundy, Piper, Kiss, and Dr. Cream—and breaks a fresh egg into each bowl. Not until she has finished breaking the last egg into the last bowl, and given them a verbal command accompanied by a hand signal, do they rush forward to begin eating.

When they are finished, the woman lets the dogs out through the front gate via the sally port. They split up in six different directions to do their business as far from the kennels and each other as possible, and return within minutes without having to be summoned.

"Good dogs," says the woman, locking the front gate behind them and leading them back into the kennel, leaving the door between the kennel and the sally port open. "Now give me my lovies."

As she drops stiffly to her knees, the dogs line up before her like obedient schoolchildren and present themselves one at a time to be petted by those skeletal fingers and kissed through that silken mask until the woman's heart is eased and her fear of abandonment temporarily assuaged.

Now only one chore remains, her least favorite: a visit to the drying shed. She decides to put it off until after lunch.

4

DR. IRENE COGAN HAD ONLY interviewed a patient under full restraints twice before. The first, Paul Silberman, was a nineteen-year-old who'd murdered his mother up in Woodside. Hacked her to pieces in the tub. The papers had called it the *Psycho* murder, though in fact Mrs. Silberman had been bathing, not showering. Paul claimed he hadn't known it was really happening, that everything seemed so strange and distorted that he thought he was dreaming. Claimed he was as powerless to stop himself as he would have been in a dream.

Irene, a specialist in dissociative disorders, had been called in by the defense to testify that Paul suffered from a depersonalization/derealization disorder. Her testimony had been effective—the boy had been found not guilty by reason of insanity, and was now receiving treatment in a private, locked facility in Palo Alto.

But Irene Cogan was neither a patsy nor a defense whore. When a murdering pedophile named David Douglas Winslow claimed to be suffering from dissociative identity disorder, Irene had testified for the prosecution that the similarity of optical functioning among Winslow's alleged alter personalities, along with their nearly identical GSRs—galvanic skin responses—indicated that he was feigning DID.

Winslow's current address was death row, San Quentin. Dr. Cogan, though she opposed the death penalty, would shed no tears for him when his appeals finally ran out—she'd already cried herself out for his tiny victims.

Dr. Cogan was not a forensic psychiatrist, however—she had been called into the current case because the prisoner was claiming dissociative amnesia. It was too early to say for sure whether he was feigning, but she suspected he was. The victims of dissociative amnesia she'd treated had presented very different affects than this prisoner; you didn't need a medical degree to read the abject confusion and uncertainty in their eyes.

But why fake amnesia? For a man as intelligent and well versed in psychology as the prisoner appeared to be, paranoid schizophrenia, for instance, would be a much easier symptomology to feign—and a more viable defense as well.

Suddenly she realized that the prisoner had asked her something. "Excuse me?"

"Spaced out, eh?" The prisoner chuckled. "I asked if you'd brush my hair back the way you did before."

"Why? It's not in your eyes."

He met her gaze boldly—Irene wondered if those mildly amused gold-flecked eyes had been that poor eviscerated girl's last sight on earth. "Just for the touch."

She was momentarily jarred. His use of the word *touch* was somehow striking in its intimacy. "I'm sorry, I don't think that's appropriate," she managed, after a moment.

"Please. It's important."

"Why? Why is it important?"

"It just is. Please, trust me. I won't hurt you—I give you my word."

Tough call. It was a small enough request, but there was the physical danger to be considered, as well as a potential skewing of the doctor-patient relationship. On the other hand, by asking for her trust he was, in effect, offering her his. And his trust was something she was going to need if she hoped to make an accurate evaluation.

Or so she told herself as she leaned across the desk. Gingerly she brushed the comma of hair back from his brow, then quickly drew her hand back as his eyes rolled up and to the right, and his eyelids began to flutter. By the time Irene had settled back in her chair, the prisoner's cockiness, his certainty, the gleam in his eye and the set of his jaw, had all disappeared, leaving behind a small pathetic figure slumped over and sobbing like a child, knees drawn up, shoulders heaving, chains rattling.

Here it comes, thought Irene. He *is* going to change his symptomology. But not to schizophrenia. She composed her features to hide her suspicion, and waited patiently for the weeping to end.

And sure enough, when the prisoner looked up, he was a different man. His heart-shaped face had grown more oval as the set of his jaw relaxed. His eyes were wider, rounder, lighter. And his voice, when he apologized, was tremulous, and pitched an octave higher.

"I'm sowwy."

So it was to be DID after all. Dissociative identity disorder, formerly known as multiple personality disorder. And she had to admit, if he was faking it, he was good. Better than good, certainly better than the monstrous David Douglas Winslow.

But perhaps that was to be expected, with the prisoner's apparent background in psychology and his obvious talent for impersonation. He knew that eye movement was a classical marker for a switch between personalities, commonly referred to as "alters," hence the roll and flutter. He knew that extreme facial and vocal changes between alters were to be expected, and that many alters were juveniles, so he'd raised the pitch of his voice, let his cheeks go slack, widened his eyes to take in more light.

If, on the other hand, he wasn't faking it, Irene understood that this might prove to be the most important case of her career. For the moment, she decided to proceed as if the DID was genuine. If he were faking, she might not get to the truth quite as quickly, but if he were not, this approach would do the least harm.

"Hello," she said softly. "What's your name?"

Panic, confusion. The eyes rolled, the lids fluttered—and the child was gone.

"Excuse me?" The first alter again. A quick, wary glance around the room; the prisoner's manacled hands nervously patted his thighs. Both the glance and the self-touching Irene recognized as grounding behavior, orienting gestures commonly seen after a switch of personalities.

And indeed, the prisoner appeared to be unaware that his face was ashen beneath its olive complexion, and tear-streaked, with a bubble of snot in one nostril—he seemed surprised when Irene handed him a tissue from her purse.

He grasped the situation quickly, though. "Guess I kinda wimped out on you."

He drew his knees up, hunched his shoulders under the orange jumpsuit, and ducked his head in order to blow his nose. When he came up his voice had changed yet again—this appeared to be yet a third alter, roughly the same age and appearance as the first, but more vulnerable, with less of an edge. "It's just so hard keeping up that front all the time."

Irene waited, neither agreeing nor disagreeing.

"You can't let them see any weakness, you know. If they sense weakness, they'll tear you apart. Even the guards." He let the tissue fall to his lap. "Especially the guards. Now what was it you asked?"

"I asked what your name was."

This time the eye roll and flutter was so quick and short-lived only a therapist with extensive experience treating DID patients would have noticed it.

"How quickly they forget," said the prisoner, in the voice he'd used originally. "You wouldn't happen to have a cigarette on you, would you?"

Irene knew better than to ask him his name again—this was clearly Call-me-Max. "I believe the entire building is nonsmoking."

The prisoner laughed easily. "Realistically speaking, what's the worst they can do if they catch us? Hell, we're risking a death sentence every time we light up."

"Good point." Irene was intrigued—and encouraged. Whether he was faking the DID or not, the patient's—*prisoner's*—use of the first-person plural was a good sign, as was his evident warmth toward her. They seemed to be moving toward a rapport that usually took much longer to establish—she definitely wanted to encourage it.

And frankly, a cigarette right about now didn't sound like the worst idea in the world. Irene rummaged around in her purse for her pack of Benson and Hedges and her lighter, then went through the desk drawers looking for an ashtray. Finding none, she took an empty Sprite can out of the wastebasket, placed it on the desk in front of the prisoner, placed two cigarettes between her lips, lit both, and handed him one, aware as she did so that it was an inappropriately intimate gesture.

The prisoner inhaled deeply, squinting to keep the smoke out of his eyes. "I feel better already."

So did Irene; she leaned back in her chair and took a deep drag of her cigarette, drawing the smoke luxuriously through her nostrils. It felt deliciously sinful and retro to be smoking with a patient again. When she leaned forward to tap her ash into the Sprite can, she caught the prisoner looking her over appreciatively.

Irene sat up, drawing the lapels of her suit jacket together over her chest and tugging her skirt down over her knees, though her legs were out of sight beneath the desk. It occurred to her that she was losing control of the interview.

"All right, I trusted you," she said. The voice-activated Dictaphone began to whir again on the table between them. "Now will you trust me?"

"With what?" he replied, exhaling a thin blue stream of smoke along with the words.

"With the truth."

"What do you want to know?"

"To start with, do you ever feel as if you were more than one person?"

"You say you want the truth?"

"Yes, of course."

He ducked his head down to his hands to take the cigarette out of his mouth, then popped back up with a maniacal grin. "Well you caan't haandle the truth!" he declared in an exaggeratedly flat monotone, his eyebrows drawn up into devilish peaks.

Irene let out a startled laugh. "So you worked in that Jack Nicholson imitation after all."

"Pretty good, huh? Want to see my—"

"No!" She cut him off sternly; time to get back to business. "When I asked you your name earlier, you told me to call you Max. Is Max your name?"

"That depends," he said pleasantly.

"Depends on what?"

"I can't tell you."

"Why not?"

"I can't tell you that, either."

Irene tried a different tack. "When you came into the room this morning, you told me your mood was appropriate to the circumstances. A young girl died horribly, apparently at your hands. How does that make you feel?"

He had ducked down again; he came back up with the cigarette between his lips. His face was blue-tinged under the fluorescent lights.

"Lost," he said softly. Irene had the impression he'd switched personalities again, down where she couldn't see the eye roll. This was the third alter, the handsome, vulnerable young man. "Lost and frightened. And alone—at least until this morning."

"What happened this morning?"

"I met you."

His cigarette had burned down almost to the filter. When Irene reached forward to take it out of his mouth for him, she felt his lips brush the back of her fingers as delicately as butterfly wings. So light and ephemeral was his touch that Irene wasn't entirely sure contact had even taken place, much less whether it had actually been a kiss.

But in her heart she knew it had. She felt a pang of excitement, close to fear but so quick and sharp it was almost sexual—and decidedly inappropriate. It occurred to Irene that when she next saw *her* therapist, they would have something juicier to discuss than they'd had in weeks. Months. Years. She took a hard pull on her cigarette, and inhaled a mouthful of burning filter.

5

"Pender, you got more balls than Hoover had high heels," said Aurelio Bustamante. The longtime Monterey County sheriff was seated behind an enormous desk crowded with awards and mementos. "First you interrogate—"

"Interview." Pender slouched in his chair so as not to tower over the sheriff, a short round man in a brown western-cut suit and a sunny white Stetson. Pender had started to remove his own hat—he rarely wore it into a room—but changed his mind: when in California . . .

"You *interrogate* one of my officers, an injured officer, let me add, without my knowledge or permission. Now you want to interrogate one of my prisoners, but you don't want to share what you got? Unh-unh, I don't think so. You gonna fuck me from behind, my frien', you goddamn well better give me a reach-around."

When dealing with local law enforcement officials, FBI agents could count on a range of reactions from hero worship to bitter resentment, depending on how much contact the locals had had with the bureau. The sixtyish Bustamante was clearly no virgin.

Nor was Pender—he decided to see if he couldn't turn the sheriff's animosity to his own advantage.

"Believe me, Sheriff, I sympathize completely with you. I started out as a sheriff's deputy in upstate New York. And if *I'm* fucking *you,* then it's a daisy chain, because I've got my boss so far up my ass he has to wear one of those coal miner hats with the little flashlight on top."

The crow's-feet at the corners of Bustamante's eyes deepened almost imperceptibly at the piquant image.

Pender pressed on. "Sheriff Bustamante, if you think the FBI is piss-arrogant to you and yours, you should see how they treat their own—especially old-timers like me. I'm two years short of mandatory retirement, they're trying to force me out early, my last fitness report referred to me as the worst-dressed agent in the history of the bureau, my personnel file's been flagged for so many petty bureaucratic violations it reads like a rap sheet, and if I have to get a court order to interview your prisoner, his lawyer's gonna be on it like stink on shit, and I'm gonna go home with nothing."

"Now I'm suppose' to feel sorry for you because you're a fuckup?" scoffed Bustamante. "I let you in to see this guy without his lawyer present and he walks on account of it, it's gonna be my ass on the line, too."

"Sheriff, I give you my word I won't ask him a single question about the current case."

"Then you're not gonna get anything out of him anyway—he claims to have *amneeesia*." Bustamante weighted the word with contempt.

"Just give me a shot, that's all I ask."

"And if I do that for you, what do you do for me?" Bustamante spread his hands out, palms up, and waggled his fingers toward himself in the universal fork-it-over gesture.

Pender picked up a foot-long brass nameplate—AURELIO BUSTAMANTE, SHERIFF—and placed it in the middle of the desk, facing the sheriff. Then, in a semicircle behind the nameplate, he arranged a Kiwanis Club man-of-the-year pen-and-pencil set in an engraved marble holder; a baseball autographed by the last roster of the now-defunct Salinas Peppers; a gold-framed photograph of the sheriff and Mrs. Bustamante, a smiling Hispanic-looking woman with upswept white hair, standing behind a passle of children and grandchildren; and a silver badge engraved with the words GRAND MARSHALL, SALINAS RODEO, mounted onto a four-inch-high wooden plaque with an angled base.

"This is you at your next press conference." Pender tapped the nameplate, then each of the other items in turn. "And here's your valiant Deputy Jervis, here's the mayor and the DA and whoever else in your department you'd like to reward with a little face time, here's your wife and family, and here's the FBI resident agent from Monterey in a dark suit and conservative tie.

"Ladies and gentlemen . . ." Pender lifted the nameplate up and down with each syllable, manipulating it as if it were a hand puppet. "I'm Sheriff Aurelio Bustamante, and I've called this press conference to announce that the Monterey County Sheriff's Department has been responsible for the capture of one of the most dangerous and sought-after serial killers in the history of law enforcement."

Bustamante reached across the desk and tipped the Grand Marshall plaque representing the FBI over onto its face, then leaned back, his fingers tented over his round belly. "If it's him, I've already got him—what do I need you for?"

"Because otherwise it goes like this. . . ." Pender tipped the nameplate over and moved the plaque up to the front of the grouping. "Ladies and gentlemen, I'm Special Agent Photo Op of the Federal Bureau of Investigation. A few weeks ago a young woman was brutally stabbed to death within sight of a MONTEREY COUNTY SHERIFF'S DEPUTY, who was in turn caught unawares and skewered like a fucking shish-ka-bob. Eventually the suspect was apprehended, but unfortunately, the MONTEREY COUNTY SHERIFF'S DEPARTMENT had absolutely no idea who the fuck they were holding. Fortunately, the FBI was able to determine through its own resources that—"

Bustamante cut him off. "Put everything back where it was, then wait outside."

Hurriedly, Pender rearranged the desk; as he left the room, he saw the sheriff reaching for the telephone. He cooled his heels in a straight-backed wooden chair in the hallway for forty-five minutes. When the sheriff's secretary ushered him back into the office, Bustamante was tilted back in his leather chair, with his cowboy-booted feet up on the desk.

"I just got off the phone with the district attorney. Both our offices, we want to cooperate with the FBI in every way possible without compromising the investigation. However, he says there's absolutely no possibility of him allowing you to question our prisoner without his lawyer being present."

"That's—"

"Let me finish. We can't let you *question* the man without his lawyer, but since the Supreme Court ruled that a prisoner in jail has no expectation of privacy, exclusive of conferences with his own attorney, there's nothing that says we can't put an undercover man in the cell with him in order to, and here I quote the district attorney, 'further ongoing investigations into crimes unrelated to those for which the prisoner is currently charged.' "

"It has to be me." Pender began to marshal his arguments. "It would take days to get one of your—"

"It's you."

"—people up to sp— Oh. Great. Thanks. How soon?"

"Tomorrow afternoon. There's no way we're putting you in with him here. It's too dangerous, and besides, he's been single-housed for a month—he'd know something was up if we gave him a roommate. But he's due in court for a procedural hearing tomorrow. The old jail next to the courthouse has been closed down since 'seventy-one, but we still use the east wing to house prisoners between court appearances. We can put you in one of the holding cells with him without too much danger—he'll be in restraints. Of course, so will you, but that can't be helped. We'll get you in place, then bring him over a little early—that'll give you some time alone with him."

"I want you to know how much I appreciate—" Pender began.

The sheriff cut him off. "Before you thank me, I have something I want you to read."

Bustamante took his booted feet off the desktop, leaned forward, and slid a photocopied document across the desk to Pender. It was a medical report detailing the injuries received by one Refugio Cortes, the prisoner's former cellmate, in the county jail, on the prisoner's first day in custody.

Pender skimmed it: depressed fractures of the orbital bones surrounding both eyes, broken nose, broken ribs, crushed pelvis. The doctors had managed to save the penis, though it would never function again save as a conduit for urine; the testicles, however, were gone, along with the rest of the contents of the scrotal sac.

"I wish I had some pictures to go along with that, my frien'," said Bustamante. "Just so you know what you're getting into."

6

IRENE COGAN HAD SPENT the rest of the morning administering the Rorschach and Thematic Apperception tests, and the hundred-question Dissociative Experiences Scale, saving the personality index for the afternoon session—it took most people a couple of hours to get through the 567 questions of the full MMPI-2. But the clinical interview had gone so poorly that after a lunch break—the prisoner was taken back to his cell; the psychiatrist picked at a dubious salad from a roach coach parked on Natividad Road near the jail—Irene decided to make another stab at it before moving on.

"What's the last thing you remember *before* waking up in the car next to the—" She censored herself midsentence. The dead woman, she'd been about to say, but she didn't want to risk upsetting him with any charged words. "Before waking up in the car?"

"Making love." This appeared to be the third alter again, the vulnerable one.

Making love. Irene wondered if those words had ever been spoken before in this lifeless room with its glaring fluorescent lights. "Go on."

"In the backseat. Parked in a redwood grove. Sunlight in long thin columns pouring through the trees. She's kneeling—" His eyes grew dreamy. "Kneeling on the backseat, leaning against the rear window ledge. I'm behind her. When she leans forward, a shaft of sunlight catches her hair. She has such beautiful strawberry blond hair. I part it at the back of her neck and kiss her nape every time I—" His eyes closed; his belly muscles tightened, and his pelvis thrust forward in a humping motion. "And every time I kiss her she says my name."

"What does she say?" Irene couldn't pass up the opportunity. "What does she call you?"

The prisoner's eyes opened; the dreamy look had faded, replaced by a cold, glittering intelligence. "Tell me," said the alter who called himself Max. "I haven't looked in a mirror for a while— do I have 'stupid' tattooed across my forehead or something?"

Rats. "I'm sorry—please go on."

"Thank you, I'll pass."

"No, really. I apologize—I shouldn't have interrupted you."

"Too late for that now," he said coldly. But just as Irene was telling herself that perhaps she was the one who should have *stupid* tattooed across her forehead, the prisoner changed his mind.

"Christopher," he whispered, leaning toward her as far as the shackles would permit. *"She* called me Christopher."

"I see. Is that your name, then?"

"That's for me to know and you to find out." Common enough childhood repartee, but there was something in the careful way he said it, in the steady, amused look in his eyes, that suggested something more to Irene. A challenge perhaps—or an offer, or an opportunity.

In order to take the Minnesota Multiphasic Personality Inventory, Max/Christopher would need a hand free to hold a pencil. The deputy reluctantly agreed to unhook the cuffs from the chain around the waist, but left the wrists cuffed together, and insisted on remaining in the room with his can of pepper spray and his short-handled riot stick at the ready.

"There are five hundred and sixty-seven statements in this test," Irene explained. "I want you to—"

"Like you said earlier, I know the drill," he interrupted.

"I need to be sure that—"

"Don't insult my intelligence, Doctor," he said, each word carefully measured. "Don't *ever* insult my intelligence."

Irene handed him the blunt, soft-leaded pencil, and saw for the first time that the inside surfaces of his manacled hands were badly scarred. When he caught her looking at his hands, he started to clench them into fists, then changed his mind and opened them for her, palms up. She managed not to wince. His fingertips were bony, nearly skeletal—she could make out the shallow hourglass shape of the distal phalanges beneath the shiny scar tissue, and there were livid white patches of unlined skin stretched tightly across his palms.

"What happened?" she asked him.

"I had the bright idea I could put out a fire with my bare hands."

"Those are grafts?"

"From the buttocks." He laughed bitterly. "I suppose I should be grateful I don't have a hairy ass."

"How old were you?"

"Old enough to know better."

"It must have been terribly painful."

"The pain was welcome."

"Oh?"

"Guilt, you know. Burns hotter than fire." Then, seeing Irene's eager expression: "And that's all I have to say on that subject." He took the pencil in his left hand. "Ready when you are, Doctor."

"All right. . . . Begin."

Irene checked her watch and made a note of the time—1:04 P.M. She also noted another eye roll and flutter—apparently one of the other alters was going to take the test. Or at least that was what he wanted her to think.

She'd brought along several journals to read, under the assumption that the MMPI would take at least two hours, but she'd scarcely finished the latest edition of the *American Journal of Psychiatry* when the prisoner announced that he was done.

Again Irene checked the time—2:02—and shook her head disbelievingly. "You do understand that if you answered randomly, it'll show up on the results."

"The F scale, I believe." He grinned proudly. "Give me another one."

"Beg pardon?"

"Let me take another MMPI—did you bring another?"

"Yes, but—"

"Let me do it again."

"But why?"

He leaned forward; the deputy, seated behind and to the side of the prisoner, half rose from his chair.

"You'll find out," whispered the prisoner. Then, in case she hadn't made the connection, he whispered the words again. "You'll . . . find . . . out."

As in: *That's for me to know and you to find out.* Irene reached into her suitcase and brought out another answer sheet.

The prisoner finished the second MMPI in just over an hour. He had again switched alters both before and after the test, but kept his head down diligently during it, so Irene couldn't read him.

"How long will it take you to get the results back?" he asked, as the deputy once again fastened the prisoner's wrists to the chain around his waist, then left the room carrying his folding chair.

"Back?"

"Yes, back. You do send them out, don't you? To get them scored? Or do you do them yourself?"

Irene sidestepped the question. "Why do you ask?"

"Just wondering how long until our next session."

"At this point, I can't even tell you whether there'll be a next session. I may not need to see you again to perform my evaluation—it depends in large part on the test results."

"I'm not worried about that," he replied confidently. "Once you get the results back, you'll want to interview me again—I guarantee it."

"Oh? And why is that?"

"Because you've never seen anything like me."

"In that case," said Irene, "I'll be sure to pay particular attention."

"*I'll be sure to pay par-tic-u-lar atten-shee-un.*" Again, the devastatingly accurate imitation, this time with a petulant twist. Then, in his own voice: "Don't patronize me, Dr. Cogan. I haven't done anything to deserve that tone from you."

"You're right, and I apologize," said Irene promptly. "I'll be evaluating the tests tonight—if I need a follow-up interview, it'll probably be within a day or two."

"I'll be looking forward to it," said the prisoner.

For the first time that day, Irene turned her back to him as she lifted the receiver of the black telephone on the wall.

"We're about done here," she told the female deputy who picked up on the other end. The woman told her someone would be right in. When Irene turned around again she had the impression she was meeting yet a fourth alter—his posture had slumped, as if he were suddenly exhausted, and he had developed a mild tic in his right eye.

"There ih-ih-is one thing," he said—the stammer on the initial vowel sounds was new. "If it were possible, if circumstances were uh-uh-altered, so to speak, would you consider taking uh-us ah-ah-on a-as uh-uh-a patient?"

"I'm not terribly comfortable with hypotheticals," said Irene, her suspicions heightened—true multiples, who'd spent their entire lives trying to disguise their dissociated identities, rarely used the first person plural until after months of therapy, if then. She hauled her leather briefcase onto the desk and began to pack up her things. "In any event, I wouldn't be able to say for sure until after I'd reached a working diagnosis. I have a small, rather specialized practice, and I couldn't tell you at this point whether you fit the parameters. I *can* tell you this much, though—I couldn't treat a patient who doesn't trust me enough to even give me his name."

"Fair eh-eh-enough," replied the prisoner. Another eye roll, another alter switch, as the deputy entered the room behind him. Then, in a whisper: "By the way, next session, if you get a chance, maybe you could pick up a pack of Camel straights on your way over. There's not enough nicotine in those Benson and Hedges to pacify a lab rat."

"Maybe," said Irene. "If there is a next time."

"Thanks," he said hurriedly, as the deputy tapped him on the shoulder.

"On your feet, Doe—let's go."

"Whatever you say, boss—you're the ace with the Mace."

"Good-bye, Christopher," Irene said, snapping her briefcase shut. She wanted to see how he would react to the name.

"Call me Max," he said with a wink, shuffling toward the door with the deputy at his elbow.

"Good-bye, Max." Irene wasn't sure what, if anything, she'd learned from this latest gambit.

The prisoner turned and and gave her another wink, broader this time. "Good night, Irene," he called, as his guard hustled him out the door. "See you in my dreams."

7

SHERIFF BUSTAMANTE'S WARNING aside, Special Agent E. L. Pender knew better than most what he was getting into. (E.L. stood for Edgar Lee, but no FBI man named Edgar used his first name professionally for long.) He'd joined the FBI in '72, at the age of twenty-eight, after working six years as a Cortland County sheriff's deputy and earning a degree in criminology in his spare time, then spent his first five years with the bureau paying his dues at the resident agency in Arkansas before being transferred to the New York field office. His wife Pam had paid her dues too, trying to make a go of it in New York on the same salary he'd earned in Arkansas—in those days there was no cost-of-living differential for FBI agents.

In the late seventies, Pender had been transferred to Washington to help his old FBI Academy roommate Steve McDougal form a unit to coordinate multijurisdictional, multivictim homicide investigations. Never again, it was hoped, would a serial killer be able to gain an advantage by moving from one jurisdiction to another.

And for the next ten years or so Pender was one of the bureau's golden boys. He'd hunted serial killers all around the country, moving from one task force to another, going wherever his skills were needed, and spent his spare time interviewing jailed serial killers for the VICAP—Violent Criminal Apprehension Program—files.

But by the time the nineties staggered around, both Pender's career and his marriage were in tatters. Too many road trips, too many affairs on both sides, and too much booze. If Steve McDougal hadn't put his considerable clout on the line, Pender would almost certainly have lost both his job and his pension along with his wife.

In time Pender had managed to pull his life together, but neither his marriage nor his career ever recovered. After the divorce, and a leave of absence to dry out, he spent most of his time behind a desk searching the national crime databases, looking for patterns that might indicate a serial killer was plying his trade.

Occasionally McDougal would send him out to interview a convict who was suspected of multijurisdictional crimes, but it was understood by all concerned that Ed Pender would never work another case as a field investigator, not after the fiasco back in 1994. In fact, he'd been lucky to keep his job at all in light of the stunt he'd pulled, holding a press conference in Reeford, Pennsylvania, after the special agent in charge had expressly forbidden him to go public with the investigation.

The missing woman was over eighteen, the SAC had argued, she had left behind a moonstruck note to the effect that she was eloping with the man of her dreams, and there was no evidence of a forced abduction: nothing, in short, to justify alarming the public by declaring that a new serial killer was on the loose.

But Pender, who had searched the NCIC missing persons files, was able to inform the SAC that as far as he could determine, this particular missing woman, Gloria Whitworth, just happened to be at least the sixth strawberry blond in the past six years to "elope" with the man of her dreams, then drop from sight.

"The whole thing stinks to high heaven," Pender had argued. "We have these women, their looks range from plain to downright homely, except for their hair—they all have beautiful strawberry blond hair. None of them has much in the way of a social life—no boyfriends.

"Then suddenly they fall in love with a mystery man. He avoids being seen by the women's friends and families. No photographs, no prints left behind, but the descriptions tally for the sightings we do have—short, slight, good-looking, dark eyes, hair either dark or bleached.

"And within a week of meeting this mystery man—two weeks at the outside—they run away with him and are never seen again. My God, man, what more do you want?"

"How about a body?" the SAC had responded. "A sign of a forced abduction? Something better than a vague general description that would prove it's even the same man? A single piece of evidence to indicate any of the women was even harmed, much less killed? The bureau hunts serial killers, not serial seducers."

Pender had been with the FBI long enough to understand the reasoning behind the SAC's decision. The bureau had always been a reactive, not a proactive, organization. An ambitious manager moved up through the bureaucracy by padding his stats, allocating his resources to investigations like interstate car thefts that produced quantifiable results, and letting the local authorities handle the loser cases.

But every instinct Pender had—and by this time he had been hunting serial killers for the better part of two decades—told him that going public in order to warn all the girls with the strawberry curls to beware of short, dark, charming seducers, could do nothing but save lives.

So he did, SAC or no SAC. And within an hour of that first and last press conference, broadcast only on one local TV station before the bureau put the kibosh on it, Pender had been summoned back to Washington to face disciplinary action from the OPR—the Office of Professional Responsibility. McDougal managed to save his ass again, but he'd spent the next stretch of his career performing routine background checks of prospective federal employees—the classic FBI punitive assignment.

In the years following Reeford, several more strawberry blonds disappeared, but in none of these cases had anyone caught so much as a glimpse of the mystery seducer. So in the long run all Pender's press conference had managed to accomplish was to drive the already wary Casey deeper into the shadows—and that hurt Ed Pender far worse than the official reprimands.

By the time McDougal agreed to form the Casey task force (or exploratory committee, as he preferred to call it—McDougal, too, knew how to cover his ass: you didn't get as far as he had in the bureau without a Ph.D. in CYA), Pender was out of the doghouse. And as recognition for his apparently having been right about Casey's existence all along, McDougal had given him a seat at the table.

As time wore on, however, and no bodies were discovered, Pender's judgment was called into question again. Eventually the task force evolved into a one-man crusade. At least once a week Pender would search the NCIC missing persons database and a half dozen other systems to see if any more women with hair described as reddish blond or strawberry blond had turned up missing.

When Donna Hughes's name popped up on the NCIC database in June 1998, Pender's first reaction was that she was too old, too good-looking, and too married to fit the victim profile. But the more he reviewed the file forwarded from the Dallas field office, the more convinced he was that Casey had struck again. Though he was unable to persuade McDougal to send him to Texas, he was successful in having Mrs. Hughes added to the list of Casey's possible victims.

Now there was Paula Ann Wisniewski, the young woman from Santa Barbara whose death had resulted in the first decent Casey suspect since the investigation began. Only a man as obsessed as Pender would have had Thom Davies, an FBI database expert, compiling lists of all disappearances or violent deaths involving females with red or blond hair on a weekly basis, or noticed, on his follow-up, the discrepancy between the hair color on the police report—blond—and that on the coroner's—red.

Pender had immediately asked for the postmortem photos to be color-faxed to him. Unfortunately the coroner's flash Polaroids, though gruesome enough, were not much help, chromatically speaking. But since the man in custody fit the description of the suspect in the first seven suspected Casey abductions and had used a knife purchased in Texas, the state where the last Casey abduction had taken place, and most important, because McDougal had no one else available, he had reluctantly agreed to send Pender out to California to interview the suspect.

And after talking to Deputy Jervis, so strong was Pender's hunch that the man in custody was Casey that if he could have been equally as sure that all the victims were accounted for, Pender would never have put his own life in jeopardy trying to tie him to the other crimes.

Instead he'd have flown back for a VICAP interview after the trial, gotten what he could out of the monster, then returned to D.C. to accept the retirement that the bureau was so anxious to foist upon him, and let California take care of Casey. They had lethal injection in the Golden State now; too good for scum like that, but what could you do?

But in addition to the probability that Casey's victim count was higher than currently suspected, there was something else to factor in: the possibility that one or more of the strawberry blonds still survived. Admittedly far-fetched, still it was a fantasy of Pender's, never to be spoken aloud, barely acknowledged even to himself except as a vague mental image: he'd open a cellar door, and there they'd all be, Gloria, Donna, Dolores, and the others, staring up at him through the darkness, somewhat the worse for wear, but alive. Alive.

It was that image—that and the autopsy photos—that made up his mind for him. Fortunately, a seasoned player like Pender knew the first rule for getting along in the bureau-cracy: Better to ask forgiveness than permission. So when he called his office later that afternoon after checking into the Travel Inn in Salinas, he reported only that he had scheduled a jailhouse interview the following afternoon, Wednesday, July 7, and expected to be back home no later than Friday.

Then he put out the Do Not Disturb sign, showered, and climbed into bed stark naked save for his sleeping mask and earplugs, intending to make up for the sleep he'd lost the night before.

But no sooner had Pender closed his eyes than faces began to swim through the blackness behind the sleeping mask. Poor puzzled Paula Wisniewski, watching her own entrails spilling out onto her lap. Terry Jervis, skewered through both cheeks with a souvenir bowie knife. Gloria Whitworth and the other strawberry blonds, faces he'd seen only in snapshots, yearbooks, or in framed photos on their parents' mantels, but animated now by his imagination, pleading to him from the darkness. Don't forget us, don't forget us, don't forget us.

And most disturbing of all, Pender saw the ruined visage of Refugio Cortes, who was still lying in the locked ward of Natividad Hospital with his nose splashed halfway across his face, wondering what it was going to be like going through life with an empty scrotal sac and a dick like a trodden Polish sausage.

8

EVERYBODY KNEW "GOODNIGHT IRENE." Irene Cogan's father, Ed McMullen (Easy Eddie, as he was known at the firehouse and the Hibernians) used to sing her to bed with it, when he wasn't working night shifts at the station.

So Irene wasn't particularly surprised when the prisoner told her he'd see her in his dreams. It was not until she had reached her car that it struck her: she'd never told him her first name. Shaken, she hurried back into the jail and told the deputy at the reception station that she had to speak to the prisoner again.

"Sorry—he's back in his cell."

"It's important."

"I'm sure it is. But we don't have the manpower to be fetching prisoners back and forth on request."

"Let me in to see him, then. I'm doing a court-ordered evaluation, and—"

"Out of the question. They'd have to search you, you'd need an escort, we just don't have—"

"The manpower—I know."

"Whatever it is, it's going to have to wait until tomorrow. Call in the morning."

The deputy's tone of voice was final, dismissive; Irene bowed to the inevitable. But she couldn't shake a sense of unease. She worked the mystery in her mind as she drove home. First she took the Dictaphone out of her briefcase and rewound the tape to the beginning, then played back the first few minutes to be sure she hadn't used her first name when introducing herself. She hadn't.

She then pulled over to the side of Highway 68 and with the

briefcase in her lap went through everything he might have seen—the tests, the paperwork, the back of the Rorschach and TAT cards—to see if her first name appeared on anything. It did not.

Irene lived in a two-story board and batten house in Pacific Grove, a small town thirty miles west of Salinas, just below Monterey on California's central coast. Also known as Butterfly Town, USA, for the monarchs that wintered there, and the Last Home Town, for the ambience, it was the sort of place you either loved or hated. Irene both loved and hated it, for the same reason—too many memories—but she couldn't bring herself to leave the house where she and Frank Cogan had lived too happily for too short a time.

Irene parked her Mustang convertible under the carport. She'd originally bought the car as a present for Frank on the occasion of his fortieth birthday.

"Just jumping the gun on your midlife crisis," she'd told him.

"Great," he'd said. "And where's my nineteen-year-old blond to go with it?"

"Where's mine?" she'd replied.

The mailbox was full, but as Irene walked around the side of the house she shuffled through the ads and circulars in vain looking for a personal letter—Tuesday was junk mail day.

She tossed the mail into the garbage bin behind the house, then let herself into her office through the back door, draped her jacket over the back of her chair, booted up the Psychometrics Software program that would score and interpret the MMPIs, then scanned the prisoner's responses into her PC before heading into the kitchen.

Irene poured herself a glass of Chablis and sipped at it as she made a tomato and avocado salad to eat at her desk. While her computer scanned and scored the second MMPI, she reviewed the first.

"Well, I'll be . . . ," she muttered, though the results were not altogether unexpected. While administering the Rorschach and the TAT, she had noted that the prisoner's responses were so sane and low-key as to border on the banal. He hadn't seen any monsters in the inkblots, nor had the stories he'd made up in response to the pictures on the thematic apperception cards shown any sign of disordered thinking.

But it would be easier for a patient with sociopathic tendencies to manipulate the projective tests than it would be for him to fool the MMPI, which had several validity scales designed to detect dissemblance. Yet when she examined the dissemblance scales on the MMPI graph, there was no indication that he had fudged his answers in any way.

As for the diagnostic scales, none of them revealed any signs of mental disorder. The paranoia reading was low for someone with the prisoner's apparent intelligence, nor had he scored high in psychopathic deviation, schizophrenia, hypomania, depression, hysteria, masculinity/femininity, psychasthenia, or social introversion. He had a little spike in the hypochondriasis scale—but then, who didn't?

The problem was, the profile was largely incompatible not only with the standard DID profile (which typically showed an F scale so high as to render the results technically invalid, extreme depression, and a polysymptomatic reading with an elevated schizophrenia scale), and the prisoner's score of 90 on the DES, but also with what little she knew of the man's history. It seemed to Irene that someone who'd butchered a young woman and knifed a cop while in a dissociative fugue would show *some* evidence of mental illness, but according to this computer analysis, Max/Christopher was as sane a man as ever drew breath.

Before going over the results of the second MMPI, Irene booted up her RORSCAN program and uploaded the prisoner's responses to the Rorschach, carried her plate back to the kitchen and washed it, then went upstairs to take a shower. When she returned in her bathrobe, with a towel around her damp hair, she eagerly snatched the multipage RORSCAN printout off the printer tray, only to read that the unidentified murderer with whom she'd spent the day was by all accounts a well-adjusted individual with a great capacity for empathy and marked altruistic tendencies. No indication whatsoever of the diversified movement responses or the labile and conflicting color responses typical of DID patients.

In normal circumstances, Irene's work would have been all but over at this point. An open-and-shut case: yes, your honor, not only is the defendant perfectly capable of understanding the charges against him and assisting in his own defense, but with a little cramming, I suspect he could do a better job in court than the overworked public defender who's representing him. That'll be eighteen hundred dollars, nice doing business with you.

But then she picked up the printout for the second MMPI, and *boom*, everything changed. The spike in the graph for the Pd scale measuring psychopathic deviation towered over the foothills of the other scales like a lonely Everest. "Poor impulse control . . . aggressive . . . angry . . . violent . . . feels put upon . . . demands immediate gratification . . . unable to learn from experience . . . psychopathic characteristics will surface under stress. . . ."

In other words, a classic Cluster B sociopath. Not only did the results of the two MMPIs appear to have been taken by two different individuals, but the two individuals had about as much in common as Mother Teresa and Jack the Ripper.

DID? Very possibly. But if it was, it was a new manifestation of the disorder, one in which the dissociation of identity was severe enough, and the break clean enough, that at least one personality tested within the normal range, while one or more of the split-off identities, the alters, harbored the entire psychopathology.

Irene's heart began to pound. She was already nationally known in her field, but only by her peers in her subspecialty. To be in at the beginning of such an unusual, and potentially highly publicized, case might be the sort of break that could launch a psychiatrist into the next stratum.

Irene stopped herself, embarrassed at letting her daydreams get the better of her. There was still a long way to go before she could even be sure of her diagnosis. And she needed to be sure: in recent years there had been far too many cases of iatrogenic DID, misdiagnosed or implanted in patients by charlatans and incompetents, creating a virtual epidemic of false memory syndrome and giving legitimate dissociative disorder specialists such as herself a bad name.

In any event, the prisoner had been right about two things: Dr. Cogan had never seen anything like him, and she would indeed be visiting him again soon.

And as she poured herself another glass of wine and lit up a Benson and Hedges, it occurred to Irene that somehow this case, this man, represented a watershed moment in her life. She knew, without knowing how she knew, that one way or another, when their business together was completed, nothing would ever be the same for either of them.

9

LYING IN THE ISOLATION CELL that night, Max was distinctly pleased with his day's work. Except for a minor glitch, during which that whining infant known as Lyssy had briefly seized control of the body, everything had gone Max's way.

Christopher had initiated a flirtation with the psychiatrist. And by taking the Dissociative Experiences test himself, having Ish take the next three tests, then sending Kinch out to take the second MMPI, Max was sure he had successfully pointed Dr. Cogan toward a diagnosis of DID—a diagnosis she would think she'd arrived at on her own.

And if he cared to, he knew, he could just as easily manipulate her into declaring him temporarily unfit to stand trial, permanently unfit to stand trial, or fit to stand trial but not guilty by reason of insanity.

But the system of identities known collectively as Ulysses Christopher Maxwell Jr. had no intention of hanging around Monterey County long enough for a trial. Too many pressing responsibilities back at Scorned Ridge. Still, until Max could engineer an escape, he would take advantage of the opportunity to be seen by an eminent and attractive psychiatrist, who was probably still trying to figure out how the hell he knew her first name.

Not that he held it against her, her not wanting to be on a first-name basis with a prisoner. He wouldn't either, were he the semi-famous Dr. Irene Cogan, specialist in dissociative disorders and author of "Derealization Disorders in Post-Adolescent Males," *Journal of Abnormal Psychology,* 1993; "Speaking in Tongues: Dissociative Trance Disorder and Pentecostal Christianity," *Psy-*

chology Today, 1995; "Dissociative Identity Disorder, Real or Feigned?" *Journal of Nervous and Mental Diseases,* 1997. To name just a few.

Mose, the system's MTP—Memory Trace Personality, or mnemonics expert—hadn't recognized her right off the bat (she'd changed quite a bit from that little black-and-white picture in the Contributors column of *Psychology Today*), but Max had put two and two together immediately after she introduced herself.

A little older, hair a little longer, still a looker. Who'd have thought she'd be passionate, too, under that cool blond exterior— Max had sent her fumbling for her buttons without dropping his eyes below her neck, while a kiss on the hand from Christopher had her all but dripping.

But the frost job! No, no, no—Miss Miller would never have approved. That Princess Di shade was all wrong for her complexion. Max would have been willing to bet her original color was something closer to a strawberry blond. All she'd need to get it back would be a splash more red to put a little blush in her cheeks, until her natural color grew in. She could still carry it off, at least as successfully as Donna Hughes had.

At forty-five, Donna, whom Christopher had seduced away from a wealthy and unfaithful husband in Plano, Texas, a year before, had been the oldest of the strawberry blonds. Paula Ann Wisniewski had been one of the youngest.

Max sighed, thinking back. Paula Ann Wisniewski. Dumb as dirt, ugly as sin—except of course for that hair. It had gone well at first. He'd picked her up easily enough—she was a waitress at a Carrow's in Santa Barbara. Lonely, homely, ready to be swept off her feet. Not a virgin, but she'd never had her body worshiped sexually the way Christopher could, and certainly never had a man fall head over heels for her the way Christopher had.

But it was Max who'd come up with a new story about why the relationship had to remain a secret—he was a "Mystery Diner" for the Carrow's chain, and if it was learned he was dating a waitress, they'd both lose their jobs.

Within three days Paula Ann was willing to follow Christopher anywhere—not a personal record, but damn good. As usual, Maxwell had left a month's worth of supplies back at Scorned Ridge, so he decided to enjoy a little honeymoon on the way up, take the coastal route the whole way.

Things started going bad almost immediately. Paula Ann was

homesick before they reached Pismo Beach, and whined all the way to Cambria. Finally, just south of Lucia, they pulled off the highway and followed a dirt fire trail a few hundred yards east to a turnout under a stand of redwood trees, beside a rushing stream.

There Christopher had romanced Paula Ann as only he could. Things were going well; then the stupid cow tried to stop him in the middle of the act. He thought she was being coy, that she wanted him to be more forceful. Then she freaked out big time. Bad mistake—Christopher couldn't handle fear. Max could, though—Max loved fear. It turned him on. And when Max was turned on, nothing short of impotence or premature ejaculation could discourage him. Then when it was over, she carried on as if he'd raped her.

When I rape you, you'll know it, Max wanted to reply. He would have killed her on the spot, but he'd always made it a cardinal rule never to leave a body behind, so instead he loaded her into the front seat and let Ish, the system's internal self helper and an unlicensed wizard of a therapist, deal with the hysterical girl for the next sixty miles.

Given enough time, Ish might have been able to mollify Paula Ann at least long enough to get her back to Scorned Ridge. A leisurely honeymoon drive, however, was definitely out of the question—Ish cut over on Highway 68 and headed east to join 101 in Salinas, intending to take 152 to Interstate 5: a faster and more direct route to Oregon. Unfortunately, while attempting to convince Paula that Max's mistake was both innocent and understandable, Ish's attention wandered briefly from the road, and he ended up running that red light near Laguna Seca.

Max took control of both the body and the wheel when the siren went off and the tricolor light bar of the white Sheriff's Department cruiser began flashing in the rearview mirror. Instead of pulling over immediately, he stepped on the gas in order to put a little distance between himself and the cruiser. It was never Max's intention to try to outrun the souped-up Crown Victoria in the sorry Chevy Celebrity—he was only trying to buy some time in which to have Kinch silence her. (Max could have done it himself, but why deprive Kinch of his only real pleasure?)

One last word from Paula as Kinch plunged the souvenir bowie knife Max had purchased for him at the Alamo gift shop the year before into her right lower abdomen, and drew it toward him in a downward, then upward arc. One word—"Oh!"— then silence.

Kinch thought at first he'd pulled it off—there were no other cops in sight when the cop brought her face within knife range—but she grabbed onto him as he hurried out of the car to finish her off, and hung on with a death grip, despite the enormous knife skewering her from cheek to cheek.

When the second patrol car arrived, Kinch ceded control to Max, who quickly realized there was no hope of immediate escape. Instead he'd turned his energies to facilitating a getaway at a later date—before they were on him, he'd managed to disengage the deputy's key ring and scatter the other keys as widely as possible to disguise the fact that he'd swallowed her inch-long, hollow, single-flanged handcuff key.

Afterward, back at the jail, three deputies beat the crap out of poor Max for half an hour. Two would hold him while the third walloped him in the gut with a riot stick. *Whack*—"This is for Terry." *Whack*—"This is for Terry." *Whack*—"This is for Terry."

"Who the hell is Terry?" he asked, when they took the rubber gag out of his mouth.

Turned out she was the nosy deputy who'd been the cause of all the trouble in the first place. When they told him she was still alive, he said it was a damn shame, and an oversight he'd be taking care of some day. It wasn't just bravado, either—more like a promise.

It had taken the body two days to shit out the key—fortunately Max was already in isolation, or it would have been mighty embarrassing, pawing through his own turds. Now all he needed was an opportunity to use it. He suspected that chance would come tomorrow, on the way to or from his court appearance.

And as he lay back with his arms laced behind his head, staring up at the bottom of the unoccupied overhead bunk, it occurred to Max for the first time that there would be no need for him to put himself at further risk searching for another strawberry blond to bring back to Scorned Ridge with him.

He had, he realized, already found Donna's replacement—one who would serve not only Miss Miller's rather specialized needs, but also the system's. Sometimes a fella just gets lucky.

10

IRENE COGAN OFTEN BROUGHT her work to bed with her. There was plenty of room: the other side of her king-size BeautyRest had been unoccupied—screamingly unoccupied—since Frank had passed away three years ago. Finding a warm male body to fill it wouldn't have been difficult—at forty-one Irene was an attractive woman—but finding a *man* was by now beginning to seem darn near impossible. A man like Frank Cogan, anyway.

She and Frank had both been scholarship students at Stanford. He was a big guy—six-four, with gorgeous wavy blond hair and an athletic physique. They'd married in college; he'd given up his own dream of becoming a painter and dropped out of school a year shy of his degree to support them. He'd gone into construction, and worked his way up from hod carrier to owning his own construction company in Sand City. Neither his hair nor his physique had lasted—Frank was too fond of beer and pizza—but his good humor had never failed him, and though untrained by Irene's standards, his was a first-rate intelligence.

Even three years after his death it was still possible for Irene to pretend that Frank was only in the bathroom, washing up, that any minute the bathroom door would open and there he'd stand in those ridiculous pajamas she'd bought him as a joke one—

She stopped herself. Thinking about Frank and falling asleep were mutually exclusive activities. Irene felt a quick flash of anger—at Frank, for dying; at herself, for still missing him; at God, for the whole mess of existence. Then it passed; she picked up the prisoner's file and went through it again from the first page, a copy of the arrest report, to the last, a copy of the sheriff's department incident report on the Cortes assault.

Irene tried to picture the slight, boyish man she'd interviewed performing the atrocities attributed to him in the report, but she couldn't do it. Had the stress of being threatened brought out Max's homicidal alter, the persona who had filled out the second MMPI? If so, was there a possibility she could evoke this other personality by threatening him, or otherwise provoking a stress response? It might be worth trying, as long as the prisoner was in restraints.

Eventually Irene dropped off to sleep, which is not to say she got much rest. Her first dream took place in the basement office where she and the prisoner had met. Max was led in, fettered and cuffed. It wasn't until after the guard left that Irene realized that they were both nude. Max explained to her that it was a new type of therapy. She said that she was the doctor and that it was her job to determine the proper treatment.

Not anymore, said Max, coming around the side of the desk, his hands raised in front of him, palms down, thumbs touching in the classic strangler's pose.

Irene looked down and found herself handcuffed to her chair. She opened her mouth to scream, but instead of choking her, he knelt and gently, without a key, unsnapped her cuffs. He helped her to her feet; naked, chest to breast, they embraced.

Then she heard the applause. For the first time she looked up and saw that she was in a packed operating theater—tier upon tier of masked and gowned figures were applauding the two of them. Max—or was he Christopher now?—dropped to his knees again and began kissing her belly, then worked his way down just the way she liked it, just the way Frank used to do it. The applause deepened; it was deafening now, a roar like the surf as the waves of orgasm began to overtake her. . . .

According to an article Irene had read in the *Journal of Human Sexuality,* although damp dreams were not uncommon among women, only a relatively small percentage reported actually dreaming to climax. But it wasn't so much the orgasm that bothered Irene, who up until a moment before awakening had gone without one, sleeping or waking, for three years, it was the identity of the partner her subconscious had chosen.

Fortunately, she had an appointment with Barbara Klopfman,

her own shrink (and her best friend: not an arrangement the American Psychiatric Association would have approved of, but it worked for them), on the jogging trail at 7:00 A.M. She and Barbara always managed to fit in either a little gossip or a little therapy when they ran—tomorrow morning it would be a bit of both.

11

AFTER SUPPER (Buff Orpingtons, in addition to having gorgeous plumage and being superior winter layers, are also first-rate table birds, white-skinned, plump-breasted, and juicy), the woman retires to the myrtlewood rocker in the parlor with her sewing basket and works by the western window until the light fades.

The piece the woman is working on tonight is nearly completed. Thirty to forty thousand separate reddish blond strands, each knotted into a transparent micro-mesh foundation by hand, using a tiny needle curved like a fishhook. But the hands that fed the golden chickens, gathered the eggs, and caressed the Rottweilers that morning are little more than skin grafts over bone—she can only tie a few hundred strands a night before her fingers start to cramp.

Still, her surgeons would be pleasantly surprised to learn that those hands are able to manage such delicate work at all. Although the interosseous muscles of the palm retained enough of their gripping strength to wield a knife (or an ice pick), it had taken hours of reconstructive surgery to repair the intrinsic lumbricates to the point where the thumb and first three fingertips of each hand could meet, much less grasp a tiny needle.

But pain aside, the woman enjoys the work. It's relaxing, contemplative, even meditative. And there's more creativity involved than one might think—not only must the strands be sorted by length, but color gradations must be matched and blended to create the all-important natural look.

In addition, the work keeps the woman's mind off her problems. The boy has been away nearly five weeks. Even the trip to Texas last year to obtain the raw material for the piece she's sewing tonight took less than a month. And if something's happened to him? If he never returns? What then of this life they've carved out for themselves, isolated on a ridgetop, no neighbors, no telephone, far from rude stares and pitying—or horrified—glances? She knows she can't survive up here alone. She also knows that while she is wealthy enough to hire attendants or retire to a first-class nursing home, there's probably not enough money in the world to procure *all* the services the boy provides, not for a woman in her condition.

And of course there are other complications, thinks the woman. The drying shed, for one.

The drying shed! "Drat," she says aloud—she's forgotten all about it. No harm done, though—missing a day here or there is no big hoo-ha, she tells herself, plucking another red-gold strand from her sewing basket and holding it up to the fading light. But it slips from her aching fingers and slithers back into the basket like a snake charmer's cobra in reverse. Time to call it a night.

A steep, narrow staircase leads to her second-story bedroom. She undresses, rehangs the green gown—she has two green dresses and two black, which she wears in rotation and washes by hand. The mask comes off last, in the bathroom; there are no mirrors in the bathroom. She washes it in the sink and hangs it on the towel rack to dry, then brushes her teeth by feel. That goes quickly—it's easy to brush your teeth when your lips have been burned away to the gum line. No bath tonight—nobody to bathe for. She splashes warm water under her arms and between her legs, then slips on a gossamer silk nightdress. She can only bear the touch of silk against her skin—her scar tissue, rather.

So the sheets and the comforter on her double bed are silk as well. She sits on the edge of the bed and from the night-table drawer removes a small ampoule of pharmaceutical morphine sulfate she had taken out of the refrigerator that morning. She raises her right leg until her heel is on the bed, hikes her nightdress up over her raised knee and lets it fall until her leg is bared, then jabs the needle into the back of the right thigh—good skin and plenty of meat there. It's a two-handed operation: one skeletal hand holds the ampoule, the other presses the plunger.

There's not much of a rush—the drug takes hold slowly when

injected intramuscularly. She dabs away a dot of blood from her thigh with a cotton ball before pulling her nightie back down. Then, with a pleasurable sigh, she switches off the bedside lamp, slips into bed, and pulls the silken covers up to her chin. She's gotten through another day without him, but it hasn't been easy—she misses him the way she misses her own breasts.

12

WITH HIS LEFT WRIST CUFFED to the chair, the prisoner extended his right hand across the table. Irene shook it without thinking, but when she tried to pull away, the prisoner's hand tightened around hers. She had a moment to think about how much stronger the slender man was than he appeared to be; then he loosened his grip.

"I did," he said.

"Did what?"

"See you in my dreams."

There were dozens of ways to handle a patient's aggressive transference; for some reason Irene couldn't remember any of them. Instead she was mortified to hear herself ask, "What was I wearing?"

"Not much," replied the prisoner, opening his mouth to laugh. His jaw dropped and kept on dropping, his face became impossibly elongated, and when he bared his teeth she noticed for the first time that there was something inhuman about them. Too small, too sharp, too many. She felt around under the desk in a panic—there should have been an alarm button—and touched his foot instead. He had extended it under the desk and was sliding it between her thighs.

She grabbed it to push it away; a soft black slipper came off in her hand, and she realized that the foot nudging her thighs open was hard, cloven, and hairy—a hoof. She cried out, jerked her hand away; the back of her hand collided with the alarm button. A distant buzzer sounded. At first she could scarcely hear it over the prisoner's laughing, but it grew louder and louder. . . .

Irene opened her eyes and saw that it was her alarm clock making all the noise. She stumbled into the bathroom, performed an abbreviated toilette, pulled a pair of sweatpants and a Stanford sweatshirt on over her jogging bra and panties, laced on her new Reeboks, and set out for Lovers Point on foot.

Lovers Point, formerly Lovers of Jesus Point, is a rocky spit of land topped by a manicured lawn, with a shallow bathing cove at one end and a great heap of boulders tumbling into Monterey Bay at the other. Barbara Klopfman was already down by the seawall doing her stretching exercises. Behind her, upthrust boulders jutted from the water like the raw material for Easter Island statues; beyond the rocks, an otter floated on its back in the kelp, picking with clever, childlike paws at an abalone shell balanced on its chest.

"Didn't think you were going to make it," called Barbara. Then, squinting in Irene's direction as Irene drew closer: "Did you get *any* sleep last night?"

"Not much." Irene stretched with her shorter, darker, plumper, and immeasurably more Jewish friend and therapist for a few minutes, then they set out on their waterfront jog, trotting side by side where the path was wide enough, Irene taking the lead where it narrowed. Across the bay the sun was rising over Moss Landing; the light on the water was dazzling.

"I did a psych evaluation of the man who murdered that girl in his car the other week," Irene began. Below them to the right, the tide was low enough to uncover the deep green moss of the tidepool rocks. White western gulls wheeled and screamed; fat harbor seals, brown and mottled gray, climbed onto the offshore rocks to begin their hard day's basking.

"That what kept you up?" Barbara was already breathing hard. Neither of them had been a runner for long; between Barbara's weight problem and Irene's cigarette habit, their pace was necessarily unhurried.

"More or less. I kept having these erotic dreams about him."

"Do tell, do tell."

By the time Irene finished her story, the two women had rounded Point Pinos, the rocky outcropping where John Denver's plane had gone down two years earlier, and collapsed, winded, on a concrete bench.

"Well, what's the verdict?" asked Irene, when she had caught her breath. Below them the Pacific waves were pounding themselves into misty foam against the rocks; a flight of pelicans crossed in front of the sun in a straight line.

"Verdict? . . . Odd choice of . . . words. Feeling . . . guilty about something?" Barbara said between gasps.

"It's only a figure of speech."

"Yes, Irene—and a cigar is only a smoke." Barbara mopped her face with the hem of her oversize T-shirt. "Listen, honey, it's not all bad."

"Tell me the good news first."

"You're obviously starting to reconnect with your own sexuality. And not a minute too soon, in my opinion. How long has it been, three years?"

"Three and a half. But why *him?*"

"Because on the one hand he radiates sexuality, with a whiff of danger, and on the other hand, being a patient *and* being behind bars, he's relatively safe to fantasize about."

"Then what's the problem?"

"The problem is, he's *not* safe to fantasize about. The way you've described him to me, he sounds like a charming, attractive, intelligent, and *extremely* manipulative sociopath who's trying to get under your skin. And doing a pretty good job of it, apparently."

"So what do you think I should do?"

Barbara patted Irene's knee. "Put up your psychic shield, wrap up this evaluation as quick as you can, then let me play *shadchen* and fix you up with some guy who's not a patient, is not going to be behind bars for the rest of his life, and is hopefully not a psychopathic multiple either."

"Where's the fun in that?" said Irene—but she did feel better. Somehow talking to Barbara always made her feel better.

When the sheriff's deputy showed Irene into the interview room via the visitor's door around eleven o'clock, the first thing she did was examine the desk. She was relieved to be reminded that it did indeed have a solid front, as she'd vaguely recalled—at least she wouldn't be spending the entire interview worrying about Max playing cloven-hoofed footsies with her under the desk.

A few minutes later the prisoner was led in through the inmate's door, and they exchanged perfunctory greetings. As soon as the deputy left the room, Irene took out the pack of Camels she'd bought for the prisoner, slit the cellophane with her manicured thumbnail, shook one out, tamped the end expertly, placed it between his waiting lips, and fired it up with the jade-and-silver lighter Frank had given her for their last anniversary.

"Try one," he urged her, his face wreathed in smoke as she placed a brown plastic battery-powered smoke-sucker ashtray in front of him. "See what a real cigarette tastes like."

"Some other time. I have a few follow-up questions I wanted to ask you."

"I thought you might." Holding the Camel in one side of his mouth, he worked a shred of tobacco out of the other with the tip of his tongue, which was unusually pointed and, like his lips, a surprisingly dark shade of red.

"To begin with, how did you know my first name?"

"Educated guess. The monogram on your briefcase. How many women's names begin with the letter I?" Then, in an exaggerated brogue: "Especially colleens with the map of Oirland writ large across their loovly countenance."

Irene thought back—it was true, he hadn't used her name until after she'd set the briefcase on the desk while packing up at the end of the session. And her heritage *was* Irish as Paddy's pig on both sides.

Feeling somewhat relieved, she took the Dictaphone out of her briefcase, set it on the desk, and turned it on. Rather than ask him outright if he had DID, she tried an indirect approach. "Next question: yesterday you told me about coming to in the car next to the young woman's body. Has this ever happened to you before?" Recurring fugue states and time loss were classic markers for DID.

Max cocked his head, amused. "No."

A sociopath with an above-average ability to manipulate standardized psychological tests, then. Irene felt curiously disappointed. "I see."

"That's no, I've never come to in a car next to a young woman's body. Good lord, Irene, you've had nearly twenty-four hours to frame that question, and that's the best you can do?"

The shred of tobacco still clung to the corner of his lips—when he stuck his tongue out to lick it off he accidentally pushed it farther onto his cheek, where he could no longer reach it. Irene found a tissue in her purse, reached across the desk (she was wearing a summerweight cotton turtleneck under a navy blue blazer today), and removed it for him. He thanked her with a winning grin; she made a mental note that along with his need to feel mentally superior, as exemplified by his last statement, he also seemed comfortable with being infantilized.

"I'll rephrase the question. Have you—"

"The answer is yes."

"I see. Have you ever heard voices?"

The amused cock of the head again. "You mean other than, say, yours, now?"

"I'll rephrase: I mean voices that no one else can hear, originating from either inside or outside your head."

"Yes—inside. But you know what's even scarier than hearing somebody else talking inside your head?" He'd been speaking out of one side of his mouth, squinting against the smoke; now he leaned forward and carefully placed the cigarette in the ashtray with his mouth.

"What's that?"

"It's the feeling that there's somebody else *listening*."

13

PENDER HAD NO TROUBLE locating the Monterey County court-house complex on West Alisal Street in Salinas. Three buildings surrounded a courtyard with curved walkways and waist-high hedge mazes. Glass catwalks atop pillared porticos connected the older east and west wings to the ugly rectangular box of the north wing at second-floor height. Stone heads of figures from California history—helmeted conquistadors, Indians with pageboy bangs, pioneer women in bonnets, ranchers in narrow-brimmed hats—stared down blankly from the cornices of the exterior walls, and the windows of all three buildings were trimmed in a surprisingly festive Aztec blue. In the center of the courtyard was a garden island of tall purple flowers and orange bird-of-paradise.

The old jail, a crumbling three-story, yellow-beige fortress with arched, grilled windows and a false parapet, was located next door to the courthouse, separated from the west wing by a narrow alley. The thick walls and straight rise of the front of the building reminded Pender of the Alamo, but the ornate dark green, wrought-iron window grilles and ornamental lamppost-sconces set into the front wall evoked old New Orleans.

Pender parked the Toyota in the county lot behind the jail and placed the paper placard he'd been given at the sheriff's office in the windshield. He checked his watch and realized he had a couple of hours to kill before he was to meet his assigned liaison, Lieutenant Gonzalez. Then he remembered how his mother used to correct him when he talked about having time to kill. Don't kill it, she would say, spend it!

Right, Mom. Pender set off to explore the courthouse complex.

The first thing he noticed was an egregious lack of security. There were no metal detectors in use—he was able to wander freely through the entire complex carrying a semiautomatic in a shoulder holster.

Nor was he challenged when he stationed himself in the alley to observe the chained prisoners in red, orange, or green jumpsuits being convoyed back and forth between the white GMC vans stenciled with the motto "Keeping the Peace Since 1850" and the holding cells, or marched across the courtyard between the holding cells and the courthouse, in full view, and reach, of the public.

Shaking his head sadly—the place was a disaster waiting to happen—Pender reentered the west wing of the courthouse and took the elevator up to the snack bar on the second floor.

There was an embarrassing delay at the cash register—it took Pender a moment to realize that the cashier was stone blind.

"I have a tuna fish sandwich and a cup of coffee," he said, handing the man a five-dollar bill. Another pause. "It's a five."

"You must be from back east," said the cashier as he made change.

"Upstate New York," replied Pender, wondering how many customers in the course of a day handed the man a single and told him it was a five—or a ten, or a twenty. "How could you tell?"

"You said tuna *fish*. Out here, we just assume if it's a tuna, it's a fish."

Pender sat alone at a corner table. He felt surprisingly calm, for a man who was preparing himself to be locked into a cell with a murderer. It had been years since Pender had conducted an undercover interview—as he sipped at his black coffee, looking out over the pleasant courtyard, he mulled over his approach.

It would be best, he knew, if the subject initiated a conversation. If not, Pender planned to start out either by bitching about his lawyer—every con in every cell in America had a beef with his attorney—or by talking about his travels: nothing suspicious in chatting about places you'd been to. He'd drop a lot of place names, sprinkling in mentions of one or two relevant towns— Plano, Texas; Sandusky, Ohio; San Antonio, where the knife had been purchased—and seeing if any of those elicited a response.

Once he had the subject at ease, Pender planned to work the conversation around to sex, admit to a rape or a little rough stuff himself, and see if he couldn't draw the man out. He wouldn't be expecting a confession at this point, or much in the way of specifics, but a good round of jailhouse bragging could be remark-ably instructive, and Casey, if it were Casey, might well drop an incriminating detail here or there.

Suddenly it occurred to Pender that he hadn't prepared himself for the interview as thoroughly as he might have, that he'd failed to interview the one person who'd had more contact with the subject than anyone since the unfortunate Refugio Cortes: the psychiatrist who'd been evaluating him.

But how to contact her? He didn't even know her name. He moved his chair closer to the window—Pender never really trusted cell phones—and called Lieutenant Gonzalez, who was not in his office. He had Gonzalez's voice mail kick him back out to the oper-ator, who connected him with Visitor Reception at the jail on Natividad Road.

"This is Special Agent Pender of the FBI. I'm trying to find out the name of the psychiatrist who visited—" He started to say Casey, but stopped himself. "your John Doe—prisoner number . . ." He flipped open his notebook and read it off.

"I'm sorry, I can't give out that information over the telephone," replied the female deputy who'd answered. Then, to Pender's sur-prise, as he was gearing up for a little bluff and bluster: "But according to the log, she's inside interviewing the prisoner. She'll have to log out when she's done—I could give her your number and ask her to call you."

"Ohhhhkey-doke." Though not a superstitious man, Pender had learned from experience that luck, bad or good, came in waves—perhaps he'd caught a good one.

14

"ALL RIGHT, sweetheart, we're going back further. It's your birthday again—do you have a cake?"

They were ten minutes into the age regression. The hypnosis had gone smoothly—like most multiples, Max/Christopher had proved eminently suggestible. After a short relaxation technique (not easy, with the prisoner seated, fettered and manacled, in a cold, relatively bare, brightly lit room with nothing but hard surfaces and right angles—but she pulled it off), Irene had him concentrate on a black dot she'd drawn on a sheet of blank notepaper, explained in a calm, low-pitched voice that he was getting sleepier and his eyelids heavier, and sent him to his safest place. She'd then implanted a code word to use as a cue for waking him up. That was pretty much all it took—Hypnosis 101, no bells, no whistles.

When he was deeply under, she began regressing him, walking him backward through his birthdays. When she reached five she observed his eyes rolling upward beneath the closed, fluttering lids—it was his first switch of the session.

"Choc'lit cake. Choc'lit icing. I like choc'lit." His voice was chirpy, his body language fidgety.

"Does it have candles?"

"A course—it's a *birthday* cake, you silly."

"Can you count the candles?"

"Five candles, one two three four five."

"Can you read the writing?"

"My name—that's my name—Lyssy, el why ess ess why."

"Happy birthday, Lyssy. Five years old, isn't that something. Did you open your presents yet?"

"After the cake—doncha know you can't open presents until after the cake?"

"How about your presents from your mommy and daddy?"

"I got a two-wheeler. In my room when I woke up in the morning. It's a red Schwinn, just like Walter cross the street, only red. Daddy said I was way too old for my Big Wheels. And no training wheels—Daddy says only, you know, *sissies* use training wheels."

"Tell me about your mommy and daddy. Do they ever do things you don't like? Hurt you or touch you?" Leading question, right on the border of suggestion. But Irene's time with the patient was limited, this was diagnosis, not treatment, and every verified DID patient in the literature had a history of early, horrendous abuse— not just your passing pat on the fanny, but really egregious stuff.

"Daddy sometimes—but maybe I was dreaming. Mommy says I only dream it."

"Dream what? Tell me about one of the times Daddy did something and Mommy said it was a dream."

"Okay, the first time I was all tucked in, I was lyin' in bed lookin' at the wallpaper. I have party balloon wallpaper in my room—pink and blue party balloons, on account a they didn't know if I would be a boy or a girl. And alla sudden I can see right through the wall into their room, Mommy's and Daddy's room. They're sitting up in bed watching TV like usual, Mommy in her nightgown, Daddy in his T-shirt.

"Only their faces are different: they look like the monsters in *Where the Wild Things Are*. Daddy has a lion face, Mommy's face is all scary and furry and pointed like a fox. And their regular faces, their people faces, are lying next to them on the bed, all empty and rubbery and wrinkly, like these monster faces are their real faces, and the regular faces are just masks they put on in the daytime."

"That *does* sound like a dream, doesn't it?"

"I know. I even dreamed I woke up. And I was staring at the wallpaper again, I couldn' see through *any* more. I'm still scared. I wanna call Mommy. But that's scary too. 'Cause what if what I saw was real? All they'd have to do is put on their people masks—how would I know?

"So I climb out a bed, ssh, real quiet, and open my door. The house is all dark for the night, except for the night-light in the hall, you know, for when I have to get up to go peepee. Tippy-toe down the hall. I can see light through the bottom a their door. I'm pos' to knock, always knock before you come in Mommy and Daddy's room, only then I think about how quick they could put their people masks on. So I try and turn the doorknob. But it's locked. But I know how to open it, cause one time Walter locked hisself in the baffroom and Mommy got the ice pick outta the drawer and stuck it in the little hole in the doorknob and it opened up.

"So I go into the kitchen and I get the ice pick outa the drawer and go back to Mommy and Daddy's room and stick it in and it goes pop and then the knob turns and I open the door and there's Mommy and Daddy with their regular faces on. Only they're not watching TV. Mommy is sitting in a chair all bare naked and she's all tied up and Daddy is standing over her, he's bare naked too and his peepee is all red and sticking out and he's holding this red candle, and he's dripping hot drips, I see the red drips on her boobies.

"Then she sees me, she says, 'Oh fuck, honey, it's the kid.' So he turns around—his peepee's pointing at me and I can't move and I can't scream, just like in a dream only I know it's real. Then he's standing over me. He pulls the ice pick outa the doorknob and looks down at it in his hand, and I know, I just *know* he's gonna, *wham*, stick it right down through the top a my head, only instead he picks me up and carries me over to the bed and tosses me on the bed and pulls down my pajama pants and I don' wanna talk about it anymore and you can't make me."

Irene had no intention of forcing him. Even using hypnosis so early in DID therapy was unconventional—pressuring him at this point could be disastrous.

"Lyssy, honey," she said soothingly. "I need you to know you never have to talk about anything until you're ready. But when you *are* ready, I need you to know you're safe telling me anything at all—nothing you tell me can ever come back to hurt you. Now, you said your mommy told you it was all only a dream?"

"A nightmare—next morning she said I had a nightmare. I axed her how do *you* know, she says I yelled in my sleep. Then she axed me to tell her about my nightmare. She says I hafta or it will never go away.

"So I say I saw through the wall, and you and Daddy took your faces off and you were both monsters and I woke up and I went into your room to see if it was true and he was hurting you, and then he pulled down my pants and he hurted me.

"And she says that proves it's only a bad dream because Daddy would never hurt us. She crosses her heart and hopes to die. But my butt still hurted, so you know what I think?"

"What, Lyssy?"

"I think either both dreams hafta to be real, the one where I see the animal faces through the wall and the one where I go into their bedroom, or both a them hafta be dreams. And sometimes I think what if everybody wears a people mask? What if everybody has a animal face under their skin. And sometimes in the bathroom I stand on my old potty stairs from when I was little, and I look into the mirror real hard, and I try to see what kind a animal I have under *my* skin."

He was starting to grow agitated again. Irene glanced at her watch. It was just past twelve-forty. She only had until one o'clock with the prisoner, and it was important to leave at least fifteen minutes at the end of a hypnotherapy session to bring the patient back and give him time to reorient.

"All right, Lyssy. I understand. Thank you for sharing with me."

"Sharing's good. You're 'pos to share."

"Yes you are, honey. You did a wonderful job. Now I want you to think about your safest place, the place in the world, it doesn't have to be real, you can make it up, where you feel the best and the safest, and I want you to go there for me. . . . Safest place . . . You there yet . . . ? Attaboy. Okay, here we go. Five, four, three, two, one . . . *applesauce!*"

Once again, Irene observed a radical alteration in the prisoner's body language. The fidgeting and squirming ceased. There was a tense stillness about him. His neck stiffened. His scarred hands, which as Lyssy he'd used expressively, within the range of the manacles, now curled into protective fists. When he opened his eyes, they darted nervously around the room, then fixed suspiciously on Irene.

"What happened?" He was acting out his grounding behavior again, rubbing his fists against the coarse orange fabric of his jumpsuit.

"It's all right, you just came out of hypnosis."

He moaned. "Who did you talk to?"

Irene's turn to go still and watchful. It was a crucial moment in their relationship—the closest Max, as Max, had come to acknowledging the nature of his dysfunction. "I'm not sure I understand your question."

"Cut the crap, Irene." His hands strained, twisting against the manacles. "We both know I'm a multiple—now who the fuck did you talk to?" It was the first time she could remember hearing him swear; his face had darkened with anger.

Recognizing that she'd erred in pretending to misunderstand his question, she tried to make up for it. "A little boy named Lyssy."

"That titty-sucking wimp? What'd he tell you?"

It took all the self-control Irene could muster not to draw back in her chair—she couldn't remember ever seeing an expression so purely murderous. "He told me about the first time he was molested by his father."

"I bet he didn't tell you how he provoked it—did he tell you that? Did he tell you it was his own fucking fault?"

"No, he didn't feel that way. Do you remember the incident?"

"No, I don't *remember* it," he said, spitting out the words with unconcealed contempt. "I wasn't there. But I know about it. Little fucker breaks into his parents' bedroom while they're going at it—what the fuck did he expect?"

"All right, all right, I understand you're angry. I wish we could deal with it now, but our time's almost up for today. So let me just give you a little food for thought—something to toss around until our next session. Your anger at Lyssy—do you think it's possible it might be displaced? That you've turned the anger you feel for your father in on yourself because it's not safe to be angry with your father, Max?"

The prisoner turned his head to the side and spat violently onto the linoleum floor of the interview room. When he turned back to Irene, he was calm again, or at least under control, and when he spoke his voice was level, reasonable.

"Food for thought, is it? I'll give you some food for thought, Dr. Cogan. One: I'm not Lyssy, and Lyssy is not me. Two: I don't *have* a father, and I never did. And three: you're not my therapist. This is a court-ordered evaluation—as far as you know, there's not even going to *be* another session. So if you're not going to be treating me, Dr. Cogan, I'd appreciate it if you wouldn't fuck with my head. You have no business fucking with my head."

Irene had no problem apologizing to a patient—dealing with multiples was always a process of trial and error. "You're right. I'm sorry. I had no intention of messing with your head."

His eyes were downcast; he nodded warily without raising his head.

"But about that last point you made." Irene struggled to keep the eagerness out of her voice. "If I could arrange it, would you *like* for me to treat you, to be your therapist?"

"I-I-I'd like that very much," said the prisoner softly. When he raised his head, Irene saw that he'd executed another switch—this was the exhausted, defeated-looking alter with the slumped shoulders, the vowel stammer, and the tic in the right eye. "But he'll never let ih-ih-it happen."

"Who? Who'll never let it happen?"

"Max."

"What if we could convince Max that therapy would be in his best interest as well?"

"You couldn't—he wouldn't."

"Why not?"

"Because . . . he's . . ." Irene watched in astonishment as the personality sitting across the desk from her began to disintegrate. The tic worsened, until both eyes were twitching violently; the face clenched like a fist; the head began to tremble violently as he fought to get the words out. ". . . he's a demon. His name is Car—"

The prisoner went limp; he sagged down in the wooden chair, then toppled forward, striking the top of his head against the edge of the desk as he fell. Irene jumped up, started toward him, then thought better of it and reached for the phone on the wall instead.

15

PENDER WAS on his second cup of coffee when his cell phone began chirping in his pocket. "Pender."

"This is Dr. Cogan. Irene Cogan. I understand you've been trying to get in touch with me?"

"You're the psychiatrist who's been evaluating the John Doe who knifed that young woman in June?"

"I am. What can I do for you?"

"I'm investigating a series of abductions of females whose descriptions match the current victim—I'd be interested in anything you can tell me about the suspect."

"Even if I had the time, Agent Pender, I'm not sure it would be ethical for me to—"

Pender, with forced calm: "Doctor Cogan, this man is a prime suspect in a dozen unsolved abductions. In less than half an hour I'm due to be locked in a cell with him. I assume you know what he did to Refugio Cortes?"

After a short pause. "I do."

"Yes, well, anything you can tell me that might help give me a handle on him could save me from a similar fate."

Pender could almost hear her thinking it over. He crossed his thick fingers and pushed her a little harder. "I give you my word that anything you can tell me will be held in absolute confidence—he'll never even know we've spoken."

A few more seconds passed. "Agent Pender, are you familiar with dissociative identity disorder?"

"I don't believe so."

"How about multiple personality disorder?"

"Oh, sure. Like *Sybil,* or *Three Faces of Eve.*"

"Exactly. Or rather, not exactly—forget what you've seen in the movies. The disorder was renamed a few years ago, to take into account the fact that the split-off identities—we call them alters—aren't really separate personalities, but aspects of the same, dissociated identity."

"How does that work?"

"Every case is different, of course. But they all have in common a history of horrendous abuse beginning early on in childhood—in some cases infancy—and continuing for years."

"Sexual abuse?"

"Sexual, physical, emotional, even satanic—you name it." Irene, who had been lecturing and writing about the disorder since 1989, switched onto automatic pilot: "With no way for the child to escape the abuse, the child's mind dissociates in self-defense, creating a more or less coherent system of alter identities to help the child deal with the trauma.

"Now the reason we use the word *system* is that despite the outward appearance of chaos, internally the alters function together to help the child, and later the adult, cope with his or her world. Over the years we've identified dozens of different classes of alters. For instance there's the host identity, not to be confused with the original identity. The host is the one who tries to hold the system together. There are also child identities, frozen at whatever age they were created, who hold the memories and affects of the original traumas.

"And one of the best examples of how the alters function together is the interaction between the persecutor or suicidal identities, who attempt to punish the individual to alleviate feelings of guilt, and the protector alters, whose function is to protect the body from harmful or neglectful alters—they'll usually step in to keep the persecutors from going too far. In some instances a suicidal alter or a substance-abusing alter will take an overdose, and the protector will call an ambulance.

"There are also ISHs—internal self helpers—who are like internal therapists, providing perspective and giving advice, and MTPs—memory trace personalities—who maintain a coherent memory of the patient's life history, regardless of which alter was in control at the time.

"Then you have cross-gender and/or promiscuous identities to act out conflicting sexual urges, as well as administrators and obsessive-compulsive identities who come out to perform work-related activities. There are autistic and handicapped alters who emerge in highly stressful times; alters with artistic skills; analgesics who don't feel pain; impostors who can imitate not only other people but also other alters; substance abusers who attempt to self-medicate and dull the pain. Some alters believe themselves to be demons or spirits.

"During the course of a day, the patient can switch between alters with different voices, postures, and affects hundreds of times, dozens of times, or not at all. And it's important to understand that the patient's body image, or self-image, actually changes depending on the alter. When a male patient is under the control of a female alter, he will actually see himself as a woman, while a child alter will see itself as a child, no matter what the patient's chronological age. And not just *see* itself—I once treated an anorexic sixteen-year-old girl with an older male alter. He came out once when she was hospitalized for tube feeding, and it took three strong attendants to subdue him—her."

"You're telling me she actually had the *strength* of a grown man?"

"It's not at all uncommon."

"All these alters—do they know about each other?"

"It varies. Every system has its own rules and manner of functioning. Some systems have subsystems of alters, who share memory and consciousness, and others who are isolated. In therapy, one of our first jobs, with the patient's help, is to map out the systems and subsystems."

"Sounds complicated."

"It is."

"What can you tell me about this particular individual?"

"The first thing you'll need to recognize is how he manifests his alter switches. When he's about to change, you'll see his eyes roll up to the right, then his eyelids will flutter. Sometimes the alter who's just taken over will look around the room, perhaps rub his thigh—it's called grounding behavior. As for the alters themselves, the identity that seems to be in charge of the body most of the time calls himself Max."

"Is Max the, what did you call it? The host?"

"I'm not sure at this point. Max's affect is all wrong. Most hosts are depressed and anxious. I did meet another alter who filled that bill—he even asked me for help. But he definitely wasn't in charge—

he referred to Max as a demon, and I think Max punished him for coming out to speak with me. I don't know his name—if you see him, you'll recognize him by his stammer, and the tic in his right eye. There's also a child alter named Lyssy—that's L Y S S Y—and a sexually seductive identity known as Christopher. I think Christopher might have been the alter who abducted the Wisniewski girl."

"How would I recognize Christopher?"

"There's nothing overt. A little more eye contact, perhaps—a softer manner than Max. But that may have been because I'm a woman. *You* might not meet Christopher—unless of course he's bisexual. Or there might be a female alter, or an alter with a homosexual orientation."

"So what have we got? Max, the host with the tic, Lyssy, and Christopher. Just the four?"

"That's all I've met so far. I think two others took some of the standardized tests for me yesterday. One of them was textbook well-adjusted—he tested saner than I do. That might be the ISH. Another tested as a classic sociopath—he's probably the one to watch for, the one who committed the murder. Then again, you might meet an entirely different set of alters than I did—I would expect the dynamic to be quite different in a more stressful environment."

Pender glanced at his watch—1:50. "Thank you, doctor—you've been very helpful. Can I call you after my interview if I have any more questions?"

"Sure—just call my office." She gave him the number; he jotted it down in his notebook. "If I'm not in, you can leave a number with my service—they'll know how to get in touch with me."

"Great. Thanks again, Doctor Cogan."

"No problem. Oh—one more thing, Agent Pender. If I were you, I would definitely take every precaution. Because the only thing I can tell you for sure about any of this individual's alters is that one of them is homicidal. At *least* one of them."

16

THE BODY OF ULYSSES MAXWELL lay motionless on its bunk in the county jail on Natividad Road, an icebag balanced on its forehead. The skin was unbroken, the swelling had gone down, and the nurse at the jail, in consultation with Dr. Cogan, had already determined that there was no concussion, else Maxwell would have been transferred to the county hospital just up the road. The reason the body lay as if unconscious was that for the moment, there was no one in charge.

Inside the head, though, things were anything but quiet. Max raged about traitors, traitors who should be burned, traitors who could be expelled or banished into the darkness of non-being forever, while Lyssy the Sissy whimpered that it wasn't his fault, that he hadn't wanted to come out, that the doctor had made him, and Ulysses, the deposed host alter, known to the others as Useless, pleaded for his very existence—when he could get a word in edgewise.

In the end it was Ish who brought peace to the system, pointing out that the debacle in the interview room was at least partly Max's fault, in that it was Max who, in the mistaken belief that he could control the situation, had given the psychiatrist permission to attempt to hypnotize them in the first place.

Ish was the only alter who was allowed to criticize Max, or at least call some of his actions or decisions into question. He pointed out, in a diplomatic fashion, that although their system represented a new and superior order of multiple personality, DID was still DID, and every one of the interlocking identities, even Max, an alter like no other, was by nature enormously suggestible.

I'm sure you'll take that into account in the future, Ish suggested reassuringly. *For the moment, though, instead of blaming each other, our time might be better spent figuring out how to limit the damage.*

Eat shit and die, replied Max. He'd already figured out how to limit the damage.

A moment later the reanimated body drew a deep, calming breath, the long-lashed eyes fluttered open. Max took off the ice-bag and sat up slowly. He could hear a guard circling the pod; he waited until the footsteps had passed his cell before rolling up his sleeve and reaching into the urine-filled toilet beside the bunk. The toilet and sink were one stainless steel unit, sink above, toilet below. Max fished around in the bottom of the bowl, removed the inch-long handcuff key, washed it off in the sink, dried it on his jail-issue, postage-stamp washcloth, and slipped it into his mouth.

Max had been to court before—as Dr. Cogan would have said, he knew the drill. There was no metal detector for prisoners leaving the new jail on Natividad, no cavity search for prisoners being transported to and from the courthouse, and no metal detector at all at the old jail on West Alisal.

Prisoners returning to the new jail did have to pass through a sensitive, state-of-the-art metal detector on their way in, Max knew. He had no intention, however, of returning to Natividad Road, with or without Terry Jervis's handcuff key, which he planned to return to Deputy Jervis personally, at the earliest opportunity.

17

JUST AFTER TWO O'CLOCK on Wednesday afternoon, Lieutenant Rigoberto Gonzalez of the Monterey County Sheriff's Department—early forties, perfectly pressed uniform, carefully trimmed black mustache—met Pender in the alley next to the old jail, abandoned now except for the ground-floor cellblock in the east wing, and led him from the brightness of a sunny Salinas afternoon into the gloomy half-light of the jail. Directly ahead of them were sliding barred doors. Gonzalez turned right instead, and Pender followed him into a messy, crowded, claustrophobic little room that looked more like the office of an old-time two-pump country gas station than the command post for a metropolitan jail.

"You carrying?" asked Gonzalez, unholstering his own weapon, the sheriff's department standard-issue Glock .40. Pender handed his SIG Sauer to Gonzalez, butt first; the deputy checked it out. "I thought you guys carry Glocks now."

"I'm more comfortable with the SIG."

"Not as much stopping power with a nine as with a forty."

"The dual action is faster, though. I figure I can always shoot 'em twice." Pender hadn't actually fired a shot in anger since his days as a Cortland County sheriff's deputy, but he remained range-qualified with both pistol and shotgun.

After locking up the guns and introducing Pender to Frank Twombley and Deena Knapp, the two deputies on duty, Gonzalez led Pender through the office—they were now on the other side of the sliding barred doors—then to the left, down a narrow corridor to the jail's old visiting room, bare save for a single metal bench suspended like a shelf from the back wall. The windows that had once separated the inmates from their loved ones were boarded up, the telephones gone, their torn wires sticking out from the wall at three-foot intervals.

"You can change in here." Gonzalez handed Pender a paper bag containing an orange jumpsuit, a gray T-shirt, white socks, and rubber sandals.

Pender asked Gonzalez if there was any significance to the variety of jumpsuit colors he'd seen the inmates wearing.

"Orange is for your violent felons, red for nonviolent felons, green for misdemeanors."

"So I'm a violent felon?"

"You'd have to be, for us to put you in with the Ripper. We keep the prisoners strictly segregated in the holding cells."

"You call him the Ripper?" asked Pender, unfolding the jumpsuit and checking it for size. XXL—close enough.

"Did you see what he did to that girl?"

"Unfortunately, yes—I saw the autopsy photos."

Gonzalez left Pender in the visiting room, returning a few minutes later with a full set of handcuffs, leg irons, chains, and a padlocking belt to pull the ensemble together. When he finished securing Pender, he stepped back and nodded approvingly. Bald, scowling, immense, the FBI man might have been the enforcer for a gang of over-the-hill outlaw bikers.

"Agent Pender, you could give mean a bad name. What do you want to be in for?"

"What do I look like I'd be in for?"

Gonzalez narrowed his eyes, gave Pender an exaggerated once-over. "How about rape? No offense."

"None taken. But with a face like mine, who'd ever believe *I* had trouble getting any?"

The deputy grinned. "With a face like yours," he said, "we should probably make it serial rape."

The holding cells were at the opposite end of the corridor. Gonzalez opened the metal cabinet containing the door control panel beside the entrance to the cell block. Inside the cabinet were four vertically sliding knobs above a solid steel wheel eighteen inches in diameter. All four knobs were down in the red, or closed, position; Gonzalez raised the fourth until it showed yellow, then cranked the big wheel clockwise.

Ready? mouthed Gonzalez.

Pender nodded.

"THEN LET'S GO, PENDEJO!"

Gonzalez stepped behind Pender and shoved him through the portal into the darkness. Pender stumbled forward down the dim corridor. A high windowless wall loomed to his left. To the right, his peripheral vision picked up dozens of shadowy figures stirring restlessly behind floor-to-ceiling bars, visible only in silhouette and motion, like nocturnal animals in the zoo when the infrareds are turned off. Then, before Pender's eyes had a chance to become accustomed to the tenebrous light, Gonzalez slid the last door open, shoved Pender inside, and he was one of them.

18

FORTY-FIVE MINUTES AFTER the cell door clanged shut behind Pender, it slid open again. Max shuffled in and took a seat on the iron bunk suspended from the wall, as far from his temporary cell-mate as possible. When his pupils had adjusted to the dim light—weak fluorescents flickering behind a dense mesh grille in the ceiling—he saw that the other man in the cell was another god-damn gorilla, every bit as large as the almost-late Refugio Cortes, and just as mean looking.

Max could feel Alicea pushing him to make a switch. *No fucking way,* Max told her. *We're not going through that again.*

Ish would have concurred, had he been consulted. It was Ish who'd analyzed the vicious cycle after the first time around. Feeling sexually threatened by the brutal Cortes, Max had dispatched Alicea to deal with him. But Alicea's feminine charms only inflamed the passions of Cortes, who had been doing a three-month stretch of county time for possession of methamphetamine. Whereupon Cortes had told Alicea, in his charmingly accented Pachuco, to "save up your spit, *puto,* or maybe you like a dry *verga* up your *culo?*"

But when Cortes showed up after lights-out (actually, they only dimmed), it wasn't Alicea waiting for him, but Lee. Lee was the alter who'd studied both karate and kung-fu, wrestled in high school at a hundred and twenty-eight pounds, and boxed in Juvie. When Lee looked into a mirror, however, he saw, not a slender junior lightweight but a light-heavyweight with a twenty-inch neck and pectorals like Batman's breastplate. And since everybody on the outside saw him as a little guy, this actually provided him a formidable advantage when he was picking on somebody his "own" size.

When he was up against a gorilla like Cortes, Lee's speed and agility were even more valuable than his strength. What gave him a real edge, however, was a trick his best friend Buckley had taught him to help him survive the no-holds-barred call-outs that were a primary source of evening entertainment at the Umpqua County Juvenile Ranch.

It was simple enough, the Buckley maneuver, but it took a fearful amount of will and practice. Decide on your first offensive move, then start counting down from ten in the mind. The trick is to make the move any time before reaching one.

Three, five, even nine—the count doesn't matter, so long as it hasn't been predetermined. That way the opponent never sees any of the usual warning flickers, the tensing of muscles, the shifting of eyes, that normally precede an attack. This makes the maneuver especially effective against experienced fighters, men who have trained themselves to watch for precisely those clues.

So here comes Cortes with his rank smell, and his dick waving in the dark. And although such behavior was personally repugnant to Lee, he impersonated Alicea long enough to put the brute at ease . . . *ten* . . . kneeling before the big man . . . *nine* . . . fondling him until he was hard . . . *eight* . . . then giving him a twisting, two-fisted hand job . . . *seven* . . . as if in preparation for oral sex to follow. *Six . . . five . . .*

At four he struck, bending Cortes's penile shaft in the middle like he was breaking a celery stalk in half. Cortes was momentarily paralyzed by what must have been excruciating pain, giving Lee enough time to straighten up, deliver a blow to Cortes's Adam's apple with the side of his left hand and another, with the heel of his right hand, to his nose.

Cortes was unconscious before he hit the ground, which did not deter Lee from jumping up and down on his rib cage, then stripping down his jumpsuit, turning him over, spreading his legs apart until his privates were on the floor, and grinding them under his heel as if he were putting out a cigarette butt.

The deputies in charge of the pod responded quickly, but it was too late to save anything but Cortes's life—the whole episode (from soup to nuts, in Max's humorous phrase) had taken no more than three minutes. And this time it was Lee who took the beating from the guards. Lee didn't mind pain—it only made him stronger.

In the end, the encounter with Cortes worked out satisfactorily for Maxwell. It ensured that he would be housed alone for the rest of his stay, and gave him a certain cachet among both the guards and the other inmates. But there was nothing to be gained by another such episode. For one thing, Max had learned over the years that you had to space the major thrills out, or you'd get jaded. For another, you might get away with destroying one cell-mate, but do it twice and your jailers would start taking extraordinary precautions, which was the last thing he wanted.

So this time he kept Alicea rigidly suppressed. *You so much as try to come out,* Max informed her, *and I will slice up this face until it's so hideous not even Miss Miller will be able to look at us.*

Then he called Mose, his memory trace personality, into co-consciousness with him, narrowed his eyes until they were nearly, but not entirely shut, lest the new gorilla try to jump him despite his restraints, and had Mose reread him the last chapter of *Ulysses,* Molly Bloom's soliloquy, while waiting to be brought from the cell to the courthouse, where he figured to have his best chance at escaping.

Ulysses was their favorite book. Max remembered the first time they'd seen it. "Look!" the nine-year-old had cried, spying it in the bookshelf in Miss Miller's living room. "Look, a book about me!"

A few hours later Miss Miller, her breasts perfumed like Molly's, had read him—or rather, Christopher—that last chapter out loud in bed. And though he was too young to understand much of it, like Leopold Bloom's, Christopher's own heart was going like mad, and yes he said along with her, yes I will, Yes.

19

THE ART OF AFFECTIVE INTERVIEWING, as practiced by Ed Pender, sometimes involved mirroring the interviewee's body language. In this case, with both of them cuffed and chained, sitting on a hard steel bench, that was already accomplished.

The difficult part for Pender was controlling his own excitement at being less than six feet away from Casey after all these years. Unbelievable. But he knew he'd have to proceed slowly, feel his way along. The ideal would be to wait for the other man to initiate the conversation, but the way Casey seemed to have withdrawn into himself, Pender knew he couldn't count on that.

"Hey," he said, after a good five minutes had passed.

No response.

"Hey—I'm talking to you."

"You talkin'a *me?*" Casey looked up slowly, his eyelids lowered sleepily and his eyebrows drawing together. And again: "You talkin'a *me?*"

A perfect Travis Bickle. Pender's laugh came easily. "Not bad."

"Not bad?" said Casey. "When did you ever see better?"

Celebrity impressionists—you never knew what was going to kindle a connection. Pender took the ball and carried it in the direction he wanted to go—place names. "I saw Rich Little do De Niro in Vegas . . . well, tell you the truth, you're about as good as him. But I saw Fred Travelena do him in Dallas—now *that* guy's a genius."

"I do a better Nicholson," said Casey.

"Lemme see."

The eyebrows peaked, the lips widened to a leer. *"Heeere's Johnny!"*

"The Shining, right?"

"Right. I can also do Christopher Walken: *I hid this uncomfortable hunk of metal up my aass two years. . . ."*

"Man, you *are* good." Pender slid a little closer toward Casey. "My name's Parker."

"Yeah, whatever," said Casey.

Pender told himself he hadn't really expected the man to give his true name, but he was disappointed anyway—even an alias might have helped. He shook it off. Back to work. "You ever done that kinda thing professionally? You should give it a try."

"Ah, bullshit."

But Pender could see that Casey was pleased. A little less guarded, too—the manacled hands, balled into fists at first, had relaxed. "No, really. You should go to one of them, what do they call 'em, open mike things. They had one in that club in Dallas. Actually, I think it was Plano. You ever been to Plano?"

Casey shrugged; Pender, with a Ph.D. in shrugs, read it as a positive response: not a *Fuck, no,* but a *Yeah, what of it?*

Oh-ho, thought Pender. Oh-ho was his version of Bingo! or Eureka! or Gotcha! On to topic number two. "In my opinion, it's basically a suck-ass town. Wall-to-wall stuck-up bitches. Man, I couldn't get laid in Plano to save my life."

"You couldn't get laid in Plano? Jeez, I got more pussy in Plano than the ASPCA. 'Course, I'm better looking than you are. I can get a woman anyplace. Shit, I can get a woman in jail. There's this shrink they sent to check me out—the bitch has already got the hots for me. We fooled around a little in the interview room—we're talking about getting together soon as I get out."

Oh-ho. Drilling randomly, Pender had struck a gusher. Casey was speaking freely now, not at all guarded. Pender modeled a receptive posture, hands as wide as the manacles permitted, shoulders relaxed, chest open but not thrust forward, as Casey slid a little closer, until they were only three feet apart.

"Of course, a guy with your looks, what *you* might want to do if you ever get back that way and you're horny, there's a motel called the Sleep-Tite in Dallas. Vietnamese hookers. Ask for Anh Tranh. Tightest little piece I ever had. All you gotta do is call the desk, tell the guy you want number one girl, make boom-boom."

Pender decided to narrow the focus a little. "They got any white girls there?"

"Just 'Mese."

And a little narrower. "Naah, I like white girls. Blonds or red-heads—nothing like a pale-haired pussy."

"You're crazy—pussy's pussy," Casey said quickly. Then he shut down, thud, like an asbestos fire curtain coming down in the middle of a scene.

Pussy's pussy. Max knew immediately that he'd gone too far. That locker-room bullshit about Irene Cogan. And why on earth had he felt compelled to tell Parker about the Sleep-Tite? He knew what Ish would say: that it had something to do with a need for approval from older men—apparently any older man would do. Or not so much approval as acceptance—he wanted to be accepted as a man, by men. He also suspected that this compulsion toward sexual boasting had as much to do with Mr. Kronk as it did with Ulysses Maxwell Sr. It would be nice to ask Dr. Cogan about it when he got her back to Scorned Ridge and they started therapy again for real.

The abduction of Dr. Irene Cogan: now *that* would be a challenge worthy of Max. He'd known he'd have to attempt it when he awoke from his hypnotic trance that afternoon—he'd been so damn smug, so sure she could never put him under. But she'd not only put him under, she'd made contact with little Lyssy.

Lyssy the Sissy, his—their—original personality, was the only identity with whom Max did not share memory, so there was no way for him to know whether or not the little tattletale had let slip some clue as to their identity, or the location of Scorned Ridge. In any event, it was not a chance he cared to take.

But self-preservation was only one of two reasons Max had determined to bring Irene along with him. The other had to do with his admittedly unique psychological makeup. Although he understood that to the rest of the world, DID was a disorder, personally Max liked to think of it as a new and superior order. Still and all, it was a great strain on Max, the de facto host alter after Useless had been supplanted, the personality who dealt with the world most of the time, whose job it was to hold together the complex and contradictory bundle of personalities known collectively as Ulysses Maxwell.

It was for that reason that Max had turned to the study of psychiatry seven years earlier. With all the resources of the system, of course, there'd been no need for formal education. He'd simply bought a small library of psychology books down in Medford, plus every textbook on MPD or DID he could get his hands on, and subscribed to every journal and magazine that came to his attention. Max read them, Mose memorized them, and Ish, who'd come into being during this period, integrated the insights into the system.

But lately Max was beginning to think they'd taken their therapy about as far as they could on their own. And since Dr. Cogan was a specialist—an attractive specialist—in dissociative disorders, and since he needed to remove her from the general population for his own protection ASAP, why not bring her back to Scorned Ridge with him to continue his therapy?

Max recognized that this was an insane idea on the surface of it. But since Paula Ann Wisniewski was dead, and Irene was—or could again be—a strawberry blond, he'd be killing two birds with one stone.

Strawberry blonds! Suddenly it struck him. Parker's crap about liking blonds and redheads—what the fuck was that? And mentioning Plano to boot. Max thought back—were there any comedy clubs in Plano? Any clubs at all? Mose couldn't tell him—Mose only recorded what other alters read, observed, or heard. But Plano, though the Chamber of Commerce would deny the appellation, was really more of a wealthy bedroom community, a glorified suburb of Dallas. Dallas was where the nightspots were.

So was it a trap? Was Parker a cop? There was definitely something familiar about the man, beneath that Bluto act. Max couldn't quite put his finger on it, so he instructed Mose to go through the archives, and report back when he had a hit.

Seconds later Max sensed the MTP's excitement. Quickly he brought Mose up to co-consciousness, and was rewarded with a vivid recollection of sitting in a hotel room in Williamsport, Pennsylvania, in 1994, watching Special Agent E. L. Pender holding a press conference in nearby Reeford, asking the public for assistance in locating one Gloria Whitworth, a coed at Reeford College, and in particular asking any strawberry blonds in the area to report suspicious contacts with strangers.

Dear Gloria. Aptly named—though she was otherwise nothing to write home about, Miss Whitworth's waist-length strawberry blond hair was glorious indeed. It had been her pride and joy— how she'd wept the first time it was harvested.

And now Pender had finally connected him, not only to Gloria but also to Donna Hughes in Plano. God double fucking damn the man. Time to book on out of here. And never mind waiting until he was taken to the courthouse to make his escape—Max, with Lee's help, had business to take care of right here in this cell.

Pender knew he'd blown it. He could sense Casey shutting down on him. Following Plano with the blonds—too much, too soon. He did what he could to repair the damage. "Yeah, you're right. Pussy's pussy."

But Casey ignored him. He'd turned his back on Pender, picked his teeth, and fiddled with his manacles, but he hadn't moved any farther away. Pender was just thinking how that was a good sign when he heard the unmistakable click of handcuffs being unlocked.

Then, before Pender could call out, Casey turned, one of the handcuff bracelets clenched in his left fist, and Pender learned with a sick sad sense of surprise exactly what Deputy Jervis had meant when she said that if you hadn't seen the fucker, you couldn't imagine how fast the fucker could move.

20

SHERIFF'S DEPUTY FRANK TWOMBLEY was a single man; Sheriff's Deputy Deena Knapp was a single woman. That being the case, Twombley couldn't see why Knapp wouldn't give him the time of day.

It was hard on a man, working in close quarters all day with a woman so attractive, so petite, and at the same time so youthfully and firmly stacked beneath that crisp tan uniform blouse that it was said of her by the male deputies, out of her hearing, of course, that she would be taller lying on her back than she was standing up.

"C'mon, just a drink to unwind after our shift," he begged her for the last time, on Wednesday afternoon. "No harm in two"—he searched for the word—"*colleagues* having a little drink after work."

"Gimme a break, Frank." Knapp was sitting at her desk with her back to the room, cramming for her criminology final. "I don't drink, and I don't date . . . *colleagues.*"

"Oh well, you can't blame a guy for trying."

"One time, no. One hundred times, you're skating on thin ice, harrassment-wise."

"Well, excuuuse me."

"I don't need this shit, Frank. I'm trying to better myself here, and—"

"DEPUTY! EXCUSE ME, DEPUTY!" Someone calling from inside the cell block.

"Sounds like our G-man," Knapp remarked.

"I'M NOT FEELING SO GREAT. COULD YOU LET ME OUT NOW? I HAVE EVERYTHING I NEED."

"Jesus Christ, how unprofessional," said Twombley. "I better get him out of there." He flipped up the fourth knob on the door control panel, and cranked the wheel, then entered the dark cellblock. Twombley hurried past the first two cells, one packed with red-jumpsuited prisoners, the other with orange, past the third, left empty to provide a buffer for Pender's interview, and peered into the fourth cell—Pender was lying on his side on the floor, with his back to the bars.

"I dunno, first he said he had a headache," shrugged the man whom the deputies referred to as the Ripper. He was sitting on the bench with his knees drawn up as far as his shackles permitted. "Then he just fell over, hit his head on the *cee*-ment."

Twombley slid the door open and entered the cell. "You stay right there," he warned the Ripper.

"I ain't going anywhere," the man replied, rattling his chains for emphasis.

Twombley knelt by Pender, saw the blood pooling around Pender's head, black as crankcase oil in the dim light. Pender's eyelids fluttered—his mouth opened and closed but no sound emerged.

"Just take 'er easy now," said Twombley. "Everything's gonna be—"

The last word would have been *okay,* but Twombley never got it out. The chain came around his neck from behind; the links cut deep into his throat, shutting off his air. He heard a roaring in his ears; then, as he tried to reach for his pepper spray, he heard a popping sound, like knuckles cracking, only a hundred times louder.

It was, he understood as his body crumpled beneath him like a marionette whose strings had been cut, the sound of his own neck being broken; he noticed as he lay dying that there were little rainbows floating in the black pool of Pender's blood.

Deputy Deena Knapp, too, was thinking about blood, or more precisely, blood splatters.

"If a blood spot on level ground is 4 mm wide and 11 mm long, what is the angle of impact?" read the question on her sample test.

She punched in four divided by eleven on her calculator, came up with .363636, and was in the process of converting that into a sine function when she sensed Frank Twombley's presence just behind her. She thought it was odd that she hadn't heard him returning from the cell block—normally the jingle-jangling of Twombley's keys drove her crazy over the course of a shift.

"Back off, Frank," she said without turning around. "You're invading my personal space."

Instead, he grabbed her by the hair, jerked her head back, and fired a burst of pepper spray into her face from point-blank range. Her chair tipped over, the back of her skull hit the linoleum with sickening force. She saw a flash of red against a field of black, then another as he grabbed her by the hair and slammed her head against the floor again.

Blinded, suffocating, in pain, she fought him as long and hard as she could. She clawed for his face with her nails, hoping at least to mark him. His weight shifted on top of her. He was straddling her upper chest now, pinning her arms with his knees. She forced her eyes open, saw a blur of orange through the tears, realized it wasn't Frank after all, but one of the inmates. She tried to scream; he fired another burst of pepper spray directly into her open mouth.

This second burst sent her into convulsions. Her eyes rolled back in her head until only the whites were showing; pink froth bubbled from her mouth. And although Max had climbed off her immediately after she lost consciousness, and hurried back into the cell block, Deputy Knapp's body continued to flop and jerk for a good five minutes afterward, as if she were still trying to buck him off.

21

THE COMMOTION WAS BUILDING in the other holding cells as Max raced back into the cell block, unbuttoning his jumpsuit as he ran. Lee had done his job and slipped back into the darkness of their mind—now it was up to Max to get them to safety.

"Shut the fuck up," he shouted breathlessly to the red- and orange-clad prisoners as he jumped over Twombley's body, which lay athwart Pender's, blocking the entrance to the holding cell. "I'll open the doors, but you gotta keep it down." The last time he'd been here he had estimated, counting off the seconds in his mind, that no more than fifteen minutes ever elapsed between the arrival or departure of prisoner convoys with armed escorts. This meant he had only five minutes left, ten tops, to make good his escape.

Stripped down to his jail-issue underwear, he hauled Twombley's body off Pender and began undressing the deputy, while his mind worked frantically. An ordinary man, he knew, would simply walk out of the jail through the office door. In which case, when the alarms began to sound and the sirens to blare, that hypothetical ordinary man would find himself stranded within hailing distance of the jail, the courthouse, city hall, and the Salinas Municipal Police headquarters.

And what then would be the ordinary man's options? Run for it? Try to bluff his way through the cordon of security that would surely be thrown up, relying on a deputy sheriff's uniform for camouflage, when they already knew his face, and would realize soon enough that Twombley's uniform had been taken? Hotwire or hijack a car in that overpoliced neighborhood?

No doubt about it, thought Max, unbuckling Twombley's heavy

belt and tightening it around his own slender midsection: an ordinary man, even if he'd managed to get out of the jail in the first place, would almost certainly be captured within minutes.

But Max was no ordinary man. He was *extra*ordinary, and possessed both the foresight to come up with an extraordinary solution and the courage to carry it out. Time, however, was in short supply. Max hurried out of the cell, giving Pender's body a wide berth so as not to step in the blood still pooling out around the head and risk leaving bloody footprints behind.

The other prisoners were crowding up against the bars, calling to him in both English and Spanish. Max tossed Deputy Twombley's handcuff key into the first holding cell on his way back into the office, then fumbled through the rest of the keys until he found one that opened the gun cabinet. He grabbed a Glock with a clip already inserted, slipped it into Twombley's holster, closed the locker again, then looked around for a telephone book. There was one on the desk; as he thumbed through it looking for the two addresses he needed, something began nagging at Max, something he'd left undone.

Unfortunately, there was no time to call on Mose. But it would come to one of them eventually—it always did, Max told himself as he located the panel that controlled the cell doors, flipped the three remaining knobs up into the yellow position, then cranked the wheel, opening the doors to the rest of the holding cells. Immediately a dozen or more prisoners, mostly orange-jumpsuited felons, elected to take early parole and began spreading out through the streets of the West Alisal neighborhood, exactly as Max had planned.

But Max was not among them. Instead, he turned back into the jail and used another of Twombley's keys to open the iron door leading from the holding cell corridor to the long-abandoned interior of the jail.

Inside, it was dark as a moonless night. Max locked the door behind him, then used Twombley's big cop flashlight to navigate his way past an obstacle course of loose wires and cables, jagged-edged water and sewage pipes, boulder-sized chunks of collapsed masonry, overturned furniture, shattered glass, rusting cell doors hanging crookedly from one hinge or fallen entirely and blocking the narrow aisles.

As he picked his way toward the interior staircase leading up to the second and third floors, Max could hear sirens going off all around him. He was in the process of congratulating himself on making the right decision when he realized what it was he'd left undone earlier: Pender, the FBI man—in all the hurry and commotion, he hadn't stopped to finish off Pender.

It wouldn't have taken but a moment or two, Max realized ruefully, knuckling himself on the forehead the way Miss Miller used to when he'd screwed up: *Hello? Anybody home in there?* He could have stomped Pender, strangled him silently, suffocated him—shit, he could have stood on Pender's throat while he was changing clothes with Twombley, and not lost a single goddamn second. Maxwell's adrenaline began flowing again—he broke out into a sweat.

Steady—steady now. This is not the time to panic. Max slowed his breathing, calmed himself, and began reasoning through the problem. In the first place, he didn't know for sure that Pender was still alive. Max didn't remember seeing him breathe—and he sure as shit wasn't moving.

In the second place, even if Pender had survived, after three whacks on the skull—three Lee whacks—his brains were probably so scrambled he'd be lucky if he could remember his own name.

And in the third place, even if Pender were both alive and compos mentis, there were no Lone Rangers in the FBI. Anything Pender knew, other agents almost certainly knew—and if they'd had any reason to connect him to Scorned Ridge, they'd have been up there digging a long time ago.

No harm, no foul, Max reassured himself—he hadn't put the system into any further jeopardy by failing to finish Pender off. Which meant all he had to do now was find a secure place inside the jail to hole up until the fuss around him died down.

So moving as quietly as he could in Twombley's leather-soled cop shoes, which were two sizes too large for him, Max made his way up to the second floor, where the cells were stacked wall to wall, floor to ceiling, with court records in cardboard boxes. Alarmingly, the corners of the floor-level boxes had been chewed through by rats.

Max shuddered and backed away—he didn't care for rodents. Eventually he found a windowless isolation cell deep in the interior of the building. The door had been removed and was leaning against the wall; just inside the entrance the flashlight beam picked out the skeleton of a pigeon lying in the dust, undisturbed by rodents, skull and ribcage intact, the long bones of the wings, feathers still attached, fanned out in perfect deltas.

It was ideal for his purposes—if the rats hadn't come in here to eat a dead pigeon, they certainly wouldn't be bothering a live human. He could hear sirens in the street below, pounding footsteps, urgent voices. A Chinese fire drill, he chuckled. They seek him here, they seek him there.

Enormously pleased with himself, he switched off the flashlight and settled down with his back to the wall to wait them out. It was pitch-black; he literally couldn't see his hand in front of his face. Which didn't bother Max any—he wasn't afraid of the dark. He knew who was, though, and it occurred to Max that perhaps the time had come to teach Lyssy the Sissy a lesson, once and for all.

22

THREE TIMES THE HANDCUFF BRACELET clenched in Maxwell's fist had come crashing down on the crown of Pender's skull. He felt only the first blow, as a jarring sensation, followed by the sort of breathless, welling nausea that usually follows a swift kick in the nuts.

Stunned, all but paralyzed, he saw the prisoner's hand rise and fall, rise and fall again, but couldn't make sense of what he saw. Couldn't hear anything, either, until he closed his eyes and began to tumble through darkness. As he fell, and fell, and fell, all the hollow, distant sounds of the jail, fragments of Spanish from the other cells, a toilet flushing, the sleighbell jingle of chains and fetters, washed over him with a roar like breaking waves.

He opened his eyes. The surf sounds abruptly ceased—the world was devoid of sound. He saw the cell bars, inexplicably horizontal—it wasn't until the deputy appeared in front of him that Pender understood that he was lying on the cell floor, on his side. It dizzied him to try to focus on the face filling his field of vision—it was distorted longitudinally, as if through a fish-eye lens. Then it disappeared. Pender felt an urge, not framed in words, to apologize to somebody about something, and as he closed his eyes and gave in to the darkness, he was overwhelmed by regret.

Time had passed—how much, Pender couldn't say. Now that the pain was in his head, his mind was paradoxically clear. He saw Twombley's underwear-clad body lying a few feet away and realized from the angle of his head that there was nothing that could be done for him.

McDougal will be so pissed, thought Pender. Got to help. Help me do this.

That last was a prayer—and Pender was not a praying man. But the results surprised him. Time slowed. Despite the pain he managed to raise himself up on his hands and knees, head hanging; he could see the blood from his scalp falling to the cement floor, drop by drop. Sometimes there were three or four drops in the air at the same time, like black rubies strung on an invisible chain.

Along with the clarity of vision came an increasing clarity of mind. His thoughts raced along swiftly, transparent and weightless. What have I learned that can help them? The motel in Dallas? The hooker? Old news. What's current? The shrink—he said something about hooking up with the shrink. What was her name? Hogan? No, Cogan.

Swaying, his left hand pressed against the dripping scalp wounds to slow the bleeding, he dipped his right forefinger into the warm pool where his head had rested on the cement floor, and wrote the following in his own blood:

Kogin akomplis?

Pender's strength failed him at the end. He drew the question mark lying on his belly. His use of phonic spelling was inadvertent. Whatever circuits in the brain governed that particular function must have been scrambled—he didn't even notice the misspellings until he found himself looking down from somewhere around ceiling height. From that lofty vantage he saw the two bodies below him, his own and the deputy's, the pool of blood, the clumsy scrawl. Then the walls and bars disappeared—he was in the dark; a tiny figure was walking toward him, the light streaming from behind it.

I don't believe in this crap, he thought, hurrying forward to meet whoever it was. It's a dream—it's only one last dream.

But what a dream. The figure grew larger. It was Pender's father, not as he'd been at the end, shrunken by cancer, but strong and tall and broad-shouldered in the bemedaled dress blues that he wore in the Veteran's Day parade every year in Cortland when Edgar was growing up. As a kid, Ed knew what every medal and ribbon represented, which was the Purple Heart and which the Silver Star. They'd buried the old man with them.

"Daddy?"

"It ain't Elvis, son," said First Sergeant Robert Lee Pender, USMC, Ret. "You ready to go?"

"I don't know."

"What do you mean, you don't know? Got any unfinished business?"

"The guy that killed me—he got away."

"The one that killed all them women?"

"That's the one."

His father laughed. "Well, shit, boy, he ain't killed you yet. Call me if he does, I'll come back for you. And don't forget, quitters never win, and Penders never quit."

And with that, Sergeant R. L. Pender executed a smart about-face and marched back up the slope, leaving Ed alone. He looked down, saw his body lying on its face, right arm extended, as if pointing to the words he had scrawled in blood on the cell floor. It was still bleeding, still breathing—and a moment later he was back inside it.

I still don't believe in this crap, thought Pender. Then the pain hit him, and he lost consciousness again.

23

LYSSY THE SISSY was frightened. He didn't like the dark. And this dark was worse than the closet his father used to lock him in. Because at least in the closet, even if you couldn't get out, you knew nothing else was going to come in.

But this dark was more like the basement. Bad things happened in the basement—it was the worst place he knew.

Although he had a watch, a big man's watch, Lyssy couldn't tell time, so he had no idea how long he'd been in this place. All he knew was that he was forbidden to cry, and he was forbidden to use the flashlight. Even so, soon his terror got the better of him. He struggled with the heavy switch—it was hard for his little fingers to operate it. Finally, using both thumbs, he managed to turn on the light, and immediately wished he hadn't.

Because there, lying only a few feet away from him on the dusty gray floor, was the skeleton of a dead bird. Seeing those empty eye sockets, that hungry beak, was worse than the dark. Lyssy tried to turn off the flashlight, but the switch wouldn't budge. He tried to cover the light with his hand. His fingers glowed red—he could see through them—he could see his own bones.

Please, he said, his lips moving silently. *Please help me.*

Then he heard the voice again.

Lyssy?

Yes?

You want my help?

Yes.

You know you've been a bad boy. It was not a question.

Yes.

If I help you, will you do what I say from now on?
Yes.
No more talking to the nice doctor unless I give you permission?
Okay.
No more talking to anybody unless I say it's allowed?
Okay.
You promise?
I promise.
Cross your heart and hope to die.
Cross my heart and hope to die.
You also have to promise to share what you know with me.
Sharing's good.
Sometimes. Tell me what you told the doctor this afternoon.
I told her about the dream—the dream about the masks. And what Daddy did.
Did you tell her about the other people, or where we live now?
No.
About me?
No.
Cross your heart?
And hope to die.
Attaboy.
Can I leave now? Can I go to sleep?
Yes. But when you wake up again, remember what we talked about. And don't forget your promises. Do you know what will happen if you break your promises?
I don't want to talk about it.
I'll put you back in the dark, and the dead bird will come to life and peck out your eyes. Or I'll burn you—remember how bad it hurted you, last time?
You're bad. You're scaring me, and you're bad.
Well ain't that the truth, little man. I am bad. And I am scaring you. But that's nothing compared to what I can do if you ever break your promise.
I won't. I said I wou'n't, and I won't.
All right then. Off you go.

Max opened his eyes. The body was still charged with adrenaline—he took a few deep breaths to calm it down and quiet the pulse pounding in his ears, then switched off the flashlight and listened in the dark. No sirens, no sounds from below—nothing but a little traffic out on Alisal Street. He pushed the illuminator button on

Twombley's Indiglo watch. Nine P.M. Full dark. Suddenly Max was immensely hungry. Hungry and horny. He yawned, stretched, rose to his feet. Time to book on out of here for real. He had places to go, people to see.

Max started to give the dead pigeon a wide berth on his way out of the cell, then realized that his repulsion was only a leftover from Lyssy the Sissy's time in the body, and gave it a good boot with the toe of Twombley's shoe. The skeleton dissociated as it skidded along the floor; by the time it hit the wall it was only a pile of bones and feathers.

24

IRENE COGAN'S BATHTUB WAS big enough for two—she and Frank had made sure of that—and took forever to fill. While she was waiting, Irene tweezed her eyebrows, then the nearly invisible granny hairs growing at the corners of her mouth. Granny hairs aside, she thought, her face was standing up pretty well to the rigors of the big four-oh, thanks to a good Garbo-esque bone structure—the younger, *Queen Christina* Garbo.

Before climbing into the tub, Irene put up her shoulder-length hair, placed her Dictaphone on the toilet seat, fast-forwarded the tape for thirty seconds or so, then pushed play and adjusted the volume. As she slipped into the steaming water, she heard Max's voice:

" . . . what spooks me, Irene, is not that there's somebody else *talking* inside my head—it's this feeling I can't shake that there's somebody else *listening.*"

Irene nodded approvingly at the classic image, reached up, dried her fingers on the bath mat, and fast-forwarded again in spurts through the relaxation exercise and most of the regression, then pressed the play button—"five candles, one two three four five"— sank back into the water, and closed her eyes.

Twenty minutes later she heard her own voice. ". . . I need you to know you're safe telling me anything at all—nothing you tell me can ever come back to hurt you."

Irene sat up, shivering, turned off the Dictaphone, let some of the cooled water out of the tub, and ran some more hot in, thinking all the while about little Lyssy. She pictured him as a five-year-old—cute little heart-shaped face, wide gold-flecked brown eyes, shock of hair falling across his forehead. If only she could go back in time. How she'd like to take that poor child in her arms and hug him close and tell him everything was all right, that what had happened wasn't his fault, and that he mustn't blame himself.

But of course you couldn't go back in time, and everything *wasn't* all right—the little boy had grown up to be a murderer. Then it occurred to Irene that that wasn't precisely true. If Lyssy were suffering from DID, then only *part* of him had grown up to become a killer, as a subconscious response to unfathomable psychological pressures.

Irene sighed and slid deeper into the bath until the hot water reached her chin. Perhaps she could still help that little boy to exorcise the animal under his skin, she thought—that is, if the great state of California didn't murder him first.

After listening to the Lyssy tape in the bath, Irene had promised herself she'd take the rest of the evening off. To fail would be an admission that she was slipping back into her workaholic mode— Barbara Klopfman would give her holy hell.

But if television was a vast wasteland, then Wednesday night was surely its Death Valley, so Irene took her laptop to bed with her and reviewed her notes on her last sessions with Donald Barber and Lily DeVries, the two patients she'd be seeing the next day.

Around eleven-thirty Irene went downstairs to raid the refrigerator. She made herself a cup of Sleepytime tea, cut a slice of carrot cake as thick as her thumb, and ate in front of the TV, switching back and forth between *Letterman, Leno,* and *Politically Incorrect.*

Around the time Irene came to the admittedly paranoid conclusion that all three networks had synchronized their commercial breaks, she thought she heard someone moving up the walkway that led around the side of the house—someone with leather-soled shoes.

Speaking of paranoid . . . She quickly muted the TV. There was no doubt about it—she could hear footsteps out back now, behind the office. Had she listened to the news that evening, she would have been even more alarmed; as it was, her heart began to pound and her throat tightened. Irene had only been in physical danger a few times in her life, and never since moving to Pacific Grove seven years earlier. The phone—where had she left the cordless phone?

In the office. But if someone was breaking in, he'd be coming through the back door, the office door. What now?

Suddenly the front doorbell began to ring out the first thirteen notes of "The Caissons Go Rolling Along."

Over hill, over dale. . . . The tune was the legacy of the house's previous owner, a retired infantry officer from Fort Ord. Irene hated it, but Frank had liked it, and after he died she couldn't bring herself to have it taken out. Irene hurried to the front door and, peering through the peephole, saw a man in a sheriff's uniform shifting nervously on her doorstep.

"Are you all right, Dr. Cogan?"

"I'm fine. What's—"

"Could you open the door for us, please?"

Irene pulled her bathrobe tighter around her silk nightie, unlocked the door, and opened it.

"Would you step out onto the porch, please?"

"I'd rather—what are you doing?" For he'd grabbed her roughly by the elbow and yanked her out of the way while two men from the sheriff's TAC squad in bulky Kevlar vests and helmets with tinted visors charged past her into the house, guns drawn.

The deputy hustled Irene down the porch steps and onto the lawn. She heard shouting, pounding footsteps, doors crashing open, police radios squawking, tires squealing, car doors slamming, sirens in the distance, then the percussive whomp-whomp-whomp of a helicopter. A moment later, a blinding light in the sky directly overhead turned night into blazing white day.

"Will someone *please* tell me what's going on?" she shouted to the cop, who ignored her. When she began to struggle, trying to break his hold, he twisted her arm behind her back and forced her to kneel. Her nightgown and bathrobe were rucked up behind her, and the grass was damp beneath her bare knees.

Emotions flooded her—rage, helplessness, shame. She lowered her head and found herself looking down at a pair of pointy-toed black cowboy boots polished to such a gloss that she could see the reflection of the searchlights dancing on them like miniature white suns.

"Thanks, Jerry, I'll take it from here." Irene caught a whiff of cologne as the owner of the boots, an older Latino man in a white cowboy hat, helped her to feet.

"I demand to know what's going on here." Irene flexed her shoulder, tugged at her nightgown, adjusted her bathrobe.

"I'm Sheriff Bustamante."

"I know who you are—I voted for you last election."

" 'Preciate it. Where's my prisoner?"

Though still half in shock, Irene was somehow not surprised. "In your jail, so far as I know. I haven't seen him since this afternoon. Now can you tell me why you're breaking into my house?"

Bustamante handed her a sheet of paper. "Here's the search warrant. He escaped from custody late this afternoon."

"Well, he's not here. Why have I been frightened half to death, manhandled, humiliated, and dragged out of my house in my bathrobe?"

"Because we had reason to believe he might be heading here."

"What possible reason—"

"During his escape the prisoner attacked an FBI agent working undercover in his cell."

"Pender!" exclaimed Irene. "I spoke to him on the telephone this afternoon."

"Before he lost consciousness, Agent Pender wrote the words *Cogan* and *accomplice* on the cell floor with his own blood." Bustamante didn't mention that there was a question mark after the second word, or that due to the misspellings it had taken the crime scene investigators several hours to figure out what the now-comatose Pender had been trying to tell them. "Why would he go and write something like that?"

"I have no idea." Feeling weak at the knees, Irene tried to visualize the scene. *Accomplice* was a long word—there must have been a lot of blood.

"All clear inside, Sheriff," one of the TAC squad ninjas called from the open front door.

"Thanks. Have your men stand down, I'll be with you in a minute."

Bustamante turned back to Irene, looked her over, and made one of those snap judgments that lawmen live or die by every day. "I'm sorry for the inconvenience, Dr. Cogan. Perhaps there's been a misunderstanding. Just in case, though, what I'd like to do, with your permission, is arrange to have a call-trace unit put on your phone line, and leave a couple of my men behind to watch the house if he does decide to pay you a visit."

"I don't know about tapping my phone—"

"I can also do that without your permission; it's just easier and more courteous this way."

Irene's Irish was still up. "Oh, by all means, let's start being courteous now."

"I have been courteous, Dr. Cogan. Do you see that man over there? The fellow in the jogging outfit, talking on a cell phone? He's from the U.S. Marshal's Service. If he'd been in charge of this operation, they'd have rammed down your front door instead of ringing the bell—I talked him out of it."

Irene wanted to keep arguing but realized she was overcompensating, trying to regain a measure of control over the situation. She'd also begun trembling—and not just from the cold. "Thank you, Sheriff," she said hurriedly. "Do whatever you need to do. May I go back inside now?"

"Yes, of course. I'll ask my men to be as unobtrusive as possible."

"I'd appreciate that," said Irene, with as much dignity as she could muster. But once inside the house, Irene not only locked the front and back doors, she also threw the deadbolts that hadn't been thrown since she and Frank first moved to the nearly crime-free Last Hometown, and double-checked the windows, even the ones on the second floor, to make sure they were locked.

Not that there was any reason to think Max would be coming after *her*. That was probably the last thing on his mind, Irene told herself as she climbed into bed and pulled the covers up over her head.

25

DOORBELL CHIMES ECHOED through the little ranch house in Prunedale. Sheriff's Deputy Terry Jervis, well sedated, murmured "Whazzit?" through her wired-up jaw.

"Ssh, it's all right. Go back to sleep. I'll see who it is." Aletha Winkle pulled a corduroy bathrobe on over her T-shirt and padded sleepily down the hall to the front door. She made sure the chain was fastened, then opened the door a crack. A sheriff's deputy she'd never seen before was standing on the doorstep, his face shadowed by the visor of his cap. Harmless looking white guy in an ill-fitting uniform, as best she could tell.

"What is it?"

"Sorry to bother you—has anyone notified you yet?"

"About what?"

"Terry's last collar, that Doe. Didn't you see the news?"

"Tell you the truth, we were watching *The Simpsons.*"

"He broke out of the old jail this afternoon. Sheriff thought there was an off chance he might be heading here. They didn't call you?"

"Nobody called."

"Fucking typical. You haven't heard any suspicious noises, though? Anything out of the ordinary?"

"No, it's been quiet."

"Probably a false alarm, then. Terry inside?"

"She's out like a light from the sleeping pills and painkillers."

"That's good—they say rest is the best thing. How's she feeling?"

"Better every day."

"Good to hear. Listen, when she wakes up, tell her Frank Twombley said hi, and he hopes she's feeling better."

"I'll do that."

The deputy started to leave, then turned back. "You know, as long as I'm out here I might as well take a look around back, just to be on the safe side. Any dogs?"

"No."

"Good deal. I'll just take a quick look, make sure everything's, you know, copacetic, then I'll be out of your hair."

"Better safe than sorry, I guess."

Aletha watched through the crack in the door as the deputy disappeared around the corner of the house. A few seconds later she heard a tapping out back, hurried into the kitchen, peered through the curtained window of the back door. Deputy Twombley was squatting down, examining the edge of the screen door by the yellow light of the bug lamp.

"What is it?"

"There are some scratches on the corner of the screen here— looks like somebody tried to force an entry. Could you take a look for me, tell me whether they're fresh?"

Aletha opened the back door, stepped out onto the concrete walk. "Where?"

"Right down here, around the bottom hinge." He stood up and stepped back to give her room. She stooped to take a closer look. The first blow of the riot stick caught her across the back of the neck and dropped her to her knees; the second, equally swift, equally savage, smashed into the back of her skull with enough force to cause a radiating fracture of the occipital bone, one of the strongest bones in the human body.

And in the brief instant between the blossoming of a thousand stars and the onrushing blackness, Aletha Winkle had time for one last thought: *I'm sorry, Terry.*

"Mama, you are a *load!*"

Max grunted as he dragged Aletha Winkle over the threshold into the kitchen. Though he appeared slender when clothed, he was in fact about as strong as a hundred-and-thirty-five-pound man could be without sacrificing speed and flexibility. But hauling two hundred and fifty pounds of dead weight—half dead, anyway—took every ounce of strength, sweat, and leverage he could muster; he was breathing hard by the time he was done.

No rest for the wicked, though—before moving on to the fun part of the evening, Max still had to switch cars. He found a set of keys hanging from a nail in the kitchen. A door led directly from the living room into the garage, where he had his choice of two vehicles, an old black Honda Civic or an equally old Volvo station wagon painted an unlikely shade of avocado green. He opened the garage door, backed the Volvo out, drove the Plymouth into the garage, and locked the door behind him.

Back inside the house, Max turned out the kitchen light, then tiptoed down the hall toward the bedroom. The door was open; the room was dark. He flattened himself against the wall and held his breath, listening. He heard regular breathing, a nasal snort every few inhalations. He drew the can of pepper spray from his belt and peeked around the door frame. No movement from the bandaged figure lying on its back on the near side of the canopied double bed. Terry Jervis was either asleep, or one hell of an actress.

With a firm grip to prevent them from jingling, Max took Deputy Twombley's handcuffs out of his belt as he approached the bed. This was almost too easy. Max could feel Kinch yearning for her blood. But a fresh victim, her spirit not yet broken? This was too new and shiny a toy (Hours of Indoor Fun!, he thought) to let Kinch play with just yet.

Later, Max told him. *You can have her at the end. As usual.* He flicked on the bedside lamp and jingled the handcuffs. "Wakey, wakey."

Her eyes fluttered open, pale blue above the ghost-white bandages. Max waited for the shock of recognition to enter them. He drank in her terror. It was delicious, exquisite, intoxicating—Kinch could never have appreciated it. Then, as her hand went under the pillow for her gun, he sprayed her.

Over the course of the long night, they all had their turns. Max was a sadist and a bugger, Christopher a sensualist and a fantasist, and Kinch . . . well, Kinch was a hacker.

Christopher went first—he was already in place when Terry Jervis recovered from the pepper spray. Tenderly he bathed her eyes and unbandaged her jaw. He brought in pillar candles and aromatherapy oil lamps and scented oils from the bathroom, and by their soft flickering light he made tender love to her. He dressed and half dressed and undressed her in outfits from her lingerie drawer and from the back of her closet; a whore in a Merry Widow, a farmer's daughter in overalls, a deputy sheriff wearing only her uniform shirt, somebody's wifey in a shorty nightgown, a teenage slut in a short teddy, a little girl in flannel pajamas. He positioned and repositioned her on her back, her side, her stomach, propped on pillows, kneeling by the side of the bed, lying on the carpet, leaning over a chair, bent over her pink and white vanity and pressed against the vanity mirror.

But however he posed her, at all times he handled her so gently and with such tenderness that gradually a glimmer of hope that he might let her live blossomed in her breast.

At which point Max took over. By design—terror wasn't half as tasty without hope to season it. The lighted candle and hot lamp oil were soon put to entirely different uses, the scented oils and lubricants employed for his ease of access rather than her comfort. Unlike the priapic Christopher, Max suffered from occasional erectile dysfunction as well as premature ejaculation, forcing him to make extensive use of the sex toys from Terry and Aletha's bedside drawer.

By the time Max was done with Terry she was still alive, but torn and trembling, a wide-eyed wreck of no damn use to either Max or Christopher. Aletha Winkle, however, though she had never regained consciousness, was also still alive, and save for the wound at the back of her head, unmarked. *She* was no damn use to Max— you can neither terrorize nor torture an unconscious victim—but Christopher wanted her, so Max let him have her.

Hauling Aletha around was a chore, so once Christopher got her up onto the bed, there she stayed. Even dressing and undressing her took a lot of energy; to save his strength, Christopher slit the outfits he wanted to dress her in up the back (or the front, depending) before putting them on her. He tried to persuade Terry to join in the fun, but it was no use—she was too far gone. Eventually he settled for undressing both women and arranging them *en tableaux*; the contrast between Aletha's massive, inert brown flesh and Terry's taut quivering pale skin was both aesthetically intriguing and sexually arousing.

But all good things must come to an end. By daybreak Christopher was sated and Max was bored; then came Kinch's turn.

Tuckered out and sweaty from the long, eventful night, Max helped himself to a long hot shower followed by a hearty breakfast.

The phone rang while he was eating. He answered it in Terry's voice—raised pitch, clenched teeth.

" 'Lo?"

"Oh—hi Terry. This is Mary Ann at El Sausal Middle. I have a fourth-grade teacher out. Does Aletha want to sub today?"

"She's sick. She has a cold."

"Okay, on to the next victim."

You said it, sister, thought Max, hanging up the phone. Suddenly he understood that this put a different light on things. With neither woman expected anywhere, the Plymouth hidden safely in the garage, and no reason for anyone to look for him here, he could think of several reasons why he might be better off hiding out for a day or so.

For one thing, it was already light out—there was a good chance one of the neighbors might see him driving away in the Volvo. For another, if the cops had thrown up roadblocks last night, they'd likely be down by tomorrow night.

Then there was the necessity for a disguise. A layover would give him time to change his appearance. And though he wasn't sleepy yet, he knew he would be soon: at twenty-eight he could no longer pull all-nighters with impunity. Plus the next part of his plan might prove tricky to execute; surely a good rest now would make for sharper wits later.

First, though, his hair. "We had ourselves a time, didn't we, girls?" he said to the two women as he passed through the bedroom on his way to the bathroom, where Terry kept her bleach, fixer, and hair coloring.

No response—not that he'd been expecting one.

26

ROADBLOCKS, HELICOPTERS, a mustering of off-duty officers in both the Sheriff's Department and the Salinas PD, door-to-door searches of the neighborhood surrounding the courthouse complex, a widely broadcast BOLO (Be On the Lookout For) describing both the fugitive and the Plymouth that had been stolen from the county lot: all for naught so far as the Ripper was concerned. By dawn on Thursday it had become apparent that although all but two of the other escapees had been recaptured, the man who'd sprung them had somehow slipped through the security cordon.

The manhunt would of course continue—but from here on in the FBI, citing the likelihood that the escaped prisoner was an interstate fugitive, would have jurisdiction over the investigation. Which was fine with Sheriff Bustamante, who hadn't survived three contested elections by personally associating himself with the sort of disaster this business was turning out to be. One citizen disemboweled within sight of Deputy Jervis; Deputies Jervis and Knapp grievously injured, along with the FBI agent Bustamante had personally allowed into the prisoner's cell; Deputy Twombley dead. Worst of all from the standpoint of accountability, there had finally been a mass breakout from the old jail that a Monterey County grand jury had recommended be closed over a year ago.

By ten o'clock on Thursday morning, the sheriff's deputies at Irene Cogan's front and back doors were replaced by a fully equipped, innocuous-looking FBI surveillance van from San Jose with "Coast Heating & Cooling" painted on the side. The FBI's lower profile was appreciated by Irene, who had two patients coming in that day; the presence of armed guards would not have been conducive to the atmosphere of trust and relaxation required for hypnotherapy sessions.

Her first patient was a middle-aged civil engineer from Santa Cruz who'd awakened in Reno one morning with no idea how he'd gotten there. It was your classic dissociative fugue state, which often involved physical as well as mental and emotional flight *(fuga* in Latin) from an intolerable set of circumstances.

In Donald Barber's case, he'd been served with divorce papers while at work. Up to that point a timid gambler and a faithful husband, he left his office without saying a word to his secretary and woke up three days later next to a hooker in a high-roller suite in the Silver Legacy.

Even more surprising, he was up fifteen thousand dollars. Irene was thinking about using a humorous subtitle—"The Art of the Fugue"—for an article she planned to submit to the *Journal of American Clinical Psychology.*

But there was nothing humorous about Irene's afternoon patient. Lily DeVries was a fifteen-year-old girl who'd been unspeakably abused by both parents as a toddler. And unlike most such cases, the abuse was amply documented—photographs of Lily's decade-old sex torture were still turning up on the Internet and in the archives of pedophiles.

By the time Lily was placed in the custody of her paternal grandparents in Pebble Beach, her personality had long been fragmented—thus far Irene had identified thirty-seven distinct alters. Sessions with Lily were always interesting, if exhausting.

After hypnotizing the girl, Irene began every session by speaking to Queenie, Lily's host alter. She would then let Queenie help her decide which alters to call up—an unconventional approach. But Irene believed that many therapists did more harm than good to the overly suggestible patients, either implanting false memories with overaggressive hypnotherapy or, like incompetent exorcists, reinforcing malign alters by calling them up too often. Letting the patient's host personality assist her was a way of avoiding those pitfalls.

The subsequent parade of alters required Irene to be a jack-of-all-trades: some were children, some male, some bipolar, some schizo-affective. Whomever else she "saw" during a particular session, however, Irene tried to end every session by speaking with Lily, the original personality who had been so long buried. She was not always successful—Lily was a shy flower of a three-year-old—

but on Thursday afternoon she came out, and for the first time as Lily, relived her earliest memories of abuse directly, without Irene having to resort to the split-screen distancing technique.

It was a breakthrough for the patient, but the sheer accumulation of horrific detail left the therapist absolutely drained. After the session, Irene called Barbara Klopfman to invite herself to dinner that night for a little gemütlichkeit therapy with the Klopfman family.

"You'll have to take pot luck—and no shop talk at the table," Barbara had warned her.

Small danger of that—as always, Barbara's husband and two teenage sons monopolized the conversation with baseball talk. Apparently the Giants were clinging to first place, a game ahead of a team called the Arizona Diamondbacks—which came as a surprise to Irene, who'd hadn't even known Arizona had a team. But the dinner—pot luck turned out to be pot roast—and the banal sanity of Sam Klopfman and the boys were just what Irene needed.

After dinner Sam and Irene retired to the front porch while Barbara and the boys did the washing up. The evening fog had drifted in from the bay, blanketing the cozy little seaside town with a soft grayish-pink light. Sam Klopfman, bespectacled and round-bellied as a Teletubby, lit up a twenty-year-old Kaywoodie prime grain imported briar filled with a custom blend of vanilla and rum-flavored tobacco from old Mr. Hellam's tobacco shop in Monterey.

"That smells so good," said Irene, rummaging in her purse for her cigarettes. "It reminds me of my grandfather."

Sam chuckled. "I've found women have a two-stage response to a man's pipe. The first stage, when you're dating, is 'That smells wonderful.' The second stage, after you're married, is 'Not in my house, buster!' "

Instead of her own Benson and Hedges, Irene came up with the pack of Camels she'd bought for the prisoner. Seeing them, she shook her head regretfully. "I still think I could have helped him," she said softly.

"Really?" asked Sam, just to get her started. He was an attorney, but understood as surely as his psychiatrist wife that Irene needed to talk about some of the issues they'd avoided all through dinner.

"Absolutely." Irene absentmindedly fired up a Camel, then looked down at it in surprise when the toasty smoke lit up taste-buds long dormant after years of smoking Benson and Hedges Lights. "Maybe not an integration, but at least some fusion."

"What's the diff?"

"Integration involves a complete and final psychic restructuring. Fusion is more of a consolidation—you map the alters, get them all communicating and working together, consolidate some of the subsystems, and with the help of the other alters, teach the more extreme personalities less extreme coping techniques. It's not a dramatic cure like you see in the movies, but as Dr. Caul, one of the pioneers in DID therapy, always said, what you want after treatment is a functional operation, never mind whether it's a big corporation, a limited partnership, or a one-owner business."

"So we get a more efficient homicidal maniac?" said Sam. "Swell. Seems to me this guy's functioning better than our sheriff's department already. By the way, let me know if you want to sue the bastards for last night. I'd take it on pro bono just for the fun of deposing old Bustamante."

Irene thought about it for a moment, then shook her head. "Thanks anyway, Sam—I'd just as soon put this whole business behind me."

By Friday morning, it seemed that Irene was a little closer to her goal of putting the incident behind her. When she woke up, the FBI surveillance van outside her house was gone. Special Agent Thomas Pastor, who'd been brought down from the field office in San Francisco to take charge of the botched operation, had come to agree with Bustamante's conclusion that Irene was neither an accomplice nor a potential victim, despite the words Pender had written in his own blood on the floor of the cell. The injured agent's opinions were not currently held in high esteem by the powers-that-be.

Pastor did, however, call Irene at ten o'clock to make an appointment for an interview later that afternoon. Pastor also asked Irene if she wouldn't mind typing up her case notes for him. Apparently he was unaware that the sessions had been taped—and she had no intention of telling him.

Irene finished typing her notes into her PC around eleven-thirty, but when she attempted to print them out, she discovered the print cartridge on her HP was bone-dry. There wasn't time to pick up another before her jogging date with Barbara, so she drove down to Lovers Point instead of walking, intending to swing by the Office Depot in Sand City after her jog.

It was another gorgeous day in the Last Home Town. Soon

enough the summer fog would be rolling in to blanket the town day and night, but for now it was still beach weather. Irene pulled the red convertible into the Lovers Point parking lot. The obsessively punctual Dr. Klopfman was waiting for Irene down by the seawall.

Five minutes later, after completing their stretching exercises, Irene and Barbara set off down the jogging trail that wound through the shining lavender-pink iceplant carpeting the long curve of the downtown shoreline park.

"This always reminds me of the field of poppies in the *Wizard of Oz*," said Irene. She was wearing an oversize tanktop over white running shorts. Barbara wore dark green shorts and a Friends of the Sea Otters T-shirt.

"Iceplant is non-native," said Barbara disapprovingly.

"It sure is pretty, though."

"That I'll grant you. Did you see the paper today?"

"Nope."

"Your boy Max was all over the front page. The FBI thinks he might be a serial killer they've been after for years."

"I'm not surprised," said Irene. "But you know, I still believe what I told Sam last night. There was real promise there. Three of the alters had a genuine sweetness about them—little Lyssy, Christopher, and that poor host-type."

"Too bad there's no way to just lock up the evil alters."

"Evil? You know as well as I do that evil is no more a psychological concept than good. There's only healthy and unhealthy, and both of those are relative points on a continuum. It's a slippery slope—once you start labeling people with mental disorders as evil, it's like you're saying they don't deserve care or treatment."

"Just because something's not a psychological concept doesn't mean it doesn't exist, honey," replied Barbara, falling in behind Irene as the jogging trail narrowed to a thin track hemmed in on both sides by iceplant.

A moment later they came upon a sight so pitiful it was almost funny—a blond man in a pink nylon jogging suit and incongruous black wing tips, trying to jog despite a severe case of what appeared to be some form of either palsy or chorea. His feet were splayed, his knees were pressed together, his butt was pooched out, his head was tucked sideways into his right shoulder, his left arm was jammed into the elastic waistband of the pink pants, and his right arm waved feebly in the air, hand flapping like a drag queen's. He stepped, or rather lurched, aside as the two women trotted up behind him, so they wouldn't have to follow his pace until the path widened. They thanked him without turning to look as they jogged by.

Warmed by the sun, soothed by the sound of the waves, and with a renewed sense of gratitude at being able-bodied, Irene and Barbara jogged beyond Point Pinos, and were feeling the effects by the time they sighted the unfortunate man again on the return trip. He was not far from the point where they'd first seen him, but ten yards off the path, struggling through the ankle-high iceplant, heading toward the road that paralleled the shoreline trail, then falling, or rather sinking, exhausted, into a semi-squatting position as they passed him. Neither woman hesitated; they left the path and waded through the tangled pink groundcover that snatched at their socks and scratched their ankles. Barbara asked him if he needed a hand.

"Thaaank yeeoo." His voice was a tortured howl, his head was twisted down and to the side, half buried in his right armpit, and his left hand was still jammed into the elastic waistband, as if to keep it from jerking upward involuntarily. They each took an elbow, helped him to his feet, and walked him the last few yards.

"Thiiis eeis myeee ca-err," he said with great difficulty as they reached the green Volvo station wagon parked by the side of the road.

"You drive?" said Irene in surprise. As soon as the ill-considered words were out of her mouth, she wished she could take them back, but before she could stammer out an apology, he straightened up and turned into Max. The transformation was that sudden, a Siegfried and Roy materialization. One moment Max wasn't there, and the next he was. There should have been a puff of smoke and a fanfare. Instead he drew a snub-nosed revolver from under his waistband and jammed it into Barbara's side.

"Decision time, ladies," he said, stepping close to Barbara and angling his body to block the gun from the view of the passersby. "Who wants to live?"

27

"IF YOU TOUCH ME THERE AGAIN, you're going to have to marry me. Or at least kiss me."

Nurse's aide Rosa Beltran, sponge-bathing the comatose patient in room 375, leaped back from the bed, spilling the basin of warm soapy water over the patient, the bed, and herself. "Muy gracioso," she said—border slang for "very funny"—and hurried off to fetch the charge nurse, who immediately paged the resident on call.

"What time is it?" was Pender's first question, as the resident, a Bengali woman half his age, checked his pupils while Rosa remade the bed.

"One o'clock," she said in a musical, singsong Indian accent.

"I hate to ask this, but what day?"

"Friday—you have been unconscious since Wednesday after-noon. How are you feeling?"

"Like I just broke the Guinness World Record for hangovers."

"I'm not surprised—in addition to the concussion you sustained, it took twenty sutures to close up the scalp lacerations. Fortunately, there is no fracture."

"My ex always said I had a thick skull. How about something for the pain?"

"Just a few minutes longer, please. The neurologist must examine you first."

By now Pender's mind had filled in the remaining memory gaps. "Did they get him?" he asked.

"I beg your pardon?"

"Casey—did they get him?"

"You can ask your friend all about that."

Pender couldn't tell whether the look the young doctor gave him on her way out of the room was one of pity or compassion. Either would have been appropriate: Special Agent Thomas Pastor, in a bureau-approved blue suit, conservative tie, and well-shined Florsheim wing tips, entered Pender's room wearing an expression that would have been more appropriate in a seafood store—a seafood store with insufficient refrigeration, thought Pender.

"I just want to get a few things straight for the record," he informed Pender after introducing himself. "My understanding is that you not only identified yourself as an FBI officer while still in the cell with the prisoner, thereby provoking the prisoner to attack you and resulting not only in the prisoner's escape, but in the death of one deputy, and the severe injury of another—"

"What are you talking about? I never—"

Pastor, standing over the bed, pulled out his notebook. "According to Deputy Knapp, you called out to Deputy Twombley to let you out of the cell, that you had everything you needed."

"I was already unconscious. It must have been Casey—he's a brilliant impersonator."

"I'm sure he is," said Pastor drily. "It's a moot point anyway. According to Steve Maheu"—Maheu, known to Liaison Support staffers as Steve Too, was Steve McDougal's second in command—"you weren't even authorized to be in that cell in the first place."

"Bullshit. Sheriff Bustamante told me—"

"I don't give a fuck *what* Sheriff Bustamante told you—no one in the bureau ever authorized a known fuckup like E. L. Pender to go undercover for a jailhouse interview. So if you want to blow smoke up somebody's butt, save it for the OPR boys—they have filters up their ass. All *I* want to hear from you is what you learned from Casey, if anything, that might help us get him into custody—to get him *back* into custody."

A wave of dizziness washed over Pender. He closed his eyes and fought against the debilitating throbbing in his head. Muzzy as he still was, he understood now which way the wind was blowing. The FBI rarely admitted to a mistake—when it did, you could bet it already had a scapegoat saddled up and ready to ride.

Which meant, Pender knew, that the best outcome he could hope for was to be offered his pension in exchange for his badge. In other circumstances, the deal would have been acceptable, even welcome—at last he'd have a chance to work on his golf game, see if he couldn't whittle his handicap down into the respectable teens.

But everything had changed in the last forty-eight hours. Now more than ever, Casey was his responsibility—and when, inevitably, the monster waltzed with another strawberry blond, she would be his responsibility too. And so would the next, and the next, and the next.

Suddenly Pender realized that there was nothing he wouldn't do, nothing he wouldn't risk, including his pension. Besides, he thought, gingerly fingering his bandaged head, this thing was personal now.

"Pastor," he said miserably, opening his eyes, letting the tears well helplessly.

"What?"

"He wouldn't tell me a fucking thing."

"Now why doesn't that surprise me?" Pastor pocketed his notebook, handed Pender his business card. "Write it up anyway, mail the report to me. Preferably from another state."

The worst-dressed agent in the history of the FBI left Natividad Hospital against his doctor's orders, but with a smaller bandage on his head and a bottle of Vicodin in his pocket. He was wearing the same loud sport coat, brown Sansabelt slacks, iridescent gray Banlon polo shirt, and stingy-brim herringbone hat he'd worn to the jail Wednesday afternoon. Two days in a paper sack had not improved the drape of the clothes; the hat sat crookedly on his rebandaged crown.

Pender cabbed back to Alisal Street, and after retrieving his gun from the jail office and the rented Toyota from the parking lot, headed for the nearest McDonald's (not counting the IV drip, he hadn't had any nourishment since that sandwich in the courthouse Wednesday afternoon), ordered a #1 Extra Value Meal to go, and brought it back to his room in the Travel Inn, where he pondered his next move.

The big problem would be getting information from official sources, he thought, washing down his second Vicodin of the afternoon with a super-sized Coke. He had a shadow copy of the entire Casey file with him (he knew it more or less by heart anyway) but very little data on Paula Ann Wisniewski, the young woman whom Casey had disemboweled. That wouldn't even be in the NCIC computer yet—he'd need someone with access to the sheriff's department records to get it for him.

But who? Pender was in no better favor with the sheriff's

department than he was with the FBI. Then he thought of calling Terry Jervis. It was a long shot—and he'd have to get by the formidable Ms. Winkle—but if anyone wanted Casey worse than Pender did, it would be either Deputy Jervis or Deputy Knapp, and Knapp was back in the trauma ward of Natividad Hospital, heavily sedated.

Nobody picked up the phone at the little ranch house in Prunedale, however—after six rings, Pender heard an answering-machine message in Jervis's lockjaw voice:

"We're not home. We're going up to Reno for some R&R. Leave a message at the beep, we'll call you when we get back."

Pender hung up. There was something wrong here. Plenty wrong. First, the woman he'd interviewed Tuesday morning would not have been in shape for an R&R jaunt only three days later. Second, no cop would leave a message like that on an answering machine. Third, and most telling, even if she had been well enough to take a vacation and foolish enough to announce to prospective burglars that the house would be empty, why would Terry Jervis have been the one to record the message, with her jaw wired shut and every word a painful effort?

His cop radar went off like a car alarm; the problem of his next move was solved. Pender bolted his Big Mac and took a quick shower with a plastic laundry bag over his head to keep the bandages dry. On his way out of the room he stuffed the cardboard container of fries into the roomy side pocket of his plaid jacket to snack on as he drove.

Two newspapers on the lawn. The mailbox stuffed. The bright flowers drooping in their beds for lack of watering. Pender reached inside his jacket and unsnapped the leather flap on his holster— the women who tended this house with such care would not have gone off on vacation without notifying the paperboy or the post office, or arranging for a neighbor to pick up the mail and water the flowers.

At this point, according to the rules, Pender should have been calling for backup. Of course, according to the rules, he shouldn't have been there in the first place. No sense sneaking around, he decided—if he were being watched from inside, that would only telegraph his suspicions. Instead he marched boldly up the walk and rang the bell with the tip of his ballpoint pen so as not to smudge any latent prints. No answer.

"Terry, it's Agent Pender," he called softly—it would have hurt his head to shout. "I just have a few more questions for you."

Still no answer. He put his ear to the door—no sounds coming from inside the house. He walked around the side of the house to the back, saw what appeared to be drops of dried blood on the cement walk a few feet from the unlatched screen door, and a wider, streaky stain on the doorstep. Pender knelt, read the blood splatters like a tracker. Like tracks, they had a story to tell.

He nudged the screen door open wider, and with his feet straddling the stain, peered through the window in the kitchen door, trying to see through the crack in the gingham curtains on the other side of the glass. He could just make out a long reddish brown streak across the kitchen linoleum. Looked like more blood; looked like drag marks.

Pender now knew what was waiting for him inside; his reaction would have been difficult for anyone but another seasoned investigator to understand. Along with a whisper of dread, he felt a sense of awe so profound it was almost religious. There, on the other side of this thin door, lay a hushed, virgin crime scene.

Virgin—could *anyone* appreciate what that meant to Pender? Even FBI field agents rarely arrive at a murder scene first—they are almost always called in by the local authorities. As for visiting firemen like the so-called profilers of the Behavioral Sciences Unit, or the Investigative Support or Liaison Support operatives like Pender, they considered themselves lucky if they were even called to a crime scene.

And if they were, it was rarely until long after the local yokels had trampled the lawns and carpets, bagged key evidence instead of leaving it in situ, picked up items and put them down in *almost* the same spot, turned bodies over before photographing them, that sort of thing.

Yet a good investigator operated by reading a crime scene as if it were a work of art. It wasn't simply a case of looking for fingerprints or checking the redial on the phone. Everything in the painting, from a single brush stroke to the total gestalt, revealed something about the painter. And inside this house was Casey's most recent masterpiece—there wasn't a chance in hell Pender was going to call for backup just yet.

He looked the back door over carefully, peered through the curtains again—no deadbolt. Just the door lock—a thumb-latch with a keyhole. He had a lock pick that he'd carried in his wallet for nearly thirty years and hadn't used in twenty, but he didn't want to start mucking up the entry surfaces before the latents had been lifted.

He halfheartedly tried the thumb-latch, crooking his forefinger around the base where no prints were likely to be found, and pulling downward; to his surprise, he felt it move and heard a click. The door sprang open—it hadn't been locked in the first place. Pender stepped inside and closed the door behind him.

Already he had an idea of how Casey had gained access. The blood spots outside the house were few, tight, and round. They had to have come from a victim close to the ground, or the pattern would have been more spread out, and the splatter points more elongated. But the drag marks beginning at the door and extending across the kitchen floor were broad and bloody; a heelmark on the linoleum showed Casey digging in, leaning against a heavy load.

So: it was probably Aletha, Pender reasoned. (He always thought of victims by their first names when he was working a case.) Somehow Casey had lured her outside, or she'd heard something and gone out to have a look. Casey knocked her to the ground from behind—she didn't start bleeding until she was down. He had to have used a club, probably Twombley's nightstick, as there wasn't enough blood for a knife, and he wouldn't have risked a gunshot. She fell face forward; Casey started to drag her inside, discovered it was harder to drag a body facedown, turned her over to get her through the door.

Where the drag marks ended lay a pool of blood, dried and cracked like mud—here Casey had left her lying. But for how long? Pender was vaguely aware that the dishes in the sink, the dirty pans on the stove, and the empty cartons of milk and eggs on the counter had been left behind, not by one of the tidy housekeepers who lived here, but by Casey. Still Pender ignored them for the moment—they were out of place chronologically. Casey hadn't come here to dine.

Then why *had* he come? For Terry. For revenge. Casey didn't know Aletha from a hole in the wall. So he dropped her clear of the door, left her lying in the kitchen. But at some point he must have stepped in all that blood—his tracks led out of the kitchen and into the living room, where they grew fainter before disappearing entirely at the door leading into the garage.

Inside the garage, Pender inspected an old Honda and a careworn Plymouth. The ignition wires of the latter were hanging out from under the dashboard—it was probably the car Casey had boosted from the lot behind the jail. No sign of the green Volvo Pender saw in the photograph on Terry's nightstand Tuesday, though. Working hypothesis: Casey arrived in the Plymouth, spent enough time here to eat several meals, then departed in the Volvo.

As Pender reentered the house and made his way down the hallway toward the bedroom where he'd interviewed Terry three days earlier, his excitement at being in on a virgin crime scene was tempered by a foreknowledge of what was waiting for him behind that half-open bedroom door. He understood that everything would change when he stepped through it: he would no longer be alone.

You are a camera, Pender warned himself as he slipped sideways through the door. You are an investigative tool. You are a stand-in for the killer. Get inside the killer's head, not the victim's.

In short, he told himself everything he'd been trained to tell himself at such moments, and it didn't help worth a damn when he opened the door and saw the two corpses posed side by side, propped up against the headboard.

28

"EXCUSE ME?" IRENE SPOKE for the first time in nearly an hour. "We're getting low on gas."

They were still on Highway 1, just south of Big Sur. Barbara was huddled in the far left corner of the backseat, her skin crawling, trying vainly to shrink away from the tip of her abductor's wicked-looking boning knife, with its outcurved, razor-sharp, nine-inch blade. Max had pulled up the hem of Barbara's T-shirt and was idly tracing a figure eight along her love-handle. He could feel Kinch yearning for control.

You'll get your turn, Max told him. *Don't you always get your turn?*

He still hadn't decided what to do with Barbara yet. He couldn't just let her go, but if he were to let Kinch hack her, Irene might find it impossible to warm up to Max. It seemed unfair somehow—still, he'd find a way to work around it. "What's the gauge show?" he asked Irene.

"About an eighth of a tank."

"How much did we have when we left?"

"I didn't look."

"That was a mistake," he said quietly. "Sins of omission are punished the same as sins of commission. Are we clear?"

"We're clear." She echoed his own words back to him, to calm him. "What do you want me to do?"

Maxwell looked out the window, saw the gated entrance to the Henry Miller Library on the left. He closed his eyes and activated Mose's extraordinary memory. "The next gas station is down in Lucia. Pull over and pump it yourself. Use this credit card." He reached into the carpet bag he'd taken from Terry and Aletha's house and handed her Terry's Visa card—he'd wanted to leave a trail pointing south anyway.

The stretch of coast highway between Big Sur and Lucia is as spectacularly scenic as any road on earth. The rocky cliffs and crags, the crashing surf hundreds of feet below, the blue slate Pacific stretching endlessly to a wide, curved horizon, the gold and silver play of light on the water—no one in the Volvo paid the slightest attention to any of it. Irene drove grimly, both hands on the wheel; Barbara cowered against the left rear door, trembling, eyes shut tight; Max was lost in plans and contingencies.

As they crossed Big Creek Bridge, with four miles to go until Lucia, Max leaned forward and spoke confidentially into Irene's ear, just loud enough for Barbara to overhear. "Do you know what Paula Ann said when she died?"

Irene had to force her mind through a reasoning process—she could no longer respond unself-consciously. So: what exactly had been asked? What would be an appropriate response, one that would neither encourage nor anger him?

"No, I don't."

"She said 'Oh.' Just 'Oh.' Isn't that pitiful? I mean, of all the things she might have said."

"She was probably in shock."

"Well, my goodness, can you blame her?"

Facetious, thought Irene—he was bantering. Did he want her to banter back? She decided to take him literally instead—less danger of setting him off. "No, I can't."

"Me either. I'll expect better of Barbara if I have to kill her, though. I mean, if you try anything the least bit funny at the gas station. You know, try to signal anybody, or leave a note."

"I won't—I promise."

"Keep in mind, Irene, I don't have anything to lose. If they catch me, they're already going to execute me for Paula Ann. So what are they going to do, give me *two* lethal injections? One in each arm? I think not."

Max sat back, leaned even closer to Barbara. "Just in case Irene does anything stupid, you might want to get some last words ready. And try to do better than 'Oh.' "

He stroked her side with the flat of the blade. "You could try something funny—you know, like, 'You can't say I don't have any guts.' Or something nice and chilling. You know what my favorite last words are?"

Neither woman responded.

"They were from a girl who was dragged out of her tent by a grizzly in Yellowstone twenty years ago. It was in the paper—I was fascinated by that sort of thing when I was a kid. Her last words, as the grizzly's dragging her off into the bushes to eat her, she calls out, 'I'm dead.' Not 'Help,' or 'Ouch,' just, 'I'm dead.' Has quite a ring to it, don't you think?"

Again, no response. He jabbed Barbara with the tip of the knife, not quite hard enough to break the skin. "I *said:* quite a ring to it, don't you think, Babs?"

"Quite a ring," Irene answered hurriedly for her friend, who appeared to have gone into shock.

The pit stop passed without incident. Maxwell lay across the backseat with his head in Barbara's lap and the knife between her legs. Irene used Terry's credit card at the pump. No bells or whistles went off, but Max knew a record of the purchase would show up on the Visa computer.

But he still needed one more dot for the cops to connect, one more clue that would point them south, away from Scorned Ridge. When Barbara started blubbering again as they pulled away from the gas station, he decided to kill two birds with one stone. Leave the superfluous brunette behind. Someplace where she would be found—but not right away.

Max tried to think back. Christopher, then Ish, had been driving, so Max had only a vague memory of the route. He closed his eyes and brought Mose up to co-consciousness. Together they studied the roadside as Mose recalled it from traveling north with Paula Ann Wisniewski a month ago.

The turn-off. What marked it?

Sign: a flame with a bar through it.

But we're approaching from the opposite direction. What's north of the turn-off?

Mose narrated the scene for Max. *Girl in the front seat crying. Ish driving. To the highway. Wait for a white van to pass, pull out behind it. Landslide cleared to the right—bulldozer tracks. Steep chalk cliff on the right. Caltrans porta-potty across the road on the left.*

Good man, Mose. That'll do. Max opened his eyes, leaned forward. "When you see a yellow porta-potty on the right, Irene, slow down and get ready to hang a left across the highway."

29

"THIS IS SPECIAL AGENT PENDER. Let me speak to— Yes, I am well aware that everybody and his grandmother has been looking for me. Who's around from the Casey task force? . . . Okay, lemme speak to Special Agent Walters. . . . Walters, this is Pender. . . . Yeah, I know—I'll get it handled. Listen, you have a BOLO out for Casey, right? Okay, he's probably driving a green Volvo station wagon with California plates. I don't have the plate or VIN numbers, but if the DMV shows a Volvo registered to either Aletha Winkle, W I N K L E, or Terry Jervis, that's the vehicle he's in. Also, his hair color has changed—he's blond now. . . . Yeah, I'll wait while you put it out."

If the system worked the way it was supposed to, within minutes every law enforcement official in California would have access to the BOLO; it would actually appear on the screens of the onboard computers in the CHP cruisers.

"Yeah, I'm still here. Here's the next thing: you still have the ERT down here?" Evidence Response Team. "Who's the criminalist? She any good?

"Because I'm on the scene of a double homicide, that's why. Jervis was Casey's arresting officer—looks like he took out both her and her roommate Winkle. . . . Yeah. . . . No, I'm alone at the crime scene. It's extra-virgin—I thought we might like to get our people here first for a change. . . . Don't *worry* about the jurisdiction. . . . Look, do you want it or not . . . ? Good choice. But for shit's sake keep this off the air or we'll have every Barney Fife in the county trampling over our nice fresh scene. . . . Yeah, I'll be here. Wild horses couldn't drag me."

After giving Agent Walters the address, Pender hit the kill switch, then a programmed number—Steve McDougal's direct-dial extension at FBI headquarters—and reached McDougal's fierce and faithful secretary.

"Hi, Cynthia. This is Ed. Steve around? Yes, *extremely* urgent. . . . Hey, Steve, it's Ed. Can you get everybody off my back? I want to stick with this case. . . . Don't laugh, I'm dead serious. I've got two more corpses here—the arresting officer and her, uh, significant other. Sex torture. He's killing cops and their families now—we have to get this guy off the street. . . .

"Yeah, well, Pastor's an asshole. I know it's my responsibility—that's why I want to work this one. Besides, from what I've seen of this guy, he'd have gotten out of there sooner or later—he had a handcuff key—and the jail was a fucking sieve. They were sup-posed to close it down years ago. . . .

"Steve . . . Steve . . . Steve, I—Yes, but—Okay, are you done now? Excellent. Now listen to me: I *will* work this case. I give you my word it'll be my last one—I'll send you an undated letter of res-ignation, you can fill in the date yourself when it's over. But in the meantime, I'm calling in all my chips—and I do mean *all,* including the fact that we sat on this Casey investigation all those goddamn years without even trying to warn the public about—The hell I wouldn't. . . .

"Blackmail's an ugly word, Steve. And you know I'd never inten-tionally do anything to cause embarrassment to you *or* the bureau. Unless of course my back was to the wall. . . . I'm sorry you see it that way. But that should give you some idea just how goddamn serious I am. Now, can you get Pastor off my back, and cover my ass with OPR this one last time? I should say, *will* you—I already know you can.

"Excellent. Steven P. McDougal, you're a prince among men. I'll keep you informed."

Pender folded his flip phone and slipped it back into his pocket. Having spent an hour inside the house, he had some idea of what the women had gone through before they died. Casey had had himself quite a party. A costume party: intimate apparel, lingerie in both women's sizes, negligees, bras, panties, much of it stained with blood and/or semen, strewn all over the bedroom.

Judging by the various ligature marks on Terry's wrists and ankles, she'd been tied, cuffed, strapped, and bound a number of times, in a number of positions. Aletha hadn't been—from the lack of ligature marks, the amount of blood in the kitchen, and the severity of the wound to the back of Aletha's skull, Pender doubted she'd even been conscious.

Not that that had spared her Casey's attentions—as best as Pender could tell without disturbing the bodies, he'd molested both women repeatedly, growing more and more frenzied, at times using their own sex toys, some of which were also scattered around the bedroom.

Nor had they been spared one final indignity, the tableau in which Casey left the bodies to be discovered. The two were propped up in bed naked, side by side, the sheet pulled up to their waists. They were posed leaning against each other, each with an arm draped companionably across the other's shoulder, their faces turned sideways to each other as if for one last, never-ending kiss.

It hadn't been enough for him to torment them while they lived, thought Pender angrily—he had to humiliate them after they were dead.

I'll get him for this, gals, Pender said to himself as he heard the first Bu-cars pulling up outside the house. I swear by everything that's holy I'll get him.

30

A SOFT CARPET OF FALLEN needles in the clearing under the red-woods. Overhead a lacy pattern of green boughs and blue sky. The cheerful, human-sounding babble of a nearby stream freshened by late spring rains. In the distance, the sound of waves crashing along the rocky coast.

Irene and Barbara lay next to each other on their backs. After draping a car blanket over them to hide the fact that Irene's left ankle was cuffed to Barbara's right, Maxwell had cleared the red-wood needles from a patch of ground nearby and was sitting in the dirt, having Mose memorize the AAA maps of central and northern California he'd found in the glove compartment of the Volvo, then burning them.

"How are you doing?" whispered Irene. Maxwell had given them each an apple and a bottle of springwater to share, then allowed each woman to urinate in relative privacy in the low brush.

" 'I'm dead,' " Barbara whispered back, in what may have been a stab at black humor. Her panic attack had passed. As long as that knife was out of sight—and as long as she didn't think about Sam and the boys—she thought she could maintain for a little while longer.

"Not necessarily." Irene was feeling better too—even hopeful. "Think about it—he didn't kill that girl until he was about to be captured. And why would he have gone to all that trouble to kidnap us, if he didn't want us alive?"

"You, not us. You're the one he came after. I'm extra baggage."

"That can work in our favor. I'm sure I can make him understand that whatever he wants from me, he won't get it if he harms you."

Barbara tried to roll onto her side, but the cuff was fastened too tightly around her ankle; she turned her head instead. "I have a feeling that whatever he wants, he takes," she whispered into Irene's ear.

"I think this alter is intelligent and rational enough to understand that there are some things that can't be taken. If he wants to kill both of us, there's not much we can do about it, but if he wants my cooperation, he'll have to let you go first."

"I won't go—I won't leave you alone with him."

"Of course you will. And when you get back, you'll give Sam and the boys a big kiss for me. I'll be all right—he didn't go to all this trouble just to kill me."

"But why *did* he go to all this trouble? What do you think he wants from you?"

Irene turned her head, looked into Barbara's eyes, so dark they were almost black in the dappled shade under the trees. "Help," she said softly. "I think he wants help."

"And if you're wrong?"

"Then you can say a kiddush for me."

"That's kaddish," said Barbara, smiling in spite of herself. "Kiddush is the blessing over wine."

"So I'm a shiksa," said Irene. "So sue me."

It wasn't easy memorizing maps. Just glancing at them didn't work—Mose couldn't visualize later what wasn't captured visually now. He had to scan the big sheets slowly, left to right, then top to bottom. When he finished one map he'd test himself before burning it and moving on to the next—once the information was fixed in Mose's memory, it would always be available.

When the last map was in ashes, and the ashes ground into the dirt, and the redwood needles scuffed back over the ashes, Max took over and pondered his next problem, how to get rid of Barbara without alienating Irene.

He weighed the pros and cons of letting Barbara live. Pro: not only would Irene be grateful, she'd have more incentive for cooperating with him in the future. Con: Barbara would be able to tell the cops about the pink jogging suit, the blond hair, and the green Volvo.

But dead or alive, she would still serve to point the cops southward. And once the bodies in Prunedale were discovered and the house searched, he'd have to ditch the car anyway, so why not do it sooner rather than later? No sense taking chances. As for clothes, and a hat to disguise the hair, he'd pick them up along with his next car—once he turned north again, he'd need to be less conspicuous anyway.

He felt himself leaning toward letting the chubby brunette live. The only joker in the pack was Kinch. He would be mightily pissed off—maybe even pissed off enough to try to take control himself. And once Kinch got going, there was no stopping him—Max might lose Irene along with Barbara.

So whom should he try to please, Kinch or Irene?

Sometimes having a dissociated identity was no frigging picnic.

31

AFTERNOON IN THE LOWER CASCADES. The sky is high and sparkling blue above the ridge, and the air so clean and clear you want to sip it like water from a mountain spring.

For the woman in the green dress and mask, however, summer afternoons at an elevation of a thousand feet are a little too warm for comfort. In her case, the delicate thermal equilibrium of the warm-blooded mammal has been disturbed by the loss of roughly one-third of the body's two to three million exocrine sweat glands: she can't afford to let herself get overheated.

So after feeding the dogs and the chickens (she estimates there's less than a week's worth of food remaining for the animals; after that she could buy herself a little more time by feeding the chickens to the dogs) and scratching around in the garden for an hour, the woman retires to her air-conditioned bedroom for a nap.

But instead of sleep, come visions. The nearly empty feed bins. The drying shed she hasn't visited in days. And most important, the six morphine ampoules in the vegetable bin of the refrigerator. Though the Percodans she takes for pain are sufficient unto the day, she doesn't think she can make it through the night without her morphine. Which means in less than a week she'll have to take some kind of action.

The woman considers her options. There is no telephone on the ridge. There are half a dozen vehicles in the barn, but only two of them, Donna Hughes's Lexus and their own Grand Cherokee, are operable. She can't drive the latter, and won't drive the former for fear of discovery. Which leaves what? The mailbox at the bottom of the ridge. It's a long hike down the hill, but she can manage it, at least during the cool of the evening. Then a letter to her lawyer. At the prices he charges, he'd be delighted to make whatever arrangements she deems necessary.

Necessary—that's the key word. Once she asks for help, a chain of events will be set in motion. Her peaceful solitude will be broken, and for the first time since she had the boy released from Juvenile Hall, there will be strangers on the ridge. Strangers with staring eyes, pitying eyes, prying eyes. Strangers to be kept away from the drying shed and out of the basement. No sense opening up *that* can of worms.

So the timing will be absolutely critical. She glances at the complimentary calendar from the Old Umpqua Pharmacy on the wall over her writing table. Today is Friday. She'll give him the weekend, but if there's no sign of the boy by Monday, she will post a letter to her attorney in Umpqua City. He'll have it by Tuesday; help will be on the way by Wednesday.

But the worms, once loosed, will never fit back into the can.

Damn that boy—where *can* he be?

32

WHEN MICHAEL KLOPFMAN'S mother failed to pick him up at the Pacific Grove golf links at two-thirty that afternoon to drive him to a Pony League game, he paged his older brother Doug, who was just about to head for the beach with some friends to catch the high tide.

Grumbling, Doug agreed to chauffeur his brother to Jack's Field in Monterey, then meet his friends at Asilomar. On his way back from Monterey he stopped by his house to pick up his board and wet suit. His mother's car was still in the driveway; her purse was on the table by the front door.

Alarmed, he checked her bedroom to see if she were ill, then called his father at work. Sam, who knew about the jogging date, called Irene. When she failed to answer either her private or business lines, he left an urgent message on her machine, then called the Pacific Grove police.

Upon learning that Barbara Klopfman had been out jogging with Dr. Cogan of recent notoriety, and that both women were missing, the PG police immediately contacted the sheriff's department and the FBI. An updated BOLO was issued within minutes, and by four o'clock the hunt for the fugitive had been upgraded to a potential kidnapping/hostage situation.

Two hours later, Motorcycle Officer Fred Otto of the California Highway Patrol was cruising north on Highway 1 when he sighted what appeared to be a body wrapped like a mummy lying on its back in the dirt at the entrance to one of the fire trails leading into the Lucia Mountains.

As he pulled over to investigate, Officer Otto was surprised to see the mummy raise its knees, dig its heels into the dirt, and shove itself another foot or so closer to the highway. He called in his location and requested an ambulance, then hurried over.

"Hang on," he said, kneeling by the side of the mummy, which was wrapped in a cocoon of filthy gauze bandages and adhesive tape from head to foot, legs together, arms inside, with only a fleshy nose protruding from the front and a shock of dark hair sticking out from the top. "Just hang on there, you're gonna be okay now."

He used his jackknife to cut through the layer of adhesive tape securing the top of the gauze, then, cradling the head in his left arm, he began to unwind the bandages. A pair of dark brown eyes opened, blinked shut against the light, then opened again warily.

"I made it," she said, when he'd freed her mouth—it was as much a question as a statement.

"Do you have any injuries under there?"

"I don't think so. I'm just sore all over—I've been crawling for hours."

"What happened?"

"I was kidnapped by the man who escaped from jail in Salinas. He has my friend Irene."

Otto had received the latest BOLO over the radio. "Are they still in the green Volvo?"

"They were when they left."

"Let me call it in, then we'll get you loose. There's an ambulance on the way."

"Have them call my husband."

"Of course."

And so the BOLO was updated again: a blond man in a pink jogging suit and a blond woman in white running shorts and tank top, heading south in a green Volvo station wagon.

Unfortunately, the corrected BOLO was already inaccurate on almost every count.

33

"BILL, I'M GOING TO ASK you a series of questions," said Max to the elderly man tied to a wooden chair in the kitchen area of a double-wide trailer located at the top of a steep driveway in the Big Sur mountains. He and Irene had driven the back roads for nearly an hour looking for just the right place—an isolated driveway with only one mailbox. "Your life depends upon your answering truthfully. Isn't that right, honey?"

Irene was standing in the doorway of the trailer, watching the driveway, as she'd been ordered to do. She turned around, saw the man looking at her imploringly over his gag.

"I believe it is," she said. Not strictly true—after her success at talking him into freeing Barbara, Irene was inclined to the opinion that Max, though extremely disturbed, was not the homicidal alter. She almost *had* to believe that. Her nerves were frayed to the breaking point, but she understood instinctively that if she let herself give in to the fear, even for an instant, she would be lost. It was an emotional balancing act, and if she fell, there would be no climbing back onto the high wire.

"Okay, here's your first question, Bill," said Max. "Are you expecting any visitors?" He'd parked the Volvo under a lean-to garage with a corrugated green plastic roof and positioned Bill's own battered white Dodge Tradesman van at the top of the driveway, pointing down the hill, ready to roll.

Bill shook his head.

"Anybody else live here?"

Shake.

"Anybody else *ever* lived here?"

Another shake.

"That's a lie, Billy-boy. *You* never hung those curtains."

Irene glanced over her shoulder, saw that the curtains were white, flounced, and feminine, with little blue windmills. Observant fellow, that Max.

"Honey, you're supposed to be watching the driveway."

She turned around again quickly. By cooperating with Max, Irene hoped to help him lower his stress level and maintain his dominance over the other personalities.

"Now, Bill, I'm goin' to give you a second chance," Max said softly, almost gently. "See, we just robbed us a bank up in Carmel. We're not interested in doing you any harm—we only want to get out of here. But the situation is heatin' up pretty fast. What I want from you is first, the truth, and second, your van. What I'll do for you in return is, I'll leave the keys in the Volvo—it's a better'n even trade, and you'll get the van back anyway once we're done with it. Now, do we have a deal?"

Bill nodded.

"Swell. Who hung the curtains?"

"My wife—she died last year. Cancer."

"Well, I'm sorry to hear that, Bill. Were the two of you married long?"

"Thirty years."

"Man, but life can be cruel." Max tsk-tsked. "Tell ya what I'm gonna do. I'm just gonna leave you tied up here for a couple hours while we borrow your van. If you can get to the phone before then, more power to you—if not, we'll give somebody a call to come get you loose. Any family around here? Any close neighbors?"

Bill shook his head. His daughter lived nearby—she was working the dinner shift at a restaurant down by the highway—but he'd be damned if he was going to give her name to these two characters.

"How about if I call some local business then? I'd just as soon not phone the police, you know how it is."

"Nepenthe—call Nepenthe. The restaurant—they'll be open."

"Nepenthe it is. Let's go, honey."

Max followed Irene out of the trailer and, in a bit of excessive chivalry, helped her up onto the passenger seat of the van. Then he slapped his forehead. "I almost forgot, we'll need clothes and supplies. Be right back."

He cuffed her left wrist to the steering wheel. Irene didn't mind as much as she thought she would. In a way it was a relief, not having to decide whether or not to make a run for it. She watched through the rearview mirror as he entered the trailer, still wearing that ridiculous pink suit, and emerged a few minutes later dressed in jeans and a blue flannel shirt, wearing a black knit watchcap over his blond hair and carrying a cardboard box, which he tossed in the back of the van.

"There's some clothes in there." He climbed up into the driver's seat and uncuffed Irene. "They look like they might fit you, but you need to change even if they don't. There's also a wig for you—Mrs. Bill must have lost her hair before she died."

A dead woman's wig—Irene could feel her scalp contracting involuntarily. "Do I have to?"

"You have to do everything I tell you. That's how this works."

As the van bumped down the long steep driveway, Irene crawled into the back and went through the contents of the cardboard box. Food: peanut butter, jelly, bologna, white bread, apple juice. Clothes: cranberry-colored polyester slacks; polyester blouse, mauve, with plastic toggle buttons. Mrs. Bill must have been quite a pistol in her day.

Irene sat on the ribbed steel floor of the van and pulled the blouse and slacks on over her tank top and shorts, then removed the wig from the box. It was Bozo red. She clenched her jaws, fought against an urge to vomit, tasted bile as she slipped the wig on and tucked her hair under it all around.

"Irene?"

"Yes, Max?"

"There's a carton of Camels in that box somewhere. Bring me a pack, would you?"

His tone was casual, conversational. Irene mirrored it. "Lucky for you he smokes your brand. I hope you left him a pack."

Silence. A long silence. Irene realized she might have overstepped her bounds, been too flip. Squatting in the back of the van, she felt a sudden wave of dizziness, and realized she was holding her breath.

"No, no, I didn't," Max said eventually; to Irene's relief, he sounded more amused than upset. "It wasn't necessary—I happen to know that the old man just quit smoking."

34

PENDER LEFT THE BEDROOM shortly after Harriet Weldon, the FBI criminalist, pulled down the sheet that covered the women to their waists, to reveal one last ghastly surprise Casey had left behind for the investigators. Below the waist both women had been hacked so savagely as to be all but unrecognizable—too many stab wounds to count had reduced their private parts to a pulp of blood and splintered bone.

Shortly after sunset, when the bodies, along with most of the FBI agents (including an extremely agitated Thomas Pastor, who had refused to speak with, or even look at, Pender), had departed, leaving the crime scene to the MoCo Sheriff's Department, Weldon found Pender in the backyard.

"I have something I want to show you," she said, leading him into the darkened bedroom, closing the door behind them, and plugging in the portable black light laser. "Quite a love machine, your Casey."

"God-*damn*," said Pender. Ghostly white stains glowed like distant stars on the bed, on the carpet, on the cushion of the vanity chair, on several of the items of lingerie strewn about the floor, and even on one of the walls. "Hard to believe all that came from one man."

For each of the stars almost certainly represented an ejaculation—seminal fluid glows white under ultraviolet light. Later an acid phosphatase test would verify the presence of semen, but under the circumstances, the investigators could already be reasonably certain of the origin of the stains.

"We won't know for sure whether it's all from Casey until the

DNA comes back," said Weldon, a short, pleasantly homely woman whose dark-framed spectacles, lumpy nose, and bushy eyebrows made her look as if she were wearing a Groucho mask. "But everything else points to one perp, so unless one of the victims had a boyfriend who'd visited her after the sheets were washed, I'd wager my per diem on it. Tell you what, though—I've never seen anything like it."

Pender agreed. "Generally speaking, most serial killers commit rape not because they love sex, but because they hate women. Wham, bam, thank you ma'am, if they can get it up at all."

"I wouldn't say this one was all that fond of women, either." Weldon switched on the room lights, knelt to unplug the black light.

Pender took one last glance around the room as they left. Chalk marks, measurements, crime scene tape, fingerprint powder—he found himself almost nostalgic for those first heady moments when he'd been alone in the house. "I don't suppose you've come up with anything that'll tell us where he came from or where he's taking Dr. Cogan?"

"Dream on."

"How about the Chevy he was captured in?" They walked back down the hall to the kitchen, where Casey had apparently fixed himself several meals, which he'd eaten in the living room, probably while watching television. He'd also slept on the couch.

"The Celebrity? Zip so far. Same with his suitcase, same with the bankroll. I'll go over everything in the lab for trace evidence, but until then, he's a blank."

"Figures."

"What do you mean?"

"One of the theories we came up with early on is that Casey is a chameleon. Which squares with Dr. Cogan's DID diagnosis. When he goes out hunting for one of his strawberry blonds, he more or less effaces his identity—becomes whatever they want him to be in order to get them to fall in love with him—not just in love, but willing to run away with him, leave home, hubby, momma, whatever."

"The consummate seducer. But how does that"—they were in the backyard; Weldon glanced toward the window of the bedroom they'd just left—"that *mess* fit in?"

"Revenge. Deputy Jervis was the arresting officer. I think up until she pulled him over, he thought of himself as not just superior to everybody else, but practically immortal. He had to punish her for bringing fear into his life, for bringing him down to our level."

"But the other woman? And all that sex?"

"I think that was just opportunistic."

"He sure made the most of it—his opportunity, I mean."

"I'm guessing he always does." Pender handed her his card. "I need a favor—call me if any trace evidence turns up. Call me first—even if somebody tells you not to."

"I heard you were in the shit," said Weldon. "I didn't know how deep."

"In the shit, but still on the case."

"Wellll . . ." She took the card. "I guess I owe you one. That was the freshest crime scene I was ever called in on." Then, glancing down at the card: "The mobile number?"

"The sky pager—it vibrates." As Pender patted the pager in his inside pocket, it went off, startling him. "Speak of the devil." He made a wiggling motion with his thick fingers—a W. C. Fields/Oliver Hardy disconcerted flutter—then used his cell phone to return the call from the backyard.

"Pender. . . . Thanks—I'm on my way." He pressed the kill switch and folded up the phone.

"Can somebody tell me how to get to Pacific Grove?" he called to the sheriff's deputies standing by the back door.

"Yeah," said one of them, a black man. "First of all, be rich and white."

"That's Carmel," said another.

"Naah," replied the first deputy. "Carmel, you gotta be born there."

35

FROM THE POINT SUR LIGHTHOUSE to Highway 156 at Castroville, the self-proclaimed Artichoke Capital of the World, from 156 to 101 at Prunedale, then north on 101 past Gilroy, the self-proclaimed Garlic Capital, Irene managed to maintain a facade of relative calm. She rode shotgun, chain-smoking Camels, feeding peanut butter and jelly sandwiches to the driver, and lighting his cigarettes for him. But the closer they drew to San Jose, the more agitated she grew, until she found herself trembling involuntarily like a victim of hypothermia.

Max couldn't help but notice. His custom, when an abductee needed to be calmed, was to dispatch Ish to handle the situation. He waited until he had a relatively clear road ahead of him and to both sides to make the switch. Momentarily driverless, the van veered to the left before Ish grabbed the wheel and corrected the line.

"What's the problem, Irene?" he asked quietly.

Irene, her trembling head buried in her hands, missed the switch entirely; nor was she in any condition to pick up on the subtle differences in voice and manner between the two alters. On the mistaken assumption that she was still dealing with Max, she decided to volunteer some personal information in the hope that it might help him see her as a person, not an object or a victim.

"We're getting near my hometown," she said, gaining control over her voice with some difficulty.

"San Jose?"

"Born and raised."

"Any family still live here?"

"My older brother. My younger brother lives up in Campbell. They're both firemen, like our dad."

"Parents still living?"

"My mom died five years ago. My dad remarried. He lives up in Sebastopol with his second wife—she's a year younger than I am."

"How does that make you feel?"

"I was very happy for him—I just wish he lived closer."

"You miss your mother?"

"Very much."

"Close family?"

"I suppose. We fought a lot, my brothers and I, but I always knew they'd be there for me. They're big bruisers, both of them—nobody messed with me in high school, I can tell you that."

"Sounds idyllic," said Ish wistfully.

For the first time, it occurred to Irene that she could be in the presence of one of the multiple's other alters. Less guarded than Max, perhaps this personality would be more forthcoming as well. "Tell me about *your* family. Any siblings?"

The response, worthy of a trained psychologist—"We're not here to talk about *my* family, Irene"—was Irene's first indication that she might be dealing with an internal self helper. She decided to take a chance—ISHs were rarely if ever violent—and see if she couldn't establish some sort of rapport with him. It seemed to her, as her head began to clear, that regaining the therapist's role might provide her with her best chance of surviving. In any event, it seemed preferable to being a victim in waiting.

Irene glanced out the window. They were driving through the heart of Silicon Valley—she could remember when this area was all prune orchards. Now it was all money.

"Am I still talking with Max?" she asked, in as conversational a tone as she could muster.

"No," said Ish, responding almost automatically, as a professional courtesy.

Encouraged, Irene tried one more question. "So what's *your* name?"

It was very nearly the last question she ever asked.

36

No one escaped the clutches of Klopfman hospitality. After a real cluster-fuck of an interagency meeting at the Pacific Grove police headquarters with representatives from the PG cops, the state police and CHP, the California DOJ, the Monterey County sheriff's department, the U.S. Marshals, and of course Agent Pastor of the FBI (he did his best to ignore Pender's presence), at which jurisdictional matters were discussed, voices were raised, and fingers were pointed, Pender showed up at Sam and Barbara's doorstep around eleven o'clock to try to wangle an interview.

Barbara had already taken two Valium and gone to bed, but upon learning that Pender had spent the last two nights in the hospital, Sam Klopfman had insisted that he stay in their guest bedroom.

Rather than driving all the way back to the Travel Inn in Salinas, then returning the next morning, Pender, exhausted and in pain, accepted. Under the assumption that he wouldn't be operating any heavy equipment for the next six hours, he took two more Vicodin tablets—not excessive for a man his size, he felt, despite the dosage recommendation on the label—and was asleep within minutes. Some time later he awoke in the dark, his mind frighteningly and deliciously blank. Someone was tapping at the door—but what door, what room?

It all came back to him when he switched on the bedside light, saw the cow-themed lamp, bedspread, statuettes, paintings, and knickknacks of the Klopfman guest room. Then he heard the tapping again.

"Yes?"

The door opened; a round, double-chinned, dark-eyed, dark-haired woman appeared in the doorway. "Agent Pender?"

"Dr. Klopfman?"

"May I come in?"

"Please."

Barbara closed the door behind her and tiptoed into the room, wearing a too-tall man's bathrobe that trailed the floor, over a comfy-cozy thick cotton nightgown. "I couldn't sleep—Sam told me you were here and wanted to talk to me as soon as possible."

"The sooner the better," said Pender doubtfully, sitting up, pulling the covers to his waist. He was feeling warm, toasty, affectionate, and muzzy. As he glanced at the clock on the wall, noting with some amusement that the little cow was at one and the big cow at six, he remembered about the pain pills. One-thirty in the morning, stoned on Vicodin.

Fortunately, Dr. Klopfman was under the influence of her own medication and either didn't notice or didn't care. Before long they were calling each other Ed and Barbara, and flirting harmlessly as she told him her story.

Pender had never conducted an interview half stoned, sitting up in bed in his underwear, but it didn't seem to affect his prowess. Barbara found the big man's presence comforting. He prompted her gently, elicited details she didn't know she remembered, and even held her hand at the scariest parts.

When she had finished, Pender asked her if she thought there was any possibility that Casey was faking DID.

"I doubt it," Barbara replied without hesitation. "He could fool me easily enough, but when it comes to dissociative disorders, Irene's the very best there is—it'd be hard to fool her. She ran a full battery of tests, did a clinical interview—she even put him under for a regression."

"I wish to hell I'd been a fly on the wall for that."

"You could always listen to the tape," said Barbara.

Pender appeared startled. "She taped her sessions?"

"Of course."

"Well, I'll be." Upon learning that Dr. Cogan had been abducted, the FBI had broken into her office, but there was no sign of the notes she'd promised to type up for them. Case Agent Pastor had confiscated her PC and was having an FBI computer security expert sent down from San Jose to break her password, but it would take at least another day. Once again, Pender was one jump ahead of the investigative curve.

"Where would she keep the tapes?" he asked Barbara.

"Her office, I suppose. I know where she keeps the spare key—I could take you over first thing tomorrow morning."

"Tomorrow morning, hell," said Pender, starting to throw back the covers, then remembering that he was in his underwear. "Didn't anybody ever tell you, the FBI never sleeps?"

"I sleep," replied Barbara.

"Irene won't," said Pender—that clinched the deal.

37

IN ORDER TO HELP THE system protect itself, Max, with Ish's help, had years earlier put in place what might be termed an emergency response reflex. If any alter but Max was ever asked his or her name, a switch would be executed instantaneously; only Max would be allowed to respond to such a question.

Unfortunately, Max had never anticipated a contingency in which the question was asked while another alter was driving a car at high speed along a fairly crowded highway. Though the driver's eyes were off the road for only a few seconds, the van veered sharply to the left again—apparently old Bill didn't believe in spending a lot of money on alignments. Then Max, seizing control, overcompensated, jerking the wheel to the right; the van lurched so sharply that it rocked briefly on two wheels.

Irene screamed and closed her eyes. When she opened them again, the van was back in the center lane, horns were blaring, and her captor had drawn the snub-nosed revolver from his waist for the first time since he'd pulled it on the old man.

"Irene, Irene, Irene, what have I ever done to make you treat me with such disrespect?"

The voice was a husky whisper, the accent Italian or Spanish. A second wave of fear, colder, deeper, and somehow even more threatening than the pure physical terror of the near wreck, all but swamped Irene's reason. Was this the homicidal alter she had dreaded meeting? With her adrenaline pumping and a brassy taste in the back of her throat, Irene struggled for control over her runaway emotions. She knew her survival depended on her mind, on her training. He's mentally ill, she told herself, and you're a psychiatrist. Use it, for God's sake: work it.

And when she had mastered her terror, or at least subdued it temporarily, the answer came to her—this wasn't an alter at all, but another of his impressions. *"The Godfather,* right?" she asked shakily.

Max nodded, and slipped the gun back into the waistband of the jeans. "I'd better explain before we end up running off the fucking road. Irene, when I first showed up on the scene, Ulysses Christopher Maxwell Jr. was an unholy mess. Chaos—absolute chaos. Alters popping up randomly at all the wrong moments, rarely communicating with each other. You said Lyssy told you about the first time he was molested. Hell, he doesn't even *know* about the first time—the abuse had been going on for years by then. And frankly, what happened that night was a walk in the park compared to the earlier abuse—by the time he was five, he'd split off half a dozen alters to deal with it.

"And Ulysses, the so-called host, was a joke—Useless, I call him. Completely powerless—he didn't even know he was part of a multiple. This system was heading straight for the funny farm, Irene— if it even survived long enough.

"Enter Max. I restored order, established communications, laid down a few simple rules of conduct, one of which is that I'm the only alter allowed to answer questions about our identity. So from now on, no more asking for names, no more peeping around until we're in a more or less formal therapeutic setting."

Therapeutic setting, thought Irene. So she'd been right when she told Barbara that what he wanted was help. But her relief at having been right on that score was tempered by a troubling thought: he'd told her his name. Which meant he had no intention of ever letting her go.

She could feel that cold wave of terror threatening to swamp her again. Of course he had no intention of letting her go—she told herself that on some level she'd known that all along. But it still didn't equal a death sentence. Escape, rescue—those were very real possibilities. As long as she managed to remain alive. By using her mind. Her training. Work it, she reminded herself. Listen.

"Now, once we start our therapy, I have no objection to your speaking to whomever you please," Max was saying. "As long as you don't try to take advantage of the situation, that is. Keep in mind—I'll *be* there, I'll be listening, I'll know everything any of them tells you, and hear everything you tell any of them."

Not any, thought Irene, remembering Max's confusion after the hypnotherapy session. Not Lyssy.

"And if you try to persuade any of them to do anything against the system's best interest, I will terminate the therapy with extreme prejudice. Are you familiar with that term?"

"Not exactly."

"I got it out of *Apocalypse Now*. It's a euphemism. A termination with extreme prejudice is invariably fatal."

"I'll keep that in mind," said Irene. "But may I speak frankly?"

"Always."

"If in your opinion you have the system operating so smoothly, why are you seeking therapy?"

He looked over at her sharply, then turned back to the road unspooling ahead of them. Traffic had begun to clear. They were cruising at fifty miles an hour, the van's maximum speed. That was why he'd stayed on 101 instead of cutting over to the interstate: doing fifty on Route 5 could get you pulled over for obstructing traffic.

"You're not being sarcastic by any chance, are you Irene?"

"No—I think it's a legitimate question."

"Then I'll give you a legitimate answer. It's no goddamn picnic being a multiple. You're always one slip away from humiliation. Hard to hold down a job. And as for a relationship, forget it— who'd want a relationship with a whole theatrical troupe? You'd never know whom you're making love to."

Irene decided not to point out that the DID literature was rife with examples of multiples' spouses (usually male spouses of female multiples) who actively subverted therapy because being married to a multiple was like having your own imaginary harem.

"I'm still a little confused," she told him instead. "You said you've restored order to the system. Why not just stay in control yourself?"

"I wish to hell I could. But it doesn't work like that. The only way I can stay in control is by letting the others all have their turns. If I don't, they're apt to force their way out. Sometimes they do anyway—that's how you met Useless the other day."

Irene thought back to what the hapless host alter had said—that Max wouldn't allow any therapy. Now she was beginning to understand. "So what you're telling me is that you want to go into therapy not to achieve integration, but to maintain more effective control over the other alters. I don't know how much progress we can make under those ground rules."

"A little fine-tuning, for a more efficiently functioning system? That's just textbook fusion, Irene—a textbook therapeutic resolution. I think it's doable, and I think it's worth a shot. How about you?"

Irene knew better than to ask him what her alternatives were. Suppressing a shudder, she turned her thoughts to the work ahead of her. Fusion was difficult enough to achieve in the best of circumstances—and time-consuming: three years at a minimum. But who could say for sure? This multiple was different from any of the others she'd treated—perhaps with a powerful alter like Max in charge, instead of the usual ineffective host, the possibility of an early resolution might not be all that far-fetched.

In any event, it would surely beat termination with extreme prejudice. So: start therapy, keep Max happy, keep your eyes open for any crack or weakness in the system that might be exploitable—and most important, stay alive.

"I suppose I'm game if you are," she told him. Then she turned to her left, reached across the space separating them, and gently pushed that unruly comma of hair, blond now, back from his forehead, and tucked it under his watchcap for him.

38

ED PENDER HAD TOSSED his share of houses in his time, and one of the conclusions he'd come to was that it was often easier to find something that had been deliberately hidden than something that hadn't. Cops, like burglars, knew all the hiding places—mattresses and drawer bottoms, freezers and toilet tanks, wall safes and crawl spaces.

But Irene Cogan hadn't been trying to conceal her Dictaphone, which meant it might be anywhere. After a thorough search first of her office, then her living room, kitchen, bathroom, and bedroom, Pender had learned almost as much about Dr. Cogan as he would have from meeting her face to face—certainly more than she would have volunteered.

He knew her late husband had been named Frank, that he'd been a builder and a golfer and an amateur painter. He knew that either she and Frank hadn't been able to have children or didn't want any—although there was obviously no shortage of money, they'd purchased a small home with only one bedroom.

He saw that she was neat, but not a fastidious housekeeper, that she was a conservative dresser who preferred department stores to couturiers. He knew she was slender, small in the top and long in the legs, and that she had her hair dyed at the hairdressers but touched it up occasionally with L'Oreal. Her scent was Rain, her favorite color was blue, and she was probably proud of those long legs—she had more dresses than pantsuits, more skirts and shorts than slacks, and although she wore plain white cotton panties from Olga, she wasn't averse to shelling out the big bucks for high-end pantyhose and stockings, and understood the value of high heels.

From the journals and books on psychology in every room of the house, and the dearth of fiction in the bookshelves, videos in the TV stand, or publications other than professional in the bathroom, he gathered she was a workaholic. He also knew that she smoked Benson and Hedges, had recently taken up jogging, subsisted largely on salads, and probably didn't care for chocolate.

Pender could also make some informed assumptions as to Dr. Cogan's sexual habits. There were no signs that she'd entertained an overnight visitor in the recent past, much less that she was involved in a long-term relationship. Only one toothbrush in the bathroom, and one dainty Silk Effects razor by the bathtub. No man had left his pajamas folded in one of her drawers or hanging in her closet—there was no indication, in fact, that anyone but herself had been in that bedroom in a long, long time. No snazzy lingerie in her underwear drawer—just those Olga panties and a utilitarian-looking beige garterbelt for her beloved stockings— while the sexy satin nightgown in her closet had gone unworn for so long that there were deep-scored hanger marks pressed into the shoulders.

Most telling of all, there was no diaphragm in the bathroom, nor spermicidal jelly, contraceptive foam, or birth control pills, and no condoms, oils, or unguents in the drawer of the bedside table— there wasn't even a vibrator in evidence. All of which suggested strongly to Special Agent Pender that Dr. Irene Cogan had not (to put it crudely) been getting any lately.

Oh, and one other thing. He knew from the wedding picture of the Cogans on the mantel over the small fireplace in the living room that before she started coloring her hair, Dr. Irene Cogan had been a strawberry blond. He only prayed that Casey didn't know it.

But despite all that he had learned about Dr. Cogan, Pender still had no idea where the hell she'd stashed her Dictaphone, and after two hours of searching, his head was absolutely killing him.

Might as well call it a night, he told himself, entering the upstairs bathroom for the second time that evening. This time he wasn't looking for anything except relief for his bladder. When he bent forward (carefully, on account of his pounding head) to raise the toilet seat, he noticed that the decorative guest towel hanging from the rack on the wall behind the toilet had been pulled down until it brushed the top of the toilet tank. The *front* of the top of the tank—it wasn't hanging parallel to the wall.

And now he knew—he knew almost before he flipped the towel

up. Thirty years an investigator, a re-creator of events, Pender tended to think first in terms of reverse process. Dictaphone on toilet, hidden by towel. Not hidden—shielded. From what? To protect it from getting wet—it's in a bathroom.

But why a bathroom? Of course: Dr. Cogan was a workaholic. Pender already knew she worked while eating. How about while bathing? You bet. So she put her expensive Dictaphone on the toilet seat, where she could reach it, but where there was no danger of it falling into the tub.

Once he had Dr. Cogan in the bath listening to the Dictaphone resting on the toilet seat, Pender worked forward again. Splish, splash, she steps out of the bath. Wraps a towel around her—not the guest towel—and maybe another to make a turban for her hair. But she needs to sit down, dry her toes or whatever. Moves the Dictaphone to the top of the toilet tank. Pulls the towel on the rack down to cover the apparatus so it won't get wet when she unwraps her turban.

All this Pender saw in his mind's eye within seconds of lifting the decoratively hemmed bottom of the towel to reveal a pearl-gray, state-of-the-art Dictaphone the size of a paperback novel, with one tiny tape cassette beside it and another still inside. At the same time, though, he understood full well that for all his investigative prowess, he would never have discovered it if he hadn't needed to take a piss.

It's better to be lucky than smart, Ed Pender reminded himself, not for the first time in his long career.

39

FLASHING LIGHTS IN THE passenger-side mirror.

Please, I want to live, thought Irene. Maxwell pulled the van over to the side of the highway, steering with his right hand while reaching across his body to draw Terry Jervis's snub-nosed off-duty .38 from the waistband of Bill's jeans with his left.

"What's going to happen?" Irene asked him.

His eyes were fixed on the rearview mirror as he lowered the revolver out of sight between the edge of the seat and the door. He knew what he had to do—he also knew it would be better for his relationship with Irene if he pretended that one of the other alters had done it. Luckily, he could imitate them all.

First, though, he had to feign a switch. "I don't . . . I don't know," he stammered, as if he were in the process of stressing out, then closed his eyes and blinked them violently several times before continuing in Kinch's rough, reluctant voice. "The fuck do I know? He probably calls in the plates first. They're looking for this van, he stays in his unit, calls over the loudspeaker for us to put our hands up, keep them in view.

"That happens, I either hold the gun to your head, see how much leverage you buy me as a hostage, or I put a few rounds through his windshield and run for it."

"And if he only wants to give you a ticket or something?"

"He asks me for my license, I have to kill him. Don't make me have to kill you, too—I don't want Max to have to start all over with another therapist."

For the next few seconds the wheels of Irene's mind spun inef-fectually. If the highway patrolman got out of his car, this new alter would kill him. If the cop didn't get out of his car, the alter would kill her. She couldn't pray for the latter and wouldn't pray for the former. But when she heard the door of the cruiser opening, her first reaction was pure relief, followed quickly by shame and a sense of impending horror. She closed her eyes.

Footsteps on gravel, then Maxwell's voice—his new voice: "What's the problem, officer?"

"Did you know you have a taillight out?"

He sounded like a young one. Irene kept her eyes shut tight— she didn't want to see his face.

"No, I didn't. I'll get it fixed at the next town, I—"

"Can I see your license and registration, please?"

"Got 'em right here."

The pistol cracked three times. The noise was unbearable in the confines of the van. Irene covered her ears. Maxwell opened his door, stepped out. Another shot. Irene buried her face in her hands and began sobbing.

"Oh, knock it the fuck off." Maxwell slammed the door and peeled out. He steered the van across the grassy, depressed median strip, executing a wide U-turn; they roared south on 101, past the orphaned highway patrol car with its lightbar flashing and its radio squawking. The left sleeve of Max's blue flannel shirt was splattered by blowback—blood and soggy, spongy beige brain tissue from the point-blank coup de grâce.

He switched the pistol to his right hand, leaned toward her, and shoved the end of the short barrel against her neck; the steel was still hot. "Calm down or I'll blow your head off, right here, right now."

"Okay," she managed. "Okay, okay. . . ."

Okay okay okay. . . . Pounding the side of her fists against her thigh to the rhythm. *Okay okay okay. . . .*

By the time she stopped, her thighs were sore, but the panic attack was over, replaced by an exquisite spiritual and emotional numbness. Irene sat up, looked around—they were off the highway, driving east up a steep mountain road. "I'm okay," she told him.

"So I heard." He was hunched forward, concentrating on the road.

"Do you know where you're going?"

"I think so. If not, I'll find somebody who does."

"And kill them?"

"When I no longer need them."

"Are you going to kill me when you no longer need me?"

Max gave her his best Kinch glare—ordinarily, when a woman saw it, it was her last sight on earth.

"Frankly, lady, I don't need you now."

Max had bigger problems to attend to than a hysterical woman—though he *had* expected better from a psychiatrist. He knew it wouldn't take long for the CHP to realize they'd lost one of their officers. He needed another vehicle, quickly—he figured he had no more than fifteen minutes to get off the highway, then find a way north without running into any of the roadblocks the CHP would be throwing up on 101.

In fact, it took less than ten minutes for a motorist who'd apparently seen his share of cop shows on TV to spot Officer Trudell's body in front of the orphaned patrol car, pull over, and use Trudell's own radio to call in the emergency.

"Officer down," he'd shouted self-importantly into the dashboard mike. "Officer down!"

Since Trudell had followed standard procedure, calling in the description and license plate of the vehicle he was stopping, within minutes of the discovery of his body the CHP dispatcher called in a 10-28—a request for vehicle registration information from the California DMV—and was able to ascertain that the suspect vehicle was a white '72 Dodge van owned by a William Stieglitz, of Big Sur. By then, roadblocks had already been thrown up on 101 in both directions, and the CHP had a plane in the air, while a few hundred miles to the south, the Monterey County Sheriff's Department dispatched a deputy to the Stieglitz residence in Big Sur.

Deputy Gerald Burrell was perhaps not the sharpest blade in Aurelio Bustamante's department. He located the driveway eventually and raced his cruiser up the steep hill, fishtailing and kicking up dust behind.

"No van up here," he called into the dispatcher. "Just a green Volvo station wagon."

"Of course there's no van there," replied the dispatcher, who was familiar with Burrell's shortcomings. "It was north of Ukiah two hours ag—Whoa, whoa, say again the vehicle on premises?"

"Volvo station wagon, green, license three niner niner—"

The dispatcher didn't even wait for Burrell to finish. "That's the guy who broke out of County—Jesus Christ, Gerry, don't you read the BOLOs?"

Burrell found Bill Stieglitz lying on the floor of the trailer a few minutes later, his head nearly severed by the kitchen cleaver embedded in his throat and his body, in full rigor mortis, straining against the ropes that had bound it in life.

Within minutes of Deputy Burrell's discovery, the BOLO was updated to include the van, and the search for Officer Trudell's killer was folded into the Casey manhunt, which was moved north to Mendocino County.

By then Max had turned off 101 and was heading east, toward Covelo. When he heard the planes buzzing and the helicopters whop-whop-whopping to the west, he turned off the main Covelo road, followed a mountainous two-lane county road for a twisting half mile or so, then pulled the Dodge off to the side of the road into a copse of trees, where with any luck it wouldn't be seen at least until daybreak.

Irene was still numb in the aftermath of the cop's murder and her subsequent panic attack. She allowed Max—it seemed to be Max again—to drag her from the van and march her back up the hillside, then lay docilely in the heavy brush by the side of the road for what seemed like an eternity while he waited for a suitable vehicle to come along. It was nearly dawn when he finally scooped her up in his arms and stepped out into the road to flag down a blue Cadillac.

As the driver ran toward them, Irene saw that she was only a girl, a beautiful young Native American girl. *Enough is enough,* she thought—not the most elegant thought anyone ever decided to die for.

And as Irene began to struggle and shout, trying to warn the girl away, knowing that it would probably cost her her own life in return, her biggest regret was not having to die, it was that she hadn't found the courage to begin fighting earlier, in time to warn the highway patrolman. At least then her death would have put an end to the killing.

Bernadette Sandoval, a twenty-three-year-old Pomo Indian, drove a powder-blue '78 Coupe de Ville her mother had named Maybelline, after some old fifties rock-and-roll song. Eight cylinders, eighteen feet long, and bench seats front and back, wide enough to screw in comfortably. This last was important, as

Bernadette lived with her mother and grandmother in Willits, while her fiancé Ernie was currently living with his father in the hills east of Covelo.

Since attaining her majority, Bernadette had been working as a night-shift cocktail waitress at the Pomo casino on the Round Valley Reservation north of Covelo. After her shift ended on the morning of Saturday, July 10, she detoured by Ernie's father's place, turned into the driveway, shut off her engine and turned off her headlights, then coasted down to the house in the dark. Ernie was waiting for her on the front step. They enjoyed a quick one, then a slow one, in Maybelline's spacious backseat.

Bernadette tore herself away from her lover just before dawn, and was not far from the Covelo Road when she spotted a man staggering out of the brush, carrying a woman in his arms. She jammed on the brakes and pulled as far over onto the side of the narrow road as she could, set her flashers, grabbed her car phone, and hurried back down the hill to help.

Her first thought was that the couple had gone off the road nearby—it could be treacherous if you weren't familiar with it—but as she approached them she saw that the situation was more complicated than she had assumed. The woman was struggling; her red wig was askew, and the man had his hand over her mouth.

Before Bernadette could decide what to do, the man dropped the woman in the dirt by the side of the road and drew a snub-nosed revolver from the waistband of his jeans.

"Thanks for stopping," he said conversationally, as if he weren't pointing a pistol directly at Bernadette's chest. "Lots of people wouldn't have, nowadays."

40

IT DIDN'T TAKE LONG FOR Pender to realize that he was being frozen out of the investigation. For one thing, no one had told him about the murder of the highway patrolman, or that the manhunt was being shifted to the north. He heard about it accidentally when he showed up at the resident agency on the outskirts of Monterey bright and early Saturday morning to have Dr. Cogan's tapes transcribed for distribution, copied, and messengered back to Behavioral Science's psycholinguistics consultant in Maryland for further analysis.

His next hint came when he inquired about a seat on the Bu-plane that would be leaving within the hour for Mendocino and was told it was full up by case agent Pastor.

"Okay, fine, how about a Bu-car?"

"Sorry, Pender, can't spare one," said Pastor brusquely.

"What the hell's going on?" Pender demanded.

"My question exactly. You come waltzing out here from Washington. You don't bother to check in with the RA. You piss off the locals, start a prison break, and get a sheriff's deputy killed. You stumble on a crime scene you had no business investigating and take your own sweet time for a walk-through before you call in the BOLO, which gives our fugitive another hour's lead. Possibly contributing to the subsequent murder of a California Highway Patrol officer."

Pastor paused for breath; it sounded to Pender as if he were reading a list of charges that had already been filed.

"But when the SAC calls McDougal yesterday to have your ass jerked back to Washington, instead of turning you over to OPR,

McDougal tells him to find you something to do. So *you* tell *me* what the hell's going on. You got pictures of McDougal and the director burying a dead whore or something?

"On second thought, don't tell me. All I want from you is a full report, ASAP, pronto, immediamente, stat, on everything Casey said and did while you were together, and I particularly want a detailed account of any and all events leading up to his escape, and I want it by this evening. And that's *all* I want from you. I don't care what McDougal says, you stay the fuck away from my investigation."

Pender had taken off his hat upon entering the office; he looked down and saw himself twisting it in his hands like a nervous supplicant.

I'm KMA, he thought. I don't have to take this shit. KMA was Bu-slang for an agent who'd already qualified for his pension; the initials stood for Kiss My Ass. He drew himself up to his full height, towering over the younger man, who stepped back involuntarily.

"Fuck you," said Pender, with what he hoped was at least a degree of dignity. "And while I'm at it, fuck the RA, fuck the SAC, and fuck the locals."

Then he handed Dr. Cogan's two Dictaphone minicassettes to Pastor, who up until that moment hadn't even known they existed, put his crumpled hat back on, straightened the brim and crease as best he could without a mirror, and turned his back on Pastor and the bureau.

41

WITH BERNADETTE BEHIND the wheel of the blue Caddy, Irene to her right, and Max in the back holding the pistol to Irene's head, the old land yacht navigated the back roads of Round Valley, a shallow dish twenty miles in diameter, surrounded by a circular rim of mountains, then cut through a corner of the Mendocino National Forest and worked its way steadily northeast through Trinity County while the search planes circled ever nearer.

Max was starting to feel the strain. He not only had to keep an eye on the planes and on Irene, but also on Bernadette, who had promised to find him an escape route via unmapped roads, to be sure she didn't try to double-cross him. And as if that weren't enough stress, he had to do it all while monitoring a chaotic interior free-for-all. The system was in a nearly ungovernable panic, and with his attention splintering off in several directions at once, Max wasn't sure he could maintain his dominance over the others much longer.

Then it occurred to him that there was a way he could kill two birds with one stone and relieve the stress on the system while they were hiding from the air search. He ordered Bernadette to pull off the county road onto an abandoned dirt logging road. With Maybelline's belly occasionally dragging the ground, they climbed until the road gave out in the deep woods at the edge of a stand of shallower second-growth scrub pine. He had Bernadette park the Caddy under the cover of the trees, then ordered her out of the car.

Irene started to get out as well.

"You stay here," said Max, holding the gun on Irene with one hand, and removing a set of handcuffs from Terry Jervis's carpet bag with the other.

"What are you going to do to her?"

"None of your—No, wait, I guess it is your business."

Max suddenly realized that he could make it three birds with one stone, hiding from the air search and relieving the stress on the system while at the same time providing Irene with a damn good incentive to go forward with therapy. He leaned in through the open driver's door. "It's chaos in here," he whispered, tapping his temple with the muzzle of the .38. "I'm losing control. If I don't give them what they want, I can't guarantee her safety or yours."

"No!" said Irene. "Max, this isn't the way."

"Of course it isn't," he said softly, cuffing her left wrist to the steering wheel. "You *know* the way. Therapy. Fusion. Unfortunately, we don't have time for that at the moment."

Bernadette Sandoval stood trembling by the side of the car, her black hair glistening in the morning sunlight that filtered through the pines. The trembling stemmed not so much from fear as nervous resolve: she had already made up her mind to go for the gun at the first opportunity. If this Max creep killed her, he killed her, but she would not be raped—and he wouldn't have been the first who'd tried. She had an uncle who still bore the scar of her nail file across his temple.

"Pick out a soft spot and lie down." Max waved the pistol around to indicate the general area he had in mind, in the carpet of needles under the pines to the right of the car.

Bernadette did as he asked—she couldn't go for the gun until he brought it within reach.

"Pull down your panties and show me your pretty."

Bernadette told herself it was nothing—kindergarten stuff. She hoped he wouldn't make her undress all the way before he brought the gun within reach, but told herself she could do that too if she had to.

"Now unbutton your blouse, Bernadette, and let's see—"

The car door opened. Maxwell whirled, gun in hand. Bernadette tried to run while his back was turned, but her panties were around her ankles. She fell, tried to crawl away. The gun barked; a bullet whizzed over her head and tore into a tree trunk, sending chips of bark flying. She fell onto her face, her arms covering her head, trying futilely to protect it from the bullet she knew would be coming.

When the bullet didn't arrive, Bernadette rolled onto her back and saw Max pointing the gun at her. Behind him, Irene was leaning out from Maybelline's open door as far as her handcuffs would permit. Her mouth was moving; it took a few seconds for Bernadette's brain to start processing the words.

"—take me, not her. If you want my help, you're all going to have to cooperate. Leave the girl be, or so help me God you'll have to kill us both."

Bernadette was afraid to look up at Max again. She kept her eyes on the other woman's face. Usually she could read white people easily—unlike Indians, everything they were thinking or feeling showed up on their faces. This Irene was deep, though, no shit. She'd been through the fires. Bernadette believed what she'd said. Again she steeled herself to die.

Fortunately, Max believed it too. "What the fuck, any port in a storm," he growled, as much to the others as to himself. Then he gestured with the barrel of the pistol for Bernadette to get up.

42

PENDER'S RESOLVE LASTED A good forty-five seconds—he was still in the elevator when the slide show began. He saw Aletha Winkle and Terry Jervis alive; he saw them on the bed, shamed and butchered, then posed in a humiliating tableau. He saw the faces of the strawberry blonds. He saw his mother's face—how proud she'd been of him when he joined the bureau. A picture of her Eddie receiving a citation from Judge Sessions had gone with her to the nursing home where she died.

And lastly, he saw his father walking toward him in his dress blues, medallions gleaming. *Quitters never win and Penders never quit.* Then the elevator doors opened, and Pender caught sight of a big bald bozo in a loud sport jacket and crumpled hat reflected in the glass doors of the building entrance.

"Special Agent E. L. Pender reporting for duty, sir," he said aloud, then saluted the comical figure in the glass the way his father had taught him—hand straight as a blade, upper arm parallel to the ground, and *snap* it off, boy, *snap* it off.

Where to?

That was the first question for Pender. No longer welcome in Monterey, he thought about jumping in the rented Toyota and driving north to Mendocino. But there was nothing he could do up there that wasn't already being done. Same for Santa Barbara, home of Paula Ann Wisniewski, the most recent strawberry blond—the L.A. field office would have agents all over Santa Barbara.

So his next question was, What do I know that nobody else knows? What do *I* have to bring to the party?

At the moment, he knew from listening to the tapes that the killer had multiple personalities, that he used the names Max, Christopher, and Lyssy, and that he'd been abused as a child. But within hours, transcriptions of the tapes would be available to every investigator, and the bureau would begin investigating DID patients, hospital records, DID support groups, as well as searching the national crime databases for name concurrences. (It occurred to Pender that Pastor would almost certainly take credit for finding the tapes; he was surprised to note that he didn't particularly care.)

So what other information did Pender have? He asked himself what salient facts would have gone into that report that Agent Pastor had requested, and was now about as likely to get as he was a blow job from the attorney general.

Easy: Dallas. The Sleep-Tite motel where you could call for a number-one girl to make boom-boom. A number-one girl named . . . what was it . . . think back . . . no, *go* back . . . *pussy's pussy . . . call the desk . . . tightest little piece I ever* . . . Ann something . . . Ann Tran!

Where to? Suddenly Pender had the answer to his first question.

43

FOR HER DAY AND AGE, and taking into account her profession and the corner of the world she lived in, Irene Cogan's sexual experience was somewhat limited. She knew everything that people did, she just hadn't done much of it herself. And what she had done, she'd done with Frank—she'd remained a virgin until shortly after they became engaged. Their sex life was fulfilling, if not adventurous, a phrase that might have been applied to the rest of their marriage as well. The last time they made love was the night before he died. It was sweet; the next morning he was cold beside her. She hadn't made love to a man since, except in her dreams.

And now this. While Max handcuffed Bernadette to the steering wheel, Irene took a blanket from the trunk, spread it across a bed of pine needles, and stood beside it—for some reason it seemed important to her not to be lying down waiting for him. Then he was standing before her, face to face, and it was as if she were back in that dream of the operating theater, where they were naked, and he'd dropped to his knees and kissed her to orgasm.

If he drops to his knees, I'll die, she thought. Instead he took off her red wig, tossed it into the bushes, then leaned forward and kissed her. She realized he wanted her to open her mouth, to kiss him back. And she should have, she knew she should have—two lives were at stake—but she just couldn't bring herself to do it. She averted her face; or rather her head turned itself away from him— that was more how it felt.

"Even better," he whispered into her left ear, which she'd unwittingly presented to him—at these close quarters there was no escaping intimacy. He brought his hand up, splayed those smooth, bony fingers across her left cheek, and shoved gently, turning her around, all the way around until her back was to him. One of his arms was around her chest, the other behind her, fumbling; she heard a zipper.

He was pressing the length of his body against her now; if he had an erection, she couldn't feel it. He grabbed the waistbands of her slacks and running shorts, and tugged them down to her lower thighs, his weight still pressed against her.

She toppled forward, her pants around her knees; the strong arm around her chest supported her, lowered her gently. Then she was on her hands and knees and his weight was on top of her, his arms around her. He slid his hands under Mrs. Bill's polyester blouse and pulled up her jogging bra to caress her breasts. She could feel his penis pressed against her panties, her homely white Olga panties. He began humping, rubbing his still soft penis against her buttocks, but making no attempt to lower her panties or enter her. Then he withdrew his hands from her breasts and began slapping her across the shoulders and the back of her head.

It didn't last long, a minute, maybe two. He moaned; his weight came off her. As she crawled on her hands and knees to the edge of the blanket, she heard him swearing under his breath. When he didn't come after her, she stood up, pulled her shorts and slacks up over her panties, rearranged her bra, started to turn around. His face was red; he was wiping his hand on his jeans.

Premature ejaculation, thought Irene, turning away again quickly, before he caught her looking. Frotteurism. Erectile dysfunction. Her inner voice had turned self-protectively clinical.

"I changed my mind," said Max after another minute had passed. "It'd probably screw up our therapeutic relationship, don't you think?"

And that was that—it was over. Of course it would never *really* be over. Irene's neck and shoulders still stung from being slapped, and her breasts retained the sense memory of those slippery smooth fingertips. But she'd been preparing herself for far worse, so along with the shame and anger was an enormous sense of relief. And he'd never entered her, never been inside her—for some reason, that made more of a difference than she ever could have imagined.

Another cause for relief: afterward, Irene managed to talk Max into leaving Bernadette behind, arms cuffed behind her and ankles tied, but otherwise unharmed. He'd even helped Irene make the

girl as comfortable as possible, gathering armfuls of pine needles to
make a bed, and spreading a blanket over them.

"I promise we'll call somebody to come get you as soon as we're
done with Maybelline," Irene promised Bernadette loudly, as
Maxwell returned to the car to fetch a second blanket from the
trunk. Then, whispering: "You'll be safer here."

"Don't worry about me—I can get loose, I know I can. I've seen
people do it in movies—you work your hands behind your back
and under your legs. I can walk back to the county road, somebody'll come along. Plus there's a good chance my mom reported
me missing and they're already looking for the car. I'll keep my fingers crossed for you."

"I'll keep mine crossed for you."

"Thanks for what you did back there—I'll never forget it."

"That's all right. I'm just sorry—"

But Maxwell had returned. "Get in the car, Irene. I want to
check these cuffs, and give Bernie here a word to the wise."

This next part would be the trickiest for Max. He knew how the
Bucharest thrust worked theoretically—he'd have to get behind
Bernadette and slip the blade of the boning knife between her first
and second cervical vertebrae—but he'd never actually attempted it
himself. None of the alters had. And the timing would have to be
perfect—he'd have to do it while Irene's back was turned. Nor
could he let Kinch out to handle this one—subtlety was not
Kinch's strong suit.

But if Max did pull it off, Irene would never know, and Bernadette would scarcely feel the knife. Of course, even if she did, she'd
have neither the time nor the neural connections to enable her to
cry out.

"Here, let me help you get settled," he said, kneeling behind the
girl and tilting her head forward to spread the vertebrae.

"Thanks."

"Don't mention it."

44

FOR ONCE, TRAVELER'S LUCK was with Pender. Not much Saturday traffic from Monterey to San Jose, oldies on the radio, no trouble returning the Toyota at the airport, plenty of seats left on the Southwest flight, plenty of time to fill out the forms required to bring his weapon onboard. And on the connecting flight to Dallas's Love Field, Pender even had room to stretch out for a much-needed nap—he hadn't slept but two or three hours in the last twenty-four—before the plane touched down.

Love Field. Was it possible for a man of Pender's age to hear the name and not think of Jack Kennedy? Pender had been nineteen at the time of the assassination. His first year at college. He was still living at home, still driving the '53 Plymouth his folks had given him as a graduation present (it was the only car they could afford), struggling to cover his expenses by holding down two jobs (washing breakfast dishes at Dan's Deluxe Diner, and pumping gas at the Flying A), chronically short of sleep, time, and money—and yet he found himself looking back on those years with considerable nostalgia. The past was like an old whore, he had read someplace—the farther away you got, the better she looked.

At the Enterprise counter, Pender rented another Corolla—about all that was left on a Saturday evening. He asked the gal if she'd ever heard of the Sleep-Tite Motel. She hadn't, but looked it up for him, then gave him directions reluctantly—apparently it wasn't in the best of neighborhoods.

Pender treated himself to a steak dinner at a restaurant with steer horns mounted over the entrance, and located the Sleep-Tite shortly after nine o'clock. A downwardly mobile strip. Twenty shabby units painted a faded pink, two wings of ten rooms each with the office in the middle. ACANCY ACANCY ACANCY blinked the neon sign, a rusting, smartly raked post-Deco affair that looked as if it should have been holding up the canopy of a drive-in restaurant back in the fifties. OOMS were $26 a night. Hourly rates available, no doubt.

Pender parked the Corolla in front of the office window where the desk clerk would be sure to see it. Thanks to the carjacking epidemic that began in the early nineties, rental cars were no longer marked as such, but anybody who paid attention to that sort of thing would know the provenance of a clean, white, late-model Toyota. Single guy in an airport rent-a-car late at night equals traveling salesman—the very identity Pender planned to assume.

Apparently the corny hat and rumpled plaid jacket didn't hurt the disguise any—the middle-aged Asian man behind the desk greeted Pender without interest or suspicion.

"What c'I do fo you dis e-ven-ing, nice room twenty-six dollah, tv, no cable, local call free." All in one singsongy breath—sounded like a Chinese accent to Pender.

"Here's the deal, friend," he said, putting his elbows on the high counter and leaning toward the man confidentially. "I have a buddy back home, told me he got the best blow job he ever got in his life from this Veetnamese gal in the Sleep-Tite Motel in Dallas last June—and believe me, this is a man who knows his blow jobs. So I figured, as long as I'm in town . . ."

"One year long time. Big turnover. Whassa name?"

"Not sure. He might have used Max or Christopher or—"

"Not *his* name, man, *her* name." The desk clerk rolled his eyes.

"Ann Tran, something like that."

"Dunno. I'll ask da girls, see wh'I can do. Twenty-six bucks for the room. In a'vance."

"I'll pay cash—just make sure it's the same girl who did my friend—otherwise you're wasting her time."

"Yeah sure, same girl," said the man carelessly. But there was a watchfulness in his eyes that hadn't been there before.

Anh Tranh, five feet two inches tall, eighty-five, ninety pounds tops, heavily made-up and wearing a peach-colored halter top and a short, tight, lime-green, vinyl-looking skirt, came waltzing into room 17 of the Sleep-Tite Motel chattering away like a Saigon street whore.

"Hey, G.I., any frien' your frien', frien' a mine. I give you extra special numbah one suckee suckee, same like him, fitty dollah, long time, hunn'ed dollah boom-boom, whaddaya say, G.I.?"

Pender closed the door behind her, reached for his wallet, flipped down his badge.

"Have a seat," he said, nodding toward the bed.

"Oh, bite me," the girl replied, in an unaccented Texas twang. "What's the problem, Wong forget to pay off Vice this month? Or you just lookin' for a freebie?"

"I'm not Vice, I'm FBI, and I need your help." He had a copy of Casey's mug shot in his wallet; he showed it to her.

"Christy," she said without hesitation, though she hadn't seen him in over a year. She sat down on the bed. "Wha'd he do, kill somebody?" More intrigued than resentful.

"Lots of somebodys." It had suddenly become obvious that Anh Tranh was wearing transparent panties under the short skirt. Pender, who hadn't had sex in months, forced his eyes upward, past her bare midriff and tiny haltered breasts to her face, which was sweet and round as a lollipop. Pretty little thing, if you scraped about half that gunk off her face. "What's with the fuckee-suckee talk?"

"Pretty good, hunh? I ain't even 'Mese—I'm Cambodian. But we get a lot of guys your age, you know, 'Nam vets, they eat that shit up, come back for more. It's like, nostalgic. Hey, did you know your head was bleeding?"

Pender reached up—he'd removed his hat upon entering the room—and touched the bandage gingerly. It was wet, and when he looked at his fingertips, there was blood on them. "Son of a bitch," he said.

"Did Christy do that to you?"

"With a pair of handcuffs." Pender mimed a stiff-armed stabbing motion.

"God-dayyum," said Anh Tranh—she seemed to be impressed.

45

THE POWDER-BLUE Coupe de Ville scraped its exhaust pipe a few times on the high crown of the dirt logging trail as Maxwell drove back down the mountain, and the next stretch of narrow, twisting county roads definitely cramped Maybelline's style, but when she reached Interstate 5, she was in her element. She ate up the miles and crossed the forty-second parallel into Oregon shortly after seven P.M.

Not that Irene knew anything about parallels or borders—Maxwell had ordered her into the trunk just before they joined up with the interstate at Redding. He allowed her out to pee only once, at a gas station near Weed with sufficiently isolated restrooms. The rest of the time she lay in a darkness broken only by the intermittent white flashing of the brake lights, and later, after dark, by the hellish red glow of the taillights.

Oddly enough, Irene found herself almost welcoming the worst stretches of road, the steepest climbs and drops, the sharpest turns. At least the constant vigilance and sheer physical effort required in order to prevent herself from being tossed around the trunk like loose luggage helped keep her mind from dwelling obsessively on the horrors and indignities of the recent past or, even more terrifying, the foreseeable future.

After a few hours on the interstate, another forty-five minutes of gently winding highway, then one more bumpy stretch of nauseating serpentine loops, S curves, and switchbacks negotiated at minimal speed, Maybelline finally came to a full stop. Maxwell climbed out, leaving the motor running. Irene heard the sound of a gate creaking open, and understood with a sense of relief mingled with dread that the end of the journey was at hand.

But there was one last hill for Maybelline to climb, a hill so steep that Irene had to brace herself with both hands to avoid being slammed against the back of the trunk. Then the car stopped again, and the trunk lid opened. Maxwell stood over Irene, his face lit eerily from below by the taillights. He asked her if she were all right. She couldn't think of an answer—words would not come.

Max reached in and helped Irene out of the trunk. She was weak, sore, and queasy, but the fresh air was a revelation, delicious, intoxicating; greedily she filled her lungs, leaning against the car until she felt able to stand on her own.

When she tried to walk, though, Irene's legs gave way beneath her. Max put his arm around her and half carried her around to the front seat of the car, helped her in, then closed the door behind her. She stared dazedly through the windshield, saw Maybelline's headlights illuminating a mysterious looking tunnel fifteen feet high and twenty feet long, made of chain-link fencing overgrown with vines and briars, with locked gates at either end. On either side of this sally port, a high, electrified chain-link fence extended on into the darkness as far as she could see.

"Wait there," called Max, stepping into the glare of the head-lights. "And whatever you do, don't open your door or roll down your window." Then he unlocked the gate and was immediately swarmed over by a pack of stocky, savage-looking black-and-brindle dogs. Irene shrieked and closed her eyes, certain that Maxwell was about to be torn to pieces.

When she opened her eyes again, Maxwell was on the ground and the dogs were worrying at him, nipping and darting and growling in their throats. Then she heard Max laughing at the bottom of the pile, and realized it was only play.

After roughhousing with the pack for a few minutes, Max shooed them back into the kennel, unlocked the inner gate, returned to the car, drove straight through the sally port, and relocked both gates behind him.

"In case you ever wanted to leave here in a hurry, this would be a real bad way to go out," he informed Irene diplomatically as they started off again.

The blacktop forked on the other side of the fence. Maxwell took the left fork, a short spur that petered out at the edge of the woods, overlooking a vast expanse of meadow sloping downward toward a dark ravine.

"Oh my," said Irene, when Max switched off the headlights.

Beyond the meadow, across the ravine, a jagged, two-horned mountain peak broke the horizon. Above it was the most spectacular night sky Irene had ever seen, a dust storm of silver stars splashed against a backdrop of incomprehensible blackness. When her eyes focused on the blackness, the stars glittered and pulsed like a living sea. When she focused on the stars, the blackness seemed to drop away dizzyingly, leaving her teetering on the edge of the universe.

Maxwell turned off the engine, and he and Irene sat together for a few moments in a deep silence that was somehow enhanced rather than broken by the clicking of the cooling manifold, the scraping of the cicadas in the meadow. Then he started up the engine again, switched on the lights, threw Maybelline into reverse, backed her up slowly until they reached the fork in the road, and this time took the right fork, which wound north along the crest of the forested ridge.

"Here we are," he announced, as the headlights picked out a long, narrow, three-story house at the edge of the forest. "Welcome to your new home, Irene."

Home. The word chilled Irene something awful. What a permanent sound it had. How she wished he'd used some other word. *House, room*—anything but *home*.

46

ANH TRANH INSISTED ON examining Pender's wound. She had him sit on the edge of the bed. He could feel the heat of her as she leaned over him and gently tugged the adhesive tape away from his scalp, then dabbed the wound clean with a damp washcloth.

"Not too bad," she reported. "One of the stitches pulled loose, but it don't look infected. Wait here, I'll be right back."

She returned with the first aid kit from the office, applied what he thought was an antibiotic ointment, fastened a small butterfly strip where the stitch had given way, then rebandaged it expertly. It wasn't until she was patting the adhesive tape into place that Pender noticed the small round tin container with oriental writing on the bedside table.

"What is that, what did you put on there?" he asked nervously.

"Calm down—it's this amazin' Chinese shit Wong gets. Take it with you, put it on every day."

"You sure it's safe?"

"My girlfriend got herse'f sliced to shit by a trick last year. Wong made her put this stuff on it every day—six months later you could hardly even tell she got cut."

Anh stepped back to admire her handiwork, then began taking off her skirt.

"Whoa there," said Pender.

"It makes my ass sweat. You want me to be comfortable, doncha?"

He did indeed. What they were about to go through would be not unlike a therapy session: without the aid of hypnosis he would try to get her to relive that evening a little over a year ago. But while

Pender wanted her to be comfortable, he also wanted to be able to focus on the job at hand, so he suggested a compromise and she agreed.

Which is how Special Agent E. L. Pender found himself sitting up in bed in a cheap Dallas motel/whorehouse conducting an affective interview with a prostitute who was wearing one of his long-sleeved white shirts over a halter top and transparent panties. Having conducted an interview in bed in his underwear the night before, he was less bemused than he might have been.

At least he was dressed this time, in polyester Sansabelt slacks and a brown Banlon shirt. He had removed only his hat, blood-stained now, his jacket, and his Hush Puppies. He had his pocket notebook in one hand and a pen in the other. "Comfy now?" he asked Anh.

"I guess."

"All right, I want to take you back to that night with Case—I mean Christy."

"Man, what a creep. He was one of those johns, he didn't just wanna fuck me, it was like he wanted me to fall in love with him, too, you know what I mean? He—"

"Hold on there, Annie. When I say take you back, that's what I mean. See, the part of your brain that sums things up, and makes judgments, and compares things to other things, that's an entirely different part of your brain from the part that stores the memories themselves. And that's the part we need to get at tonight—that's where the details are. And you know what they say, the devil's in the details. I'll start you off. What room was it—this one?"

"Unh-unh. Nope. Twenty. Other wing, far end."

"Okay, you walk up to the door. It's closed. It's right in front of you. Picture the numbers on the door. A two and a zero. You knock. He says . . ."

"*It's open.* He says, 'It's open. . . .' "

"Sometimes you see a trick, you think what the fuck's *he* doing, payin' for it. This one's cute, he's young, he smells good, fresh, like limes when you just cut 'em open. And I can tell he's already hard, even before he forks over the cash. Some guys're twitchy about the money part, but this guy, it's like it's part of the fun.

"The second time—and I'm just catchin' my breath, like maybe a minute went by, no lie—so the second time, I'm suppose to pretend like I'm his little girl. I been ast that before, lots, I guess on

account of I'm small. And small here, you know. I tell him the second time's extra, and playin' let's pretend is double extra, and
nobody hits me. He says my love, start the meter. I get called lots of
things—'my love' ain't usually one.

"The spooky thing is, the second time, it's like he's a whole different person. He moves different, he talks different, he even fucks
different. . . ."

Of course, Pender didn't really need *all* the details. The trouble was,
you didn't know which ones you needed until you had them all.
Casey was priapic, a chameleon, liked to play games, carried a thick
wad of cash. Nothing new in any of that; he'd had over two thousand dollars—hundreds wrapped in twenties—in his possession
when he was arrested.

The third act of the drama was more revealing: this time Casey
was the naughty little boy and Anh was the teacher. . . .

"I dunno what I'm suppose to be spankin' him for, but *he* sure do.
'I'm sorry, I'm sorry I'm sorry I'm sorry.' He's lying on his stomach,
I'm whalin' on him pretty good, then he grabs me, turns me over,
and fucks me like an animal. I don't mean just doggy-dog, I mean
like you couldn' a got him off me with a bucket of cold water, you'd
a had to blast him with a farhose. But it ain't personal—it's like *I'm*
not even there. He starts off apologizin' to this teacher, then he's
bangin' the shit outta me, then he wants to ass-fuck, where I do
not go, I'm very sorry, but he don't care 'cause I ain't me, I'm this
teacher. He knocks me down, he sticks it in, he says something like
'Meet Max, how do you like Max,' shit like that.

"Now old Wong might be a dickhead, but he do try to watch out
for us. I start screamin', he sends Big Nig—his name's Ng but ever-
body calls him Big Nig—to check on me. Nig uses the passkey, all
holy hannah breaks loose.

"And Big Nig, you gotta understan', his mama got raped by a
black GI, so he's half 'Mese, half black, and pure pissed off. Plus
he's twice Christy's size, plus he's suppose to be a big karate expert
and all. Anyway, he come bustin' in, see if the john's killin' me or
what. Two seconds later, Big Nig's on his back and Christy's sittin'
on top of him bangin' his head against the floor. I mean, dayum, if
the carpet in this place was any thinner, Nig's brains would of been
all over it before Wong shows up with his horse pistol.

"Christy, he hears Wong drawin' the hammer back on that big

ol' Colt, he climbs off. Says we had a misunderstandin'. I say well I don't *think* so. So he gets his pants off the chair, pulls his roll out, starts peelin' off Franklins—when he gets to five I say okay, I misunderstand now.

"But here's the part that really frosted my ass. Him and Nig start talkin' while he's gettin' dressed, Nig talkin' bout what the fuck move was that, man, I got me a *black* belt and I never saw it comin'. They start talkin', next thing I know they goin' out for a drink together like they best buds or some'pn. And *I'm* the one cain't siddown, know what I mean?"

"Sure do!" said Pender with absentminded enthusiasm, his attention having strayed briefly—he was planning his next interview in his head.

Anh Tranh giggled like the schoolgirl she should have been. "Why, Agent Pender, I would'n a figured you for the type."

47

TONIGHT THE SILK DRESS is black. Black as her mask, black as her mood, black as the forest through which she moves. The woman has watched the sunset from the front porch, but it has brought her no peace. And afterward, she cannot bear to go back into that empty house again, so she throws a shawl over her shoulders and hikes down to the kennels.

It's a short hike, but she is winded by the time she arrives—her lungs were badly damaged in the fire. While she catches her breath, the dogs perform their eerily silent gambol to show their pleasure at this unexpected appearance (she rarely visits them at night), then line up for lovies. Dr. Cream joins Lizzie at the head of the line. Lizzie is the oldest, Doc the largest and fiercest-looking member of the pack, but beneath that black-and-brindle skin beats the tenderest of hearts. (Unless of course you are a stranger, in which case Doc, like the others, will be delighted to tear you into surprisingly small and numerous pieces, which, pending permission from his master or mistress, he will then devour.)

When the woman kneels, Dr. Cream assumes the kowtow position, forepaws extended, and slouches toward her to receive her first caresses, while Lizzie circles around behind her, pushes her muzzle under the tumble of red-gold curls, and nuzzles the nape of her neck. The woman drops her chin to her chest; her sigh is not unlike the sigh that issues from her after her nightly injection of morphine.

Suddenly her body stiffens; she raises her head.

"Hush," she says, though the dogs aren't making any noise. Soon there's no mistaking the sound of an engine: a vehicle is climbing the blacktop driveway that zigzags up the eastern side of the ridge. The dogs rush into the sally port, prepared to greet their master or silently ambush an intruder. A headlight beam snakes through the trees, pointing this way, then that, as the road doubles back on itself. The woman crouches behind the kennel as the Cadillac pulls into view, stops in front of the sally port. The driver's door opens; Ulysses steps out. Relief—wild, manic joy—surges through the woman. In her mind she rushes into the sally port to open the gate for him and throw herself into his arms.

Then in the space of a heartbeat the relief gives way to fury. "How dare you!" she says under her breath, still crouched behind the kennel, as he walks around to the back of the car and helps a slender, unsteady woman out of the trunk. "How dare you leave me alone here while you go gallivanting around the countryside with some floozy."

And as he helps the floozy around to the front seat of the car, the woman in the silk mask sees that she has blond hair. Frosted blond hair, not even close to strawberry blond.

"How *dare* you!" she whispers again, outraged beyond outrage. Her injured hands, in some atavistic reflex, try to clench themselves into fists, but feebly curled claws is all they can manage.

48

THE OFFICE OF THE Sleep-Tite was empty, but Pender could hear voices in the back room. He rang the push-bell on the counter, and Wong bustled out.

"FBI, hunh?" He waggled his finger. "You no tell Wong truth."

"Mr. Wong, why do I have the feeling that you speak English better than I do?"

"Ha ha, very funny, wha' c'I do fah you now, you wan' money back? I give you money back fah room."

"Keep it—I need to speak with Mr. Ng."

"Don' know, never heard." But although Wong's eyes hadn't flickered, his body shifted almost imperceptibly toward the door he'd just come through.

"Big Nig, I believe you call him," said Pender, strolling around the counter and heading for the back room.

"Not me, I don' call him that." Wong hurried in front of Pender, not to block him but to precede him. Dropping in unexpectedly to Wong's nightly *pai gow* game was a good way to get yourself killed. "You bettah not either, you know what's good fah you."

The door opened, Pender followed Wong inside. His first impression was one of disorientation, dislocation—it was not the sort of gathering Pender had expected to stumble upon in Dallas, Texas. He didn't know there *were* any Chinese in Dallas.

And the six Chinese gentlemen seated around the green baize poker table seemed equally surprised to see Pender materializing in the smoky haze. A seventh man, a mountainous, dark-skinned Afro-Asian in a jungle-print Hawaiian shirt, who'd been slouching on a stool in the back of the room, sprang up and was reaching behind him for his weapon when Wong gave him the chill-out sign, pushing down with his palms on an invisible table.

Pender waited in the doorway while Wong and Ng conferred, then Wong went back to his game while Ng followed Pender into the office, where Pender showed him Casey's mug shot.

Ng, who was nearly as tall and broad as Pender, shrugged. "Don't know him."

Pender sighed. "Very good. I'll be sure to pass the word along to my numerous underworld contacts that Ng is a real stand-up guy. Now tell me everything you know about this murdering sack of shit before I open up a can of soup on you."

Not exactly your textbook affective interview, but Pender's head was starting to throb again.

"Soup? What're you talking about, soup?"

"Alphabet soup. You know: FBI, ATF, DEA, IRS, INS . . ."

Ng weighed his options. It didn't take him long—the Fed seemed serious as a heart attack, and the murdering sack of shit was only a one-time casual acquaintance. "He said his name was Lee. He gave one of our gir—He gave a friend of mine a hard time. I kicked his ass. We had a drink, talked about martial arts. I don't remember much—it was like a year ago."

"I already know you didn't kick his ass," said Pender. "He kicked yours. Next thing you tell me that doesn't jibe with everything else I already know, you're going to find out how much trouble an FBI man with a hard-on can make for you."

The roll of muscle above Ng's massive supraorbital ridge lowered in concentration. "I asked him how he whipped me. He said speed plus surprise equals power."

"What else?"

"Said he coulda had a black belt only he wouldn't kiss the *sensei*'s ass."

"Black belt where? In what?"

"Karate. Said he also wrestled in high school, boxed in Juvie."

Juvie, thought Pender. Juvenile Hall. An institutional past—pure gold. "Where? Did he say where?"

"I don't . . . Wait, hold on, . . . Someplace in Oregon? Yeah, that's it—Oregon. I remember he said it like 'Organ.' a ranch. Said he learned a move there. He even pulled it on me, this move. We're sitting at the bar. He says, tell me when you're ready, I'm gonna bust a move on you and you won't be able to stop me, even if you know it's coming.

"So I'm looking right at him, no way somebody's gonna get to *me*, I'm ready for him. But sure 'nough, next thing I know—*shoop!*" Ng's hand, stiff as a trowel, shot toward Pender's throat, stopped just short of his Adam's apple.

Pender's head jerked back ineffectually—he understood that if Ng had meant to kill him, he'd be drowning in his own blood by now.

"He wouldn't tell me how he did it. Said this kid called Buckley taught him in Juvie."

Oh-ho, thought Pender. "Buckley—would that be a first name or a last name?"

"Dunno. Only reason I remember, back in school I used to date a sistah named Chaniqua Buckley."

It didn't matter, for Pender's purposes. Databases could be searched either way. First thing in the morning, he decided, he'd put a call in to Thom Davies, the database whiz. Then he remembered that tomorrow would be Sunday. Not that it made any difference—he'd just have to wake up early enough to catch Thom before he left for the golf course.

49

THE PARLOR WALLPAPER WAS patterned with delicately scrolled dark green vines on a pale pink background the color of flesh. A brass floor lamp with a rosy stained glass shade provided a cozy light. In the corner near the stone fireplace a grandfather clock that had traveled westward from Philadelphia by covered wagon ticked off the seconds; a handmade myrtlewood rocking chair creaked at regular intervals.

After all those hours in Maybelline's trunk, Irene found herself enjoying the gentle, reliable motion of the rocking chair—at least it was under her control. Still she couldn't get Maxwell's words out of her head. *Welcome to your new home, Irene.*

He'd left her alone in the parlor half an hour earlier, with a chillingly understated admonition: "Stay here, make yourself comfortable. I have some business to take care of, but if you leave this parlor, I'll know."

So here she sat, though she'd clearly heard the front door slam when he left the house. It was partly because she was afraid of him that she obeyed him, and partly because she was exhausted physically and worn out emotionally, but there was also an element of wanting to please her captor, or at least to avoid displeasing him. Stockholm syndrome, early stages, she told herself—how strange to be able to put a name to one's behavior, to diagnose it clinically, and yet to be unable to alter it.

So she rocked, and waited, and when she heard someone moving around in the kitchen down the hall, Irene congratulated herself on her restraint. Somehow he'd been able to sneak back into the house without her hearing him, she decided. If she *had* left the parlor, he'd have caught her for sure.

Unless of course it wasn't him. *Oh lord.* Irene quickly braked the rocking chair with her feet, intent on the sounds coming from the kitchen, though her heart was pounding so violently that the pulse in her ears nearly drowned them out.

Someone was moving around in there, all right. Whisking eggs in a glass or ceramic bowl, boiling water in a whistling kettle, sizzling up some bacon—now she could smell it. Soon she heard footsteps, light, shuffling footsteps, leaving the kitchen, coming down the hall toward the parlor. Irene's chair faced the fireplace. She sensed a presence behind her, heard raspy, tortured breathing in the doorway, but would not, could not, turn around.

Then she heard a silken rustle. Irene kept her eyes fixed resolutely on the round hooked rug at her feet. The skirt of a floor-length black dress entered her field of vision, then a pair of fleshless claws covered with a taut mottled patchwork of shiny pink scar tissue and smooth white grafted skin lowered a supper tray onto the chess table next to the rocker.

And Irene knew somehow, as she steeled herself to look, that the woman was steeling herself to be looked at.

"I thought you might be hungry." The diction was overprecise, the voice thin and muffled behind a black silk surgical mask cut from the same cloth as the woman's high-necked dress. It was impossible to read her age: the flesh around the edges of the mask resembled melted candle wax, all drips and ridges and runnels, mottled ivory in color, but streaked with blue-black soot, while her eyelids had evidently been surgically repaired, and her glorious strawberry blond hair, though glossy and abundant and apparently made of human hair, was obviously a wig.

You're a doctor, Irene reminded herself, struggling to keep the horror she was feeling from showing on her face. You've seen disfigurements before. "Thank you. I'm Irene Cogan."

Instead of introducing herself in return, the woman extended one of her gruesome claws as if for a handshake. But when Irene reached out to take it, she snatched it away, grabbed a lock of Irene's frosted blond hair between her skeletal thumb and forefinger, and yanked.

"Ow!" Irene yelped and drew back. "What did you do that for?"

The woman ignored her. "A clever boy, that Ulysses," she muttered aloud, calmly examining Irene's roots by the rosy light of the stained-glass lamp. "Wicked, but clever. Now finish your supper, and I'll show you to your room."

Welcome to your new home, thought Irene, scalp stinging, sudden tears blurring her vision.

50

IN ROOMS 15 AND 19 of the Sleep-Tite Motel, the whores and johns came and went. In room 17, Pender stuffed his thirty-two-decibel-proof foam plugs into his ears and began mapping out the initial computer search in his head.

Step one: Juvenile records were sometimes expunged, but not if the juvenile went on to become an adult criminal. Assume that was the case with Buckley—a statistically supportable assumption. Then look for hits on criminals with a first or second name of Buckley who'd done time in juvenile facilities anywhere in Oregon between—Casey looked to be in his late twenties—between '82 and '92. . . .

Step two: hope to hell step one came up with a manageable number of hits. Because that was about as far as the search could be narrowed on computer: step three would require a face-to-face interview with every Buckley on the list, in the hope that one of them just might recognize the boy whose name was Max or Christy or Lyssy or Lee from the adult Casey's mug shot.

All that would take time, manpower, and luck, Pender knew, and even if he managed to find out who Casey was, he would still be faced with the daunting task of tracking him down without the considerable resources of the bureau behind him. The sense of exhilaration he'd felt after interviewing Ng suddenly drained away. In its place, exhaustion, discouragement, and a wicked headache.

I'm too old for this shit, thought Pender. He went into the bathroom, washed down two Vicodins with a cupped handful of tepid water scooped out from under the tap (the plastic glass did not claim to have been sanitized for his protection), then brought his bound shadow copy of the Casey file back to bed with him, and while waiting for the medication to kick in, opened it at random like a born-again Christian seeking inspiration in a Bible.

A photocopy of Dolores Moon's eight-by-ten glossy stared up at Pender. Impish grin, curly strawberry blond hair. Tiny little thing with a great big voice. Born Huntington, Long Island, 2/12/69. Last seen, Sandusky, Ohio, 4/17/97. In between, a career playing itself out just below the show-biz radar line—her last role was Snoopy in a Sandusky dinner theater production of *You're a Good Man, Charlie Brown.*

Pender flipped backward a few pages. Tammy Brown. Born Pikeville, Kentucky, 9/22/78, last seen Pikeville, 7/3/96. Kentucky collegiate heavyweight power-lifting champion out of (where else?) Pikeville College. Not one of your buffed, ripped, steroid power-lifters, however, but rather a shy, fat, good-natured, drug-free Christian with a round, multiple-chinned face right out of a Botero painting. The polar opposite of Dolores Moon: heavyset, intro-verted, by all accounts virginal. The two women had nothing in common but strawberry blond hair and bad luck.

The Vicodins were starting to kick in. Pender closed his eyes, saw the vision that in one form or another had been haunting him, driving him on, for the last several years. This time it was Dolores and Tammy staring up at him through the darkness. Waiting. Waiting for him. His eyelids fluttered open again, and he forced himself to turn to the back of the file, to Casey's last victim but one—two if you counted Dr. Cogan.

Donna Hughes. Born Sanford, Florida, 12/20/56. Last seen, Plano, Texas, 6/17/98. Casey did most of his hunting in the spring or summer months, leading the investigators to speculate that he lived in a climate where the winters were not conducive to travel. Pender wondered if Pastor knew that. It might help narrow the search.

"I should *be* there," he said aloud, his voice sounding strange and distant with the earplugs in. "I should *be* there—they'll never catch him without me."

But he wasn't there, he had to remind himself. Instead he was here. In Dallas. Which was right next door to Plano. And suddenly, though he was by now so wrecked on the painkillers that he could scarcely think, Ed Pender understood to a stone certainty exactly what his next move had to be.

51

ANGER. DENIAL. DESPAIR. BARGAINING. Acceptance. These were the stages the human mind passed through when faced with the prospect of its own demise. Irene Cogan had been going back and forth between anger, denial—or at least dissociation—and despair for thirty-six hours. Now, alone in what under other circumstances she would have considered a charming little third-floor guest bedroom with an antique brass bed, big maple bureau, night table, escritoire, and adjoining bathroom, she had reached the bargaining stage.

She began by apologizing to the Virgin Mary for the things she'd said about Her Son and His Father after Frank died, and for not having been to mass since then, but pointed out that she had tried to live a good life, hadn't sinned much, at least in deed, and had helped quite a few souls in need, professionally (although she had to admit she had been well paid for it). She promised Mary that if She did intercede on Irene's behalf, she would go to mass every Sunday and volunteer her services at one of the free clinics in Seaside, Watsonville, or Salinas.

That was how Irene bargained in her head after the woman had locked the bedroom door behind her. It brought her little if any peace. Then she went through the contents of the bureau and the closet and slipped into deeper despair. For in the top drawer of the bureau she found underwear in a variety of styles and sizes, bras ranging from 32C to 40DD, barely-there bikini panties and capacious bloomers, bobby socks, knee socks, pantyhose, all showing signs of wear. Similar range of sizes for the neatly folded T-shirts, jerseys, and blouses in the second drawer—smaller sizes to the left, larger ones to the right—and for the sweaters, slacks, and jeans in the bottom drawer.

Inside the deep, narrow closet were skirts, dresses, coats, sizes 6 through 16. On the closet floor were shoes, sneakers, sandals of varying sizes, all previously worn. Irene slammed the closet door and backed away, then sat down heavily on the bed. How many women had contributed to this collection? she wondered. Dear God, how many women?

She dropped to her knees and began to pray in earnest, not with her head this time but with her heart. Dear Jesus I'm so frightened. Help me Mother Mary, I can't do this alone. Holy Spirit, give me strength. Give me wings. Help me our Father in heaven hallowed be thy name I'll believe in You with all my heart I'll never forsake You again. And even if You can't save me, even if it's part of Your plan that I die here, please, please, *please* be with me. Don't leave me alone here. Jesus. Please.

She didn't realize she was crying until the first teardrops hit the hardwood floor. But by then the worst of the despair had passed. Irene tried to tell herself that Jesus had answered her, but she couldn't help thinking about something one of her professors once said on the subject. The comforts of religion don't actually require the existence of a deity, he'd informed the class—only a belief in one.

"Thanks anyway," she said aloud, climbing to her feet and wiping away her tears. Then, with bravado, only half-joking: "I'll take it from here."

Normally—previously—Irene hadn't been much of a believer in what the New Agers call affirmations. Saying, "I am a radiant being," into the mirror every morning, that sort of thing. As a psychiatrist, she knew too much about the subconscious for that, knew that every time you say, "I am a radiant being," your subconscious replies, "Are not." A hundred affirmations a day, a hundred *are nots*—a person would be lucky to break even.

But desperate times require desperate measures. She made up an affirmation on the spot: "I *will* stay alive. Everything else is secondary. I *will* stay alive."

And it helped. She was nowhere near the acceptance stage, but at least she felt able to function. She opened the closet door again. Hanging from a hook on the inside of the door was a floor-length cotton nightgown the color of marigolds. As she reached for it, something nagged at the back of her mind—something about the clothes. So after undressing and slipping the nightgown on over her head, Irene did a little detective work, forcing herself to go through the bureau drawers again, taking a closer look at the dresses in the wardrobe. Different sizes, yes; different styles, too. Small women and large, younger women and older, chic women and women with no taste whatsoever.

But there was one thing the clothes all had in common: the color scheme. Warm Spring on the seasonal charts. Delicate tones. The neutrals were camel browns, creams, and grays. Some true greens and golden yellows, but no true blues, only aquas, turquoises, and teals.

Not quite a redhead's palette, though: the clothes on the red end of the spectrum were not the brighter shades that would have flattered a classic redhead. Instead, salmons, corals, pumpkins, peaches, and roses, the softer pastels she herself had favored before frosting her own strawberry blond hair.

Irene backed away from the closet, her mind spinning. The women who had left these clothes behind—were they all strawberry blonds? Was that why that hideous creature in the glorious strawberry blond wig had plucked her hair out—to examine the roots?

The implications were unthinkable. Suddenly Irene felt unbearably claustrophobic. She staggered over to the small four-paned sash window, opened it, stuck her head out. As she gulped in the sweet mountain air, she caught a glimpse of Maxwell trudging across the meadow toward the house, his head down, his blond hair white in the starlight.

I *will* stay alive, Irene told herself, quickly pulling her head back inside and lowering the window again. Whatever's going on here, I *will* stay alive.

Will not, replied the little voice in her head.

52

FOR A MOTEL THAT RENTED rooms by the day or hour, the beds in the Sleep-Tite were fairly comfortable. The alarm on Pender's watch woke him from a sound sleep at seven. At seven-thirty he phoned Thom Davies, the British-born database specialist.

"Morning, T. D. Hope I didn't wake you."

"Pender? For God's sake, man, it's eight-thirty on a Sunday morning."

"It's only seven-thirty here, and *I'm* up."

"Central time? I thought you were keeping regular in Prunedale."

"I'm in Dallas. How's my account in the old favor bank?"

"I believe you still owe me several lunches and your firstborn child."

"Care to make a deposit on my second-born?" He told Davies what he was looking for.

"I'll get on it first thing tomorrow morning," said Davies.

"Not quite what I had in mind."

"Ed, it's Sunday morning."

"He's averaging two murders a day since he escaped, Thom. You do the math."

"How about a shit and a shower? Do I have time for a shit and a shower?"

"You could probably skip the shower," replied Pender. "I doubt there's going to be anybody else in the office."

Plano was a northeastern suburb of Dallas, though the town had enough of a history that it preferred not to think of itself as suburban. "It's plain to see/Plano is the place to be," read the Chamber of Commerce sign.

The Hughes house was a white colonnaded near-mansion in the pricey Lakeside addition. Pender, a Yankee to the bone, half expected Hattie McDaniels or Butterfly McQueen to open the front door. Instead the maid who answered the doorbell was Hispanic; Pender wondered if that represented progress.

The maid informed Pender that Señor Hughes wasn't home, but he could hear voices out back. He turned and started down the walk, then cut around the side of the house. Sure enough, Horton Hughes was sitting poolside, wearing a white polo shirt and twill slacks, Italian loafers, no socks, reclining on an upholstered chaise longue, reading the Sunday paper. Behind him a tanned twenty-something brunette in a well-filled white bikini was swimming laps in the azure pool. Whitewashed wrought-iron chairs were grouped around a whitewashed wrought iron table shaded by a yellow canvas umbrella.

Hughes looked up. "Who the hell are you?"

"Special Agent Pender, FBI." As he flashed his credentials, Pender realized he must look like day-old shit in his wrinkled plaid sport coat, with his bald head clumsily bandaged under a blood-stained tweed hat.

"Is it Donna?" asked Hughes. "Have they found Donna?"

It seemed to Pender that there was a strange note of ambivalence to the tone, as if Hughes weren't entirely sure which answer he was hoping for, yes, no, dead, alive. He decided to Columbo the man.

"Well sir, Mr. Hughes, we think we've identified the individual she left with. May I ask you a few questions?"

"I suppose," Hughes answered reluctantly. "But we've been through all this."

"Aren't you going to introduce me to the young lady?" Pender nodded toward the girl in the pool.

"That's Honey."

She rolled onto her back and waved, then went back to her laps. Pender asked Hughes if Honey were his daughter, and received a terse, thin-lipped "No."

Now Pender understood why Hughes had seemed so ambivalent about Donna—he'd turned her in for a newer model.

In response to Hughes's shouted orders, the maid brought out another china cup and saucer for Pender and poured his coffee for him. Pender sat with his back to the pool and asked Hughes to tell him about Donna's disappearance.

"Is there really anything to be gained by going through all this again?" asked Hughes. "I've told the police, I was out of town that week. I got home, Donna was gone, along with her suitcase, her good jewelry, and her Lexus. I haven't heard from her since."

"Do you know which clothes she packed?"

"I'm afraid I didn't pay all that much attention to Donna's clothes, other than that she bought too many and they cost too much."

Two aggressive non-answers so far. Pender decided to abandon the affective approach and push back a little. Though he could empathize with the haughty rich, put himself in their shoes for the sake of an interview, as a poor boy from Cortland Pender had no objection to trying the opposite approach.

"But the jewelry, *that* you had no problem identifying as missing?" he asked in a deliberately provocative manner.

"Of course not. I bought most of it for her myself. And I can't say I approve of your tone, Agent Prender."

Oh-ho. "That's Pender. Had Mrs. Hughes given any indication that she was troubled or unhappy?"

"No more than usual." Hughes leaned forward as if to impart a confidence. "I've never pretended we had an ideal marriage, Agent *Pender*—is that right?—but frankly, that's none of your goddamned business."

"How about Honey there? Did she know Mrs. Hughes?"

Hughes shoved his chair back from the table, the metal feet screeching on the patio tiles, and rose haughtily to his feet. "This interview is over, Agent Pender. If you have any further questions, contact my—"

Pender ignored the dramatics, took a sip from the china cup; it really was very good coffee. "Hey there, Honey," he called over his shoulder—his back was still to the pool.

"Hey, G-man," called the girl.

"Did you know Mrs. Hughes?"

"I surely did—she was my momma's best friend."

Pender turned around, an arm draped over the back of his chair. "Does your momma know you're sleeping with her best friend's husband?"

"Why not?" replied Honey. "She did."

"Just a goddamn minute," said Hughes.

Pender turned back to him. He could hear Honey climbing out of the pool behind him, breathing hard, dripping water onto the tiles. "I like interviewing *her* a whole lot better than you, Mr. Hughes. Think her parents would be equally forthcoming?"

The girl padded across the tiles, toweling off her long black hair. The combination of the raised arms and the vigorous toweling imparted an interesting motion to her bosom. "You want to talk to Momma, you better get there before her third mimosa. As for Daddy, he's so long gone the only way she even remembers his name is she reads it off the alimony checks."

"How about you then, Honey? Did you see Mrs. Hughes before her disappearance?"

Pender looked down at his coffee cup as she wrapped the towel around her head in a turban and adjusted her bikini top unselfconsciously, then sat down next to him and poured herself a cup of coffee from the silver carafe. Hughes sat down as well, somewhat anticlimactically.

"Sure, about two weeks before. And I was not screwing Horty here until the bed was good and cold, I'll have you know."

She was a spoiled little rich bitch, but Pender found himself liking her—at least she was honest. An odd crime statistic he'd run across somewhere surfaced in his mind: wealthy Plano, Texas, had the highest per capita rate of teenage heroin-related deaths in the country in 1996 or '97, he couldn't remember which. "Were there any signs she was having an affair?"

"I can't picture it. I mean, I can't even picture her doin' it with Horty. The woman did not exactly ex-hude sexuality. 'Course, last time I saw her she didn't know about Horty and Momma—walkin' in on them the way she did mighta put a little itch in her britches, payback being a way of life 'round here."

"Is that true, Mr. Hughes? Mrs. Hughes found you in bed with her best friend?"

No answer. Pender didn't press it. Oh, Donna, he thought, to the tune of the old Richie Valens song. No wonder you ran away from home. Part of him wanted to believe that she'd run away with someone other than Casey, but it didn't seem likely. If she'd been poor, then sure, maybe she'd have hit the road and not made contact for a year. But she was far from poor, and in Pender's experience, nobody walked away from money.

They did sometimes walk away *with* it, though. "I understand all of Mrs. Hughes's bank accounts were untouched, Mr. Hughes.

And of course there's been no credit card activity. Would she have had any other source of cash readily available to her?"

"I've already answered that question," said Hughes.

Oh-ho. Foolish answer. Guilty answer. It probably wouldn't mean much for the investigation, but several of the other strawberry blonds had disappeared with amounts of cash proportionate to their means. "What was it, a wall safe?"

"I don't know what—"

"If you tell me here and now, I promise it goes no further. If not, the IRS is always happy to cooperate with the FBI—and vice versa."

"Yes, it was a wall safe."

"Excellent. How much did she leave with?"

"Twenty grand in hundreds and twenties, best I could tell."

"Good enough," said Pender, who over the years had developed a sixth sense about just how far you could push an interview. "Thank you for your cooperation. And now I'll leave you two to your Sunday. Here's my card—use the sky pager number if you think of anything. And Honey, if I could get your last name and your mother's address?"

"It's Comb. I was just heading home myself—you can follow me if you want."

"Honey Comb," repeated Pender, amused.

"Don't *even*," said the girl. "I've already heard every joke there is."

53

JUST STAY ALIVE. . . .

Irene slipped out of bed and crossed the room to the window. It had been a brutal night. Hard to say which was worse, the fitful bouts of nightmare-ridden sleep or the wide-awake three A.M. dreads. Probably the latter—at least you could wake up from the nightmares.

Eventually, though, she had managed to arrive at an uneasy truce with her terror by continually reminding herself that so far, most of what she'd told Barbara had come true. Maxwell wanted her help, which meant he needed to keep her alive. And where there's life, there's hope, wasn't that what everybody said? A cliché, perhaps, but one that she would have to teach herself to appreciate on a gut level.

In the meantime: just stay alive. Irene parted the white muslin curtains, raised the window, took a deep breath. Mountain air, morning dew, sweet meadow grass, Christmas tree tang of the Doug firs. The two-horned mountain to the west was blue-green and shrouded in mist; the meadow grass riffled in the wind, pale green with an undertone of shimmering gold.

And now, in the daylight, Irene was able to make out a peculiar structure half-hidden in the high grass of the meadow about a hundred yards from the house, not far from where Maxwell had been walking the night before. She stuck her head out of the window for a better look, and saw what appeared to be a sunken greenhouse the size of an Olympic swimming pool, covered by an opaque Plexiglas bubble rising only a few feet above ground level.

Then it dawned on Irene that the window she was leaning out

of was only a little narrower than her shoulders, and that directly below her was the roof of the screened-in porch. She eyeballed the two-story drop and realized that there was nothing to prevent her from climbing out the window and lowering herself to the porch with a bedsheet rope.

Not yet, though, she told herself. Not until you've figured out a way to get past the dogs or over the electrified fence.

Suddenly there was a knock at the door. With a guilty start, Irene pulled her head back inside and closed the window as quietly as she could. "Just a minute." She found an apricot-colored velour bathrobe in the closet and slipped it on over her nightgown, then opened the door.

Max, in a multicolored hibiscus-print Hawaiian shirt and mod-ishly baggy shorts. "Good morning, Irene. Did you sleep well?"

Did I sleep well? After being kidnapped and nearly raped, did I sleep well? Oh you rotten s.o.b. "Yes, thank you. Did you remember to call somebody about Bernadette?"

Max smiled reassuringly. "I called the Trinity County Sheriff's Department last night. I had to take the car phone up to the hayloft of the barn to get a signal. By now, Bernadette's probably resting comfortably in the bosom of her family. Are you ready for breakfast?"

"You know, I think I am." To her surprise, Irene realized that she was absolutely famished. The good news about Bernadette had restored her appetite.

The kitchen was wood-paneled, with a hardwood floor, a gorgeous cast-iron wood-burning stove, now fitted with electric burners, and a round-shouldered old Amana refrigerator. The kitchen table was covered with a hand-embroidered linen tablecloth. Maxwell waved Irene to the chair at the head of the table, then opened the oven door and removed a plate of scrambled eggs and bacon.

"I'll pop some toast in for you," he said, setting the plate down in front of Irene. She had taken a quick shower and was wearing a rust-colored cotton blouse over a pair of white cotton shorts.

"Can I ask you a question, Max?"

"You can *ask.*" He poured two cups of coffee from an old-fashioned bubble-topped percolator on the stove, then sat down across from Irene.

"Who was the woman I met last night?"

"Aw-aw-all in good time, lady."

Jimmy Stewart. Max's celebrity impressions seemed to be a coping mechanism for avoiding stressful topics—of which the woman in the mask was apparently one. Irene decided not to press him; she changed the subject. "These eggs are delicious."

"They don't get any fresher—I took 'em out of the coop this morning."

"Aren't you having any?"

"We've already eaten—we keep farmer's hours around here."

"What do you grow?"

"Silver bells and cockle shells and— No, I'm kidding. Just a truck garden—and of course the chickens."

But Irene's mind had already completed the Mother Goose rhyme Maxwell had abandoned so precipitously. *Pretty maids all in a row.*

While Irene finished breakfast, Maxwell set up an impromptu psychiatrist's office in the woods behind the house. He was stoked as he dragged the furnishings up from the basement storeroom and down the path. For years he'd daydreamed about achieving fusion, real mastery over the others, not just sporadic control. And now, his daydream was on the verge of becoming a reality.

It wouldn't be easy, he knew—it would take work and commitment from both himself and Irene. He'd have to be honest with her, or as honest as their unusual circumstances would permit, and he'd have to allow her access to the others—and vice versa. But if it achieved the desired effect, it would be well worth it.

And if it didn't work out? Well, he and the others would still have enjoyed the opportunity, for the first time in their lives, of telling their story to a sympathetic, understanding professional. And afterward, no matter how it turned out, they'd all have the luscious Dr. Cogan to share, for however long she lasted.

It's only therapy, Irene tried to tell herself as Maxwell led her down the dappled path. You've done it a thousand times before.

Still she was rocked, momentarily disoriented, when she first came in sight of the office he'd set up in the small clearing. A padded Windsor-style myrtlewood chair and a notebook and pen for her, a padded redwood-slatted chaise for himself, a small round three-legged table placed in the angle between the chair and the head of the chaise to hold a box of tissues and an ashtray. A Freudian layout in a Jungian wood. And the sweet smell of the needles, the mushroomy smell of the loam, reminded her sharply of the redwood grove near Lucia, of the pine grove in the Trinities—she understood now that the forest was Maxwell's safe place.

"Are we missing anything?" he asked her.

"Some water, perhaps. Therapy can be thirsty work."

After fetching a pitcher and two plastic glasses, Maxwell lay down on the chaise. Irene positioned the Windsor chair beside his left shoulder, crossed her legs, and waited with the stenographer's notebook in one hand and a green Uniball pen in the other.

She wasn't sure at first how to begin. "Do you think you might be up for another regression?" she asked him.

"NO!" Max's shout echoed through the forest, flushing the crows and jays from their boughs. Then, quietly but firmly: "No more hypnosis."

Irene felt the fear coursing through her system—she had been reminded of how vulnerable she was, dealing with a volatile and dangerous multiple without any of the customary safeguards.

Calmly, calmly: "Of course you don't have to do anything you don't want to, Max. But if we're going to have any chance of success here, the other alters are going to have to be included."

"Not a problem—I can take care of it."

"Fine. As I said, you don't have to do anything you don't want to. But I do need you to know that hypnosis and regression can be invaluable tools. Perhaps later on we can work out some ground rules, some safeguards you'd be more comfortable with."

"Perhaps," replied Max, with just the trace of a lisp—Irene's old lisp.

She let it pass. "I just thought of something, Max. I've been acting as if this session were a continuation of an ongoing therapeutic relationship. But this is actually our first session. Which means there's a very important piece of business we need to get out of the way."

After a quick conference with Ish (co-consciousness; no switch), Max came up with the answer. "A contract?"

"A contract." Not only could behavioral contracts be used to set limits on unhealthy behavior, but by establishing obligations, rewards, and punishments, they could also help nurture an appreciation for cause and effect in multiples who had generally been raised by abusive adults with erratic parenting skills.

"Can do." Max closed his eyes and conferenced with both Ish and Mose, who provided him with the contract template in general use among DID therapists. "Okay, here goes:

"I, Max Maxwell, speaking for all the alters, both known and unknown, comprising the system inhabiting the body known as Ulysses Christopher Maxwell Jr., hereby guarantee the rights and safety of our body, the rights and safety of Dr. Irene Cogan, our therapist, the safety of Dr. Cogan's property, and the safety of the property of all the alters, including any written or taped material they may provide to Dr. Cogan during the course of therapy."

"Very good. How about guaranteeing respect for the rights, safety, and dignity of all alters?"

"On behalf of all alters, both known and unknown, I promise to respect the rights, safety, and dignity of all alters."

"And do you have any suggestions for establishing the consequences of contract violations?"

"Accountable alters to be banished from consciousness for . . . forty-eight hours?"

"How about a reward for following the guidelines?"

He thought about it for a moment. "Could we go for a swim later? You and me?"

Irene thought about it. Compared to some of the things he might have asked for, a swim sounded harmless enough. And unless that structure in the meadow really was a covered swimming pool, he might even intend taking her off the property.

"Agreed. What I'll need you to do tonight, I'll need you to write up the oral contract we just made. We'll go over the document tomorrow morning, then both sign it. Between now and then—and I'm speaking to all the alters who can hear me now—if any of you can't accept the terms of the contract, you have to speak up now, or consider yourself bound by them until tomorrow morning."

Max closed his eyes. He could hear what he called the crowd noise building in his head. *Humor her,* he told the others. *Just humor her.* He opened his eyes and turned his head, glanced over his shoulder at Irene. "Looks like we're all in agreement."

"Excellent. Let's get started. Again, my preference would be a hypnotic regression, but if that's still out of the question, what I need, when you're telling me your history, is to hear in turn from each of the alters involved, rather than have all their experiences filtered through you. Would that be possible?"

"As long as you don't ask their names directly. Remember, if you do that, they automatically revert to me."

"But will they identify themselves? I have to know who I'm speaking with."

As if by way of response, Maxwell's eyes rolled up and to the right, and his eyelids fluttered. When they opened again, his lips were slightly pursed, his eye movements quicker.

"Good morning, Dr. Cogan," he said. It was a woman's voice. Not a falsetto, not the modified Julia Child vibrato of so many transvestites, but a woman. "My name is Alicea." A-*lyss*-ee-ah. "Max wants me to tell you about some things that happened to me when I was a child. Would you like to hear them?"

"Very much, Alicea. I'd like very much to hear them."

And so began one of the strangest and most horrifying tales that Irene Cogan, who'd made a career of listening to strange and horrifying tales, had yet heard.

54

THE YEAR IS 1980. A Saturday night. Nine-year-old Alicea is hiding in her bedroom. Or at least wishing she could hide. She knows what's coming—she's been through it before. In a way, it's her job. More than her job: it's her reason for being.

As nine o'clock approaches, Alicea sneaks out of her room wearing only her underpants and tiptoes down the hall to her parents' bedroom. The door is ajar. She slips inside and locks it behind her, secure in the knowledge that it cannot be opened from the outside—all these years after Lyssy's dream, and the hole in the doorknob is still clogged with Superglue.

Feeling goosebumpy all over, Alicea strips off her underpants (in the process unconsciously tucking the male genitalia of which she is unaware back between her legs) and with her legs closed stands before the full-length mirror to examine her body. What she sees is very different from what Christopher sees when he examines himself in the mirror. The contours are more rounded, as if there were an extra layer of fat beneath the smoother, moister skin. And the dark hair is longer, the rib cage longer and narrower, the nipples slightly fuller. Best of all is the delicious smoothness between the tightly pressed thighs.

Nope, no question about it—Alicea, though enough of a tomboy to the eye that no one ever acknowledges her true gender, is a one-hundred-percent all-American thank-heaven-for-little-girls little girl. This is a good thing—she understands that if she were a boy, what she is about to be subjected to would be crushing, absolutely unbearable.

Reassured, she returns to her room. Downstairs the grown-ups are getting rowdier—the speed and the booze are beginning to kick in. She turns on her radio to drown out the noise. "Another One Bites the Dust," by Queen. Alicea adores Freddie Mercury.

As always, Mother opens the door without knocking. Her eyes have that off-center look they get when she's high on meth, as if the irises were oblong and the pupils elongated.

"I see you're ready, for a fucking change," says her mother spitefully, though Alicea is nearly always ready when they come for her—sometimes it saves her a beating.

The grown-ups are waiting for her in the basement. There are four or five of them tonight, all standing back in the shadows except for Carnivean, who sits on his black throne, under the red spotlight, naked save for the short goat horns set wide apart on his forehead.

When Alicea and her mother reach the bottom of the stairs, Daddy joins them. Like the others except for Carnivean, they're wearing loose-fitting robes. They walk her to the foot of Carnivean's throne. Grandly, rather like the Duchess in *Alice in Wonderland,* Carnivean gestures for Alicea to open her robe. She does so; he looks her up and down as if he hadn't seen her dozens of times before, nods approvingly, then steps down from the throne and takes her by the hand.

Her parents move aside; Carnivean leads Alicea over to the divan against the wall. She kneels, bends forward across the soft padded leather. He lifts her crimson cape and flips it over her head, enfolding her in a soft, incongruously private, ruby darkness. She rests her cheek on the back of her crossed hands and tries to tune out the pain.

Alicea knows of course that outside this basement Carnivean is really Mr. Wandmaker who owns the Harley shop where Daddy works. She also knows she must never say that out loud. Mr. Wandmaker took Daddy in when he was orphaned and taught him to be a mechanic, and where would we be without him? With his clothes on he looks big and powerful, but naked he's just gross fat, with a big hairy belly and saggy boobies like an old woman.

When she hears him begin to grunt she knows it's almost over—and also that the worst part is about to begin. For now his weight drops down full upon her and the slapping begins—her buttocks, the back of her thighs, her shoulders and head under the cape; the thrusts grow deeper and more frenzied.

Tonight this final stage seems to go on forever. Alicea feels a funny, pins-and-needles prickling in her head as his weight begins to squeeze the breath out of her. Just before she passes out from lack of air, though, she hears a voice in the darkness—the darkness inside her head, not the darkness under the cape. A man's voice—but not Carnivean's, not Mr. Wandmaker's. A somehow familiar voice, though she's never heard it before.

Alicea?

Yes?

I'm here. I'm going to take care of us now—I'll never let them do this to us again.

Who are you? she asks.

Call me Max, says the voice.

55

"AND I KEPT MY PROMISE," said Max, rubbing his fists against his thighs. "They never did that to her again."

Irene recognized his voice. She'd missed the switch but observed the grounding behavior. From a purely professional point of view she was fascinated. The birth of an alter—terra incognita in the annals of dissociative identity disorder. "Do you have any sense of where you came from, Max? Where you were before you spoke to Alicea?"

He turned around in the chaise, amused, detached. "Do you, Irene? Do you know where you came from before you were you?"

"No—but I'm not an alter."

"Neither are any of us, as far as we're concerned."

"I don't think I'm following."

"Then let me enlighten you." He sat up and swung his legs casually over the arm of the redwood chaise. "How do you define an alter, Irene?"

She rattled it off: "'A dissociated state of consciousness, with a persistent sense of self and a characteristic pattern of behavior and feelings.'"

"Very good. Here's how I define it: an alter is everybody else in here. All the other personalities, or identities, or whatever you want to call them, who inhabit this body—those are alters. I'm just me, the same as you're just you."

"And if I asked any of the others the same question?"

"You'd get the same answer: 'I'm me—everybody else in here is an alter.' "

"Fascinating."

"Ain't it, though." Max resumed his supine position on the chaise. "Oh—and by the way, Irene?"

"Yes?"

"I'm perfectly aware that Useless and some of the others think I'm a demon."

"Why is that, do you think?"

"Because I made myself known to Alicea while she was getting fucked by a man wearing horns and calling himself Carnivean."

"I'm not familiar with the name."

"In demonology, Carnivean is the patron devil of lewdness, and his chief joy is enticing humans into obscene behavior."

Despite the warmth of the morning, Irene was beginning to feel chilled. Max's behavior while attempting to rape her the previous day, she realized with a mounting sense of horror, was quite similar to Alicea's account of Carnivean's attack on her. Multiples often internalized their persecutors as a way of gaining a semblance of control over that which could not be controlled. Which meant that it was conceivable that on some level Max identified with or embodied Carnivean, that he thought of *himself* as the patron devil of lewdness and obscene behavior.

Equally troubling was the degree of Max's control over his alter switching. Irene couldn't recall ever having met a multiple who'd switched alters so easily, or with such eerie sureness. She didn't know exactly what that signified, though, or what it might portend. All she was sure of at the moment was that Ulysses Christopher Maxwell Jr. was like no other multiple she had ever encountered.

"Irene? Dr. Cogan?"

"What? Oh, sorry."

"You need a break or something?"

"No—please go on."

"Okay—but try to stay with me, hunh? I'm not flapping my gums for the exercise."

Max's first act, upon taking possession of the body from Alicea, was to throw his head back with all the force he could summon. A crack, a moan, and the weight was off his back. He flipped the cape off his head and looked over his shoulder. Wandmaker, one of his horns knocked askew, was staggering backward across the basement, cupping both hands to his face, dark blood from his shattered nose dripping from between his fingers.

Max did not yet know how to engineer a switch without the cooperation of another alter. Consequently, it was Max who endured by far the worst beating the body had ever received from Ulysses Sr., then spent the next twenty-four hours locked in his bedroom closet in severe pain, without food or water. It would have been longer, but Monday was a school day.

Max knew how to turn both negative experiences into positives, though. He used the time in the closet to convince the others that the helter-skelter anarchy under which they had been living was a thing of the past, and that they would all benefit immensely from the change. Then, on Monday morning, he made sure that his beloved fourth-grade teacher noticed the bruises from the beating.

"Miss Miller was an angel—an absolute angel. One of those teachers that every little boy falls in love with, and every little girl wants to be just like.

"I of course (that's the collective I, by the way) had long since been identified as a gifted child. They made me take the IQ test three times because they couldn't believe the score. Eventually they also recognized that I had total recall. Hypermnesia, the specialist called it."

"This hypermnesia—is that the function of a particular alter, do you know?"

"Our MTP's name is Mose. He's a freak. Remembers everything, understands nothing."

"Thank you—go on."

"With a mind like mine, you'd think somebody would have given me some special attention, but up until fourth grade, all the other teachers expected from me was to learn the lessons and keep my mouth shut. But Miss Miller, she not only designed an enhanced curriculum for me, she gave me individual tutoring after school."

"Is that 'me' primarily Max, or one of the other alters?"

"Christopher, mostly."

"May I speak with Christopher?"

"Sure—why not? . . . Good morning, Irene."

It had taken but an instant.

"Good morning, Christopher. Nice to meet you."

"Oh, we've met. In the jail."

"Yes, I remember. I believe you kissed my hand."

A shy, winning grin over his shoulder. "A liberty—but irresistible."

"Quite all right. So how do you feel about what's going on?"

"The therapy? What's good for General Motors is good for the USA."

"I don't follow."

"What's good for Max is good for the rest of us."

"I see." One of her professors used to call *I see* the therapist's hiccup. "Tell me about Miss Miller."

He sighed—a lover's sigh. "She was in her late twenties when we first met. Delicate bones. Pale, freckled skin. Funny upturned nose. Radiant—*radiant!*—reddish blond hair she wore piled and pinned on top of her head like they used to wear it a hundred years ago. Sweet little figure. Very shy, very empathetic. You could see everything she was feeling in those big green eyes—when I showed her the bruises from the beating after Max broke Wandmaker's nose, they filled with tears. She took me down to the school nurse herself.

"After that everything happened pretty quickly. The police were called, my parents were arrested at work, and I went home with Miss Miller that afternoon—the alternative would have been a temporary group or foster home situation, or protective custody in Juvie, which they believed I would have seen as punishment."

"Understandably."

"Understandably. Anyway, Miss Miller lived in an old Victorian house within walking distance of the school. She fixed up the spare room for me. She said I didn't have to talk about anything if I didn't want to. I said I sure didn't. I remember we had Twinkies for an after-school snack—she bought them especially for me—and we watched old movies on television—she loved old movies—and I did impressions of the actors for her. Eventually I picked up all the classics—Bogart, Cagney, Stewart.

"Her bedroom was upstairs, with a spare room across the hall. She made that up for me, but of course I couldn't get to sleep that first night. So she let me sleep with her. We watched TV in her big bed, and drank cocoa. I remember watching her take her hair down. She was sitting at her vanity, wearing a long white nightgown. Her back was to me, but she knew I was watching as she unpinned it and it came tumbling down. She told me over her shoulder that she had to brush it a hundred and fifty strokes every night, and asked me to help count the strokes.

"The moonlight was coming through the window and shining off that beautiful strawberry blond hair, and when she let me do the last few strokes, I thought I was going to die from happiness. . . ."

Long silence. Too long. "What happened next, Christopher?"

Now the words came tumbling out rapidly. "It wasn't her fault, it wasn't Miss Miller's fault. She didn't get any pleasure out of what happened next, after she came to bed. *I* was the one who insisted on hugging *her*. I threw my arms around her and clung to her like a little monkey, and when she tried to push me away, I cried and clung even harder."

He stopped. Irene waited a few beats, then prompted him: "Were you aroused?"

"Yes."

"Did you experience orgasm?"

"A dry one—I was only nine."

"From frott—from rubbing against her?"

"I know what frotteurism is. And the answer is yes."

"Did she know?"

"Of course not!"

Irene couldn't miss the defensive tone, but decided not to call him on it yet. He was describing things as he'd experienced them as a nine-year-old. That was good—she didn't want to interfere with that. In the normal course of therapy there would come a time when she would need him to bring his adult perceptions to bear on the situation, in order for him to understand that as a child, he was blameless—that a woman who would allow a boy his age to have sexual relations with her, especially at such a vulnerable time, was as much a monster as Maxwell's parents. Once he understood that, she could help him deal with the anger and denial, hopefully without evoking the homicidal alter.

But this was not the normal course of therapy—not even close. With any luck, she thought, she would escape or be rescued before then. In the meantime, she had to feel her way along slowly and nonconfrontationally.

"How did your parents feel about what was going on?"

"Well, little lady, Ah guess ya could say my pop was kind of embarrassed. Soon as they got out on bail he took his double-barrel and blew mah mom's brains all over the wall with one round a double ought six, then blew his own head off with another."

A John Wayne impression. Irene sensed that he was close to cracking—still, she had to ask the question. "And how did you feel about that—your whole life changing, losing your parents? It must have been terribly difficult."

He turned around to face her. "Guilty, I guess," he said in his own voice. "And glad. And guilty at feeling glad. I killed them as surely as if I'd pulled the trigger. But there would be no more beatings, no more rapes, no more being locked in the closet or terrorized in the basement. Plus I had Miss Miller. Can we take that swimming break now? This is tougher than I thought."

"Of course. But it just occurred to me, I haven't brought a bathing suit."

"No problem," replied Maxwell. "I'm sure we can dig one up some place."

56

THE RIDGE WAS FIRST settled by pot growers back in the sixties, Christopher explained to Irene as they returned to the house. The hippies had lived in psychedelic-painted school buses at first, he told her, and with the money from their first few sinsemilla harvests they'd dug wells and paid the electric company to run power lines up from Charbonneau Road. With power for the water pumps, they were able to irrigate the next crop with drip lines and double their yield.

Rolling in dough by now, the tree-hugging hippies reluctantly cut down a few Douglas firs and built the house on the very ground where the trees had stood. They also bought an old barn in the valley, took it apart, and reassembled it board by board on Scorned Ridge to use as a drying shed. Unfortunately, summer was too short and autumn too damp in Umpqua County to allow sufficient curing time—they eventually dug a pit six feet deep in the meadow, lined it with concrete, and roofed it over with thick Plexiglas.

Mystery solved, thought Irene. It was the drying shed she'd spotted in the meadow this morning. "What happened to them—the growers?"

It was a big operation, Christopher explained—too big, even for Oregon's liberal drug-enforcement policies. In the late seventies, helicopters descended upon the plantation in the meadow. The hippies managed to escape, but the crop was burned and the property seized, to be sold at auction several years later—Miss Miller's representative just barely managed to outbid the lumber companies.

The house at the edge of the forest was high and narrow like a Swiss chalet, with a sharply peaked shake-shingled roof and over-hanging eaves. As they approached, Irene noticed that many of the dark-stained deal boards were warped, bowed, and even split.

Maxwell followed her eyes, read her thoughts. "They nailed it up green," he explained. "Someday I'm going to have to rebuild the whole damn thing."

The rear, kitchen door faced the forest; Christopher led Irene around the side of the house to the screened-in front porch that faced west, across the meadow.

"I've seen some incredible sunsets from here," he said, holding open the screen door for her.

"I can imagine."

Christopher closed the screen door and hurried ahead of Irene to hold open the heavy front door that led from the porch into the house. A dark, narrow, wood-paneled hallway ran the length of the house, passing the parlor and dining room on the right, and the steep stairway leading to the upper floors on the left, on its way to the kitchen in back.

"I'll pack a picnic lunch for us," Christopher announced. "I think you'll find the bathing suits on the top back shelf of your closet. Meet you down here in half an hour?"

Irene checked her watch, which was the only personal item in her possession, other than the clothes she'd gone jogging in two days earlier. "One o'clock, then."

The trembling began as she started up the stairs. By the time she reached her bedroom Irene was shaking so violently that the brass bedstead rattled when she sat down. She thought of the victims of long-term trauma she'd seen. The blank stares, the long silences, the sudden and unprovoked shudders and withdrawals. True, they were all still alive, but it wasn't quite what she had in mind when she'd coined her affirmation, her mantra.

Irene had always prided herself on her rational nature. She'd sometimes been accused of being too rational, of keeping too tight a rein on her emotions. But deep down inside, she'd never been able to shake the feeling that if she ever allowed herself to really let go, she'd fly to pieces like a busted watch in a cartoon. It was fear of weakness that kept her strong, fear of falling apart that held her together.

So she sat on the edge of the bed and hugged herself tightly, rocking to and fro as she struggled for control. It was only partly fear for herself that was driving her so close to the edge, she realized. There were also strong components of pity, for that little boy who'd been so terribly abused, and anger at his abusers. The pity was easier to deal with—a good psychiatrist had to be able to take in her patients' trauma without taking it on—but the anger was difficult to handle. Irene forced herself to bear in mind that little Lyssy's parents and the Miller woman had probably been abused as children—almost all adult abusers had.

When the trembling finally stopped, Irene searched the closet shelves until she found a peach-colored one-piece maillot bathing suit with a Nieman-Marcus label. For her sanity's sake, she tried not to think about, or at least not to dwell upon, the identity or fate of the previous owner. That way lay panic, if not madness.

Irene undressed in the small bathroom adjoining her bedroom, and tried the suit on. It was a little large, and loose in the bust, but she liked the way it was cut high on the leg, all the way to the hip—she'd always been proud of her legs. And when she slipped on a pair of white mules from the closet, she had to admit that her calves looked pretty darn good for forty-one. Then it occurred to her that the last thing she wanted was to appear sexually attractive—shaking her head at her own foolishness, she opted for rubber flip-flops.

Christopher was wearing a lavender T-shirt and a pair of faded jeans—how well the colors complemented his bleached hair. He looked her up and down as she stepped out onto the porch, and whistled appreciatively. She followed him across the meadow to a gate in the fence at the southwest corner of the property. Both fence and gate bore high-voltage warnings. Irene flinched as Christopher reached forward to unlock the gate—he told her not to worry, that he'd turned the juice off back at the house. She filed the information away, telling herself it might come in useful some night.

On the other side of the fence, a steep trail led down the side of the ravine. Christopher had been carrying a backpack; now he slung it on and helped Irene pick her way down to the fast-running creek. They walked along the bank until they came to a wide slow-drifting pool shaded by the overhanging branches of river willows, just downstream from a sharp bend in the creek. A classic ol' swimmin' hole. Christopher hung the knapsack on a tree branch and stripped down to a purple Speedo.

It was the first time she'd seen his torso—he hadn't bothered to take off his shirt during the attempted rape. The figure that had appeared slender, almost delicate, clothed, was instead lean, hard, lithe. Narrow but powerful shoulders and upper arms, smooth rounded pecs, a six-pack set of abs, a hard little BB butt, smooth-muscled thighs and calves—if there was an ounce of fat on the lad, it wasn't visible.

"Last one in is a rotten egg," he said, running gracefully along the bank to just above the bend in the creek, where he executed a shallow dive into the fast-moving water and let the current carry him down to the pool.

Irene followed him upstream, then slipped off her flip-flops and tiptoed into the water. She had always been a tentative swimmer, even in backyard pools, but the cold current soon proved too strong for wading—when she was knee deep it swiped her feet out from under her. She fell backward, flailing her arms, and cried out, alarmed but exhilarated, as the water swept her along downstream like the flume ride at the Santa Cruz Boardwalk.

Seconds later she found herself bobbing on her back in the still, sun-dappled water of the swimming hole, looking up at the lacy green willow boughs waving gently overhead, silhouetted against the distant blue of the sky above the ravine.

"Did you love it?" asked a soft voice behind her.

Irene turned to see Christopher treading water. His boyish face was only inches from hers, wet and shiny in the dappled light reflecting up from the marble-green water. His bleached hair was plastered back, his dark eyes were soft and vulnerable, his unnaturally red lips were parted, and he was breathing hard.

"I did, I loved it." Irene's own chest was heaving, her skin was tingling, and the adrenaline was coursing through her. She knew he was about to kiss her; how easy it would be to let him. And probably less dangerous than turning her back.

She tried repeating her new mantra to herself—*just stay alive, just stay alive, just stay alive*—as he brought his lips closer and closer to hers, but when the moment came, her head turned away of its own volition and she took the kiss on the cheek.

"I have to try that waterslide again," she said lightly, rolling onto her side and striking out for the creek bank, praying wordlessly that he would not come after her, knowing that if he did, she would have to fight him, even if it cost her her life.

And she never used her mantra again.

57

AFTER INTERVIEWING MRS. EDWINA COMB, Pender visited three more of Donna Hughes's "best friends." 0 for three. Not that he'd expected much—basically he was just killing time until he heard from Thom Davies.

The call came in around six-thirty in the evening, at the Holiday Inn off I-75 in Plano. Pender had checked in and enjoyed a long hot shower, protecting his bandaged scalp with a plastic shower cap—an afternoon with the anomic rich of Plano left him feeling dirtier than a night in the Sleep-Tite. He was in the bar listening to a cocktail pianist warbling "Michelle" when his sky pager began vibrating in his pocket. He recognized the number and hurried back to his room to return the call.

"What've you got for me, T. D.?"

"Jam," said Thom Davies. "Jammety-jam-jam."

"Remind me—in Davies-speak, jam is good or bad?"

"Jam is good. Jam is loovely. Forty-three criminal Buckleys in Oregon, nineteen of whom began their careers in juvenile facilities. Of those nineteen, eleven, representing five different facilities, are within our target age range."

"Any of those have records for assault? Strong-arm stuff, anything like that?"

A pause while Davies counted. "Six."

"How many are still in custody or on parole?" Those would be the easiest to locate.

"Five out of the six. Three in custody, two on parole. Do you have a fax there?—I'll send you the printout."

Pender read him the Holiday Inn's fax number from the placard by the phone.

"All righty, then—I'll whip it right off to you."

"Thanks, T.D. Thanks for everything. You went above and beyond—I truly owe you. Sorry I had to ruin your Sunday."

"Never mind, it's my own bloody fault. After ten years with the bureau, I should know better than to answer the phone on my day off."

58

AROUND THE TIME PENDER was receiving the Buckley printout in Texas, Irene and Christopher were just beginning their Sunday-afternoon therapy session in Oregon. The late-afternoon light was golden in the office in the forest; the forest floor still retained the day's heat, but a cool breeze had sprung up from the west.

"When we left off this morning," Irene was saying, "you had just finished telling me about your first night at Miss Miller's. Did it continue, that aspect of the relationship?"

"For seven more years. Of course, it changed as I got older. We started having intercourse after I hit puberty—I guess I was around twelve. By then she enjoyed it as much as I did, and neither of us thought of it as abuse. I knew better than to talk about it at school, though. I didn't ever want it to end. I didn't date, I didn't care about girls—I had a woman. As for Miss Miller—"

"Excuse me, Christopher. What was Miss Miller's first name?"

"Julia—but I never used it."

"Why was that, do you think?"

"I don't know—I never really thought about it."

"All right, sorry for interrupting. Go on—you were about to tell me something about her."

"Just that I think—no, I know—that she loved me as much as I loved her. We used to talk about moving away and getting married when I was old enough. We would have, too, if it hadn't . . . if it hadn't been for *him.*"

His fists were clenched; he'd twisted around on the chaise until his back was to Irene.

"Christopher? It's all right, Christopher, it's all right now," she crooned soothingly. "I need you to take a nice, slow, relaxed breath. . . . There you go. This is obviously a charged subject for you. Are you sure you wouldn't rather wait until tomorrow morning? Two sessions in one day can be awfully draining."

"No, let's keep going. I'll be okay. You need to talk to Max now, anyway."

"Fine. Just remember to breathe—and remember it's the past. Whoever *he* is, he can't hurt you now."

Ain't that the fucking truth? thought Max—he'd already executed the switch.

He was Mr. Kronk, the high school shop teacher, Max explained to Irene. Before she met Maxwell, Miss Miller and Kronk had had a brief flirtation. But she was much younger than Kronk. His size, his maleness, the smell of sawdust and machine oil, all reminded her of her late father, a widower who'd abused her sexually after her mother passed on.

So Kronk had married the high school secretary and Miss Miller turned her attentions to her new ward, who was as far removed from Kronk and her father as a male could be, and still be a male. (Sometimes, when he was cooking with her, or doing housework, it seemed a lot like having a little girl around. But she never learned about Alicea, never knew about the alters—like most multiples, Maxwell's skill at hiding his disorder bordered on genius.) And it would never have occurred to Miss Miller that she was as much an abuser as her father had been. Boys were different—boys had needs. She never forced herself on Ulysses, as she always called him—quite the contrary.

It took Miss Miller another seven years to understand that she had needs, too—needs that couldn't be filled by an increasingly strange boy half her age. Ulysses was growing ungovernable. He was already fearfully strong for such a little fellow, a varsity wrestler and a brown belt in karate. Handling the big, soft, recently divorced Kronk was probably a piece of cake in comparison.

So she told the boy that while she'd always be there for him, *that* part of their relationship would have to end. Soon he found her bedroom door locked against him. It was the same type of lock he'd picked as a five-year-old, but he withstood the temptation, telling himself he could stand not having her, as long as nobody else did. Then she began dating Kronk, staying out all night or, even worse, bringing him back to her own bedroom.

It was pure hell for poor Christopher, Max explained to Irene. He would lie in his bed, in his room across the hall, a pillowcase he'd stolen from her pressed to his cheek, smelling the scent of her hair while he listened to the bedspring serenade, old fat Kronk wheezing and snorting, and Miss Miller's breathy cries, until he was half mad with longing, fear, and jealousy. Eventually he reached the point where he no longer even wanted to come out to take his turns in the body—he preferred the darkness.

So it was Max whom Kronk and Miss Miller took out to dinner one dreadful night in the spring of 1987.

"Julia has done me the honor of accepting my proposal of marriage," Kronk explained, while she simpered and admired her new ring. But Kronk wanted Max to know that he intended to be like a father to him. He painted a pretty picture—they would go fishing, Kronk would teach him woodworking and take him to ball games.

Oh swell, thought Max. Just what Lyssy would have wanted—when he was five and his real old man was screwing him up the ass. But it was too late for all that now. What the system really needed was what it had learned to need from Miss Miller.

Hurt, humiliated, and angered, Max kept up a brave front all through dinner. When they got home, he even agreed to join them in the living room. They put on an old Dennis Day record Miss Miller used to dance to with her father, and Max and Mr. Kronk took turns waltzing with their strawberry blond.

But when the two adults retired to Miss Miller's bedroom early, a new alter took control of the body. His name was Kinch. And although this was Kinch's first time in the driver's seat, he must have been there all along, or at least since they were five, because it was with a feeling of déjà vu so strong it all but crackled that Kinch crept down to the kitchen and took an ice pick from the drawer, tiptoed back upstairs, and sprang the lock on Miss Miller's door the same way Lyssy had sprung his parents' bedroom door.

Ah, but Kinch was not Lyssy—and he was certainly not five years old. He was sixteen, Maxwell's chronological age, strong and cunning and quiet as a stalking cat. The room was lit only by candles, but there were dozens of them, on the bureau, on the vanity, on the bedside table. The light may have seemed romantic to the lovers, but it looked hellish to Kinch.

"Max?"
"Yes?"

"Could I speak to—"

"Trust me, Irene, you don't want to. You already met him once—he's the one who shot the highway patrolman. When Kinch comes out, people get hurt—and you're the only other person around."

"I suppose I'll take your word for it. But you know, sooner or later, if Kinch is going to be involved in the fusion, I will have to speak with him."

"Maybe we can work something out."

"I hope so."

Kinch tiptoed to the foot of the bed, watched impassively for a few seconds as Kronk's hairy ass rose and fell, rose and fell. He couldn't see Miss Miller at all. Then she shifted her legs and the covers slipped down, revealing her fine slim legs wrapped around Kronk, her pale thighs spraddled out obscenely, her hard little heels drumming against that hairy, blubbery ass as it pumped away and pumped away and pumped away until Kinch couldn't stand it any longer. He jumped on top of that gross, hairy back, his nostrils recoiling from the man-scent, and drove the ice pick between Kronk's shoulder blades.

The big man roared, and tried to buck him off. Again and again, Kinch drove the ice pick into that meaty back with enough force to penetrate through the meat, through the back ribs and the spine, into the heart and lungs. And he kept stabbing long after Kronk had ceased to struggle, kept stabbing until, after achieving the briefest and limpest erection compatible with ejaculation, he had climaxed. Then he was Max again, and at last Miss Miller's faint smothered cries reached his ears—he realized that she was being crushed beneath the combined weight of their bodies.

Max rolled Kronk's corpse off her, dislodging the ice pick. "It's okay, Miss Miller," he told her. "I'll take care of you now. I'll always take care of you. You don't need Kronk—you never needed Kronk."

But she wasn't listening. She pushed him away and threw herself across the body of her fiancé, weeping hysterically, trying to give Kronk mouth-to-mouth resuscitation, her face smeared with the bloody froth he'd breathed out at the last. Max, angered and disgusted, dragged her off the body, threw her on the floor. She pulled herself up and fell across the body again, began kissing Kronk's bloody lips, making no pretense at resuscitation.

This time Max threw her halfway across the room, hard enough to stun her. But she would not be denied—she began crawling toward the bed. Infuriated, he snatched up one of the candles on the bedside table and began setting fire to the sheets, while Miss Miller grabbed at his ankles, trying to pull him away.

When the flames started leaping around Kronk's body, Max grabbed Miss Miller by the wrists and tugged her out into the hall. With desperate strength she fought free of him and raced back into the bedroom, snatched the satiny polyester comforter off the floor, and tried to beat the fire out with it. Seconds later the comforter was a sheet of flame draped over her head, clinging to her flesh.

She staggered backward, arms flailing. Max threw her to the floor and tried to pull the comforter away, but the polyester had melted to her skin from the top of her scalp to her knees; flesh and fabric were inextricably merged. Max beat the flames out with his hands.

A violet hush had crept over the forest. Irene couldn't bring herself to speak. She leaned forward and placed her hand on Maxwell's left shoulder. He reached back to pat her hand; she turned his hand over to look at the scars. Again she marveled at the smoothness of his palm—no life line, no love line, nothing there to show a palmist how many children he'd have.

"It must have been painful," she said.

"I was glad for the pain. It kept my mind off the guilt."

"Do you still feel the guilt?"

"Only every fucking day of my life."

"And the woman I met this morning—the woman with those terrible scars? That was Miss Miller?"

Max nodded. "What a world, what a world," he said in a high-pitched, cackly voice.

The words of the Wicked Witch hung in the still forest air.

"Sounds like a good place to start our next session," said Irene encouragingly.

"You're the doctor," replied Max, smiling weakly.

59

PENDER HAD TO PUT ON his drugstore half-glasses to review the fax Davies had sent him. There was no background, no narrative, just names, dates, descriptions, convictions, incarcerations. Davies had highlighted the names of the five strong-arm criminals who were either in custody or on parole—the highlighter showed up as a gray bar on the fax.

Of these, one of the parolees in particular caught Pender's attention, perhaps because of the unusual first name. Cazimir. Cazimir Buckley, aka Bucky, aka Caz. African-American, six-two, hundred and eighty pounds, born Los Angeles, 1970. The closer Pender studied the tiny print, the better this Buckley looked. String of assaults going back to age twelve. Did three stretches in the Umpqua County Juvenile Facility. In a year, out a month, in a year, out a month, in a year, and on to the penitentiary. Pender read between the lines: little problem with managing your anger there, Caz? Probably not easy being black in Umpqua County. Wherever that was.

When Buckley was eighteen, they put him in with the big boys after a conviction for aggravated assault. The assault must have been aggravated as hell—they'd given him the going rate for manslaughter in Oregon. Perhaps he learned anger management in the state pen, though—Pender noted that he was paroled only six years later, so he must have earned all his good time.

Cazimir Buckley was currently under the jurisdiction of the Umpqua County Parole Board. Seemed like as good a place as any to start. Pender got the area code for Umpqua County from the operator, got the number for the parole board from directory assistance, then gave himself the rest of the night off and went back down to the bar, where he washed down two Vicodins with the help of his old friend Jim Beam—his head was absolutely *killing* him.

Jim and the Vicodins proved to be a potent combination. The big bald man in the plaid sport coat, head bandages, and crumpled, bloodstained hat finished the evening perched on the end of the piano bench, singing Everly Brothers duets with the piano player. Pender took Phil Everly's parts, his sweet tenor handling the high harmonies with surprising ease. "Bye Bye Love," "Hey Birddog," "Wake Up, Little Suzy"—he even remembered the entire recitativo of "Ebony Eyes."

They finished up with "All I Have to Do Is Dream," then Pender stuffed a twenty into the tip jar and staggered back to his room. Umpqua County, he thought, as he collapsed into bed. Where the hell is Umpqua County?

60

IRENE HAD EXPECTED TO be dining with Maxwell and Miss Miller that evening; instead he brought a covered tray up to her room. A tiny chicken, hardly bigger than a Cornish hen, baked potato, snap beans, and a bottle of Jo'berg Riesling. He and Miss Miller needed to spend some time together, he explained. So if she wouldn't mind staying in her room until tomorrow morning. . . .

The antique escritoire was in the corner of the room. Irene pulled it over to the window and watched the sun setting behind the next ridge while she dined. Living on the shore of Monterey Bay, Irene was no pushover when it came to sunsets. But this one was a keeper—it set the sky on fire and burnished the green meadow grass gold. Her heart filled, then emptied with a rush that left her breathless and despairing. She'd never known homesickness before. She missed her house, her friends. She prayed Barbara was all right. Old Bill and Bernadette, too. She wondered if she'd ever see her father and brothers again. She even missed her young stepmother.

She also worried about her patients. Lily DeVries—they still hadn't followed up on her last breakthrough. The girl would be bound to see it as yet another abandonment, another betrayal.

Hang in there, Lily, she thought, raising her head and looking out at the fiery sunset. As she did so, she caught a glimpse of her reflection in the window.

"You too," she told the reflection. "You hang in there too, Irene." And though she was not particularly hungry, she forced herself to finish the meal, washing every other mouthful down with a swig of wine as it turned to ashes in her mouth.

There were no books or magazines in her room, no television. Feeling restless, unable to concentrate on her notes from the day's sessions with Max, she decided to try her hand at a haiku. She'd gone through a haiku phase in college. Frank had illustrated some of them with his pastels—what delicate, feathery strokes his big hands were capable of. She and Frank told themselves that someday they'd publish a book of her haiku and his drawings, but of course it never happened—life, then death, had intervened.

Irene poured herself another glass of wine, turned the notebook to a blank page, began doodling green curlicues around the margins. First line, five syllables. She looked out through the window and the pen began to move. *That two-horned mountain.* Second line, seven syllables: *Black, jagged, it hides the sun.* Third line, five syllables: *And the creek runs cold.*

Quality time with Miss Miller. Supper in the dining room, with the good silver, the good china, the candelabra on the white tablecloth. Miss Miller, with effort, dissects her chicken with a knife and fork and insists that Ulysses do the same.

To eat, she unties the bottom string of her green silk surgical mask and shoves the food under. She wears only silk—she can't bear any coarser fabric rubbing against the scar tissue. After dinner, they do the washing up together—she washes, he dries—then walk hand in scarred hand to the chicken coop at the edge of the forest.

Freddie Mercury has already led his harem from the outer yard into the inner coop. Miss Miller locks the gate while Max checks the wire surrounding the yard for breaches, and examines the ground outside the fence for holes.

Reassured that the flock is safe from raccoons and foxes for another night, the master and mistress of Scorned Ridge return to the house, and Miss Miller selects a video from their extensive collection. *Casablanca*—they watch it together at least once a year. The original version, not the colorized. During the last scene, Miss Miller speaks Ilsa's lines along with her; Max does Rick and, at the very end, Renaud as well.

The act of retiring to bed is an intricately choreographed ballet—a pas de trois, though if Max and Peter execute the switch successfully, as they have for the past several years, Miss Miller will never know it.

They go upstairs together, each to his or her own room. Max

showers, gives Miss Miller time to wash up, then crosses the hall to her bedroom. She's already lying on her stomach with the hem of her nightgown hiked up to the small of her back. He sits on the side of the bed and injects her in the left buttock with one ampoule of pharmaceutical morphine sulfate, and in the right buttock with another.

While they wait for the morphine to come on, Max pulls the blinds, closes the shutters, draws the blackout curtains, and stuffs a towel under the door so no light leaks in from the hallway. Miss Miller insists on the room being pitch-black.

Now comes the tricky part. Standing by the door, Max checks the floor to be sure there are no obstacles lying around, then turns his back to the room and orients himself precisely, right hand on the doorknob, left hand on the light switch, before executing an alter switch. Exit Max, to voluntary darkness; enter Peter, to darkness on the physical plane.

Peter was one of the last alters to be created. His was a difficult birth—almost an act of will on Max's part. Peter shares little memory with the other alters, none of it visual. Born full-grown, eighteen years old and destined to remain so, Peter has been blind from birth. He's never seen a woman—never seen a human being—and only touched one. Only *met* one. Miss Miller. He knows this room intimately; once he has his bearings he can negotiate it like a sighted person.

Blind Peter finds his way back to the bed, helps Miss Miller roll over, and taking great care not to cause her pain, undresses her. She is woozy, quietly euphoric from the double dose of morphine. Her senses dulled, she finds his gentle, feathery caresses bearable, even welcome, as much for the emotional enjoyment as the erotic.

After considerable foreplay, Miss Miller rolls on her side, facing away from Peter, and he achieves penetration from a horizontal rear-entry position. The morphine often prevents Miss Miller from reaching orgasm, but tonight it only postpones, then prolongs her climax. Afterward he strokes her long soft hair, taking care not to dislodge it, until she falls asleep.

Then he falls asleep. In Peter's case, though, it's not sleep as the rest of us know it, but only a descent into a warmer, welcoming darkness. And as he fades off, without any visible signs of switching, Max awakens, feeling every bit as high on post-orgasmic endorphins as if he'd just finished making love himself. He hears Miss Miller's raspy, steady breathing and slips out of bed. He's halfway across the room when her voice freezes him in his tracks.

"Did you enjoy that, sweetness and light?"

Max winces in the dark. "Of course." "Sweetness and light" is an endearment she only uses sarcastically. He's already feeling guilty—he just doesn't know about what. Maybe she wants to be appreciated. "It was wonderful."

But that wasn't it—her tone is still biting. "Would you like to do it again some night? *Ever again?*"

"Of course." *Get to it, damn it—I can't stand the suspense.*

"Enjoying your sessions with your therapist?"

So that's it. "I'm finding them very helpful."

"So much so that you've completely forgotten that you have over five weeks of housework to catch up on?"

Oh. "No, ma'am."

"Why do I always get the shit jobs?" muttered Alicea rhetorically as she hauled the heavy Kirby back down to the basement.

Of course, Alicea knew perfectly well why she got the shit jobs—except for the old woman, Alicea was the only female of the household. Fortunately she was strong for a girl—she could lift the Kirby with one hand. And tireless—she had already started a load of laundry, vacuumed the first and second floors, and scrubbed the downstairs bathroom. Now she shifted the wet laundry from the washer into the dryer, rotated each of the bottles in the wine rack, and dusted the glass-fronted display case and its contents.

While performing this last chore, she caught sight of herself in the glass. She admired her torso under the too-tight T-shirt, and found herself wishing there were somebody around to appreciate it.

Fat chance of that, though—after the Cortes debacle, Max would probably never again let her out when men were around. Alicea wondered whether Dr. Cogan had any interest in other women—any port in a storm, as Max always said.

After dusting the display case, Alicea decided she'd earned a break, and ascended to the kitchen to make a cup of herbal tea. While she was waiting for the tea to steep, though, she put her head down on the kitchen table for a rest, and soon felt herself slipping back into darkness.

The experience was similar for most of the alters. Slipping into the darkness was like going to sleep. You didn't dream, but when you awoke, either because Max had summoned you or because the system was under extreme stress, you remembered what had hap-

pened while you were sleeping as if it *had* been a dream. And sometimes when you awoke you were in the body, but most times you
were still in the darkness. In the latter event, you could always try
to force your way back into the body, but usually Max was too
strong.

For Max, the experience was different. He only visited the darkness voluntarily, or on the rare occasions when one of the others
seized consciousness against his will. And he alone never slept in
the darkness. No need: Max was the alter who slept for real, Max
was the alter who dreamed.

Another difference: Max was capable of monitoring the others
visually from the darkness. He rarely exercised the power, however,
as the experience was both dizzying and uncomfortable, like
watching life through the viewfinder of a handheld camera, or rid-
ing in a car being driven too fast by someone you didn't quite trust.

And when Max raised his head to find himself sitting at the
kitchen table with a cup of chamomile tea (which he despised), he
recalled everything that had happened while Alicea was in control
of the body, not as if he'd dreamed it, or as if he'd experienced it,
but rather as if it had occurred in a movie he'd seen recently.

Max's bedroom was directly below Irene's on the second floor.
As he undressed for bed, he could hear her moving around overhead. He imagined her undressing up there, showering, climbing
into bed, and found himself growing sexually excited—he was even
sporting a very un-Maxlike erection.

"So now you want her?" he said disgustedly, giving his penis a
backhand slap and watching it bobble. "Where the hell were you
yesterday afternoon, when I needed you?"

61

IN THE OLD DAYS, FBI agents had to leave at least three telephone numbers so they could be reached at all times. With the advent of sky pagers and cell phones the rigid call-in procedures had been relaxed—only Thom Davies knew that Pender was staying at the Holiday Inn in Plano. So it came as a surprise when the phone in Pender's room began ringing just as he emerged from the bathroom after his shower on Monday morning, still wearing the plastic Holiday Inn shower cap to protect his injured scalp.

"Pender here."

"Pender, this is Steve Maheu. I'm calling for Mr. McDougal."

"He's not here," said Pender, just to mess with Maheu, a nondrinking, nonsmoking, crew-cut Mormon. For Pender, one of the benefits of having known McDougal since their academy days was not having to go through Steve Too to get to Steve One.

"You know perfectly well what I mean. I'm calling on his behalf, at his request. You really tore it this time, Pender—Steve specifically asked me to tell you that he's not going to pull your ashes out of the fire."

"What fire?"

"Did you interview a Mr. Horton Hughes yesterday?"

"We had a pleasant poolside chat."

"Apparently Mr. Hughes didn't find it all that pleasant. And apparently Mr. Hughes is also a close personal friend, not to mention a generous supporter, of a senator from Texas who shall be nameless. Can you see where this is going, Ed?"

"Nowhere, Maheu. Absolutely nowhere. I conducted an interview, the subject was not forthcoming, I—"

"Subject? You were interviewing the relative of a victim."

"In my best judgment at the time, I also had to consider him a possible suspect. He was screwing his wife's best friend before she disappeared, and his wife's best friend's daughter afterward. I had to elimin—"

"I don't care who he was screwing, and I'm not going to debate this with you, Pender. You're off the investigation, starting now. Come home and turn in your badge or kiss your pension goodbye."

"Has McDougal even spoken to Thom Davies? Does he know what I'm onto here?"

"You mean your printout of forty-three career criminals, one of whom who may or may not have known the subject briefly a dozen years ago? Yeah, we're all just thrilled to death, Ed—that'll break the case wide open for sure. Now get your sorry behind back to Washington on the next flight out. And consider yourself suspended from active duty in the meantime—from this point on, if you so much as ask somebody the time of day in an official capacity, I'll pull your credentials so fast your underwear'll fall down."

"Whoops," said Pender. "Couldn't hear you. Sounds like we have a bad connec—"

He made a crackling noise and hung up the phone, counted to ten, then took it off the receiver and went back into the bathroom. He removed the shower cap and bent his head to inspect his scalp. It had been torn in three places by the rounded edge of the handcuffs. Two of the wounds had required six stitches, the other had taken eight. He could see where the last stitch on the longest cut had worked loose. The butterfly bandage Anh Tranh had applied was still in place, and that Chinese salve she'd given him must have been the real deal—the ragged edges of the wound had already knitted together.

Pender took the tin of salve, a box of gauze pads, and a roll of adhesive tape from his toilet bag, cut four long strips of tape and laid them sticky side up on the chrome shelf under the mirror, then overlapped four pads on top of those, the way Annie had done. After smearing the salve directly on the cuts with his forefinger, he slipped his hands under the tape and gauze arrangement, lifted it in the air like a priest serving mass, flipped it over onto his head, and pressed the tape down firmly.

Then he brought his hat into the bathroom and set it atop the bandage, intending to trim the tape so it wouldn't be visible. But the hat was too small. It was also bloodstained and irreparably crumpled at the crown. Pender took it off and turned it in his hands.

"Hat, you've been a good old rounder and a good old pal," he declared. "For almost ten years now, through thick and thin—mostly thin—you stuck with me. And now that you've been used up in the service, I'd like to give you the official FBI send-off. Tum te *tum*, tum te *tum* . . ."

As the last note of Taps died away, Pender dropped the hat into the wastebasket under the sink, then flushed the toilet for the sound effect.

"And one more thing," he called to the hat on his way out of the bathroom. "If I were you, I wouldn't count on that pension."

62

THERE WAS NO SHORTAGE of toiletries or hair care products in the guest bathroom adjoining Irene's bedroom. She had her choice of three toothbrushes. In her old life it would have been an agonizing decision—Irene had never used another person's toothbrush, not even Frank's. But by her third morning in captivity, her second on Scorned Ridge, she found herself scrubbing away with the first toothbrush that came to hand, not obsessing at all over the probability that it had been owned and used by a dead woman.

Her mind was clear and focused. Last night before falling asleep, she'd worked out what she needed to do. When the alters had finished up their collective history, she would need to work with Max alone. If any fusion of identities was going to take place, Max was the alter who would be in charge.

But before she would facilitate a fusion, she'd have to know a little more about him. Ulysses, the old host alter, thought Max was a demon. Was it possible, despite his denials, that Max also thought of himself as a devil? He didn't present as a paranoid schizophrenic, but he might well be a Cluster B sociopath with narcissistic tendencies.

In which case, it would be wrong, morally and professionally, as well as dangerous for Irene personally, to further empower Max. What her options might then be, she wasn't sure—maybe try to strengthen one of the other alters. Christopher seemed pretty well established. But she didn't need to decide any of that until she had a better understanding of Max's makeup.

After showering, Irene donned a rose-colored Versace T-shirt that had cost some woman thirty or forty bucks new, and a pair of white Bermuda shorts from the Gap. When she opened the bedroom door, the aroma of fresh coffee filled the staircase, drawing her down to the kitchen.

Miss Miller was at the stove, her back to the room, the picture of domesticity in slippers and a silk housecoat over one of her green dresses. The only jarring note was the strawberry blond hair: instead of being shoulder-length, straight, and sleek, as it had been the last time Irene saw her, it was thick and full and curly, cascading halfway down her back.

Act normal, Irene told herself. Normal, normal, what is normal? "Good morning, Julia."

Miss Miller turned toward Irene. "Good morning, Dr. Cogan."

The hand-sewn green silk surgical mask puffed out when she spoke. In the daylight Irene could see that the eyelids above it were skin grafts, clumsy reconstructions. "Did you sleep well?"

"I never sleep well."

"I'm sorry to hear that. Perhaps I could prescribe something for you."

"I don't like to sleep. I see myself in dreams, the way I used to be."

"I understand."

"I doubt that very much."

The back door opened. Maxwell entered the kitchen wearing a Hawaiian shirt over baggy shorts, carrying a wicker basket.

Beneath the stiff bodice of the green dress, Miss Miller's bony chest began to rise and fall rapidly, Irene observed. Love or fear?

"Morning, Irene—feel these." He brought the basket over to the table. It was lined with excelsior and filled with fresh eggs.

She touched one. "It's still warm."

"Fuckin-A," said Maxwell.

"Language!" warned Miss Miller, turning back to the stove.

"I didn't hear any complaints last night." Maxwell slapped her playfully on the rump.

"Ulysses!" A pleased, simpering tone. Irene wondered if she were blushing under the mask—if she could blush.

Morning session. Max handed Irene the contract he'd drawn up. It was letter-perfect; after formally inquiring again whether any of the alters, known or unknown, had any objections to the contract, and receiving no demurs, she slipped the piece of paper into her notebook.

"Would you like to take up where we left off last session, or is there anything that's come up since then that you'd like to discuss?"

"I can't even remember where we left off," said Max with a self-deprecating grin.

"Coming from anyone else, I might be able to believe that."

"Okay, then." Max's eyes rolled up, the lids fluttered, and he began to speak in a monotone:

"Do you still feel the guilt. Only every fucking day of my life. And the woman I met this morning—the woman with those terrible scars. That was Miss Miller. What a world, what a world. Sounds like a good place to start our next session. You're the doctor."

Irene started to ask this new alter his name, then remembered Max's warning. Quickly she thumbed back through her notebook until she found it. "Hello, Mose. I'm Dr. Cogan."

"Irene Cogan, M.D. Derealization Disorders in Post-Adolescent Males, Journal of Abnormal Psychology. Speaking in Tongues: Dissociative Trance Disorder and Pentecostal Christianity, Psychology Today. Dissociative Identity Disorder, Real or Feigned? Journal of Nervous and Mental Diseases."

"How do you feel about what's going on?"

"What's Going On. Marvin Gaye. U.S. number one R&B top forty-five, week ending March twenty-seventh, nineteen seventy-one through week ending April twenty-fourth, nineteen seventy-one."

Irene jotted down the words *savant* and *autism?* next to his name. "Thank you, Mose. May I speak with Max again?"

An effortless switch. "Real ball of fire, that Mose," said Max.

"Rights and dignity of all alters," Irene cautioned him.

"Sorry. Okay—the fire. I spent a couple months in the hospital, they performed three separate skin grafts, then—"

"Excuse me, Max. I understand burns are terribly painful. Is there an analgesic alter in the system?"

"Unhappily, no. Morphine helped. So did rapid switching. And when all else failed, Lyssy the Sissy."

"May I speak with Lyssy?"

"I don't think he's available at the moment. He had rather a bad fright that night we were hiding out in the old jail—I haven't heard from him since."

"Perhaps another time."

"Perhapsssss." Irene's lisp. Max continued in his own voice.

"Okay—fire, pain, operations. A few months in the hospital, then almost a year in the Umpqua County Juvenile Facility awaiting trial on charges of murder, arson, and attempted murder. No bail— there was nowhere for me to go anyway.

"The ranch wasn't bad—that's where I learned to raise chickens. After lights out, the boys would stage fights. Call-outs, they called them. No holds barred—anybody could call out anybody else. And if you didn't fight, everybody got a free crack at you.

"Then one summer morning my lawyer comes out to the ranch to tell me all the charges have been dropped. He said Miss Miller had changed her story, told the DA that Kronk had attacked her and I had come to her defense, that the fire was an accident. I wasn't sure how to take it—whether she was trying to protect me, to make it up to me somehow, or whether she was just afraid I'd turn her in about the sex. I'd never told anybody about that.

"Then the lawyer told me Miss Miller wanted me to come back to live with her again, and how did I feel about that? I grabbed my gear out of my footlocker and drove away with him and never looked back. The only person I even said good-bye to was my best friend Buckley. Black guy from Compton. He and I had been inseparable. I was already good at martial arts and wrestling—or anyway, Lee was—"

"May I . . ." Irene began.

Alter switch.

". . . speak with Lee."

He was already there. Poised body language, somehow tense and calm at the same time. He'd puffed out his chest, and he was unconsciously pumping his fists until the veins stood out on his forearms.

"I didn't know shit about street fighting." Each word was weighed carefully before it emerged from between lips pressed so tightly together that the full, bowed shape of Maxwell's lips had become two thin, cruel lines. "Bucky whipped my ass good our first fight. After we buddied up, he taught me his secret. It saved my life more than once."

Lee paused to take a sip of water from the glass on the three-legged table. The forest animals had grown used to the therapy sessions. A squirrel scampered across the dry needles; jays quarreled in the lower branches of the firs; somewhere high overhead in the forest canopy an invisible woodpecker was noisily at work. "That's all I got to say."

The next time Maxwell spoke, it was as Christopher. Irene was attuned enough by now to recognize the soft, melodic voice.

"I remember I was confused at first. Instead of heading back towards town, the lawyer drove east, into the mountains. He told me Miss Miller had bought Scorned Ridge for us to live in. I remember thinking it was a little peculiar, the way he dropped me off near these, these *ruins*—the place was an unholy mess, the buildings falling down, the meadow overgrown. He didn't even get out of the car. Just handed me my duffel, yelled, 'Good luck, kid,' and roared off back down the hill."

Christopher closed his eyes. Irene understood that he was back there again, standing by the side of the blacktop.

"I pick up my duffel and head for the house. The screen door is swinging on one hinge. *Skreeeek, skreeeek.* Front door's boarded up. I hear her calling me from the back of the house. Her voice is so different, but still so . . . *her*. She's in the kitchen heating water for tea. Wearing an old-fashioned black dress. She turns around. Oh Jesus, oh god."

Irene reached out, put her hand on his shoulder. Christopher opened his eyes, looked around wildly, then relaxed visibly when he saw it was Irene. He tried to make a joke out of it.

"Oh, *mama!* I don't think I can go back there twice."

She told him what she'd have said to any patient. "But you must, Christopher. You have to confront the past in order to realize that it *is* the past. You have to relive it in order to get to the place where you can hold it as a memory, and not keep reexperiencing it subconsciously as a current event."

"But it *is* a current event," he moaned. "Everything's a current event. Mose never forgets anything." He grabbed his head between his hands, pressing his strange smooth palms tightly against his temples.

"It's not about forgetting, it's about forgiving," said Irene. "Understanding and forgiving yourself. You're carrying a crushing burden of guilt around with you."

It was Max who looked up, his head in his hands. "Sister, you don't know the half of it," he said sardonically.

"Tell me."

"The first one's name was Mary Malloy."

63

MISS MILLER COULD HAVE had the place renovated by professionals—her father had left her a considerable nest egg—but she didn't like having anyone else around to look at her, so Maxwell (to use the collective term) worked alone whenever possible.

Or as alone as a multiple can ever be. Mose scanned two handyman's encyclopedias and dozens upon dozens of do-it-yourself books into his prodigious memory, and the various alters turned themselves into carpenters, plumbers, electricians, painters, as necessary, according to their talents and interests. When he did have to hire outside help, Maxwell would work alongside them—he never had to watch anybody do a job twice.

And he was extremely motivated. All the energy he used to put into martial arts, wrestling, fighting at Juvie, sex with Miss Miller, he threw into the renovation, working from dawn to dusk seven days a week. By the time that first winter rolled around, the house was habitable—he'd never been prouder of anything in his life.

It was mid-March when Maxwell, as Christopher, stopped into the Old Umpqua Feed Barn to get some advice about chickens—he was thinking about starting a flock. Mary Malloy was behind the counter. A more objective observer might have noted that she was a younger Miss Miller—same strawberry blond hair, delicate cheekbones, milkmaid skin, slender frame. All Christopher knew was that he was a goner the minute he laid eyes on her.

They started talking. She said she loved chickens, used to raise them when she was a little girl, down on the farm. The more they talked, the more they found they had in common. Mary was an orphan, too. After her parents died, the Jehovah's Witnesses took her in. A bunch of them lived in one of the big old turn-of-the-century houses at the edge of town, down by the river.

Thereafter, it was always Christopher who visited the feed barn. On his third trip he got up the courage to ask her for a date. He was eighteen, but shy and backward with girls his own age—he'd never even dated one. Mary agreed, but said they had to keep it quiet. If the other Witnesses had found out she was seeing somebody outside the faith, they'd have shunned her. Kicked her out of her apartment, turned their backs to her on the street. She'd have been a complete outcast. For her it would have been like losing her home, her family, and her friends simultaneously.

So even after they started dating regularly, they kept a low profile. If they went to see a movie, for instance, she'd sneak out and meet him at the theater.

At this point, their relationship was still innocent. Bearing a burden of guilt both for the abuse he'd suffered as a child (abused children always feel guilty, as if they have somehow deserved the horrors visited on them), and for the death of his parents, Maxwell was extraordinarily conflicted about sex. Alicea was terrified of it, but couldn't help behaving seductively around men. Max, as Irene had suspected, had internalized Carnivean's predilections, along with a great deal of rage. Christopher held himself responsible for the seduction of Miss Miller. And it was sexual jealousy on the part of all of them that led to Kinch's appearance, Kronk's death, and the fire.

As for Mary, even French kissing was a big deal for her. So they took it slow. Christopher started timing his trips into town to coincide with her day off. They'd meet at a prearranged spot and she'd return to the Ridge with him. They'd feed the chickens, swim in the creek, maybe make out a little—nothing heavy.

The first few times Christopher brought Mary back to the Ridge, Miss Miller never left the bedroom. But he told Mary all about her. Well, not about the sex. If you left out the sex, then the agreed-upon fiction, Maxwell's heroism in saving his foster mother from a rapist and being burned himself in the process, cast him in rather a romantic light.

So he and Mary talked it over, and decided that Miss Miller was only being shy on account of her disfigurement. Mary certainly had no reason to suspect that Chrissy's foster mother might be bitterly, insanely jealous. Neither did Christopher. After all, Miss M had ended their sexual relationship even before the fire; the idea she might want to rekindle it in her condition was utterly, literally inconceivable to him.

Of all the alters, only the preternaturally mature Max suspected what Miss Miller was going through, and how it might end. But Max wasn't that fond of Mary in the first place, having discovered that when Christopher was in love, his personality was strong enough to threaten Max's hegemony over the system. He kept his mouth shut.

And eventually Miss Miller seemed to warm up to Mary. Who wouldn't?—Mary was that sweet. She never even flinched the first time she saw Miss M, which suggested that she either had iron discipline or that she saw the world through the eyes of an angel.

It was the happiest time Christopher had ever known—even better than when Miss Miller had rescued him and taken him to her bed. And as his relationship with Mary deepened, he began to experience the spontaneous remission of his dissociative disorder. Such remissions were, Irene knew, not uncommon as child multiples entered adulthood. Sometimes the remissions were permanent; more often the symptoms reappeared again as the multiple entered his or her thirties. But Christopher didn't know anything about that—all he knew was that whole days could go by without another alter seizing control of the body.

By this time he and Mary had reached the stage of heavy petting. But further than that she would not go. So Christopher did what normal, healthy, foolish young men have done throughout the ages: he proposed marriage.

And she accepted. That meant she'd soon be leaving her faith, her friends, what passed for her family. But now she had Chrissy—that gave her the courage to leave.

The two young lovers told Miss Miller that very evening. Christopher hadn't bought Mary a ring—he didn't have any money of his own—so Miss Miller took the engagement ring Kronk had given her off her own finger and slipped it on Mary's. Christopher was flabbergasted. He'd never allowed himself to believe that so much happiness could ever be his.

Mary and Chrissy slept together for the first time that night. He hadn't been with a woman since Miss Miller first locked her door. They made love by moonlight. It was good. He was gentle. Though she was a virgin, there was no pain and very little blood. After the first time they cried, literally cried for joy in each other's arms, then started all over again. She climbed on top and rode him as though she'd been born to it, her back arched, her small white, strawberry-tipped breasts thrown forward and her head thrown back, her hair pale and shimmering in the moonlight.

If lives have an arc, this is the zenith of Maxwell's. An instant later, in darkness and confusion, the downward plunge begins. A breeze from the open door. Footsteps, a rustle of silk. A sound like a dull punch. A puzzled cry. Mary's weight collapses on top of him. He works his way out from under her.

"And how do *you* like it, young man?" says Miss Miller. She's standing at the foot of the bed. Christopher is dimly aware of Mary kneeling beside him, supporting her weight with one hand and flailing clumsily behind her with the other, as if she were trying to brush away a bee crawling up her spine.

For a moment he understands nothing. Then he flicks on the bedside lamp and sees the hilt of the ice pick protruding from the small of Mary's back, and suddenly he understands everything.

64

"GOOD MORNING?" ALVIN RALPHS wasn't quite sure what to make of the big bald fella with the bandaged head who had just shambled into Alvin's Big Hat Big Man Western Wear shop in Dallas wearing a rumpled plaid sport coat over a shoulder holster, wrinkled Sansabelt slacks, and shapeless Hush Puppies. It was enough to make a haberdasher weep.

"Good morning." Pender wasn't quite sure what to make of Alvin Ralphs either. Alvin stood five-seven, if you counted the two-inch heels on his boots and the five-inch crown on his Stetson, his western-cut suit was powder blue, with embroidered yokes fore and aft, and with his bright eyes and fallen jowls, he looked (thought Pender) like the love child of Little Jimmy Dickens ("Does Your Chewing Gum Lose Its Flavor on the Bedpost Overnight?") and Droopy Dog, from the old Warner Brothers cartoons.

"What can I do for you?" His diction was precise, his tone lilting—no Texas twang to speak of.

"I need a hat."

"I can see that."

"And I figured as long as I was in Dallas . . ."

"Say no more." Ralphs held up his right thumb, sighted in on Pender's head like a painter checking perspective. "Eight and a quarter?"

"Bingo."

The bright little eyes narrowed. Ralphs sighted in with his thumb again, then rubbed his jowls. When the pronouncement came, it was with the finality of a papal bull: "J. B. Stetson El Patron, Silver Belly White."

He disappeared into the back of the store, returned with a box, positioned Pender before a triple mirror, climbed up onto a stepstool, and with a ceremonious air carefully lowered the El Patron onto Pender's head, making sure it cleared the bandages.

"I ask you, sir: Does Alvin Ralphs know his hats?"

"He does, indeed," said Pender, admiring his reflection—or at least the hat's reflection. "I kinda look like shit from the brim down, though, huh?"

"Let's just say from the neck down, sir."

"I was once told I was the worst-dressed agent in the history of the FBI."

"One can only hope," replied Alvin Ralphs.

65

"Do you want to finish her off, or shall we let her suffer?" asks Miss Miller, as the girl Christopher loves crumples face forward on the bed, still pawing feebly behind her, trying to remove the ice pick protruding from her lower back. Deflected by her lumbar spine, the point has slipped sideways at an angle and penetrated her right kidney. She is bleeding to death internally. "I assure you, it's all the same to me."

No answer. Christopher, backed against the headboard, hugs his drawn-up knees.

"I know what's going through your treacherous little mind," Miss Miller adds, lifting the hem of her dress primly as she sits down on the corner of the bed. "You're thinking there's still time to save her. Snatch her up in your arms, drive her to the hospital. Be a hero."

Mary has begun keening his name now—*Chrisseee, Chrisseee.* Miss Miller raises her own weak voice as best she can over the shrieking. "But before you do that, Ulysses, think about what will happen if she doesn't make it—if she dies on the way. What are you going to tell them? That *I* did it? And if I tell them you did— that you raped her and stabbed her?"

"Chrisseee. Chrisseee. Help meeee."

"Just who—excuse me, *whom*—do you think they're going to believe, Ulysses?"

Mary, weakening: "Chrissy it hurts Chrissy oh god what's happening . . ."

"You or me, Ulysses? The poor, feeble, disfigured schoolteacher, or the boy who's left his seed inside the victim, a boy who's already killed a man with an ice pick?"

Christopher covers his ears with his hands, trying to block out not just the women's voices but his own internal cacophony—the crowd noise.

" . . . it hurts Chrissy it hurts so bad help me Chrissy . . ."

"Finish her, Ulysses. It's the only way."

". . . please Chrissy oh God Chrissy I hurt I hurt so bad . . ."

Ulysses . . . Chrissy . . . Ulysses . . . Chrissy . . .

"SHUT UP! EVERYBODY JUST SHUT UP!"

Silence. Silence in the bedroom, silence in the forest. With the sun almost directly overhead, the chiaroscuro effect of the dappled sunlight was more intense than ever, luminous white columns where the sun penetrated the forest canopy, dense black shadow where it did not.

Irene Cogan closed her notebook and leaned forward. "Do you need a break?" she whispered. Maxwell was facing away from her; her lips were inches from his ear.

His head moved slowly to the left, then to the right. *No.*

"Are you sure?"

A nod.

"Go on, then. What happens next?"

Slowly he turned to face her. His eyes were dull, his face expressionless. "Kinch," he replied. "Kinch happens next."

Miss Miller watches from the doorway—she's backed away in order to avoid being splattered. When Kinch is done, she approaches the bed, leans over, taking care to keep the skirt of her dress out of the gore, picks up Mary's left hand, slips off the ring she gave her at dinner, wipes it clean on the corner of the sheet, slips it back onto her own finger. Only then does she address Ulysses.

"Clean this mess up," she tells him. Then an afterthought, as she absentmindedly fingers her current wig, a cheap polyester affair she was given before she left the hospital: "Oh, and save me the hair. I think I'm going to take up wig making."

66

BEING A MULTIPLE WAS a lot like being a sports team with a deep bench. With Christopher in hiding and Max exhausted after the traumatic morning session, it was Useless—Ulysses, the erstwhile host alter—who picked up the plum assignment: driving into town for supplies.

Before he left, he brought a lunch tray up to Irene's room, and apologetically locked the door behind him on his way out, assuring her that "Ih-ih-it's for your oh-oh-own safety." Not Jimmy Stewart—Useless had a vowel stammer of his own. "I-I-I'm locking her ih-ih-in too."

Irene, who was still trying to digest the idea that there were at least two homicidal psychopaths on the ridge—Kinch and Miss Miller—didn't touch the food. Instead she sat down at the writing table, looking over the green meadow, and began making out her will.

I, Irene Cogan, being of sound mind and body, declare this my last will and testament. All my worldly goods, I leave to be divided equally between my father, Edward McMullen of Sebastopol, and my brothers, Thomas McMullen of San Jose and Edward McMullen Jr. of Campbell, except for my jewelry, which I leave to my dear friend Barbara Klopfman, of Pacific Grove.

What else? Not much to show for a life. Not that it mattered—the document was not likely to be found. Maybe years hence, if she hid it well. Or never, if she hid it either too well or not well enough. She tore the sheet out of her notebook and slipped it under the fold-up top of the writing table, then crossed over to the bed, stripped off the sheets, and knotted the ends together. No more fooling herself about being rescued, or about achieving through therapy some miraculous fusion that would help Maxwell see the error of his ways. She'd known it was time to escape—or at least begin actively seeking out a means of escape—since midway through this morning's session, when Maxwell had uttered those chilling words: *The first one's name was Mary Malloy.*

The first one? Dear Jesus, the first one? She'd realized then that he'd never let her go voluntarily—all that would be left of her would be her panties and jogging bra in the top drawer of the bureau, her tank top in the middle drawer, her running shorts in the bottom drawer, her Reeboks on the floor of the closet. And of course her hair on Miss Miller's head, after it had grown out to its original color.

A drop of fifteen feet from the window ledge to the roof of the porch below. Two sheets and two blankets knotted together at the corners and anchored to a leg of the heavy bureau gave Irene more than enough length. She hadn't climbed a rope since high school gym class, but she could still hear Miss Hatton shouting at the girls to *use those legs, ladies, use those legs, the good lord made 'em stronger than your arms.*

Irene, in a pair of Guess? jeans and a long-sleeved green jersey, climbed out feet first, belly to the sill, hunching her shoulders together and angling them diagonally to squeeze through the narrow opening. Hanging from the sill with both hands, she hooked her left leg twice around the uppermost sheet until it was draped across her instep. Right foot on left, squeezing the rope between sole and instep, she let go of the sill and inchwormed her way down.

Thank you, Miss Hatton, she thought to herself as her feet touched the shingles—then she realized that she still had a ten-foot drop to the ground. Irene tiptoed to the corner of the sloping porch roof, dropped to her belly, and slipped over the side, lowering herself from the aluminum rain gutter, wrapping her legs around the downspout strapped to the corner post supporting the roof, then shinnying the rest of the way. When her feet hit the ground, she backed away from the porch and looked up, up, up to her bedroom window.

Suddenly it occurred to her, much too late to do anything about it, that if she didn't find a way off the property before Maxwell returned, she might not have the strength to climb back up.

Time to hustle those buns, ladies, hustle those buns, thought Irene—it was another of Miss Hatton's sayings.

Moving at a steady trot, it took Irene half an hour to understand that her first assumption had been correct—there was no easy way off Scorned Ridge. The electrified chain-link fence enclosed the entire property, and the juice was on, as evidenced by the freshly charred corpse of a rabbit just outside the fence at the northwest edge of the meadow. The gate at the southwest corner of the property that led down to the river bore a diamond-shaped yellow High Voltage sign, and the gates of the sally port at the southeast corner of the property were padlocked, and topped with triple strands of electrified barbed wire mounted on ceramic spools.

And when Irene looked through the chain-link into the dappled green darkness of the embowered sally port, the Rottweilers were waiting for her. Six of them had come trotting silently through the open door in the side of the sally port—they paced the enclosure like caged lions, their amber eyes trained on Irene as she peered through the inner gate, and following her intently as she turned back from it.

Having failed to find a way off the property, Irene decided to explore the outbuildings. She trotted up the blacktop that wound through the woods and curved to the north, following the crest of the ridge past the house, past the chicken coops, and over a hump in the ridge to a weathered old red clapboard barn with sliding double doors, a cement floor, and a hay loft at the far end.

No livestock in the barn: instead the stalls contained vehicles. A Ford Taurus, a VW bug, a blue Nissan, a Geo Metro, a forty-thousand-dollar Lexus coupe, and in the first stall on the right, old Maybelline, the powder-blue Coupe de Ville. Only Maybelline and the Lexus had license plates; the Texas plates on the Lexus had expired six months earlier. After checking out a few of the cars and finding no keys, Irene climbed the ladder to the hayloft, where hundreds upon hundreds of books, magazines, and journals of all ages and on all manner of subjects were stacked or tossed about seemingly at random.

Makes sense, thought Irene, as she explored the loft. With an MTP like Mose, Maxwell would never have to read a book twice, or find one he'd already read to look something up. In a way, the loft was like a model of Maxwell's mind: zillions of facts stored away randomly.

Encyclopedias. History. Back issues of *Scientific American, Poultry Journal*. Fiction: heavy on Joyce—at least three separate editions of *Ulysses*. Horror fiction—King, Koontz, Card. Paperback crime novels with lurid covers. True crime, mostly serial killer biographies: Bundy, Gacy, Jack the Ripper, Thomas Piper, Bela Kiss, Dr. Thomas Neill Cream. *Red Dragon* and *Silence of the Lambs*. Stacks of *National Geographics* with their distinctive yellow covers. Travel books. Spy novels. Medical books—a facsimile first edition of *Gray's Anatomy*. Stacks upon stacks of pornographic magazines, heavy on bondage and discipline. Pornographic paperbacks, most of them rape- or incest-themed, judging by their covers, were mixed up with manuals on carpentry, furniture and cabinet making, hunting, wig making, butchering, wiring, gardening.

And along the back wall, scattered haphazardly under open wooden shutters that had probably once led to a hay chute, was a collection of psychology texts and journals that surpassed Irene's own library. All the standard texts, including a valuable first edition of Rorschach's *Psychodiagnostics* and several handbooks on the MMPI and TAT—no wonder Maxwell had done so well on his standardized tests.

There was also an eclectic assortment of journals and magazines. Out of curiosity, Irene started going through the periodicals, looking for the issues that contained her pieces, the ones that Mose had cited. She spotted one right away: a copy of the *Journal of Consulting and Clinical Psychology* with her article on DID vs. MPD. Next to that, leaning against the back wall, a 1997 issue of the *Journal of Nervous and Mental Diseases*.

And there in the corner was the copy of *Psychology Today* with her article on dissociative trance disorder and Pentecostal Christianity. She thumbed through it, saw her picture in the contributor's column.

"Good night, Irene, my Aunt Fanny," she muttered. Maxwell, with Mose's help, had probably recognized her the first time he laid eyes on her.

On her way down the ladder, it occurred to Irene that she'd overlooked an unlikely, but terribly important possibility. Maybelline! The car phone! Dear God, was it possible he'd left the phone in the Caddy?

She jumped the last few feet to the ground and raced the length of the barn to the de Ville. No keys, but the cell phone was still plugged into the cigarette lighter, the charging indicator a glowing red dot in the dim light of the barn. Irene held her breath, took the phone out of the cradle, and read the green display in the handset window. NO SERVICE.

Then she remembered Maxwell telling her yesterday morning that he'd had to climb up to the hayloft to get a signal. She scrambled back up the ladder and tried the phone again. NO SERVICE. She paced the length of the loft, even leaned way out the window and held the phone over her head. NO SERVICE NO SERVICE NO SERVICE.

But Maxwell had promised her he'd called about Bernadette. She thought back to her last glimpse through the rearview mirror of the black-haired girl lying on her side, her eyes closed, unmoving, and understood, with a sick heavy feeling, that Maxwell had lied, that he had either killed Bernadette or left her there to die of exposure. Then she recalled Maxwell's cryptic words when he'd emerged from old Bill's trailer in Big Sur: *I happen to know the old man just gave up smoking.*

I bet he did, thought Irene. And Barbara? Had Maxwell lied about Barbara? Had he somehow finished her off as well? With a moan, Irene dropped to her knees and began vomiting up what little remained in her stomach of the fine country breakfast Miss Miller had cooked for her five hours earlier.

67

FEELING UNCOMFORTABLE ABOUT leaving Irene and Miss Miller alone at the ranch, even locked in their rooms, Maxwell hurried through his errands in town. It was Useless who refilled Miss Miller's prescriptions and purchased a bottle of Lady Clairol Strawberry Blonds Forever at the Old Umpqua Pharmacy, spent two hundred dollars of Donna Hughes's remaining mad money at CostCo to replenish food stocks depleted by his long absence, and stopped into the Old Umpqua Feed Barn at the outskirts of town. But it was Christopher who left the feed store with chicken pellets, supplements, dog treats, and four fifty-pound bags of dog chow— the familiar surroundings, the sweet smell of hay and alfalfa, the dusty, particulate light streaming in from the high windows, had triggered an alter switch.

With the Grand Cherokee loaded to the gunwales, the drive back to Scorned Ridge via the hairpin twists and cutback turns of Charbonneau Road took nearly an hour, but Christopher enjoyed it immensely. After his long session this morning, and a short rest in the darkness, he was feeling astonishingly well—vital, recharged. It was true what Ish's books in the loft said about the cathartic effect of talking out your innermost sorrows.

It had been the first time he'd ever discussed Mary with anyone but the unsympathetic Miss Miller, and although according to the books it was far too early to expect a complete healing, nonetheless he was starting to feel as if the worst was behind him. After all, what did the books know about the resources and capabilities of a state-of-the-art multiple?

But even a fully conscious, next-generation multiple couldn't have done it on his own. Christopher understood that he had Irene to thank for his newfound peace—he realized suddenly that he was in the process of falling head over heels in love with his shrink.

And although he knew what the books would say—transference—he had to remind himself once again that the singles who wrote those books didn't understand what it was like to be a multiple. Falling in love was Christopher's function. It strengthened the system, it vitalized the body.

It also pissed off Max no end—but that was Max's problem. He should have seen this coming—and the fact that he had not indicated to Christopher that Max's control might be weakening, that his long tyrannical reign over the system might at last be coming to an end.

Christopher drove the Cherokee into the cool green darkness of the sally port and closed the gate behind him. The dogs came out to greet him; he roughhoused with them for a few minutes and gave each of them a rawhide chew, then unloaded the dog chow before unlocking the inner gate and driving the Cherokee on through.

After unloading the groceries at the house and stripping off the scraggly gray wig he always wore into town, Christopher drove on to the barn to park the Cherokee, then hurried back up to the house. On his way out of the barn, he noticed a sour smell he hadn't picked up before—probably a dead rodent—but was in too much of a hurry to see his new beloved to look for its origin just yet.

Now that he knew he loved her, he couldn't wait to see Irene. He took the stairs two at a time, pretending not to hear Miss Miller calling to him from her room, and knocked at Irene's door. No answer. He knocked louder, then turned his key in the lock and silently opened the door.

She wasn't there. A quick moment of panic, a glance at the narrow window—then he heard the shower running. He tiptoed into the bathroom and saw her slender body silhouetted through the opaque shower curtain. His erection pressed against his trousers—it took an effort of pure willpower to back out of the room again. After all, he had guaranteed her privacy. And forty-eight hours in the darkness was far too long a time for Christopher to be separated from his beloved.

*   *   *

As Irene, exhausted emotionally from her discovery in the loft and physically from the desperate climb back up to the bedroom, turned off the water and stepped out of the shower, she heard Maxwell calling to her from the hallway.

"Be right there," she yelled back as she wrapped one towel around her, and a second around her hair. On her way across the bedroom she glanced around to be sure that everything was in order—window closed, sheets and blankets back on the bed—before opening the door.

"I brought you a present," said Maxwell, stepping past her into the room. He handed her the Strawberry Blonds Forever. "Until your natural color grows out."

Irene's mind spun trying to work through the permutations of meaning in the gesture—was he readying her for a sacrifice? A love affair? But all other thoughts were driven from her head by Christopher's next statement:

"I see you've been a naughty girl."

She blanched, turned away, struggled for control of her voice. "What . . . what do you mean?"

He gestured toward the writing table by the window. "Your lunch—you haven't touched it."

68

THE BIG BALD MAN IN the natty, western-style sport coat with embroidered yokes fore and aft, stiff new boot-cut Wrangler jeans, and shiny, silver-toed Tony Lama boots tipped his new white Stetson to the stewardess as he stepped off the commuter jet in Eugene, Oregon.

Pender's new look was not intended as a disguise. He was counting on the probability that the FBI would not embarrass itself by issuing a BOLO for one of its own agents. But as Alvin Ralphs had pointed out, a man with a brand new El Patron had certain standards to live up to—why not let somebody else be the worst-dressed agent in the FBI for a change?

On his way out of the store, Pender had revisited his transformed reflection in the window—he now stood nearly six-ten from the soles of his new boots to the tip of his high-crowned hat.

"I see by your outfit that you are a cowboy," he'd said to himself sotto voce. The new height took a little getting used to, though—he knocked his hat off going through the terminal doors.

Pender had used his own credit card for the flight. Arriving in Eugene late Monday afternoon, after the weekend car rentals had been returned and washed, Pender had his pick of the fleet. Again using his own credit card, he selected a sporty-looking Dodge Intrepid with barely enough leg room for him and clearance for his new hat, purchased a set of maps, and set off for Umpqua County.

It was full dark by the time he reached the county seat. Founded during the gold rush of the 1850s, Umpqua City, a mining town until the gold was gone, a logging town until the forests were decimated, was now struggling to reestablish itself as a tourist destination. Pender booked a room at the Old Umpqua Hotel, a three-story yellow brick establishment across the street from the Umpqua County Courthouse, and catty-corner from the Old Umpqua Pharmacy. After a long shower, he treated himself to a salmon dinner in the hotel's Umpqua Room—wood-paneled walls, white tablecloths, and waiters wearing sleeve garters.

When he got back to his room, Pender turned off his cell phone and sky pager before climbing into bed. For anyone else it might not have been that big a deal, but for Pender, it meant that for the first time in over a quarter of a century, he was beyond the reach of the bureau.

69

IRENE DINED ALONE, locked in her room again that night. Christopher would have preferred to eat with her, but he knew better than anyone how dangerous it could be to ignore Miss Miller for too long. This way when Miss M complained about being locked in her bedroom all afternoon, he could at least point out that Irene was still locked in hers.

There was, however, zero chance of Miss M receiving a visit from Peter that evening. Christopher had other plans for the body. After dinner he and Miss Miller did the washing up together, visited Freddie Mercury and his flock, and sat together on the front porch watching the sun set behind Horned Ridge, the two-pronged peak to the west.

But when that sun was gone, so was Christopher. Irene was sitting at the writing table composing a second haiku when she heard the knock. She glanced quickly over her poem—

> *Sunset on Scorned Ridge*
> *Strawberry Blonds Forever*
> *I don't want to die.*

—then closed her notebook and slipped it under the top of the escritoire.

"Yes?"

"It's Christopher—may I come in?"

"Can it wait till morning?"

He hadn't expected that. "I just wanted to say good night."

Irene decided she might as well test him now as later. "Good night, then."

"I want to come in."

"Christopher, we have a contract. You've agreed to respect my rights. As I'm sure you're aware, DID therapy can be as exhausting for the therapist as for the patient. I'd really appreciate a little space tonight—then I'll see you in the morning, fresh and rested and ready to go."

On the other side of the door, Christopher was in a quandary. He felt a nearly overwhelming desire to let Max or one of the others have her—as long as it wasn't Lyssy, at least he'd be able to access the memory. Then he realized that the urging was probably *coming* from Max.

Irene put her ear to the door—she could hear him breathing. "Good night, Christopher," she said, trying to put a kindly, caring inflection on it.

"Good night, Irene." Then, in a whisper: "I'll see you in my dreams."

Miss Miller is half asleep. Her bedroom door opens, then closes again softly. "Ulysses?" She stirs from her junkie nod as he climbs into bed beside her.

"Sshh." Christopher, as opposed to Max or Peter, hasn't made love to Miss Miller since he was a boy, but Irene has left him no choice—for Christopher, the drying shed is no longer an attractive option.

Miss M is lying on her back. He can see too much of what's left of her unmasked profile; his erection is rapidly dwindling. Hastily he shuts his eyes, nudges her over onto her side, facing away from him, and works her nightgown up to her shoulder blades. Her back is unscarred—as he traces a line down her spine and fondles her cheeks, he can just about persuade himself that it is Irene's long, slender ass he's fondling. The erection stirs again. Rather than break the spell by attempting to enter her from behind, he flips it up, trapping it between his belly and her butt, and begins rubbing himself frantically against her.

"Oh, Ulysses," she drawls coquettishly. She's mildly aroused, drugged out, and amused. "Just like the old days." She means the frotteurism.

"Sshh." He hushes her again—that voice will spoil everything— and shuts his eyes even tighter, as if that will shut out the voice. "Don't talk. Please don't talk."

Now the room is silent except for the silky, rhythmic whisper of the sheets. Five minutes, ten minutes—*wshhh, wshhh, wshhh, wshhh.* Then a moan, and it's over.

"Thank you," says Christopher.

No response—just Miss Miller's steady, raspy breathing. She appears to have fallen asleep.

"Thank *you,* come again sssometime," he replies for her, in Irene's voice, so as to prolong the fantasy. Then he chuckles silently, wipes himself on the tail of her silken nightgown, and slides backward out of the bed, carefully avoiding any further contact with that dreadful body.

70

AFTER GROWING UP IN sunny San Jose, Irene Cogan found she rather enjoyed fog—if you didn't, you didn't settle in Pacific Grove. There were few things she and Frank liked better than having coffee and cinnamon rolls in bed on a foggy Sunday morning. Two newspapers, the *Monterey Herald* and the *San Jose Mercury News,* spread out across the comforter, a silent football or basketball game on the bedroom TV for Frank, the radio tuned to classical music for Irene, and through the second-story window, the silver fog drifting lazily through the boughs of the great live oak in the front yard.

The fog on Scorned Ridge, however, was a different creature, oppressive, damp and cold and heavy. When Irene opened her eyes shortly after dawn on Tuesday morning, it seemed to her to be pressing up against the bedroom window, as if seeking a crack through which it could gain entry. She pulled the blankets over her head and tried to go back to sleep.

Some time later, she couldn't say how long, Irene found herself sitting on the toilet with her nightgown hiked up and no memory of having entered the bathroom in the first place. She tried to tell herself that it was funny, or at least ironic, that under stress the DID specialist should find herself displaying symptoms of a dissociative disorder, but it wasn't—it wasn't funny at all.

What it was, was a wake-up call. She spent the next hour sitting at the writing table going through her notebook, looking for some weakness, some crack in Maxwell's system, that she could exploit in the guise of therapy. According to her notes, little Lyssy seemed to be the only alter with whom Max and the others did not share memory.

But Max had already informed her that Lyssy was unavailable. Even if Max were lying, Lyssy could only be accessed through hypnosis, which would require Max's cooperation. And if she did access Lyssy, she would still be dealing with a weak, infantile personality who couldn't do her much good, unless he knew how to shut off the power to the electric fence, which seemed unlikely.

Mose, though—Mose would know how to shut off the power. He'd tell her, too. But unlike Lyssy, Max and the MTP *did* share memory—they might even have some sort of co-consciousness or copresence setup, in which case Max would know the moment Mose told her.

Alicea was a possibility, if Irene could establish some sort of sisterhood connection. But even if Alicea agreed to help Irene, Max could easily seize consciousness from her.

Christopher, though—what was it Christopher said yesterday? When he was in love, his personality was strong enough to threaten Max's control. That was why Max hadn't warned him about Miss Miller.

When he was in love. In love. In love . . .

Irene found herself in the bathroom again. Not sitting on the toilet this time, but standing in front of the sink, staring alternately at the box of Strawberry Blonds Forever on the stainless steel shelf, and her reflection in the mirror behind it.

For the first time in years, Christopher had been in control as Maxwell fell asleep, and stayed in control long enough to enter REM sleep. In the beginning of his dream he was down at the swimming hole with Mary. Below the dark green surface of the water, she had slipped the top of her bathing suit down for him; her nipples were puckered and hard from the cold.

By the time the dream ended, though, she wasn't Mary anymore—she had somehow turned into Irene. Which was fine with Christopher. He slipped from REM back into stage-two sleep with a peaceful smile on his face and an erection substantial enough to prevent him from turning onto his stomach for several more minutes.

But it was Max who awakened in the body the next morning. As always, he recalled, indirectly, as if he'd seen it in a movie, everything that had happened while Christopher and Useless and the others had been in control. He understood immediately what was going on. Not only was Christopher gaining power and influence from the therapy, but the other alters seemed strengthened as well.

Exactly the opposite of the results he'd hoped for—he vowed to put a stop to it.

"Not . . . guh . . . happen," he muttered aloud. "Wouldn't be prudent." A pedestrian George Bush impression, not up to his usual standards.

By ten o'clock, when the knock came at Irene's door, the fog had burned away—it was another gorgeous day in the southern Cascades.

"Just a minute." Irene checked her reflection in the mirror, primped up her slightly damp strawberry blond hair, and opened the door. She couldn't tell at first which alter she was dealing with, but whichever one it was, he was momentarily struck dumb. She prompted him: "Well, what do you think?"

He whistled softly—he couldn't take his eyes off her. "I think my dreams just came true."

It's Christopher, she decided. Thank you, Jesus. "It's a little dark, but it'll probably lighten up as it dries."

"It's perfect."

"Thank you. By the way, I wanted to apologize for last night, for not letting you in to say good night. The truth is, I had the impression you might be going through some transference, and well, the *real* truth is, I was going through some countertransference myself."

"Now my dreams really *are* coming true."

"We can't act on it—surely you understand we can't act on it."

"Of course not."

She could see the hurt in his eyes. "At least not yet," she added hastily. "We still have a lot more work to do."

"I understand," he said sweetly. But although the voice was Christopher's, for just a moment there, Irene could have sworn she saw a flicker of Max's sardonic expression gazing back at her from behind those gold-flecked brown eyes.

"Is there anything that's happened since our last session that you need to discuss?"

It was slightly chillier in the forest this morning than it had been the two previous days. Maxwell wore a bulky brown-and-white Oaxacan sweater over his hula shirt and shorts. Irene wore a cranberry-colored cardigan from the closet over a short-sleeved blouse and a pair of white ducks.

"Other than falling in love with my therapist?" He glanced over his shoulder, gave her that Christopher grin.

Irene forced herself to smile back. "We can start there if you'd like—but I'd have to give you my standard speech on transference."

"Something that happened while I was in town, then."

"Yes?"

"We must have had a spontaneous alter switch—I don't think anybody noticed. I found myself in the Old Umpqua Feed Barn."

"Where you originally met Mary."

"Right. But what I wanted to tell you—as far as I can remember, it was the first time I was back there since, I guess since she died, that I didn't feel an overwhelming sense of guilt."

"What *did* you feel?"

"Sadness. But a peaceful sadness—like I'm finally starting to put all that behind me."

"Sounds like progress. Anything else?"

"Not off the top of my head."

"All right then, let's move on. Yesterday, before you started telling me about Mary, you said something I need to ask you about."

"What's that?"

"You said something about Mary being the first one."

"No, I didn't."

"I distinctly remember—"

"Max said that."

"I see. What do you think he meant by it?"

"I'll tell you later. First I have a present for you." From the deep pocket of his sweater he removed a small packet: gilt wrapping paper folded into a rectangle and secured with transparent tape. "Happy anniversary."

"Excuse me?"

"Don't tell me you don't remember?" Genuine disappointment, even a hint of anger.

Desperately, Irene searched her memory. Finally it came to her. "It's our one-week anniversary. We met one week ago today."

"I knew you couldn't have forgotten." He handed it to her. "Go ahead, open it. Just a little something I picked up in town."

She tore open the paper; a pair of emerald drop earrings spilled out onto her palm. They were exquisite—and if Irene knew her jewelry, frightfully expensive. She realized immediately that he hadn't bought them yesterday, or they'd have been in a plush box. She tried to think how to react.

In the normal course of therapy, Irene would have had to: 1) inform him that an expensive gift was inappropriate at this point in their relationship and that she couldn't accept it; 2) gently call him on his lie about having just bought it, and try to find out why he'd felt it was necessary to lie; and 3) point out that he'd changed the subject from Max's comment about Mary being the first one.

But this wasn't about therapy—it was about surviving. So she thanked him as effusively as she could, then worked the question-mark-shaped gold wires into her own earlobes, her own flesh, despite a suspicion so strong it bordered on telepathy that Maxwell had stripped them from the previous owner's body after raping, then murdering her.

71

THE YELLOW BRICKS FOR the Umpqua County Courthouse had been fired in the first brickyard in the state of Oregon, according to the plaque on the wall outside the frosted-glass door of the Umpqua County Probation Department—a plaque Pender had become all too familiar with by the time he wangled Cazimir Buckley's current address out of Penelope Frye, the lone and harried receptionist/secretary/clerk who seemed to be holding down the fort while everybody else in the department was either off on vacation or out sick.

The problem, Miss Frye explained, was that only Mr. Harris, Buckley's case officer, could authorize her to give out personal information on the parolee. Pender tinned her, reasoned with her, begged her, and badgered her until she finally agreed to make a few phone calls—but only if he in turn agreed to wait outside: she was getting a stiff neck looking up at him.

So he paced the hall and read the plaque until Miss Frye opened the door to inform him that according to Mrs. Harris, Mr. Harris was at that moment somewhere in the middle of Crater Lake with a fishing rod in one hand and his first cold Bud of the morning in the other.

Another round of reasoning, begging, and badgering; another few phone calls; another wait in the hall until Miss Frye finally reached one of the department higher-ups. But eventually all the pacing and badgering paid off: Pender left the courthouse with an address—304 Britt Street, in Umpqua—and the distinct impression that if Penelope Frye had been in charge of security at the Department of Energy, the Chinese would never have made off with any of our nuclear secrets.

*   *   *

Lovely morning—there'd been no fog in the valley. The sky was clear, the air was cool, the surrounding mountains picture-postcard perfect above the quaint old town. Pender walked the thirteen blocks to Britt Street—the brand-new boots had his dogs howling by the time he reached the handsome blue Victorian.

He double-checked the address in his notebook: either 304 had been divided into apartments or converted to a halfway house, or else Caz Buckley was one wealthy parolee. Remembering Buckley's predilection for aggravated assault, Pender unsnapped the flap of his shoulder holster as he started up the steps. Before he could ring the bell, the door was opened by an attractive black woman in a white uniform, her graying hair pulled back into a severe bun under a peaked nurse's cap.

"Yes?"

"I'm here to see Caz Buckley."

"Well, thank the good Lord," said the nurse, her face softening as she reached out to take Pender's hand between both of hers. "Bless your heart, you're the first visitor he's had since he's been here. Come in, please."

Encouraged but puzzled, Pender forgot to duck as he went through the doorway, and nearly knocked his hat off. He reached up to catch it, and was thankful for Alvin Ralphs' knowing tailoring—his old jacket would have revealed his shoulder hoster for sure.

Once he was inside, a glance at the entrance hall cleared everything up. On a side table was a display stand with brochures—Your Hospice and You; Patient's Bill of Rights; You Are Not Alone—and on the wall was a bulletin board listing various support groups and grief workshops.

Pender weighed his options briefly, and decided that when the law enforcement gods drop a gift like this into your lap, it would be bad luck to throw it back. "I'm glad I'm still in time. How long does he have?"

The nurse shrugged, her usual response to that particular question. "Why don't you wait in there?" she told Pender, indicating the parlor to his left. "I'll see if he's still awake."

"I'd rather surprise him," said Pender. "I can't wait to catch the look on old Caz's face when he sees me."

"I really shouldn't, Mr . . . ?"

"Pender. Look, I give you my word of honor, if he's asleep, I'll tiptoe right on out." Then he looked down at his boots. "Well, maybe not tiptoe—I just bought these yesterday and they're not broke in yet."

The confidence had two purposes. First, it *was* a confidence, and confidences always invite trust. Second, it was a good way to get the woman's sympathy. Like cops, nurses knew all about sore feet.

"Well, I suppose it would be all right, if you promise not to wake him. . . ."

"Word of honor. If he's asleep, I'll sit quietly by the bed."

"It's room 302. I'll take you back to the elevator."

Pender ducked through the low doorway and shut the door softly behind him. The room was tiny, with a downward-slanting roof. According to the printout, Buckley was a hundred-and-eighty-pound African American, but the skin color of the man in the bed was a sickly yellowish gray, and he couldn't have weighed much over a hundred pounds.

His eyes were closed, his breathing shallow. He appeared to be asleep, but Pender never for a moment considered keeping his promise to the nurse. There was a wooden chair next to the bed; Pender sat down with his hat in his lap, leaned over, and whispered into the dying man's slightly cauliflowered ear.

"Cazimir Buckley, do you believe in an afterlife?"

"Who wants to know?" whispered Buckley, without opening his eyes.

"Pender, FBI."

With his left hand, the one that wasn't hooked up to the IV, Buckley reached for the buzzer to summon the nurse. Pender grabbed his wrist.

"I need some information about somebody you might have done time with in Juvie."

"Fuck you," said Buckley, with an effort.

"You're dying, Caz. You're gonna need all the good time you can get, when you're called to the Lord."

Buckley didn't have another fuck you in him. He raised the middle finger of his right hand weakly instead.

"At the moment, he's averaging two murders a day."

Finger.

"Black women." One black woman, anyway.

But the finger stayed up. So much for appealing to the man's sense of religion, humanity, or racial identity. On to self-interest, which was where Pender would have started with any con but a dying one.

"Listen up, Caz. Here comes the deal, and it's only coming by once. This is a sweet setup you have here. I don't know how you wangled it, but it's a helluva nice place to die. Only maybe you don't deserve a nice place to die. I've already talked to Mr. Harris, and if I don't get full cooperation from you, starting with my very next question, I can have your parole revoked by tomorrow afternoon."

The upraised finger wavered. Buckley's nostrils flared from the effort of breathing. Pender went on: "It's your choice, Caz. You get to decide whether you want to die here or in the hospital wing of the state penitentiary. Now, do you understand me?"

Slowly the gaunt gray man opened his eyes; the whites were yellow as egg yolks. "He killin' black women, you said?"

"The last one was named Aletha Winkle. I found her body. He fractured her skull, raped her repeatedly while she was dying, then hacked her to pieces with a butcher knife."

"You got a pitcher of him?"

Pender showed him Casey's mug shot.

"I dunno. Juvie, you said? Thass goin *way* back, man."

"He said you taught him some trick, some martial arts trick for getting the jump on somebody?"

Buckley looked at the picture again. He started to smile, then a spasm of pain wracked him.

"Leggo my hand," he said. Pender unpinned the call button from the sheet and moved it out of reach, but that wasn't what Buckley was going for. He found the handset that controlled the morphine infuser and jabbed the button with his thumb.

Pender waited a full minute. He could afford to be generous. He now had an even surer way of guaranteeing Buckley's cooperation: he could take the morphine button away from him. Ends and means. "Feeling better now?"

"Hurt less. Shit don' get me high no more."

"Sorry to hear that. You have a name to give me?"

"Might have."

"Well then, I *might* let you have that magic button back next time you need it. Now who are we talking about?"

"Max. We talkin' 'bout little Max. And you know what's really fucked up?"

"What?"

"I made up all that shit about countin' backwards and all. Flat made it up."

72

IRENE, THOUGH SHE WAS still flirting, letting Christopher rattle on about how lovely she was, how her hair set off the earrings, could feel herself starting to lose her nerve. How tempting it seemed, how easy it would be, to sit here and let him talk himself out. Then a nice lunch, maybe a swim, and another travesty of a session. A nice dinner. Maybe a video—there was quite a collection in the parlor. Her room was comfortable enough. And if he insisted on sex, as long as he remained Christopher, it wouldn't be so bad. He was gentle—he even smelled good. It wouldn't be giving up, she told herself—she'd just be staying alive, waiting to be rescued.

But for how long? This was a highly unstable multiple, living in an unstable relationship with . . . Irene made a differential diagnosis of Miss Miller on the fly: a pedophiliac with either narcissistic, avoidant, or dependent personality disorders, or all of the above, exacerbated by post-traumatic stress disorder to the level of psychosis.

So why are you still futzing around? she asked herself. Futzing—that was one of Barbara's expressions. And it was the thought of Barbara—please Jesus let her be alive—that gave Irene the strength to push on.

"What do you say we get back to work here, Christopher? I think the best way I can express my appreciation for these lovely earrings is by moving ahead with your therapy."

"Okay by me."

"Yesterday you said something I found interesting. You said that when you were in love with Mary, you were able to resist Max's control."

"Right."

"But on Sunday you told me that what was good for Max was good for the system. Is that something you really believe?"

"No, but he does." Suddenly Maxwell sat up, swung his legs over the side of the chaise, took the pen from Irene, and set it down on the arm of her chair, then pressed her hand between his two hands. "Tell me that you love me, Irene—tell me quick if you want to keep talking to me."

Was it a trick? Was it even Christopher? Irene felt an immense weariness coming over her, like someone lost in a snowstorm, who only wants to sleep, yet knows that sleep is death. The thought of saying those three little words to this man was equally repellent to her both as a therapist and as a woman. But if this was Christopher, she had to do everything in her power to help him maintain dominance over the system, over Max.

"I love you." Her voice rang strangely in her ears.

"Kiss me like you mean it."

In for a penny, in for a pound. She allowed him to press his lips lightly to hers.

"Thank you," he said. "Now I'm going to tell you a story. But I need you to hold my hand the whole time, and look into my eyes."

"All right."

"When I was fourteen I started keeping a diary. Every day that I was in control of the body, I'd make an entry. When Miss Miller and I were going good, it'd have three, four daily entries in a row. When we were fighting, there might be one a week. Then one night I discovered I had run out of pages—filled the diary up. I was looking around my room for something else to write in, and in the back of the closet I found an old composition book—you know, the kind with the black-and-white marbled cardboard covers?

"But when I opened it up, I saw that someone else had already started a diary in it. A boy by the name of Martin. A boy who'd lived in that very room. Went to my middle school. Had the same teachers I did. Slept with Miss Miller. I was so jealous I could have spit."

"So you weren't the first?" Irene said softly.

"That's what I thought, too. Then I checked the dates. February nineteen eighty-two through June of eighty-three."

"He was an alter?"

"One of us. One of us. But I'd never heard of him. So I started reading his diary. He'd been there almost from the beginning—he was one of the first split-offs. And he hated Max, he despised him. Called him an outsider. He wrote down that he was writing the diary for the rest of us to find. He wrote that Max was the devil incarnate, and was trying to destroy him. That eventually Max would destroy us all. But if only we'd work together we could fight Max, take away his power over the system.

"Ten pages in, the last entry ended in the middle of a sentence. Below it, in a different handwriting, Max's handwriting, were the words *Sic Semper Traditor*."

"Thus always . . . ?" That was as far as Irene's medical Latin would take her.

"Thus always to traitors. If it's possible for an alter to die, Martin was dead. Worse than dead—at least dead people leave memories behind. There was nothing left of Martin but that notebook."

He fell silent, but his eyes, only inches from Irene's, were eloquent: they spoke of fear, they begged for help.

"I understand what you're trying to tell me," she said. "You're afraid that what happened to Martin will happen to you if you try to resist Max—even though you know that that would be the best thing you could do for the system. But I need you to know that there's one big difference between yourself and Martin."

What? His lips moved soundlessly.

"You have me." But in her heart of hearts she was every bit as terrified as Christopher appeared to be.

73

"WHEN I COME UP FROM Compton to live with my auntie, I already done Juvie time down south."

Cazimir Buckley's yellow eyes were damp and dreamy. He kept his thumb on the infuser button for comfort. He seemed to have been energized by the social interaction, thought Pender—or perhaps he wasn't quite as indifferent to the prospect of a final reckoning as he'd pretended to be.

"So the Juvie here, man, to me it's like one a them, whatchacallem, Med Clubs, Club Meds. Big ol' farm, first horse I ever seen outside the TV that a cop wasn' ridin'. First cows and pigs I *ever* seen. And they fed us good. Best I ever ate in my life. I didn' even mind shovelin' cow shit—it's shit, but it's, like, clean shit. At night they lock us down in one big dormitory together, trusties in charge.

"Them farm boys, they ain't seen many brothers up here. I took some whuppins, give some whuppins. What save my ass from a real stompin', the trusties had this rule: all fights one on one. You want to mess with a dude, you call him out after lockdown. It's what we had instead a TV."

Buckley closed his eyes, mashed his thumb down on the infuser button. As they waited for the morphine to take effect, Pender had a delicate decision to make. His customary interviewing technique allowed for digression—sometimes you learned things going up side roads you'd never learn on the highway. But Buckley was already weakening, and he didn't appear to have much strength in reserve.

"Max," prompted Pender. "Tell me about Max."

Buckley's eyes fluttered open. "I'm *gettin'* there, man, I'm *gettin'* there. He come to Juvie straight out of the hospital, his hands is all burned to shit, got gloves on for the skin graffs. No way that li'l dude belong in Juvie, but he don' have no place to go back to, either, and wouldn' no foster home take him in, 'cause he burn that last place down.

"Li'l sweet piece like that, you reckon he gon' be somebody's butt boy his first night. But got-damn if the li'l fucker couldn' fight like a man. Ka-ra-tay! He coulda taught Jackie Chan a move or two. First dude mess with him, kid kick his cracker ass just usin' his feet.

"Then when them bandages come off and he can use his hands, nobody fuck with him, *nobody* call him out. So he start callin' dudes out his own self. Now you take *me* back then—back then Caz *like* to fight. And some dudes, they *love* to fight. But little Max, he *need* to fight.

"One night, finely he call me out. My auntie, she come out to visit me, bring me a box a homemade cookies. Max, he say how come you don' give me no cookies, dude? Share and share alike. I act all scared and shit, say here, man, take all the fuckin' cookies you want. Then when he got both hands full of cookies, I jump him. Bloody his nose, kick the shit out of him while he still down, cause I don' want no part of him after he get up.

"Now you figure, after somethin' like that, dude gonna wait his chance, get some back. Not Max. It's like he my asshole buddy from there on. Follow me aroun' like a puppy dog—how you *do* that to me, Caz, how you *do* that? What I'm gonna tell him, wait til your man got his hands full of cookies and too greedy to let go? Got-damn, he'd a kicked my ass good, he figure that out. So I make some shit up 'bout countin' back from ten, and jumpin' your man before you get to one. Anytime 'fore you get to one, so long as you don't make up your mind too soon."

"I have to tell you, Caz, you just might have been onto something there," said Pender, thinking of how fast Casey—Max—had jumped him in the holding cell.

"Got-damn if *he* don' think so. He practice and practice—he just be out there feedin' his chickens—man, he love them chickens— and alla sudden, voom!—he bust a move. Standin' in the chow line, voom!—he bust a move. Got so good at it, finely wouldn' nobody on the ranch have no part of him, so they put him on the boxin' team. Unde-fuckin-feated. They hadn'a cut him loose, he'd a been junior lightweight Gold Gloves, maybe Oh-lympics, no lie."

Buckley pressed the infuser again, but not enough time had elapsed. "Fuck me," he muttered.

"You say they cut him loose?" said Pender quickly. "How'd that work?"

"Well, like I tol' you, he never shoulda been in Juvie in the first place—all this time, he on'y waitin' trial. Finely the ol' lady he burn up, she get better enough, finely she tessify he was savin' her ass—say the man Max kilt, he was rapin' her. Say she call for help, Max jump him with a ice pick. Say the fire was a accident."

Again he pressed the button with his thumb. This time it clicked. Buckley closed his eyes and sighed with relief.

Pender waited another few seconds, then pressed on. "Do you remember her name?"

"Naw. All I remember, one day Max' PD show up, take him away to live with her."

"Have you seen him since Juvie?" asked Pender.

"Thass a good question."

Oh-ho. "How do you mean?"

"Last year. I got my parole, account of my liver cancer. Compassionate parole, they call it, but it's just, you dyin' and too sick to do nobody no harm, they don' wanna have to take care a you. You right 'bout that prison hospital—man, thass a *hell*hole. I'da been anybody else, I coulda got one a them transplants, but you a con, they don' even put you on the list.

"So I been out about a month, I got me a room and board down by the river—my auntie done passed. I guess maybe it's July. I'm comin' outta the drugstore—the ol' one on Jackson Street, near the courthouse—I see this dude comin' in. I profile him pretty good, 'cause I'm thinking, got-damn, sure look like little Max. On'y he's too old to be Max—all gray-ass.

"And damn if he don' eyeball me too, like maybe he's thinkin' that sure looks like ol Caz Buckley from Juvie, on'y it's way too old to be Caz. On account a I was down about a hunnerd ten, hunnerd twenty, no hair, skin all yellow, color of a old Laker unie. But he don' say nothin' and I don' say nothin'. On'y now you tell me cops is lookin' for him, so coulda been it really *was* him, on'y in disguise."

Buckley was at the end of his strength. His eyes had closed again, and his whisper was barely audible.

"Beg pardon?" Pender had to lean over to hear the last few words. His face was less than a foot from the yellow eyes when they finally opened again.

"I said, we done now, you and me?" asked Buckley.

Pender nodded.

"You ain' gon' make no trouble with my parole?" He clicked the morphine button again.

"No."

"Do it help any, what I tol' you?"

"It helps. It helps more than you know," said Pender, with a catch in his voice. He wasn't sure where all the emotion was coming from. It had something to do with the dying man in front of him, sure, but it was more than that. He knew this was his last case. He also knew that with the information Buckley had given him, he could break it—soon. It was a bittersweet realization, a valedictory sort of feeling.

"Good," said Buckley, as the morphine eased him again. "Like the man say, do the right thing."

"You did, Caz." Pender patted Buckley's shoulder. "Anything I can do for you before I go?"

"Yeah," said Buckley. "Gimme back the call button."

"Oh—sorry. Here you go."

"And lemme know how it turn out—you know, if you ketch him."

Pender promised that he would, then hurried out of the room. The elevator door opened before he reached it, and the gray-haired black nurse stepped out, pushing a medication cart before her.

"You all right?" she asked him.

Pender nodded, adjusting his Stetson as he stepped into the elevator.

"Will you be coming back?"

Another nod.

"Don't wait too long," she called, as the elevator door closed. She hoped he'd understood what she meant—that Buckley didn't have long to live. This big bald cowboy seemed like a strange fellow to be visiting poor Caz, but they were obviously close. She could have sworn she saw a tear in the man's eye.

74

BEING A PSYCHIATRIST INVOLVED a certain amount of acting. In some ways, a therapy session was like a long improvisation. The trouble was, Irene wasn't sure she was a good enough actress for the role she had to play.

Because as the morning session wore on, it had become clear to her just how high a price she would have to pay to maintain Christopher's dominance over Max and the other alters. Not only would she have to actively encourage his transference, she would have to feign a countertransference. It wasn't enough that Christopher was in love with her—she had to convince him that she was in love with him.

"My poor Christopher. It must have been so difficult for you, living with Miss Miller after what she'd done to Mary."

"Not really. I went away for a few months."

"Where were you?"

"It's hard to describe to somebody who hasn't been there. It's like the place you go when you're sleeping but not dreaming. Time doesn't pass."

"And when you woke up, when you came back?"

"I opened my eyes in the morning, and I was me."

"Was it of your own volition, do you think?"

"No. They needed me."

"They?"

"Max and Miss Miller."

"Tell me about it."

"I was only there for part of it."

"But you remember the rest? You and the others share memory?"

"I don't remember it directly, but I know what happened. Sort of like a dream. And of course there's always Mose, for the details. Like we always say, Mose knows."

"Do you communicate directly with Mose?"

"Yes."

"Any of the others?"

"Ish. Max, sometimes."

"Now?"

"No."

"Tell me what happened when you woke up, then—why did Max and Miss Miller need you?"

"You'll hate me."

"I won't—I couldn't."

He slid off the chaise, sat down on the carpet of needles, then reached out toward Irene. She climbed off her chair and sat cross-legged in front of him.

"Hold my hand," he said. "Hold my hand and look into my eyes. And if you see me starting to switch, kiss me like you love me."

"I will," said Irene, trying not to sound as miserable as she felt. "I do."

"The second one's name was Sandy Faircloth. It was Miss Miller's idea. Three months had gone by since Mary's death. At first Max was afraid somebody would come around asking questions, but as far as he could tell from reading the local paper, Mary was never even reported missing. The Witnesses may have just thought she ran away—who knows?

"He and Miss Miller settled back into the routine. He put all his energy into fixing up the place, gardening, raising the chickens, putting in the electric fence to keep the predators out.

"Then one day in August Max was out hoeing. Miss Miller was sitting in the shade watching him, wearing her new wig. It was hot, he was only wearing a pair of cutoffs, he had a hard-on, and frankly, he just didn't give a damn whether she saw it or not.

"She did—she said he ought to consider finding himself a girl-friend. Said a healthy young boy like him had needs. He thought she was teasing him at first, but she was serious. I think she knew she couldn't keep him penned up forever. She said if he brought another one back, he could keep her—that as long as it was a strawberry blond, and as long as he didn't get too attached, she wouldn't interfere.

"Looking back, I can't honestly tell you whether I knew what they had in mind—really, *really* knew. If I did, I was in denial about it, at least consciously. I found myself in the body. I knew I was supposed to pick up a girl, and I knew she had to be a strawberry blond. But subconsciously I must have known that once I brought her to the ridge, she wouldn't be leaving, because I didn't even bother trying to pick up any girls in Umpqua City, or even down in Medford, or over in Roseburg. Instead I stocked the freezer with enough food to last Miss Miller a week or two, then drove all the way to Eugene.

"I stayed in a cheap motel, hung around the University. I fit in pretty good, sat in on a few lectures—it was summer session. Sandy Faircloth was a secretary in Human Resources. Not much of a looker, except for her hair. But that didn't bother me. I figured it would help my chances. The prettier they were, the more likely they already had a boyfriend.

"Seducing her was a snap. It's a talent I didn't even know I had until I used it. I start off pretending I'm falling in love with the girl. Then after a while, I really do. Fall in love, I mean. Even though on some level I know I really don't. Does that make any sense?"

Irene lobbed the question back to him. "Does it make sense to you?"

"I'm not sure. But it happens every time. And then they fall in love with me. The hard part is maintaining a low profile, staying away from their friends and families. One thing about a girl in love, she wants to tell the world about it. I got better at it later. I'd tell them I had a stalker, or I was with the FBI. That's another thing about a girl in love—she'll believe anything.

"With Sandy, I didn't even bother making up a story. She had a week's vacation coming to her. I told her she could come home with me, see my place, but it had to be our secret, that she had to just trust me.

"And she did—not the brightest star in the firmament, my Sandy. I brought her back here, installed her in the guest bedroom, and screwed her brains out every night for a week—me or one of the others. Miss Miller, she laid low.

"Eventually the time came for Sandy to get back to Eugene. But by then, we were hooked. Not on Sandy—on sex. I personally couldn't imagine going back to the way things had been before. I tried everything. I told her I was in love with her, that I'd kill myself if she left. I even proposed marriage. No good—she was frightened by then, and maybe not quite as head over heels as she'd been before. She said it was over—no more sex, time for Sandy to go home now.

"I didn't know what to do, how to handle it. So Max took over. She freaked on him—he smacked her around. First time for that, for him. He liked it—it turned him on. He locked her in the drying shed when he was done. From then on the die was cast. We couldn't exactly let her go, could we?"

"I see," said Irene, making a promise to God that if she survived, she would never say *I see* to a patient again.

"Long story short, we kept Sandy another few months. Everybody got to take their turns with her—even me, I'm ashamed to say. Sometimes Miss Miller would watch. Sandy didn't like *that* at all. Eventually she stopped taking care of herself, stopped talking, even stopped begging. We had to force-feed her, wash her. Sex wasn't much fun. She'd just lie there—it was like fucking a hole in the mattress. Didn't make me feel very good about myself, I can tell you. After a while I gave up on it, personally, but for Max and the others it didn't seem to matter.

"Then one night the two of them, Miss Miller and Max, were in the parlor playing chess. Max asked Miss Miller what she wanted for Christmas. Another wig, she said—Mary was starting to fade, so she wanted another long beautiful head of strawberry blond hair, just like the girl in the drying shed.

"Of course Max knew she wasn't talking about him *buying* her another wig. So on Christmas Eve Max washed Sandy's hair, and harvested it with an electric razor. On Christmas morning Miss Miller got her present, and so did Kinch."

So little remorse, even for his own actions, thought Irene. It was almost as if Christopher were trying to paint himself in the least favorable light. Perhaps he was trying to test her. If so, she was determined to pass. She opened her arms to him. He leaned forward, put his arms around her in return. They rocked together awkwardly for a moment, then he lay down with his head in her lap. She stroked his brow.

"The third one's name was Ann Marie Peterson," he began.

I can do this, Irene told herself. I can do anything I have to do.

75

PENDER NEARLY KNOCKED his Stetson off again entering the Old Umpqua Pharmacy. It felt like going back in time, to the drugstore on the corner of Clinton and Main, in Cortland, in the early fifties. Wooden floors, ceiling fan, white-jacketed pharmacist behind a high marble counter decorated with antique apothecary jars. Pender would have bet a week's salary that the old fellow was known as Doc to the townspeople. The only thing missing was the soda fountain where you could buy a cherry phosphate for a dime.

"Good afternoon," said the pharmacist. "What can I do for you?"

Pender identified himself, flashed his tin, and slid Maxwell's mug shot across the counter. "Seen this fella lately?"

"Can't say I have."

"Does the name Max ring a bell?"

" 'Fraid not."

"Christopher? Lee? Lyssy?"

"Nope, nope, and nope."

"He was in the news about ten, twelve years ago—a fire, maybe a scandal?"

"Sorry—I only moved down from Portland five years ago. Always had a dream of owning a place like this."

Pender switched from the official to the conversational mode. "So how's it working out?"

"It was working out pretty well, up until they built that Rite-Aid across town."

"Happening all over the country, from what I hear. Damn shame, too. Listen, Doc—do they call you Doc?"

"Some do."

"Well, Doc, this fella here, I know he was in here around a year ago. My witness said he disguised himself to look older—maybe he was wearing a gray wig."

"Oh, *him*."

Oh-*ho!* Two little words, and the universe undergoes a paradigm shift.

"That's Ulysses Maxwell. Caretaker for a woman named Julia Miller. They live way out on Scorned Ridge. He first came in to get her prescription for morphine ampoules refilled not long after I bought the place. Of course I couldn't do it, just give out morphine sulfate to a third party like that. It's a Schedule Two narcotic. I told him he had to get some paperwork filled out. Oh my, if looks could kill!

"But he came back the next day with all the forms. Comes in regular, now, every month or so."

"When was the last time you saw him?"

"Yesterday afternoon, around two o'clock. Picked up Miss Miller's refills and a bottle of Lady Clairol—Strawberry Blonds Forever, as I recall."

Oh-*ho*. Oh-*fucking*-ho. "Do you happen to have an address on file?"

"Sure do. Hold on, I'll find it for you."

Just as the pharmacist disappeared into the back room, the bell over the door tinkled, and an elderly woman entered. Pender tipped his hat to her. He'd never worn a cowboy hat before—he found he enjoyed tipping it to people. Especially now that he was high as a kite on adrenaline and a sense of destiny.

Because while the extraordinary run of luck Pender had been enjoying for the last three days—Anh Tranh to Big Nig to Caz Buckley to Doc to a live address—wasn't unprecedented in his experience (and long overdue when you considered he'd gone several years without a single damn break in the case), the way the pieces were falling into place, Pender was ready to believe that destiny, or fate, or God, or whatever you wanted to call it, had selected him for this particular job.

Once again he glimpsed that mental image of the strawberry blonds waiting for him in the darkness. And although thus far Ed Pender had never seen much evidence of order to the universe (an occupational hazard), much less the hand of a micromanaging God, it now occurred to him that perhaps his whole life had been leading up to this day.

76

TUESDAY MORNING'S SESSION stretched on into the early afternoon. When Maxwell suggested they take a picnic break down by the river, Irene was leery, but agreed. Her bathing suit (or rather, she now knew, Mary Malloy's, Sandy Faircloth's, Ann Marie Peterson's, Victoria Martin's, Susan Schlade's, Zizi Alain's, Gloria Whitworth's, Ellen Rubenstein's, Dolores Moon's, Tammy Brown's, or Donna Hughes's bathing suit) was still on the line from Sunday's swim. She took it up to her room to change, while Maxwell packed their lunch.

White meat chicken sandwiches with Grey Poupon, a bottle of white wine, chocolate-dipped ladyfingers for dessert. Maxwell double-wrapped the sandwiches and cookies, first in foil, then in baggies, remembered to pack napkins, plastic cups, and a corkscrew, and went down to the wine cellar to select a bottle of wine to cool in the creek while he and Irene swam.

He switched on the cellar light and trotted down the stairs, past the display of strawberry blond wigs mounted on mannequin heads in a glass-fronted case in the dark cellar to keep the color from fading. Only a few were still acceptable to Miss Miller, but they retained one from each of the gals for sentimental reasons.

The wine rack was behind the display case. He settled on a nice Ventana Chablis. It was a Monterey County wine—Irene would be bound to appreciate that. Maxwell slipped the bottle into his backpack, crossed the cellar to the fuse box, unlocked it, switched off the power to the electric fence.

And he was in a good mood as he climbed back up the cellar stairs. A little therapy, a refreshing swim, a picnic lunch, a little alfresco sex—

a lot of alfresco sex—with a woman still in the head-over-heels-with-Christopher stage: who could ask for anything more?

A bracing swim, a delicious lunch, a short nap on the mossy river-bank, one last swim. When he made his move, Irene wasn't sur-prised. She'd known it was coming—she just hadn't known when or how, or, despite all she'd told herself, whether she would be able to go through with it.

When was during that last swim. *How* was, he came paddling up to her from behind, rested both hands on her shoulders, and began kissing the nape of her neck. And at first it seemed as if she *would* be able to handle it, even after he stripped her bathing suit down to her waist and began to fondle her breasts from behind.

It's a movie, she told herself—an attempt at deliberate dissocia-tion. Her nipples were already pebbled from the cold water. He's my leading man, and it's a movie. She started to turn toward him, but he held her in place. Until then, she hadn't really appreciated how strong he was. He seized her wrist and drew her hand behind her, down to his crotch. His penis was flaccid and shrunken—from the cold, she thought at first. He wanted her to masturbate him. It was uncomfortable, reaching down and behind her like that—it hurt her shoulder. Again she tried to turn around in the water. Again he prevented her.

And then she knew. Not Christopher, but Max. Max all along. Max performing another of his devastatingly accurate impres-sions—this time of Christopher. Max whose hand she had held, Max whose eyes she had gazed into, Max whose red lips she had kissed, and worst of all, Max with whom she'd discussed his own betrayal.

I'm dead, she thought, feeling his penis harden in her hand.

Am not, replied a little voice in her head—a dissociated little voice. And following its promptings, she hooked her thumbs into the bathing suit at her waist and rolled it down the rest of the way, kicked it off, then bent forward, as if to provide him greater ease of access.

She held her breath as he positioned himself behind her with one hand, while fondling her breasts with the other.

"Give it to me, baby," she whispered, then threw her head back sharply, heard a *crack!* saw a bright light. The arm around her went slack. She threw herself forward, kicked hard at his stomach with both feet, and struck out for the opposite shore of the river.

77

BEFORE LEAVING THE PHARMACY, Pender purchased a box of one-and-a-half-by-four-inch Band-Aids and a nail scissors. Back in his room, he removed his old bandages and inspected his scalp in the bathroom mirror. Wong's salve had done its job. All three wounds had closed, no redness, no puffiness. Using the nail scissors, Pender took his own stitches out, rubbed on a little more salve, and covered the scars with three of the big Band-Aids, overlapped.

His next order of business was to write Steve McDougal a long letter on hotel stationery, detailing his movements in the last few days, and for the first time ever, putting a name—Ulysses Maxwell—to the suspect known up until then only as Casey.

Pender stuffed the letter into an envelope, sealed the envelope, scrawled McDougal's name and fax number across the front, and gave it to the desk clerk on his way out. "You have a fax machine?"

"Sure do."

"If I'm not back by tomorrow morning, I want you to open this, and fax the document inside to this number."

"You got it," said the clerk, pocketing the twenty Pender had slipped him along with the envelope.

"Open it before then, and you're looking at a federal rap."

"Wouldn't dream of it."

"Good man. Now, can you tell me how to find Charbonneau Road?"

"No, but here's somebody who can. Hey Tom," he called to someone behind Pender. "You know where Charbonneau Road is?"

"Way out in the boonies." Pender turned to see a uniformed postman coming through the hotel door. "RFD—Remote Frickin' Delivery. What you're gonna want to do, you're gonna want to get back on the highway, follow 'er east for about twenty miles. Look for a sign on your right says Horned Ridge Lodge. The lodge has been closed about ten, fifteen years, but the sign's still up, far as I know. That's your Charbonneau Road—it's one lane wide. Loops on back to the highway east of the county line. Whatcha driving?"

"Dodge Intrepid."

"You're gonna want to take 'er easy, then," the postman said. "Unless they've done some major work since I had that route, there isn't a straight nor level stretch much longer than your car from one end of Charbonneau to the other."

Tom the mailman had scarcely been exaggerating. After turning off the highway, Pender averaged ten miles an hour the rest of the way, and even that was pushing it. Consequently, it was well into the afternoon when he finally spotted the mailbox at the bottom of a blacktop driveway to the left.

He drove by slowly. Wooden fence, six rails high, padlocked gate, blacktop driveway snaking up through the trees on the other side. He couldn't see a house; couldn't even see the top of the ridge. Which meant they probably couldn't see him, either. The bad news was that he had a fence to climb, and a long, steep walk ahead of him. The good news was, he hadn't thrown away his Hush Puppies.

Once past the driveway, Pender started looking for a spot to pull over. It was another three-tenths of a mile by the odometer before he found a cleared level spot wide enough to park the Intrepid.

He pulled off to the side of the road, changed shoes, loaded a fifteen-round clip (supposedly available only to law enforcement personnel) into the SIG Sauer, and chambered a round before reholstering the weapon. (The SIG was engineered to fire with the hammer down and a round up the spout; a heavy trigger pull served as safety.)

Pender closed the trunk and started down the road, then turned back almost immediately, popped the trunk, and tossed his new hat inside. It had occurred to him that the white Stetson was not exactly camouflage wear. Of course neither was his big bald Band-Aid-striped head, he realized, but there wasn't much he could do about that now.

78

NAKED, IRENE SCRAMBLED UP the rocky slope on the far side of the swimming hole. She could hear Maxwell splashing behind her. The muddy bank was slippery, the littoral rocks slimy. As she reached for an overhanging willow branch, her feet went out from under her and she fell face forward onto the steepest part of the bank. He splashed out of the water and grabbed her by the ankle. She kicked free and scrabbled for purchase with her fingers, then scrambled the rest of the way up the bank on her hands and knees.

She reached the top of the slope, looked around wildly. All the same, every direction. Skinny white-barked trees, sunlight slanting crazily. Before she could decide which way to run, he was on top of her, his weight crushing the breath from her. She squirmed around onto her back. He inched forward until he was sitting on her chest, with his knees pinning her shoulders. His lower lip was split, but his grin, though bloody, was joyful; in his upraised hand, a jagged rock, poised to strike.

"We—we had a contract," was all she could think of to say. She was mesmerized by the blood dripping down his chin and onto his hairless chest. It occurred to her that if he leaned forward, it would be dripping directly onto her face. Somehow that bothered her more than the rock in his upraised hand.

"The fuck you talkin' about?" He blinked slowly, like a crocodile, then turned his head to the side and spat out a mouthful of blood. "*I* never signed no fuckin' contract."

It was not Max's voice. Nor Christopher, nor Useless, nor Lee, nor Alicea. But she'd heard it before. When? Where? Then it came to her. This was the alter who'd killed the highway patrolman—this was Kinch. *I'm dead.*

Are not.

Prompted again by that tiny inner voice, Irene extended her life, at least for the time being, with a simple question. "Who are you?" she called loudly. "What is your name?"

Before Kinch could answer, his eyes rolled up and to the right, his eyelids fluttered, and Max found himself back in the body. He lowered the rock, rubbed it against his thigh to ground himself, then tossed it away. Because whatever else Max may have been—certainly a Cluster B sociopath, possibly a demon born of a demon, if you believe in that sort of thing—he wasn't the type to waste a perfectly good strawberry blond by bashing her brains out before her hair had been harvested at least once. If Kinch had had his way, Max knew, there'd have been hell to pay with Miss Miller.

79

HE COULDN'T HAVE SAID whether the majestic trees keeping the sun off his pate were redwoods, pines, or firs. After all the twists and turns Charbonneau Road had taken, he didn't know whether he was on the north, south, east, or west of the ridge. All Ed Pender knew was that it was hot, and his ribs hurt where he'd scraped them hauling his lard ass over the gate down by the road, and the jeans he'd bought yesterday in Dallas were beginning to chafe.

Pender was starting to have his doubts about going after Maxwell alone, realizing he'd be lucky to have the strength to even pull a trigger by the time he'd dragged himself up the side of this damned mountain. This *got*-damned mountain, as Buckley would have said. But Pender never seriously considered turning back—at least not without having checked the place out.

Because if he did a careful reconnoiter, the Hostage Rescue Team would *have* to consult with him before going in. He'd have a chance to remind them that Maxwell had recently killed a hostage when threatened with arrest, and stress the importance of a stealth assault.

Oh yeah, stealth. . . . Pender left the blacktop for the last part of the climb, moving uphill behind the cover of the trees, stepping lightly on the dry fallen needles, looking down often to avoid snapping twigs underfoot. Sweat was running down his bald head in rivulets and stinging his eyes. He patted his scalp. The Band-Aids were gone, sluiced away. He took out the navy blue cowboy bandanna that Alvin Ralphs had thrown in for lagniappe, folded it diagonally, and tied it around his forehead.

When he came in sight of the strange sally port, and the fence with the yellow High Voltage signs, Pender's inner voice, the smart one, told him to turn back and call in the troops.

Just lemme take a peek at that lock, he told himself, crossing the blacktop at a crouch (as if that would do any good were someone watching) and hefting the gimcracky dimestore padlock securing the gate in the outer fence. What kind of idiot would spend all this money on the security fence, he wondered, reaching for his wallet, then practically invite anybody with a lock pick through the front door?

A minute later he'd sprung the lock, opened the gate, and learned the answer to his question: it was a trap. Out of the corner of his eye he saw a dark blur. The hundred-and-fifty-pound Rottweiler hit him high, knocking him off his feet, sending his wallet and wire pick flying. He tried to grab for his weapon as he went down, and landed awkwardly on his side, driving his elbow into his ribs, knocking the wind out of himself. He lay there stunned for a moment, unable to move.

Paradoxically, the temporary paralysis saved Pender's life. If he'd struggled, or tried to run, the pack would have torn him to pieces. Instead they surrounded the interloper, hackles bristling, growling deep in their throats (but not barking: Miss Miller hated the sound of barking dogs), and waited for the command from their master or mistress that would either call them off, or give them the go-ahead to attack.

And the fact that neither their master nor their mistress was around to give either command, and might not be around for hours, made no difference to the dogs. They'd wait. They'd wait for their master or mistress until hell froze over, and then they'd wait frozen. They were good dogs, you see; they were all good dogs, and they lived to please.

80

"MAX! MAX, WE HAVE a contract."

He climbed off her, breathing hard, and sat down, bare-assed and dripping, on a warm rock, in an oblong shaft of sunlight. "Therapy's over, Dr. Cogan." He spat out a mouthful of blood. "We'll just have to muddle on as best we can without you."

"Christopher," she called hopelessly. "Christopher, I need to speak with you."

Max pressed the back of his hand against his split lip until the bleeding slowed. "Don't worry about Christopher—I've promised him he'll get his turn with you if he behaves himself. Not for a few months, though—not until you're too disgusting for the poor sap to even *imagine* he's falling in love with you."

"So it's been you all along?"

"Just since this morning." He touched his lip again—still bleeding. The pain was interesting, but not overwhelming. "Let's go, Irene. I think it's time to introduce you to your new friends in the drying shed."

"You go to hell."

"I come from hell," he replied, holding his lip.

From her bedroom window, Julia Miller watched Ulysses and the new one, the psychiatrist, crossing the meadow, both of them stark staring naked. The psychiatrist was stumbling forward, her arms crossed over her breasts; Ulysses was behind her, pinching his lower lip between his thumb and forefinger with one hand and shoving her ahead of him with the other when she faltered. It looked very much as if the honeymoon was over.

It also looked as if the new one had restored her hair to its original, strawberry blond color.

Good things come to she who waits, thought Miss Miller, leaving her bedroom for the first time that day. Ulysses would be needing his clippers. She decided to bring him one of his new guns, too. The big one.

A horizontal trapdoor, flush with the ground. A descent into a dark stairwell. Another door, vertical. A glaring, diffuse white light overhead, a stifling heat. Two women, emaciated as concentration camp survivors, each with a blanket around her shoulders, standing in the center of the room, their arms around each other's waists. The smaller one's skin was stretched tightly over her cheekbones, and her lips had drawn away from her teeth—a death's head surrounded by a nimbus of red-gold stubble. The larger one had a little more flesh on her, and her hair was longer. Same color, though, except for a touch of gray at the temples.

"Harvest time," said Maxwell, shoving Irene toward them. "Clean her the fuck up."

As Max locked the inner door, the hatch slid open above him. Miss Miller started down the steps with her sewing basket over her forearm. The soundproofed hatch closed automatically above her. Ignoring his nakedness, she handed him the basket containing his battery-powered Panasonic hair clippers, along with his new Glock.

"Miss Miller, you're a wonder." Max's lower lip had stopped bleeding, but felt stiff—a crust had formed over the split. "I was just on my way up to fetch these."

"I'm not optimistic about that new one's hair," she said. "I'll try to make it work, but you know I prefer natural color. Which reminds me, Ulysses: did you notice the old one in there is turning gray?"

"I did. I was planning to take care of her tonight," Max told her. It was the truth, too. Kinch was extremely disappointed at having been deprived first of Barbara, then Bernadette, and then, most cruelly, just as he was poised to strike, of Irene. And a disappointed Kinch was an angry Kinch, an unmanageable Kinch. Maxwell understood full well that he needed to throw the bloodthirsty alter a bone. And what better bone than Donna Hughes, the once desirable Texan, now only another mouth to feed?

"Oh, how lovely." Miss Miller was genuinely pleased. And why not?—things were finally getting back to normal on Scorned Ridge after the disruption of Ulysses's protracted absence, followed by the presence of the meddling psychiatrist. "By the way, sweetheart, I was thinking of steaming some vegetables and rice for supper— how does that sound?"

"Slice up a couple of those hot sausages I bought yesterday, and you've got a deal."

"*Have* a deal," she corrected, then turned and started back up the steps.

"About tonight," Maxwell called up to her. "Did you want to watch?"

"Thank you for asking," she said, pushing the button that caused the hatch to slide open again. "I'm a little fatigued from all this excitement. Let me see how I feel after a nice long nap."

"Whatever you decide—it's up to you."

"Of course it is, my sweetness and light. Of course it is."

81

PENDER HAD BEEN A dog owner most of his life. He liked dogs. Lost the last one, a handsome shepherd named Cassidy, in the divorce—the house he didn't mind losing so much, but he was still bitter about the dog and had steadfastly refused to get another, though he understood perfectly well that he was only punishing himself.

So shooting the Rottweilers would be no cakewalk, either emotionally or physically. Pender was lying on his left side, his right hand under his jacket. Once he'd caught his breath he began drawing the SIG Sauer millimeter by agonizing millimeter, until it was free of the holster but still concealed beneath his coat—most dogs this well trained would have been taught to recognize a weapon and disarm the bearer. Slowly, though his every instinct screamed at him to do the opposite, to protect his underbelly and his manhood by curling up into a fetal ball, he rolled onto his back.

Warning behavior from the dogs—snarls, a display of incisors.

"Good dogs. Aren't you good dogs?" Pender crooned to them in his soulful tenor. Though the muzzle of the SIG pointed to the left, he'd have to begin shooting from right to left, before the dogs on the right side got to his shooting arm. The dogs to the left he figured he could fend off with his left arm until he could swing the gun around. "Calm down, now. Nice and easy. See, I'm not gonna—"

BLAM. BLAM. BLAM. He dropped the first three with head shots, and the other three turned tail and ran whimpering for the kennel. Apparently they weren't that well trained after all, thought

Pender, climbing to his feet and mentally thanking SIG Sauer for the dual-action firing mechanism. Then he smelled something burning. He looked down, saw the smoldering bullet holes riddling his new jacket: the blood-spattered fabric had been ignited by the muzzle flash.

After slapping the fire out with his bare hands, Pender raced around the sally port, hurriedly gathering up the ID, receipts, credit cards, scraps of notes, ticket stubs, and business cards that had fallen from his wallet when the dogs hit him, then looked around the sally port, trying to work out his next move.

In one direction, an unlocked gate leading to safety; in the opposite direction, a locked gate leading to Maxwell. Pender knew what the smart move was, but once again he was blinded by his secret vision of the strawberry blonds waiting in the darkness. And even if *they* were a fantasy, he told himself, Dr. Cogan wasn't. If Pender left now, what was to prevent Maxwell from executing her, then fleeing? He had cash and cunning—how many more would die before they ran him to ground?

With no time to waste, Pender had already wasted precious seconds. He ran toward the inner fence and fired a fourth round into the lock—he figured the element of surprise was pretty much lost anyway. Then he crashed through the gate shoulder first and hurriedly left the blacktop, cutting to his right, into the relative safety of the woods.

The first structure Pender came upon was a weathered shack six feet square. A pumphouse; he could hear the high thin whine of a motor and smell the water in the deep covered well.

He ducked inside and waited, listening. Nothing out there—no barking, shouting, no gunshots, no footsteps. Where the hell is Maxwell? He's not deaf—is he gone? It was tempting to rest there in the cool darkness for a few minutes; instead he closed the door behind him quietly and moved on, following the ridge.

Pender almost missed the house at first. What caught his eye was the dark triangle of the roofline glimpsed from behind through the sweeping, upturned boughs of the firs. It was a dense geometric shape floating high in the trees where everything else was airy grace and flickering light, where the only other straight lines were the soaring verticals of the tree trunks.

He began moving toward the house, walking quietly on his rubber-soled shoes, keeping to the cover of the trees, and came upon the damnedest sight. A rustic-looking wooden chair and a

slatted chaise had been placed at forty-five-degree angles to each
other, with a three-legged table in the angle between them holding
a pitcher of water, two plastic drinking glasses, an ashtray full of
unfiltered butts, and a box of pop-up lilac-colored tissues.

Despite the oddness of the setting, Pender recognized the simu-
lacrum of a psychiatrist's office. A good omen, an excellent omen:
it almost certainly meant that Dr. Cogan was alive. Or had been,
fairly recently. He picked up one of the butts—a Camel—then
tossed it back down and followed the path through the woods to
the house, a high, narrow dwelling of dark-stained, weather-
warped deal.

He entered through the back door, found himself in the
kitchen. Bread, baggies, a knife with damp traces of mayonnaise
and mustard on the counter. It looked like someone had packed a
lunch here—not long ago, either.

A picnic or outing of some kind? Was that why no one heard
the shots?

There were two doors ahead of him, the open door to the hallway and a closed door to the right of the hallway door. Again the
vision of the strawberry blonds waiting in a cellar appeared to
Pender: apparently his subconscious mind had grasped where the
closed door led before his conscious mind could reason it out.

He switched the gun to his left hand, opened the door, felt
around for the light switch, started down the open-treaded stairs.
At the bottom of the stairs he looked left—laundry room—then
turned right, rounded a corner, and came upon the glass-fronted
display case containing four shelves, each with three featureless
white mannequin heads, all but two wearing wigs of human hair.

Pender groaned softly to see his secret hope, his secret vision, so
cruelly, surrealistically parodied. Here were his strawberry
blonds—he even recognized a few. That one with the bangs on the
second shelf from the bottom, that was Gloria Whitworth, wearing
her hair the way she wore it in the photo her roommate snapped a
week before she left Reeford. This darker one on the top shelf, with
the reddish highlights, that was Donna Hughes. And there on the
bottom shelf was Sandra Faircloth—her long straight hair had
faded badly in the ten years since she'd disappeared from Eugene,
Oregon, shortly after meeting the man of her dreams.

So much for hopes and visions. In a career spent hunting serial
killers, many of them of the type known as collectors, Pender had
seen far more obscene and gruesome displays. This one was pretty

tame in comparison. Why then was he so badly shaken, he wondered? Because he had come to believe in his hopeful vision?

Let that be a lesson to you, Edgar Lee, he told himself. Now get your fat ass out of this house and back down that hill and get some real cops in here, clear-eyed, clearheaded young ones who'll shoot first and have visions later.

Then he remembered that Dr. Cogan might still be alive. He tiptoed back up the stairs, switched off the light, closed the cellar door behind him, sidled around the doorway into the hall. His steps were noiseless, Hush Puppies on hardwood, as he started up the stairs.

When he reached the second-floor landing, Pender heard someone moving in one of the rooms. He tiptoed toward the open doorway, peeked around the jamb just as a woman in a long green dress emerged from an adjoining room and crossed to the bed, her back toward Pender. Her strawberry blond hair was short and curly. Dolores Moon, he thought, taking a step forward.

Miss Miller turned; her green eyes started to widen over the mask, but the surgically repaired lids couldn't go any higher. She tried to scream—Pender closed the gap between them in two strides and clapped his hand over her mask. A disconcerting sensation—there didn't seem to be any nose under there.

"It's all right, I'm with the FBI," he whispered. "Don't make a sound. Do you understand me?"

A nod. He loosened his grip. She tried to scream again; again he closed his hand over the mask, this time covering both her mouth and the hole where her nose would have been, denying her air. She clawed at his arm, tried to kick him. He bent backward far enough to lift her off the ground and held her dangling there, legs kicking and arms flailing, chest heaving, until her body went limp. He dropped her onto the bed, turned her over.

Please let her be breathing, he thought to himself—he didn't want to have to perform mouth-to-mouth on whatever was under that surgical mask. But the green bodice rose, fell; the silk mask fluttered. And as Pender looked around for something to stuff into her mouth to prevent her from screaming again when she regained consciousness, it occurred to him that he still didn't know whether he'd rescued a victim or captured an accomplice.

82

IT'S OVER, IRENE TOLD herself. The chase, the capture, the glimpse of her own death in that frozen moment when the rock was poised in Kinch's upraised hand, then the ordeal of being half-pushed, half-dragged up the ravine and across the meadow, followed by the stumbling descent into this glaring white hell with its two damned souls, had left her beyond exhaustion, beyond hope, even beyond terror—or so she thought.

The room was ten feet high, twelve paces wide, and thirty paces long, with cement walls, a musty green indoor-outdoor carpet over the cement floor, and an elongated, opaque, thermoplastic bubble for a ceiling. Electric fans, one to suck air in and another to draw it out, were set into the walls at either end of the room, just under the ceiling.

A single tap eighteen inches above floor level in one corner supplied water for drinking and, apparently, washing hair, because lined up against the wall nearby were at least a dozen bottles of shampoo and creme rinse. No soap, just lots of shampoo. The only other amenity in the room, the privy, was a doorless four-by-four alcove, with a wood-grained plastic toilet seat mounted on a hollow platform over a deep pit.

"Over here," whispered the taller of the two women, seizing Irene by the elbow, attempting to pull her toward the tap. "Please, it's best to do as he says."

"Why?"

"To avoid unnecessary pain," the smaller woman explained patiently, taking Irene's other elbow. "He's very good at pain."

And what Irene saw in their eyes, glancing from one woman to the other as they gently tugged her toward the corner of the room, sent the terror welling up inside her again. Because what she saw was pity—for some reason too frightening even to contemplate, these two walking cadavers felt sorry for *her*.

When she understood that they meant for her to kneel naked on the steel grate set into the concrete floor under the tap, Irene balked. Even together, they weren't strong enough to force her down; as they urged her, their eyes kept glancing back to the door in the opposite corner of the room. When it opened, they stepped away from Irene.

"Kneel," called Maxwell, striding across the room naked, with the sewing basket over one arm, and gesturing to Irene with the barrel of his pistol. She knelt.

"You two, over there." He waved the gun in the direction of the door; they obeyed, but instead of crossing the room directly, they scuttled sideways around the perimeter, blankets drawn around their throats, giving him as wide a berth as possible without turning their backs on him.

"Get your head under the faucet, close your eyes."

After the fear, and the shock of the cold water, came the humiliation. Kneeling naked and powerless left Irene feeling not so much angry, or even despairing, as defeated. No more praying, no more bargaining, no more affirmations, no more scheming. She closed her eyes and let her head loll while Maxwell, his touch as sure and gentle as her own hairdresser, lifted and separated the strands of her hair, parting and sifting them with his fingers to rinse out the mud and leaves from the riverbank, the pale green clinging seeds of meadow grass.

Under the rushing water, a sort of peace came over Irene. And although the pychiatrist in her couldn't help putting a name to it—traumatic dissociation—Irene knew that what she was experiencing was beyond classifying, beyond analyzing. How presumptuous of her, she thought, to insist on dragging her patients back to reality all these years. Because in the not-here, not-now, she had somehow managed to distance herself from the pain and the unbearable fear. The once overwhelming emotions were still there, but at a remove; hers, but not her.

And not even the gentle tugging at her scalp as Max gathered her twice-washed, creme-rinsed, strawberry blond hair in one hand, or the annoying buzz of the portable clippers as he harvested it, reached Irene in the no-place to which she had retreated.

83

AFTER POPPING DOWN TO the basement to switch the power to the perimeter fence back on, Maxwell hurried upstairs to deliver the sewing basket with its precious cargo of human hair. Miss Miller's bedroom door was closed; he tapped lightly.

"Woman of the house!" John Wayne to Maureen O'Hara in *The Quiet Man*, one of their favorites.

"*Man of the house*, Miss Miller was supposed to respond. Instead, silence. He opened the door and saw she wasn't there, that the bed was barely rumpled. Max crossed the hall to his bedroom, slipped on a pair of shorts and a fresh hula shirt, and went to look for her.

But Miss Miller wasn't up by the chicken coop. Maybe the kennel—she might have gone for her minimum daily requirement of hugs. Her lovies, as she called them—how Miss Miller loved to get her lovies from her doggies. And they loved her too. Somehow they knew to be patient and gentle with her—they never roughhoused the way they did with him, but absorbed her endless caresses with wiggly-assed delight.

Max knew Miss Miller wasn't there long before he reached the kennel next to the sally port. Something was seriously amiss. None of the dogs came rushing to the fence to meet him, not even Lizzie with her waggling tail. He opened the kennel gate, saw three dogs whimpering in the shed, crossed the kennel yard, stepped into the sally port through the side door, and stared dumbfounded at a dismal sight.

His three senior dogs, Jack, Lizzie, and Dr. Cream, lay in pools of blood on the blacktop, the backs of their heads gone, blown off, exploded from the inside out. He stooped next to Lizzie's body, stroked her short, greasy coat. His hand came away covered with blood and white flecks of bone and brain matter. He wiped his palm on her tail, which would never waggle again, then lifted what was left of her head and saw that she'd been shot through the underside of her muzzle. The top of her skull had been carried away, practically atomized by the exit wound of what must have been a hollow-point round fired from extremely close range.

But what sort of monster would do such a thing, slaughter three dogs in cold blood? Although Maxwell knew that law enforcement often carried hollow-point man-stopper rounds, Black Talons, Gold Dots, that sort of thing, it didn't occur to him that this was the work of cops. Cops didn't pick a man's lock, sneak onto his property, shoot his dogs, and carry off his teacher.

For the first time since the lights of Deputy Terry Jervis's patrol car began revolving in his rearview mirror, Maxwell experienced pure, mind-numbing panic. Crowd noise, confusion.

"EVERYBODY SHUT UP!" His cry filled the sally port; the crowd noise stilled. "I'll take care of this."

Time to play detective. Max examined the lock on the outer gate: open but undamaged. He—it had to be a man: no woman would do that to a dog—had picked it, slipped inside. The dogs had ambushed him as they'd been trained to do, knocked him down and held him. He'd shot three, then blown off the other lock to get through the sally port and enter the property.

It had to have happened when Max had been down in the drying shed, which had been soundproofed, not to keep noise out but to keep it in. Freaking goddamn irony.

Anyway, Miss Miller must have surprised the intruder somehow. . . .

But that's where Max's scenario stopped making sense. If Miss Miller had surprised a burglar, where was she? Burglars didn't carry off old women. Rapists, maybe, but not even the most desperate rapist would consider Miss Miller a likely victim. Perhaps he'd killed her and hidden the body. Or—

Out of the corner of his eye, Max saw a flutter of white. He turned his head, focused in on the piece of paper caught in the dense ivy growing up the fence. It was a MasterCard receipt from—he squinted in the dim light under the sally port—the Shell station just outside Umpqua City. And the name of the purchaser was E. L. Pender.

Pender. Thick-skull motherfucker. God double fucking damn the man again. Now time was *really* of the essence: Max had to know whether Pender had snatched Miss M and gone for help, or whether they were still on the property. But he couldn't just leave the sally port open and unguarded, so he found a twenty-foot length of dog chain in the kennel, wound it around and around the outer gate, secured it to the gatepost, and locked it with a rusty old padlock, to which the key had long since disappeared. He then hurried back into the kennel, dragged out the three remaining dogs, and closed them into the sally port.

If Pender were still on the property, Max reasoned, this would be his only way out. And if the FBI man shot the remaining dogs to get through, at least Max would hear him, and could sneak up on him from behind while he struggled to unwind the chain. And then may God have mercy on his soul, because Max would have none.

And if Pender wasn't still on the property? Grab the cash and haul ass.

But Max was always one to look for a silver lining. And there was one, he told himself, locking the inner gate of the sally port behind him with the lock from the outer gate and trotting back up the blacktop toward the house with the Glock in his hand. Much as he'd miss only the third home he'd ever known, much as he'd miss Miss Miller, he could almost convince himself that in a way, this might be the best thing that could have happened.

Because without Miss Miller to pander to—and pander for—the system known collectively as Ulysses Maxwell would no longer be restricted to picking up only strawberry blonds, or forced to keep them happy while hauling them halfway across the country back to Scorned Ridge. And no more having to fuck terrorized, half-starved skeletons, either. The system would be free to—how had Jules put it in *Pulp Fiction?*—to walk the earth. To choose any girl who caught its fancy, and do with her what it wished, when it wished.

Didn't sound half bad. But first, Max had to find out whether Pender was still on the property, and he had to find out fast. How, though? Scorned Ridge was big, with dozens of places to hide. Then it came to him. He veered off the blacktop and raced through the trees, then cut across the meadow to the drying shed.

84

"CALLING DOCTOR WILL. Doctor Will to Live."

Irene, lying on her side on the damp indoor-outdoor carpet, ran her hand over her stubbly scalp, then opened her eyes to the same nightmare she'd shut them against. The emaciated imp in the army blanket was squatting in front of her, silhouetted against the white glare of the ceiling, spouting nonsense, patting Irene's hand. Irene realized with a weary sense of resignation that the comforts of traumatic withdrawal were not for her: her mind was woefully clear.

She sat up. "Which one are you?"

"I'm Dolores—that's Donna."

"Dolores Moon and Donna Hughes."

"He told you?"

"I'm his psychiatrist." Irene looked around the room, struggled to compose herself. "Was his psychiatrist. He murdered a girl down in Monterey. I was assigned to evaluate him—he broke out of jail and kidnapped me."

"And now you're just another strawberry blond," Donna pointed out. "Welcome to the drying shed."

Dolores shushed her. "Donna, don't you see—if they caught him and he broke out of jail, at least they know he exists. They're probably looking for him." She turned back to Irene. "Right?" she said hopefully.

"I'm sure they are. They don't know who he is yet—"

"Oh." A dismayed sound.

"—but they have to be closing in," Irene hurried on. "He killed a highway patrolman in northern California on Saturday morning."

"What day is it now?" asked Dolores.

"Tuesday, the thirteenth."

"What month?"

"July."

A pause. Reluctantly, Dolores asked one last question: "What year is it?"

"Nineteen ninety-nine."

In the silence of the drying shed, the echoes of both question and answer lingered for all three women. Dolores realized that she was well into her third year of captivity—one way or the other, she knew it would be her last. Donna understood that the first anniversary of her disappearance had come and gone. She wondered if they were still looking for her. Or if anybody missed her, for that matter. Not Horton, that was for sure. Nor that treacherous, husband-stealing Edwina Comb, either.

As for Irene, she was struggling to hold on to the last shreds of her composure. At no time during his interminable recitation of atrocities this morning had Maxwell hinted that any of his victims was still alive, much less only a few hundred yards away, underground. What *year* is it? Oh dear Jesus, what *year* is it?

Dolores broke the silence. "Have you had anything to eat today? We have a little grub left."

"No, I'm fine," Irene replied. "We had a picnic down by the creek. Wine. Ladyfingers."

"Christopher took me down by the creek when I first got here," mused Donna. "Fed me and fucked me silly. I was so happy. At long last, I thought—at long last I'd found true love. Next day I met Max."

"Then you know about the DID?" Irene was mildly surprised—Maxwell could have hidden it from them if he'd cared to.

"Dee eye what?"

"DID. Dissociative identity disorder. They used to call it multiple personality."

"Oh, that," said Donna. "Sure. Didn't know they changed the name. Didn't know it had a name—we just figured he's nutty as a fruitcake."

"Well, there's that, too," said Irene. Then she surprised herself—she actually giggled. It was either a sign of returning mental health or incipient hysteria. She was trying to decide which when the door burst open.

85

"PENDER!" MAXWELL'S VOICE, FROM somewhere in the direction of the house. "PENDER!"

Miss Miller, her hands and feet bound with towels from her bathroom and a sock stuffed into her mouth under the surgical mask, kicked ineffectually at the boards of the loft. Pender had tried to talk with her a few times, but she didn't seem to want to do anything but scream, so for now he ignored her—and Maxwell—and kept working. He was stacking books at the edge of the hayloft, which smelled of dust and vomit, until he had built himself a barricade two feet high, three feet thick, along the edge of the loft. From behind it he had a clear view of the barn door, and a clearer shot at Maxwell than Maxwell had at him.

It wouldn't be an easy shot, though. The range from the edge of the loft to the door was close to sixty feet, and he'd have to figure in the downward trajectory. He'd also have to try for the kill grid: there was no guarantee that a nine-millimeter round, even a hollow-point, would knock a man down from that distance.

But at least his target would be backlighted in the doorway. And even if Maxwell did manage to squeeze off a round, Pender figured he'd be safe enough ducking behind three feet of books. Unless of course Maxwell was packing something in the nature of a .357.

Hurriedly Pender added one more layer to the barricade—a leather-bound set of the complete works of Joyce, Kalat's *Biological Psychology,* Barlow and Durand's *Abnormal Psychology,* and twelve volumes of the *Handyman's Encyclopedia*—then settled down for a long wait.

If Maxwell entered the barn before nightfall, Pender would have the drop on him. If he didn't, Pender could go back on the offensive under cover of darkness while Maxwell was out looking for him. And if they didn't find each other before morning, Pender would return here and wait for the Hostage Rescue Team that McDougal would undoubtedly be dispatching as soon as Pender's fax reached him.

However it worked out, Pender liked his chances—until he heard a woman's voice calling him from the same general direction.

"AGENT PENDER? THIS IS IRENE COGAN. MAX SAYS HE'S GOING TO KILL ME IF YOU DON'T SHOW YOURSELF."

Pender didn't want to believe it. Surely Maxwell understood that a dead hostage is no hostage at all. He decided to wait it out.

"PENDER!" Maxwell. "LOOKS LIKE I UNDERESTIMATED YOU—AGAIN. OBVIOUSLY I'M NOT GOING TO KILL MY HOSTAGE."

Obviously, thought Pender.

"WHAT I'M GOING TO DO NOW, I'M GOING TO BURN HER WITH A CIGARETTE LIGHTER UNTIL YOU SHOW YOURSELF."

Oh fuck. Pender could feel the sweat breaking out on his forehead again. *Things don't get any easier, do they?*

He took off his bandanna and wrung it out, then tied it around his forehead again. Another question presented itself: was Dr. Cogan still a legitimate hostage, or was she now acting as an accomplice? She'd been Maxwell's prisoner for over a week, more than enough time for the Stockholm syndrome to have taken effect. Especially with such a charming seducer as Maxwell—most if not all of the missing strawberry blonds were believed to have gone off with Casey voluntarily, at least initially.

Pender now faced perhaps the most difficult decision of his career. He decided to wait it out a little longer, see if he could gauge whether Dr. Cogan was really being tortured by the tenor of her screams.

Sure enough, the first one was more of a yell—a full-voiced shout, with plenty of lung power. But Pender knew he had to discount it. Maxwell might have merely threatened her into screaming the first time—that was what Pender would have done in Maxwell's situation.

But after the second scream—it rose and fell and rose again and bubbled in her throat, ending in a heartfelt "OH GOD, OH GOD, STOP, PLEASE STOP, PLEASE MAKE HIM STOP!"—there was little doubt left in Pender's mind. Some anguish and shame, but little doubt.

"LEAVE HER ALONE! I'M IN THE BARN!"

"I THOUGHT YOU MIGHT BE!" shouted Maxwell.

"The hell you did," Pender muttered.

"WHERE'S MISS MILLER? IF YOU'VE HURT HER, I'LL MAKE YOU PAY."

Oh-ho. "SHE'S SAFE FOR THE MOMENT—BUT SHE'S SCARED, AND SHE MISSES YOU. GIVE YOURSELF UP."

"NICE TO KNOW YOU HAVE A SENSE OF HUMOR, PENDER."

"I try to keep myself amused." Pender settled in behind his barricade of books, steadying the barrel of his pistol on a copy of *Finnegans Wake* and sighting in where the two sliding barn doors met, at a point approximately three and half feet from the concrete floor.

"I'm sorry I had to do that, Irene," said Max as he marched her down the blacktop to the barn. "He left me with no choice."

Irene could no more have replied at that point than she could have flown. For the first time she understood the use of the word "insult" as a medical term meaning a bodily injury, irritation, or trauma. There was no other word to describe how it had felt to have Maxwell snatch her out of the drying shed, drag her naked across the meadow and up to the chicken coop—a more or less centralized location—then bend her wrist behind her back and hold his Bic lighter to her forearm for an agonizing eternity, until her scream finally met Agent Pender's standard for sincerity. At that moment she had hated both of them, Maxwell and Pender, with equal intensity.

When they reached the barn, Maxwell forced Irene to pry open the sliding doors just wide enough to admit them, and remained crouched behind her as she entered. The barn faced to the west; the late-afternoon sun behind them cast the elongated black shadow of a four-legged woman across the dusty cement floor.

Irene looked up to the hayloft at the other end of the barn, saw the barricade of books, saw the black of the gun muzzle pointing at her, saw the top third of Pender's massive bald head above and behind it, a blue bandanna knotted around the forehead. It wasn't how she'd pictured him at all.

Maxwell saw the head too, raised his pistol, and fired a shot at it over Irene's head. The report was deafening. Instinctively she threw herself forward onto the cement floor. Maxwell was unprotected for a moment, but Pender had already ducked behind his barricade. By the time Pender raised his head again Maxwell had seized Irene by the elbow, dragged her over to the side of the barn, behind the passenger side of the blue Cadillac, then fired another shot up at the hayloft.

Pender fired a round over the de Ville. He now had ten left—one in the chamber and nine in the clip. He had no idea how many rounds Maxwell had—or how many weapons.

"Are you going to come down here, or do I have to burn her again?" called Maxwell.

Irene, lying on her bare back on the rough concrete floor, ears ringing, stared up into the rafters. That hopeless, defeated feeling came over her again. If Pender came down, Maxwell would kill them both. If Pender didn't . . .

But she couldn't let herself think about that. Because she knew that given the choice, she would choose death over burning—she just couldn't face the pain again.

86

"HURTING HER ISN'T GOING to do you any good, Maxwell," Pender called from behind the barricade. "I'm soft-hearted, but I'm not suicidal. And don't forget I have Miss Miller."

"I guess we're going to be here for a while, then."

"Not that long."

"What do you mean?"

"How far have you thought this thing out?"

"Far enough." Max's provisional plan was to wait for dark, creep up to the foot of the ladder, use his talent for imitation to impersonate Irene. *Agent Pender, it's me, Dr. Cogan. I'm coming up.* Max would have the element of surprise on his side—he'd be content to take his chances with the older, slower, fatter FBI man.

When that was over, Max told himself, he'd have to make a run for it. If Pender had managed to find him, the rest of the FBI couldn't be far behind.

So yes, Maxwell had thought this thing out far enough. "Why do you ask?"

"Just wondering how you plan to deal with the Hostage Rescue Team that'll be coming in in about an hour. That's how much of a head start they gave me."

Max felt a leaden weight in his gut, and the murmuring began in his head again. *Everybody shut up,* he commanded. *I have to think.* What Pender said had rung true and fit the known facts. FBI agents never worked alone. Of course the cavalry was on the way. Why else would Pender be content to hole up in the loft?

"Pender?"

"Still here."

"Assuming you're not full of shit, why are telling me this?"

"Because I'm prepared to offer you a deal. Once the HRT arrives, it'll be too late, it'll be out of my hands. You'll kill Dr. Cogan, they'll kill you. I don't care about you, but it's my job to see that no harm comes to her. So here's the deal: if you leave Dr. Cogan behind unharmed, I'll let you walk out of here. You can take Miss Miller, or leave her behind—that'd be entirely up to you."

"How's this supposed to work, exactly?"

"Simple as pie. You walk out that door behind you. You'll have a head start—that's about as much as I can promise you."

"How do I know you won't shoot me in the back on my way out?"

"Because I'm an FBI agent, not a hit man."

"Tell that to Randy Weaver, and all those poor crispy critters in Waco."

"My point exactly—that's what happens when you get the ninjas involved. All that armor, all those guns and flash grenades and dogs, all that testosterone and confusion. Hell, *I* might even get killed, and that's *definitely* not part of my game plan."

"That still doesn't answer my first question. Why should I trust you not to shoot me in the back?"

"Because given the current climate"—Waco was heating up again, with the discovery that the FBI had lied about using incendiary grenades—"the good old days of shooting perps in the back are behind us. And if you leave Miss Miller behind, which you'll probably want to do anyway, seeing as how she doesn't seem to be in traveling condition, she'd be a witness. She's up here, she can hear me."

"Let me speak to her."

"Not convenient at the moment. I'm not moving from this spot."

"What's to stop me from using Dr. Cogan as a shield, leaving the same way I came in?"

"Hey, go for it, fella. You think you can get far enough in an hour, on foot, carrying a grown woman, while I'm potshotting you, then by all means go for it. If not, here's the deal. As long as you leave Dr. Cogan behind unharmed, you can walk out of here anytime before it gets dark. After that all bets are off."

"I'm not sure. I need to think."

"Just don't think too long," called Pender. "I figure we have about an hour until sunset."

* * *

An hour, thought Maxwell. Not much time—for the dull normals. For a next-generation multiple, it was more than enough. He already knew what he was going to do. The old reliable had been working for him since Juvie, and he'd already beaten Pender with it once. No reason he wouldn't fall for it again.

Still, a little more darkness wouldn't hurt. Not too much, though—Maxwell needed enough light to shoot by.

"Pender!"

Pender glanced at his watch. Half an hour had passed. The light was fading inside the barn. "What?"

"No deal—I still don't trust you. But I'll make you a counter-offer."

"I'm listening." Pender's stomach growled. He remembered for the first time that he hadn't eaten since breakfast. Odd he hadn't noticed it before—he was not a man accustomed to missing meals.

"You and me, *mano a mano*. Gunfight at the OK Corral."

"How's that going to work?"

"You come down here, we count down from ten and draw."

Oh-ho, thought Pender. Years ago, before the Reeford disgrace, he was sometimes called upon to give a lecture at the FBI Academy in Quantico, "The Art of Affective Interrogation," in which he stressed to the recruits that often the key to cracking a case was not what you knew, or what you didn't know, but what you knew that the other fellow didn't know you knew.

Still, it wouldn't do to give in too easily. "How do I know you're not going to shoot me on my way down?"

"We both stand up at the same time with our guns at our sides, pointing down. Either of us makes a move prematurely, the other one'll see it."

"But I'll be at a disadvantage, climbing down a ladder one-handed." Pender pretended to mull it over for another moment. "Tell you what, you hold your gun behind your back until I'm on the ground. Deal?"

"Done," said Maxwell.

Done, thought Pender.

Irene didn't know what to think, except that it would be over soon, one way or the other, and that the chances of her survival had increased from zero to fifty percent. Not a set of odds she'd have thought much of a week ago—apparently it was all a matter of where you were coming from. Like everything else in life.

"Dr. Cogan?" called Pender.

"Yes?"

"Would you count to three, slowly?"

"Now?"

"Yes, now."

Irene looked at Maxwell. He nodded.

"One. Two. Three."

On three Maxwell stood up, the pistol in his left hand, behind his back. Irene climbed unsteadily to her feet, peered over Maybelline's roof, but at a crouch, to keep the car between Pender and her nakedness, and saw the FBI man standing in the hayloft with his gun at his side. Slowly, he began to move toward the ladder.

Irene watched Maxwell's hand—if it began to move, she was prepared to shout a warning, maybe even try to grab it. Pender started down the ladder, hanging on with his left hand, gun in his right, toes feeling for the rungs, head turned at a painful angle so he could keep his eyes on Maxwell.

"So far, so good," called Maxwell, slowly bringing his hand out from behind his back when Pender reached the ground. Then, without taking his eyes off Pender: "Irene, would you count down from ten to one—same cadence you just used."

"Wait," said Pender calmly. "I just want to be clear on this—do we draw *at* one or after?"

"What's your preference?" asked Maxwell, just as calmly.

"Could be problematical either way. How about three, two, one, *go,* and we draw on the go."

"Okay by me. Got that, Irene?"

"Got it."

"Then let's git it on," said Maxwell, in a high, pinched voice. Irene didn't recognize it, but knew it was one of his impressions.

He does that when he's nervous, she remembered. *He was nervous that first day with me.*

"Ten," she said, loudly and clearly, hearing her voice echo around the barn.

Pender was still trying to decide what number to go on when she started her count. He'd thought about it all the way down the ladder. Going before the count began would have been risky—Maxwell was watching him too closely. But Maxwell had implicit faith in Buckley's trick. Once the countdown began, he'd start to relax, he'd be in familiar territory.

"Nine."

Too soon.

"Eight."

Not yet—nerves of steel.

"Seven."

Pender cocked his wrist and fired from the hip. Seven sounded just about right to him.

87

THE HOLLOW-POINT CAUGHT Maxwell high in the left shoulder and spun him sideways. His balance and reflexes were superb. He kept his feet and even managed to squeeze off a round of his own that ricocheted off the cement floor and sent chips flying from one of the stanchions separating the stalls.

Pender managed to get off a second shot within the space of a heartbeat, but yanked it high. A rookie mistake—second shots tend to pull high due to bad initial positioning caused by the upward kick of the gun on the first shot.

You know better than that, Pender told himself. Everything but his mind was moving in slow motion. He found he had all the time in the world. Still he overcompensated downward on the third shot. The bullet smashed through Maxwell's knee as he struggled to switch the heavy Glock from his useless left hand to his right. The gun went flying, but somehow Maxwell managed to hop halfway out the barn door before falling, despite the fact that his right knee had all but disappeared in a spray of fine red mist.

Maxwell lay on his back, half in and half out of the barn, staring up at a rosy sunset sky. Pender approached him cautiously, holding the SIG out in front of him, his finger half-tightened on the trigger. When he reached Maxwell, Pender saw that he was still conscious, and that neither of the wounds was necessarily fatal. What a goddamn shame. He knelt at Maxwell's side, placed the muzzle of the SIG against Maxwell's forehead so that Maxwell could see it and feel it.

"Caz Buckley sends his regards," Pender said softly. "By the way, he said to tell you he never really liked you."

*   *   *

When the shooting began—she hadn't seen who started it—Irene had dropped to the floor and crawled under Maybelline. She was astonished at how calm she was. A week ago, she knew, she would have been either hysterical or catatonic. Instead, she waited for the gunfire to end, and didn't crawl out until she saw Pender's Hush Puppies crossing her line of vision.

She stood up, saw Pender kneeling in the doorway at Maxwell's left side, holding the gun to Maxwell's forehead. "No!" she cried. "What are you doing?"

"Just securing the prisoner," he replied, hurriedly beginning to pat down the waistband and pockets of Maxwell's shorts with his free hand, searching him for another weapon while trying to avoid the blood spurting from the damaged knee. At that point Pender himself wasn't entirely sure whether he had intended to fire a third round into Maxwell's brain from point-blank range. Probably not: though he was pretty worked up, he hadn't forgotten that powder burns on Maxwell and blowback on himself would have been a dead giveaway.

Irene approached them with a certain amount of dread, but when she saw Maxwell's wounds, her medical training kicked in.

"Here, give me your bandanna." She knelt beside Pender and pressed her thumb against Maxwell's spurting femoral artery.

He glanced over at her, did a double take, though he had to have noticed that she was naked before then, then hurriedly stripped off his torn, sweaty, bullet-riddled, blood-spattered, scorched, three-hundred-dollar jacket and draped it around her shoulders. It hung to the floor.

"Your bandanna," she said again.

"What for?"

"I have to make a tourniquet."

"What for?"

"To stop the bleeding."

"Oh—right." Reluctantly, almost resentfully, Pender stripped off his bandanna and handed it to Irene. For a disconnected moment, Pender couldn't imagine why she'd have wanted to save Maxwell's life. But of course they had to keep him alive. How else would they learn the fate of all those strawberry blonds? Unless . . .

"Dr. Cogan, while the two of you were together, did he tell you about any of the other strawberry blonds?"

"He told me about all of them."

"Names and everything?"

"Names and everything. I have them in my notebook. Hold your thumb here." She had him press against the artery while she tied the knot. Only after the bleeding had stopped did she slip her arms through the sleeves of Pender's jacket and button it around her.

"How many?"

"Twelve altogether," replied Irene.

"Counting Wisniewski?"

"Counting Wisniewski." Irene stepped across Maxwell's supine body and knelt to examine his shoulder wound. It didn't look bad. But as she tore a strip of rayon from the bloody hula shirt and pressed it into the bullet hole, she remembered from her emergency medicine rotation in Palo Alto that the exit wounds were always worse. She had Pender lift Maxwell up so she could examine his back. There was no exit wound: that first bullet was still inside him somewhere.

Max groaned as they lowered him back down—his extraordinary mind was still clicking away, though he could feel his will ebbing, floating off into the peaceful, rose-pink sky.

"Take it easy," said Irene, as they lowered him back down. "It's okay—just relax now." A blond lock had fallen across Maxwell's forehead and into his eye; she brushed it back gently with her fingers. "We have to get him to a hospital," she told Pender.

"You sure you want to do that?" he whispered. "Keep him alive, take a chance on him getting free some day?"

She stared at him blankly.

Still whispering: "Do you know how you were going to die? Number thirteen?"

"What—" She started to ask him what difference it would make, but something in his expression stopped her. "No, I don't."

Pender's eyes filled with sorrow for what he was about to do. Over the years, he had made a habit, almost a religion, of keeping the horrors he had seen to himself, at least where civilians, including his then-wife, were concerned. It helped cost him his marriage. But most people couldn't live in the world Pender inhabited. And now he had to take poor Dr. Cogan, who looked like a forlorn waif in his enormous, bedraggled jacket, with her hair all cropped to stubble, and drag her through it. Rub her nose in it.

"To start with, he would have raped you, repeatedly, in every conceivable orifice and every conceivable position. He would have tied you, posed you, costumed you, beat you, tortured you, penetrated you, and inserted foreign objects into you, over and over and over, in a growing frenzy that would have ended only in your death. If you were one of the lucky ones, you'd have lost consciousness early on—not that that would have stopped him until he was ready to stop—or died accidentally, from a skull fracture, say, or internal bleeding, or asphyxiation."

If that's lucky, thought Irene, I don't want to know about unlucky. But she made no attempt to stop him. She liked having him this close—he was shelter, he was safety. She knew that nothing he was telling her should have made any difference to her Hippocratic oath. She also knew she had to hear him out.

"But if you were unfortunate enough to be born with a strong constitution, or a fierce desire to live, it would have ended with a knife."

Pender's mind drifted back to the bedroom of the little ranch house in Prunedale. *Harriet Weldon pulls back the sheet that Maxwell had drawn up to the dead women's waists. One of the investigators gasps, another moans. The photographer snaps a flash picture; the sudden glaring whiteness sears the image into Pender's memory. How many knife blows would it take to obliterate a woman's private parts, reduce them to this unrecognizable state, he wonders. A hundred? A thousand?*

"Agent Pender?"

Pender was vaguely startled to find himself standing over Maxwell's body. "Sorry. Drifting. Must be more beat than I thought. Where was I?"

"A knife?"

"Oh, yes. A knife. A good strong butcher knife—sturdy enough to survive being driven through bone—pelvic bone—again, and again, and again, until there's nothing but a bloody—"

"No more. Please." Irene's head was spinning. She was afraid for a moment that she was about to pitch forward across Maxwell's body. Pender slipped his arm around her.

"Kinch," she said as he eased her back into a sitting position a few feet from the body.

"What?"

"Kinch—that's the name of the alter who carves the women up."

"Then you'll let me do it?"

"Do what?"

"Loosen the tourniquet."

Irene thought about it. She thought about it longer and harder than she'd ever care to admit, even to herself. In the end it wasn't her Hippocratic oath that swung the balance, it was the fact that in more than ten years of specializing in dissociative disorders, Irene had never heard of, much less treated, a multiple even remotely like Maxwell. He was sui generis. The chance to study him, to learn from him, might in the long run lead to breakthroughs in the treatment and understanding of DID that could benefit victims like Lily DeVries. Against that, her own fear, and a vaguely defined urge for revenge, didn't measure up. She shook her head no.

Pender climbed wearily to his feet. "Is there a telephone back at the house? My cell phone doesn't work out here."

"Not that I know of."

"I'm going to hotwire one of these vehicles then. Will you be all right here if I go for help, or do you want to come with me?"

"No, I think I should stay with Donna and Dolores."

It didn't register for a moment—then, for the second time that day, Pender's universe underwent a paradigm shift. "Say again?"

"Donna and Dolores—I should stay with them until the ambulance comes."

"Donna Hughes and Dolores Moon? They're alive?"

"You didn't know?"

No, Pender started to say. Then he realized that he had—that somehow or other he'd known all along. He just hadn't always believed it.

88

HUDDLED BY THE VENTILATION shaft next to the faucet after Maxwell dragged the psychiatrist out of the drying shed, Donna and Dolores held hands. An eternity passed.

"It'll be over soon," said Dolores.

"One way or the other," Donna replied.

It was the very phrase that had been going through Dolores's mind, though she'd chosen not to voice it. "Know what I keep thinking about?" she asked Donna.

Again their thoughts were in synch. "Tammy?" After going five days without a meal during the last week of Max's absence, Tammy Brown had drowned herself under the cold-water tap while the other two slept. It couldn't have been an easy thing to do. They'd found her lying on her back on the grate the next morning, her body cold, her skin slick and pebbly as a dolphin's, her parted lips blue. And after Donna shut off the faucet, they saw that Tammy's open mouth was full to the brim with clear dark water, like a fathomless lake about to overflow its thin blue banks.

"If she'd only held on a little bit longer." Maxwell had arrived that very night, dumped her body into the privy, and shoveled a bucket of lime over it.

Another eternity passed. It was nearly dark—then it was dark. They'd left off holding hands. Dolores had her back to the wall, facing the door. They heard the outer hatch sliding open. The eternity that passed between the opening of the outer hatch and the inner door, though it contained only footsteps and the tinkling of keys, was the longest eternity of all. Dolores felt her heart pounding at her ribs and thought it was about to burst.

Then the door opened and a huge blood-spattered bald man stood there holding a battery-powered lantern. Beside him, the psychiatrist had her arms full of clothes.

The alter or entity known as Max had never been entirely sure about his own nature, or origins. The fact that the other alters looked upon him as some sort of demon was of course convenient, and had helped him wrest dominance over the system from Useless and Christopher. But for himself, the possibility that he might be an incarnation of Carnivean was only conjecture based upon the circumstances of his first appearance, the perverse delight he'd always taken in activities that others saw as shameful or evil, and the system's undeniably superior level of functioning, compared not only to other multiples but to the human race in general.

It might be coincidence, it might be random mutation, but the possibility that an evolutionary leap such as he represented might also be the result of demonic possession could never be entirely discounted.

So as he found himself slipping into the darkness, once again Max managed to convince himself that it wasn't all bad. At least he didn't have to worry about hell. If it existed, he told himself, he was on the board of directors; if not, oblivion, and an end to the agonizing pain he now found himself in. And in either event, the riddle of his origins would be solved soon enough.

But no sooner had Max arrived at this state of inner peace than it was shattered by the sound of Miss Miller's voice. She had somehow managed to hump her way across the loft on her uninjured back, though her arms and legs were still securely—and painfully—bound, then work the gag out of her mouth.

"Ulysses?" she called.

Max opened his eyes, saw that night had fallen. What a sky, what a sky! "Down here. He shot me."

"I heard."

"I think I'm dying."

"Oh, you think you're dying every time you stub your toe. Remember when you were twelve and you had the flu? I've pulled you through worse scrapes than this, young man. Now get up here and untie me."

"You're safe now," Irene said soothingly, though she had to wonder whether any of them, including herself, could ever feel truly safe again. At the moment, she understood, they were all suffering from acute stress disorder, a precursor of post-traumatic stress disorder that included all the PTSD symptoms, plus severe dissociative symptoms like selective amnesia, affective numbing, and derealization. But Irene shrugged off her own problems—not only was she the least affected of the three, she was a psychiatrist, for crying out loud. "It's over—you're free. He can't hurt you anymore."

She kept repeating variations on that theme as she helped Donna Hughes to her feet, helped her get her arms through the sleeves of an orange blouse, steadied her while she stepped into a pair of shorts, helped her up the steps and out into the moonlit meadow. A moment later Pender emerged from the hatch with Dolores Moon in his arms, still clutching her blanket around her, unwilling to give it up though Irene had brought her a selection of what appeared to be her own clothes, judging by the sizes.

Irene herself had changed back into the cranberry cardigan, short-sleeved blouse, and white ducks she'd worn—was it only that morning? Time had ceased to have much meaning—she recognized that as a dissociative symptom.

Pender eased little Dolores onto her feet and put his arm around her to steady her. She leaned against him, and with his help turned a full hundred and eighty degrees, turning her back to the two-horned peak to the west, facing the house at the edge of the meadow, and behind it, the full moon rising over the forested ridge.

"Isn't that something?" she said.

Pender looked down at her, then up at the moon. Next to him, Irene and Donna were supporting each other, their arms around each other's waists.

"It sure is," he agreed. He might have been suffering from a touch of acute stress disorder himself—he couldn't access his emotions, they were too big and too deep. It was as if he'd never seen that full moon before, as if he'd landed on a planet with a whole different sky.

A lesser man, a singular man, would never even have made it into the barn, much less dragged himself all the way to the foot of the loft essentially one-armed and one-legged, and nearly bled out. It required the cooperation of all the alters except Lyssy, and the autistic Mose. Each of them took a turn, then slipped back into the darkness. In the end only blind Peter was left to drag the body the last few feet.

"Where's the ladder?" he called—up until then he'd known only the terrain of Miss Miller's bedroom. "I can't see."

What was the matter with the boy? thought Miss Miller, vexed again. The barn was certainly light enough, with the moonlight pouring in through the open hayloft shutters. Still on her back, she wedged her shoulders against the barricade of books Pender had erected and began shoving against them, trying to get to the edge of the loft to guide him to the ladder.

A paperback volume struck Peter on the back of his head. Stunned and confused, he tried to shield himself from the shower of books with his good arm as he crawled under the overhang of the loft to safety.

"Are you all right?" she called, hearing him grunt in pain. No answer. Worried that she'd accidentally harmed him, she braced her back and shoulders against the barricade again, drew her legs up, heels against thighs, and pushed backward with all her might.

Pender's original plan was to get the women settled at the house, find the keys to, or hotwire, the Cherokee, shoot the remaining dogs if they gave him any trouble, drive toward town until his cell phone kicked in, then drive back up to Scorned Ridge and await the ambulances or medevac choppers and the Evidence Response Team. There would be no further need for a Hostage Rescue Team, though knowing the bureau, Pender thought they would probably dispatch one anyway, with a video team, just for the image-positive footage.

But the original plan hadn't accounted for the possibility that neither of the two original hostages would allow him out of her sight. To them, Dr. Cogan didn't count—she was just another in a parade of strawberry blonds. So, exhausted though he was, he carried the little Moon woman up the blacktop toward the barn in his arms, while Donna and Irene followed behind, their arms still around each other's waists.

As she hiked behind Pender, sometimes supporting Donna, sometimes being supported by her, Irene couldn't shake the dreamlike feeling that when they got to the barn, Maxwell's body would be gone. It was such an overwhelmingly strange sensation, and made such an impression on her psyche, that when Pender reached the hump in the ridge first, muttered an obscenity, set

Dolores on her feet, drew his gun, called to the women to wait for him there, then set off at a trot down the slope to the barn, Irene knew in advance what she'd see when she reached the hump in the ridge herself.

Or rather, what she wouldn't see: Maxwell's body was no longer lying in the doorway where they'd left it, apparently unconscious, only fifteen or twenty minutes earlier. Where it had been, she saw only a pool of blood, black in the moonlight, and Pender slipping sideways into the barn, holding his gun at his chest.

Seconds later he emerged waving, and called to Irene, beckoning her down the hill. She hurried down the sloping blacktop, Donna in her orange blouse and shorts and Dolores in her blanket following behind, now supporting each other.

Pender was waiting with the lantern at the foot of the loft. Miss Miller lay atop a pile of books, her head twisted at an impossible angle. Irene kicked away a leather-bound copy of *Dubliners,* and several volumes of the *Handyman's Encyclopedia,* and knelt at her side. She lifted Miss Miller's scarred wrist and felt for a pulse, then looked up at Pender and shook her head.

He nodded, then raised the lantern higher to cast its light on Maxwell, lying on his back in the darkest corner of the barn, under the loft.

She hurried over to him, examined the tourniquet, tightened it one more notch.

"Mommy," he whimpered, reaching up to stroke her cheek.

She started to ask him his name, then thought better of it. The childish voice, the relaxed jaw, the oval face, the wide eyes, told her all she needed to know.

"Hello, Lyssy," she said softly.

"Mommy, it hurts." He looked past her toward Pender, standing above them, holding the lantern. "That man hurted me."

"He didn't mean to," said Irene. "He won't hurt you anymore."

"You promise? Cross your heart and hope to die?"

"Cross my heart and hope to die."

89

THE BU-CHOPPER CAME wheeling over Horned Ridge at first light, and touched down in the meadow on Scorned Ridge, discharging an Evidence Response Team complete with cadaversniffing dogs. Pender was waiting for them. He could tell by the way even the ASAC from Portland listened carefully to his every suggestion that all had been forgiven. E. L. Pender had been transformed from outcast to hero agent literally overnight.

Pender understood the responsibilities that came with the new designation: he made sure to wear a blue windbreaker with FBI in yellow letters a foot high to the press conference later that morning and to thank, with a straight face, both the Umpqua and Monterey County sheriff's departments for their cooperation.

Pender also understood that in addition to the responsibilities that came with being a hero agent, there were also perks. Everybody wanted a piece of Dr. Cogan—the FBI, the CHP, three sheriff's departments, and the rapidly assembling news media—but after the press conference, he used his newfound clout to protect her, insisting on interviewing her personally, in her hospital room.

He did decide, however, to leave it to some other poor bastard to inform the families of the victims. That, and the rest of the postinvestigation, would not be his problem—he would be heading back to FBI headquarters, where he would hand over his badge to McDougal and retire as a hero, with a full pension. He would also be handing over his gun. The uglier the Waco investigation got, the more the FBI was determined to play up this lonely public success: the director wanted Pender's SIG Sauer P226 on display in the FBI museum.

As for Pender's subsequent plans, they included sucking up his pension, possibly getting a consultant job with a private security outfit (another perk of being a hero agent), and definitely working on whittling down his handicap into the respectable teens.

First, though, Pender had one more piece of business to take care of in Umpqua City.

He could feel the effects of yesterday's exertions in his thighs as he trudged up the hospice stairs and rang the doorbell. The same dignified, gray-haired nurse who'd admitted him yesterday opened the door. She greeted him with a raised eyebrow. Everybody in the state of Oregon knew who he was by now.

"You should have told me you were FBI," she said accusingly.

"Would you have let me see Caz?"

"Hell, no," she said, on a rising inflection.

"Then more people would have died. Listen, I promised Caz I'd stop by and tell him how it came out. Is he awake?"

She lowered her eyes, shook her head.

Pender understood immediately. "I'm so sorry."

When the nurse looked up, there were tears swimming in her eyes. Pender would have thought you'd get used to death, working in a hospice—but maybe you only got used to crying.

"A few hours ago," she said. "I just finished getting him ready. Would you like to see him?"

"I'd rather remember him the way he was," said Pender. Bullshit, of course—after discovering Tammy Brown's partially decomposed body in the privy shortly after dawn, along with several other skeletons, Pender felt he had seen his quota of dead bodies for the month. Year. Millenium. "I hope my visit didn't do him any harm."

"The contrary," said the nurse. "I've never seen him so peaceful as after you left. He wouldn't tell me what the two of you talked about, but whatever it was, it helped him let go. Around here, that's a good thing."

"I'm glad," said Pender, tipping his hat. It was indeed a good hat for tipping. "You take care."

"I do," she said. "That's my job."

He thought about that on his way down the steps. "Mine too," he said to himself. "At least it used to be."

Back at Umpqua General, Pender found the media feeding frenzy in full swing. News vans took up half the hospital parking lot.

Microwave uplink dishes sprouted on the hospital lawn. Reporters were besieging the receptionist at the desk, while a video crew was interviewing the candy striper who'd brought Donna and Dolores their breakfasts.

Pender nodded to the sheriff's deputy outside Irene's door. She was at the window, dressed in surgical greens, peering through the curtains at the activity in the parking lot below. Pender handed her an FBI windbreaker and a navy blue FBI cap.

"You sure you're up for this? You want to rest a little longer, just give me the word."

"No, I want to get it over with," she replied, tugging the cap over her shorn head. "I can't stand the thought of her lying up there alone."

Pender snuck Irene out the way he'd come in, through the hospital kitchen. One enterprising freelancer intercepted them and attempted to thrust a microphone in Irene's face as she climbed into the Intrepid, parked at the bottom of the loading ramp. Pender body-checked him halfway to the California border.

When they reached the high school, they could see the Bu-chopper approaching from the east. Pender drove around the building and directly onto the football field. He parked in the end zone as the helicopter touched down on the fifty-yard line, hopped out of the car, trotted around to the passenger side, opened Irene's door for her.

"Your chopper awaits, madame," he yelled over the noise of the rotors, offering her his hand.

"Thank you, kind sir," replied Irene, taking it. It occurred to her that perhaps they were flirting—she wondered if she was doing a good job.

Irene found herself crouching involuntarily as she trotted toward the chopper beside Pender, her left hand holding his, her right hand holding on to her cap. She had always wondered why people crouched over when they ran toward a helicopter whose rotors were a good twelve or fifteen feet off the ground. Now she knew—you couldn't help it.

When they reached the chopper, Irene surrendered to a sudden impulse. She rose up onto her tiptoes and gave Pender a peck on the cheek.

"I owe you my life," she shouted into his ear.

"It was a hell of a swan song, wasn't it?" he shouted back, as he helped her up into the helicopter. "You take care now."

"You too."

Irene watched through the bowed window as Pender turned and trotted away in an exaggerated crouch. His FBI windbreaker was puffed out like a bright blue sail from the rotor wash, and he was holding on to his white Stetson for dear life.

When he reached the car, Pender turned back and waved, then took off his hat and waved that as the helicopter lifted off. Irene smiled at the sight of his big head shining in the sun. She was too good a psychiatrist not to know that her attraction to the fat old FBI man was more transference than romance. He was Frank, he was her father, he was safety, he was a rock—still, she couldn't wait to tell Barbara Klopfman about her little infatuation.

The thought of Barbara, whom she'd all but given up for dead, affected Irene like a jolt of mood elevator—biochemical sunshine. For the first time, it all came together for Irene—she realized suddenly that her prayers had been answered. I did it, she told herself. I stayed alive. Then she remembered her last haiku. Strawberry Blonds Forever, she thought, taking off her long-billed FBI cap and waving it in a wide arc behind the window of the helicopter at the receding figure in the bright green field below.

Irene knew, of course, that this feeling of exhilaration couldn't last. Sooner or later it would all catch up to her. Probably sooner— the Bu-chopper was flying Irene down to Trinity County, where a search-and-rescue team of sheriffs and park rangers was waiting for her to lead them to Bernadette Sandoval's body.

But at the moment she felt alive, truly alive, and open to all possibilities, which was more than she could have said eight days ago, on the morning the prisoner in the orange jumpsuit first shuffled into the interview room of the Monterey County Jail on Natividad Road, fettered and manacled, with a lock of nut brown hair falling boyishly across his forehead.

Epilogue

Just over a year later, enjoying a complimentary continental breakfast in a hotel room, Irene Cogan was startled, while channel-flipping, to see Dolores Moon being interviewed on *Good Morning Portland*.

There was nothing surprising about seeing Dolores on television—she'd been on *Dateline* a few weeks after being rescued, and her book tour had kicked off with a long segment on the *Today Show*. But it was quite a coincidence that they were in the same town on the same day. Irene called the station and left her name and number. Five minutes later her phone rang.

"Hello?"

"Irene Cogan, what the hell are you doing in Portland?"

"Hello, Dolores. Up until five minutes ago, I was watching you hawk your book."

"How'd I do?"

"I'd buy it—and I know how it comes out. Do you want to have dinner tonight?"

"I'd love to, but I'm leaving for Seattle in about an hour. No—San Francisco. Seattle was yesterday." Dolores laughed. It was good to hear her laugh. "And when the book tour's over, I have an audition for the role of Eponine in a western tour of *Les Mis*. Apparently being kidnapped was a terrific career move."

"I'm so happy for you. How're you sleeping these days?"

Long pause. "With the lights on, and a snootful of Valium. You know how it is."

"It'll get better."

"I know." Quick change of subject—Dolores didn't like to dwell. "So how's *your* book coming?"

"Actually, that's what I'm doing in Portland. I need one last interview with him, to give the book some closure. And me."

"He's here?" Dolores didn't bother hiding her alarm.

"Miss Miller left him a substantial inheritance. He was transferred to a private hospital—pretty hotsy-totsy, from what I understand—after being found unfit to stand trial."

"If I'd known, I'd never have let them include Portland on the tour. Just knowing I was in the same state with him was stressful enough."

"There's nothing to worry about. He's on a locked ward, maximum security."

"As far as I'm concerned, *dead* is maximum security. Anything short of that is just screwing around."

"I understand—believe me, I understand. I'm a little conflicted about seeing him myself. A *lot* conflicted—which is partly why I have to do it."

"Better you than me. Listen, Irene, I have to go. I *definitely* don't want to miss that plane out of town now."

"Okay, honey. It's good to hear you sounding so well. Call me some time when you get a chance. And good luck with *Les Mis*. I mean break a leg."

"You too. Bye."

"Bye."

Irene replaced the receiver in the cradle. The idea of a plane out of town sounded pretty good to her. But she'd had to go to a lot of trouble to arrange the interview with Maxwell—permission from his lawyers, who were also his guardians, as well as his doctor, and the administrators at Reed-Chase. If she chickened out now, then changed her mind again, she knew she might not be able to swing it a second time.

After a quick pep talk in the mirror—she was a frost blond again—Irene packed her overnight bag. On the back of the door was one of those "Have you forgotten anything?" signs. She couldn't help turning around obediently to look, and discovered that she'd left her wallet on the foot of the bed. She didn't even remember taking it out of her purse—apparently her subconscious *really* didn't want to do this interview.

Ever since she'd heard that little voice in her head on the riverbank, the one that had prompted her to ask Kinch his name, Irene had been paying a lot more attention to her subconscious. But she refused to be pushed around by it. One more pep talk—you have to *know,* she told herself; you'll feel better if you *know*—then she retrieved her wallet and was out the door before she could change her mind again. Or vice versa.

Reed-Chase Institute was a beige two-story structure set back from a pleasant, tree-lined street. Dr. Alan Corder, a good-looking, athletic fellow with a spring in his step, and all his hair, met Irene in the lobby. He was Irene's age, but flatteringly deferential. He told her he'd read everything she'd published on DID, including her recent article on Maxwell in JAP—the *Journal of Abnormal Psychology*—and asked her if she would do him the honor of having lunch with him to discuss the case.

Oh, slather it on, thought Irene—but she accepted. Corder led her down a long corridor, through a locked door, up an elevator, and through another door that opened when he punched a code into a keypad. The locked ward was situated in the back of the building by design, Corder explained. This way, the grilled windows weren't visible from the street.

"Keeps the NIMBYs off our back."

"I understand," said Irene. A NIMBY was someone who didn't mind society building high-security prisons or asylums—just Not In My Back Yard.

Corder signed Irene into the security unit, had her fill out a liability waiver, then led her down a wide hallway painted a pleasant shade of salmon.

"Has there been any change in his status since I spoke to you last week?" she asked.

"None whatsoever. He's a model patient. If it weren't for his history, and the court order, he'd have earned his way off the locked ward by now."

Irene put her hand on Dr. Corder's arm, stopping him in his tracks in the middle of the corridor. "Never," she said, staring up into his eyes for emphasis. "Never, never, never, never, never."

"I understand how you feel."

"This isn't *about* me."

"Of course not. But try to withhold judgment until you've spoken with him. I think you'll be pleasantly surprised. And don't worry—either myself or one of the orderlies will be observing you through the security window the whole time."

The last door on the right at the end of the corridor was painted pastel blue, the color of Maybelline, with a one-way glass panel set at eye level. Irene would not let herself peek in. She was afraid if she saw him, she'd lose her nerve. Corder punched a code into the keypad; the deceptively heavy door swung open on silent hinges.

At first glance, it was an ordinary, pleasant-looking dormitory room. Desk, bureau, bed. Pale blue walls. But it didn't take long for a trained eye such as Irene's to spot the anomalies. The bathroom was an alcove—no door. The glass of the four-paned window overlooking the back garden and walking paths of the institute was a double-layer mesh sandwich, the sash for show only—it wasn't built to open. The top of the bureau was padded, the corners rounded; it had open, recessed shelves instead of drawers that closed. The desk corners were padded and rounded, too, and both desk and chair were bolted to the floor. No lamps—the lights were set behind opaque white panels in the ceiling.

Maxwell, in blue pajamas with white piping, was seated at the desk, crayoning, his back to the door. He turned. "Hello, Doctor Al," he chirped brightly, in a pennywhistle voice.

"Good morning, Lyssy. Do you remember Dr. Cogan?"

"I guess." But there was no recognition in the gold-flecked brown eyes, only a guarded expression: an age-appropriate response for a polite five-year-old with no idea who Irene was, but with enough intelligence to understand that they wouldn't ask you if you *remembered* somebody unless you'd already met them.

"Hello, Lyssy. What are you drawing there? May I take a look?"

"It's a picture of Missy." He held up the manila-colored sheet. Irene crossed the room and took it from him. It was the stick figure of a woman wearing a stylized, triangular dress and long hair. Long black hair, Irene was relieved to see.

"Very pretty," said Irene, handing the drawing back to him. "Who's Missy?"

"My friend."

Occupational therapist, mouthed Corder. Then, to Maxwell: "Lyssy, Dr. Cogan would like to talk with you for a few minutes. Would that be all right with you?"

"I guess. Only . . ." He beckoned shyly for Corder to lean over, then whispered into his ear.

"Of course," said Corder. "Dr. Cogan, could you wait outside for a moment?"

Irene backed out of the room, closed the door behind her, and watched through the one-way glass as Maxwell, his arm around his doctor for support, hopped over to the bed, his right pajama leg swinging loosely below the knee. Irene winced. Until that moment, she'd forgotten about the amputation. Feeling like a voyeur, she turned away. A few minutes later the door swung open, and Corder emerged. "He's all yours."

Maxwell was waiting for her just inside the door. Irene hadn't expected to be in such close proximity so soon. She decided to take charge right away. "Hello again, Lyssy. Have a seat."

"I have a seat," he said mischievously, patting his pajamaed behind.

"Very funny. Bed or chair, take your pick."

He limped over to the bed and sat down. Not a bad limp, just a hitch and an exaggerated swing of his hip.

"You're walking very well," said Irene. She sat behind the desk, pushed his crayons and drawing pad to the side, removed her notebook and Dictaphone from her purse, and set them on the desk.

"First I had to use crutches, first. Then a cane. Now I don't even need that. They have legs you can run on, too. Someday I'm going to get one of those, if I'm good, and I could be in the Olympics for people with one leg. If I'm good and people stop being scared of me."

"Oh? Are people scared of you?"

"Some people, I guess. In the old hospital they used to keep me tied up."

"Do you know why that was?"

"I guess."

"Why?"

"Ask Doctor Al—he knows."

"I'd like to hear it from you. I need to know what *you* think."

"Because once upon a time there was a bad man who got inside my body and pretended to be me and did bad things to people."

"I see. And where is that bad man now?"

"The police man shot him and he went away."

"Do you remember anything about him?"

"All I 'member, I was in this dark jail place and I was scared and he made me stay there and there was this dead bird on the floor. Is my voice on that?"

Irene pressed stop. "Yes. Would you like to hear it?" She hit the reverse button, then play.

" . . . *this dead bird on the floor. Is my voice on that?*"

"That's not me," said Maxwell. "Is that me?"

"That's you. Everybody's own voice sounds different to them when they hear it over a tape recorder."

"How come?"

"Because you're hearing it from the outside rather than the inside." He had presented Irene with a convenient segue. "By the way, Lyssy, do you ever hear other voices inside your head?"

"You mean like the bad man?"

"Sure, like the bad man."

He looked down at his lap. "N O means no. And if I do, I have to tell Doctor Al or one of the nurses or somebody right away, cross my heart and hope to die." Then he looked up slyly—transparently slyly. "Right?"

"Absolutely," replied Irene. "Would you like to play a little game with me?"

"Absolutely," he repeated in his piping voice. He appeared to enjoy the sound of the word. "Ab-so-lutely."

"Okay, here's how it goes. I'm going to ask you three questions, and you have to answer them truthfully. You understand what *truthfully* means?"

"I'm not a baby."

"I know—I just have to make extra sure. But here's the game part—the whole time I'm asking the questions, and the whole time you're answering, you have to look straight at me. No looking away, no hiding your face or anything like that. Think you can do that?"

"Too easy," he said scornfully.

"Then shouldn't be any trouble. Okay, first question." Irene pointed to her eyes. "Look right here." Their eyes locked across the room. "How old are you?"

"Five. One two three four five."

"Very good. Second question: what's your favorite ice cream flavor?"

"Choc'lit."

"Excellent. Third question: what's your name?" This last was the only question that mattered, of course.

"Lyssy. L Y S S Y," he declared proudly, his eyes locked on hers. "Do I win?"

"You sure do." No upward flicker of the eyeballs, no flutter of the eyelids, no grounding behavior, no change in the voice, no sign of stress or struggle.

"What? What do I win?"

Irene turned off the Dictaphone, slipped it into her purse along with her notebook, then rummaged around and came up with a pack of sugarless Trident. "Chewing gum," she said, feeling a touch manic. "First prize is a pack of Original Flavor, Sugarless Trident. More dentists recommend sugarless Trident for their patients."

"Coo-ool," said Lyssy. "Are we done now? Are we finished?"

"You know, I think we are," said Irene, standing up. "I think we are at long last finished." She slung her purse strap over her shoulder, crossed to the bed, handed Lyssy his prize.

He hurriedly tore the pack open, stripped the foil off two pieces, shoved them both into his mouth. "Will you come back to see me some time?" he asked her indistinctly.

"Perhaps some day, Lyssy," she said, crossing to the door, which opened as if by magic. "I do live sort of far away."

"Too bad," he said. "You're nice."

Irene turned in the doorway. "Why, thank you, Lyssy. You're nice too." She took a backward step; the door closed.

"Well?" asked Dr. Corder, beaming.

"I'm impressed," said Irene, stepping up to peer through the one-way glass. Maxwell was still sitting on the bed, motionless save for the steady movement of his jaw as he worked at his gum.

"But not entirely convinced?"

" 'Fool me once, shame on you; fool me twice, shame on me.' He's already fooled me once, Dr. Corder."

"Please, Dr. Cogan, call me Al."

"In that case, call me Irene."

"It'd be my pleasure," said Corder, offering her his arm. "Now how about that lunch?"

"Sounds great." Irene took his arm, and together they strolled back down the salmon-colored corridor. Were they flirting? she wondered. She certainly hoped so.

Ulysses Maxwell sat motionless on the bed for another ten minutes. When he was sure they were gone, he spat his gum out onto the floor. Then his carriage changed dramatically. He lowered his shoulders and arched his neck, cocking his head slightly to the side.

" 'Why, thank you, Lyssy,' " he said aloud, forming the words carefully, almost primly, at the front of his mouth, and speaking with just a trace of a lisp—Irene's lisp. " 'You're nice, too.' "

He rose, crossed the room with only a ghost of the limp he'd put on for Irene, sat down at his desk, and with the black crayon swiftly sketched the outline of a nude woman on the top sheet of the pad. No stick figure this time: she was reclining in a modified odalisque, her hands behind her head, her small breasts tipped pertly. Then he put the black crayon back in the box and took out several other shades, peach, melon, red-orange, orange-red, apricot, and carnation, with which he sketched in first a few sparse pubic hairs, just above the triangular space between her slender thighs, then a luscious head of shoulder length, strawberry blond hair.

"Much better," he said, admiring her for a moment, then tearing the picture into narrow strips, and the strips into tiny pieces before depositing it in his wastebasket. "That Princess Di shade was all wrong for your complexion. Miss Miller would never have approved."